THE APPLE AND THE TREE

THE APPLE *and the* TREE

CLEMMIE BENNETT

The Apple and The Tree

First Edition

Paperback ISBN: 979-8-37607-637-8
Hardcover ISBN: 979-8-39145-416-8

To my nephew, Luther.

1.

THE NEXT CHAPTER
2020

Lolly had always preferred beginnings over endings, but the sun was setting over the London skyline as it had set on her life. Ella watched the orange light gazing back through the clouds, embracing her with warmth on this summer night, until a screeching cry coming from an exhausted toddler made her shiver.

Lolly was dead.

A squirrel hopped on her bench and grabbed a broken almond someone had left behind. Ella felt the ghost of a smile appear on her lips. Her phone vibrating on her lap broke their quiet agreement, prompting the rodent to flee as fast as it could with its treasure. The name of her father on the screen made her hesitate, but she picked up and let him speak first.

'Hi again, can we talk?'

'About?'

'My mother, of course. Well, it is about her.'

'I miss her.'

'I know. Ella-Grace, I am boarding soon. Can I just get to the point?'

'If you stop calling me by that name.'

'It is the name I gave you,' he replied impatiently. 'What are you planning to do with the ring she left you?'

'I told you this morning. I want to keep it.'

'Be reasonable. If my mother was right, it's worth a lot of money. Of course, if she wasn't, you will get it back and never hear another word about it. I promise.'

'This is the only thing she left me in her will and I am keeping it.'

'I understand you loved your grandmother, but twenty-year-old girls don't wear five-century-old rings! What if you lose it? What then?'

'I am not twenty yet. Fathers are supposed to remember their daughter's birthday, you know. Have a safe flight home,' Ella put an end to the conversation as she hung up the phone, irritated.

She took the jewellery box out of her handbag and opened the lid with curiosity and precaution, still getting used to the fact that the ring was now hers. Lolly had always been so protective of it, wearing it on a chain around her neck rather than on her finger and explaining to anyone who ever asked that it had been made in England in the early sixteenth century and had stayed in the family ever since.

Ella grimaced. The intricately engraved gold hoop, surmounted by its hexagonal sapphire, would never really belong to her. It would always be Lolly's. Lolly's poison locket ring. Ella would never forget how her grandmother used to dare herself, every year as a birthday tradition, to pour sugar in her tea directly from the small compartment under the blue stone.

'It makes me feel like I am in the sixteenth century,' she would then exclaim flippantly before putting the ring safely back on its chain. Ella laughed out loud at the memory, getting a disconcerted look from the couple of tourists watching the sunset nearby.

Lolly. For some bizarre reason, she had left everything but this ring to her estranged son. Life had been a bit of a blur for Ella since Covid-19 had fatally infiltrated her grandmother's lungs. Her father had flown back from his home in Norway and she had left him unchaperoned. Lolly had been cremated, her house and belongings sold, and her money transferred to her son's bank account without Ella having to lift a finger or being asked for her opinion. Now that she felt more like herself, a wall of shame prevented the air from reaching her lungs every time she thought about how little she had been involved.

Despite Ella's vivid dream about her father stealing it in her sleep, the jewellery box was still on her bedside table when she opened her eyes. To be on the safe side, she opened it. The ring was still there, as if Lolly was too.

Ella allowed herself to cry in the shower as reality hit: she was all on her own. Pretending the wetness of her cheeks was solely coming from the shower head, she spared a thought for the woman who had given her life and then taken her own shortly after.

'Postpartum depression,' Lolly had given Ella a three-word-explanation when the girl had wondered about the reasons behind her mother's action.

Nora Yalden had not found the strength to cope with being a mother and had abandoned everyone behind – was what the father of her child always said.

Ella had made peace with being one of the reasons why her mother had chosen to end her life with a stool and a rope. Her father had not. Grieving the loss of the woman he loved, Owen Buckley had realised his intentions had never involved single parenting. He had left his newborn baby to his parents and moved out of the country. He had never been present, nor reliable.

Ella spent the next hour lying naked on a towel on her bed, her fingertips distractedly tracing endless circles around her belly button. Nora and Owen had given her life, but Lolly and Pop had given her unconditional love and as much time and attention as they could afford. An aggressive cancer had won against Pop over five years ago, giving just enough time to his loved ones to say their goodbyes.

Saying goodbye to Lolly had not been an option. There had been a pandemic. The hospital had not allowed visitors. Lolly had not been in need of her bed for very long. Ella was left alone with her grief. She was left alone with her life and at a loss with what to do with it.

'What would you do, Lolly?' Ella murmured, trying to remember what her grandmother had done to grieve the love of her life.

The answer brightened up her mood. Lolly had gone back to all the places in London where she had shared meaningful moments with Pop. The Tower of London, where they had met. The open-air theatre in Regent's Park, where they had had their first date watching a Shakespeare play. The Pergola Hill and Gardens in Hampstead, where he had proposed. Postman's Park, where she had told him she was pregnant with his child.

The Horniman Gardens popped up in Ella's mind as she considered doing the same. Lolly and she would sit on a bench and admire the view for hours. It had been the theatre of Ella's tears following her first heartbreak. There, Lolly had pointed at her poison locket ring and said she could fix her problem if she wanted her to, making her laugh through her tears.

Lolly had always made her laugh. Ella would never forget their trips to every single place remotely related to King Henry VIII or one of his wives. Lolly had always managed to make learning fun.

Windsor Castle had always been her grandmother's favourite, but Ella's most cherished memories had been made in Eltham Palace. Like that day, when they had chatted so much in the underground rooms with one of the guides that they had been locked up in the palace in the evening. Or when they had danced alone in the middle of the great hall, on a cold winter Sunday. They had visited this palace so many times most of the people working there knew their names.

Ella sent a voice message to her best friend to tell her all about her conversation with her father. She barely had time to put a bra on before Iris called her back.

'He tried to take the ring from you?' she repeated, stunned.

'He did, didn't he?'

'Unbelievable. I swear, next time I see him, I'll punch him in the face! I am fuming! You're not giving it to him, are you?'

'No way José!' Ella exclaimed.

'That's right, that's the spirit!' Iris laughed. 'How are you feeling today?'

'Still a little bit sorry for myself, but okay.'

'Be patient, Els. You're grieving. Give it time.'

'I know. I am gonna go to Eltham Palace today, it might do me good.'

'You girls always loved going there together. Do you want company?'

'Thank you, but I'll just grab a book and spend the day in the gardens.'

'Let me know if you change your mind! I need to go, my mom's calling me to take the dog out. Love you!'

'Love you too. Hug Goliath for me,' Ella said and hung up smiling, thinking about this tiny black sausage dog that Iris had decided to name after the biblical giant.

She was about to send a message to Iris, requesting a photo of the dachshund, when she instead received one from her employer asking her to work late the following day. Ella sighed. How she had become a nanny when she had never had any particular passion for children was a mystery to her. She had never had a clear vision of what her life was supposed to be, so, when a couple had posted an ad about a job as a nanny for their son, she had applied. Lolly had helped her find a small studio as close as possible from her work. Almost two years later, nothing had changed.

Ella sometimes wondered what the next chapter of her life would be. When she would move on to things she would actually be excited about. As a child, she used to think twenty-year-olds were all adults with their lives figured out. She had three months left.

With her book in her hands and the September sun kissing her skin in the gardens of Eltham Palace, Ella forgot her worries. After a while, children playing nearby ruined her tranquillity, but surprisingly she did not even mind. She closed her book, sunk her elbows in the dry grass and watched the children play. The eldest had pulled down his surgical mask, making it look more like a chin guard than a barrier against any disease, and was blowing iridescent bubbles. He was followed by his younger sibling and their dog, both trying to catch them. When the little one bumped into her pet, she cried and went to hide under a ball-shaped tree until her father came to comfort her.

Ella giggled as she saw the dog hesitate between the bubbles left to burst in the air and the tears to dry on its young owner's face, but her good mood disappeared when she received a text from her father.

> *Ella-G, I am not trying to make you do anything you don't want to do, but I really think you should consider what I said about the ring. It would be for the best. Only saying that because I care about you.*

Sitting up hoping the blinding sun had made her misread the message on her phone, Ella read the text a second time, and in an outburst of rage threw both her book and phone away. Surprise and fear made the little girl cry louder and Ella apologised to her father before lying back down on the grass, her hands on her face, trying to calm herself down before even thinking about getting her phone back.

Because I care about you. The audacity! It was not for her. It was for the money. If he'd wanted to have the ring as a souvenir from Lolly, she could have been open to a discussion. But the man wanted to sell it to the highest bidder. Ella reached for her handbag, took the small box out and put the coveted jewel on her finger. She did not know how five-hundred-year-old rings were supposed to look. The large yet uneven blue stone would not have looked out of place in an antique jewellery shop, but there was little hope it was as old as her grandmother thought it was.

Forgetting about her phone abandoned on the grass, Ella silently thanked her father for giving her away to his parents. Accepting the fact that he was not fit to raise a child was the best thing he had ever done. There was not much else to be grateful for. She still had to decide which was worse between his drunk phone call on her fifth Christmas morning to tell her that Father Christmas was not real, or the one on her eighth, perfectly sober, to tell her that her birth had ruined his life.

Ella had been lying down on the grass for far too long to be able to guess the time, making the too large ring spin around her finger and wondering if altering it down to her size would damage it. Nausea took her by surprise. Her internal organs seemed to be somehow bouncing against each other; it was like her body was falling off a cliff. The overall feeling was similar to what used to often happen to her in her sleep as a child, although the nausea that came with it was a first. Ella waited for her body to wake up at the end of her fall.

Nothing happened. Her nausea disappeared, her organs calmed themselves down, but Ella did not wake up. Opening her eyes, she realised she had never been asleep in the first place and frowned. She sat up, annoyed for the beautiful blue sky to have been replaced by a dull shade of grey. Weather in London could be so unpredictable. Her arms, previously warmed by the sun, were now cold as a rock, and the wind went blowing her light brown hair in her face. Ella regretted having picked her long yellow summer dress in the morning and was about to joke with another visitor about the weather change, but the gardens had been deserted.

Something was off. Ella couldn't put her finger on what yet.

Lost and dizzy, she looked for her phone. Her blank mind wanted to ask thousands of questions. She did not know if she had after all fallen asleep or not and could not help but smile when she thought about the possibility of having been locked up again, by herself this time. But panic was soon to grow more intense inside of her as seconds went by and her phone was still nowhere to be found. Ella rubbed her eyes and tried to stay calm as it became clear that her belongings had all been stolen. She ended up swearing out loud. She had no money to buy a new phone. And it was the second time in three months that she had lost her debit card. At least, her bank would laugh.

Ella sighed and decided to walk to the palace to find someone to complain to but froze. Her lips parted to mouth a few astonished additional swearing words. Her mind was finally catching up and hit her with her surrounding reality: it was not Eltham Palace. It was a large, red-bricked building, surrounded by water. There was a moat. A proper one, full of water. Not the dry, moat-turned-grass path that had stood there earlier. It could not be Eltham Palace. For half a second, Ella considered having been abducted. She stared at the sturdy bridge crossing the moat. The possibility of having been kidnapped, without noticing, from the gardens of a palace, then dropped to the gardens of another palace, was quite thin.

But there was a moat. Her heart racing, Ella started to properly look around and spun on herself a few times before stumbling to the conclusion that she was, indeed, asleep. There was a moat!

2.

OUT OF THIN AIR

Ella pinched herself. Shut her eyes as hard as she could and opened them again. Pinched herself a second time. To no avail. She was still standing on the grass, facing a crossroad of two perpendicular neat paths. Behind her, a U-shaped, low building, and a gatehouse made of bricks. Ella was about to slap her own face when a voice made her jump. Someone was singing. A man?

She obeyed her fear and ran to her left, crossing one of the paths, reaching the nearby trees for safety. Fallen leaves and twigs crackled beneath her feet. More than trees, she had entered a forest. Ella did not try to find a rational explanation to the sudden growth of a forest. She kept running and only stopped to catch her breath once she believed herself to be far enough from the singing voice.

'You are going crazy,' she said to herself out loud. She slapped her face. It did nothing to wake herself up.

She took her head in her hands, forcing herself to breathe as calmly and fully as the yoga instructor used to teach her when she went with Lolly to her classes. The palace had been replaced by another, hundreds of trees had grown in less time than it had taken her to kill her last orchid – a green thumb was not something she could boast about – and the warmth as well as her phone and handbag had disappeared in a split second. It did not make any sense.

Ella walked further in the forest, wandering between the trees for as long as it took for her heart to stop beating in her ears. Green, brown, the woods were so dense she could not see the sky above her head anymore. There had to be an explanation. There always was one.

She reached for Lolly's ring for reassurance, hoping to hear her grandmother's voice telling her what to do.

'Oh, hell, no, no, no!' Ella cried when her fingers touched her bare skin.

The ring. It was not there.

Tears exploded out of her eyes and came running down her cheeks as she held herself in her own arms. She was cold, with no phone or money, lost and alone in woods that had not existed a few moments ago, and had been stupid enough to run through said woods wearing a ring that was too big for her finger. The one thing she cared the most about in the world was now as lost as she was. Things could simply not get any worse.

If gods or guardian angels existed, they must have considered this as an invitation. Ella tripped and found herself on all fours in the mud. Cursing all living things and whoever had invented mud in the first place, she heard something and stopped. It was weak, but it was there. Ella got back up on her feet and used her cotton dress to wipe her hands. She heard the sound again. A wail. Ignoring the wobble in her legs, she followed it.

Her stomach relaxed when she found a very small beagle with its collar stuck in a bush. The frightened pup barked at her but, when Ella extended her hand, it let her.

'I am not going to hurt you, I promise. Let me help you with your collar,' she said, round-eyed with amazement when she looked at it.

It was massive, made of red velvet, with pearls and roses embroidered on it. Ella had never seen anything like it, especially not on such a small dog. She had to be curious about what had led the owner to buy a pet collar with pearls on it and, once she had untangled the collar from the bush, examined it more closely. The roses were Tudor roses.

She laughed. 'Your owner loves the Tudors even more than my grandmother. I didn't know it was possible!' she told the dog. It tilted his head on the left. 'Who is your owner?' Ella asked before putting it down on the ground.

There was a moat. A forest. And now a lost dog. Ella took a deep breath and let it all out, waiting for the air to completely empty her belly. The beagle limped back to her, trying to get her to carry him in her arms again.

'Are you hurt?' she wondered out loud and noticed a deep cut on his paw. Ella sighed, trying to keep her heart rate under control as she realised that the only acceptable solution to help her unfortunate new friend was to find the singing man.

At least, the task was rather easy. Ella followed the singing voice until she was out of the woods, the dog barking weakly in her arms as he recognised its owner. That man would give her an explanation to what was going on around her.

'What the heck is he wearing?' she whispered when she caught sight of him. If she had not been so scared, she would have smiled. He looked astonishing, shimmering with all the jewels encrusted on his costume, yet it was the first time Ella had ever seen a man wear bright red tights. 'All right, this guy is definitely your owner. He is very committed to his role,' she added on the same tone.

Lolly would have loved him. Even Ella did. The lengths some people could go for their passions would always fascinate her, and it was nice to see people without half their faces covered by a mask, for a change.

The man was walking towards her as if he owned the place. His aura was such that Ella barely noticed the much more serious looking man following him. Over the last few feet that separated her from the man with the red tights, they locked eyes, and she found it tricky to swallow. As if something had broken inside her brain. The man's eyes were so blue and his gaze so intense it was impossible to focus on anything else.

'We thank you, for your assistance in finding our companion,' he said with a surprisingly high-pitched voice for a man so tall.

But he was not even a man. Less like an adult, more like a teen dressed up. His face was round and youthful; he could not have been any older than Ella. No sound came out when she opened her mouth. An invisible hand was squeezing her throat. She took a step back when the no longer singing man reached his arms towards her. He took the dog from her nonetheless, calmly but firmly.

'Where are we?' Ella heard herself croak.

'In the gardens of our royal palace of Eltham,' he replied as if it were evident.

'But there is a moat,' she retorted.

He laughed. 'Indeed,' he said, but then stared at her for a moment with a concerned look on his face. 'Are you unwell?' he asked.

That's one way of putting it, she thought. Unwell. Or dreaming. Hallucinating. Delusional. Or just beyond insane. There was a moat. Ella had always been a practical person, but there was a moat where there had never been one before. A moat could not appear out of thin air. Ella massaged her eyelids, fighting the irrational thoughts inside her brain that were theorizing that this person was maybe not playing dressing up after all.

But time travel is not real, her logical side remembered. Ella thought about someone pulling a very elaborate trick on her. It made even less sense.

He was waiting for an answer. She did not know what to tell him. The two sides of her brain were arguing so loudly she could not hear herself think. Trusting science meant assuming he was either some sort of a professional re-enactor or a prankster. She could remind him that none of it was funny and go on with her day. But trusting the persistent voice inside her head, that kept on repeating that no prank could create a moat around a castle, meant believing against her better judgement that she had travelled to the past. It was utter insanity.

Each second that went by made him look more suspicious. He had been patient so far, but Ella's astonishment had once again taken her voice away. If she had really travelled in time, telling him it was the year 2020 when it wasn't could have disastrous consequences. A metallic taste filled her mouth. Being burned alive for witchcraft was a risk she was not willing to take. She decided to play along, even if it turned out to be a prank. Being mocked for a while or ending up as a meme on social media was still better than being incinerated.

'Are you hurt?' he insisted.

'Your dog is,' she finally replied, resisting the urge to run away. She would not have made it very far anyway.

'He shall be seen by the Keeper. We heartily thank you for providing such kind help. What is your name?' he asked. Ella's heart dropped down to her feet.

'I... I don't know,' she stuttered, refusing to let the tears that had gathered in her eyes run down on her face. If it wasn't the twenty-first century anymore, it meant that she knew no one and that no one knew her. It also meant no money, no home, nowhere to go, no means to survive and no explanation about who she was and what she was doing here.

There was a pause. A moment of incredulous hesitation.

'You do not know?' a low, throaty voice repeated. The other, more quiet man, had spoken for the first time. Ella looked at him for a second, confused, but was drawn back to the blue eyed individual.

'I... no. I fell when I tried to help your dog. I must have hit my head. And I... I don't remember my name or anything else,' she lied, touching a pretend bump on the side of her head.

'How distressing,' the man murmured. 'We are most entirely in your debt. You provided us with help, and now help you shall get. We shall have you seen by Her Grace's physician,' he informed her as Ella tried to hide the intensity of her relief. He was going to help her. 'We shall find you suitable clothing also,' he added, giving a disapproving look to her muddy dress and sandals.

'Thank you…' Ella said. 'I don't know who you are,' she admitted, in denial of the solid guess her brain had already come up with.

'Why, this is His Grace, the K…' the other man started to say with a certain exasperation.

He was stopped by a brief sign of the hand. There was an amusement in the eyes, a laugh on the smile. 'Henry the Eighth, by the grace of God, king of England and France and Lord of Ireland,' he finally introduced himself. 'What name do you wish to answer to?' he asked.

'I don't know…' she replied.

'Then we shall call you Elizabeth, like the late queen our mother,' he decided.

Ella nodded. She was pushing away every story her schoolbooks and her grandmother had ever told her about him from the second half of his reign. The many wives and the many more executions, in particular. Lolly had never managed to convince Pop that Henry VIII had not always been a cruel tyrant. Now that she may have had him in front of her, Ella was desperate for her grandmother to have been right.

Lolly!

Ella had inherited from a ring believed by her grandmother to be dating from the sixteenth century and, days later, there she was, talking to a man claiming to be Henry VIII. It could not be a coincidence. The ring. Ella did not know how, or why, or even if Lolly had ever found out about it, but the ring had sent her five hundred years into the past and the man was telling the truth about who he was. Which meant the ring, lost in the middle of the woods, was also her way out of there.

'It is the second year of our reign, the year 1510 of our Lord Jesus Christ,' the King told Ella when she asked him.

She would have gladly sat down to process this information, had he not been walking so fast. Instead, she walked behind him in silence, with for only comfort the beagle's adorable face looking at her from over his owner's shoulder. There were so many things to consider and so many problems to solve, yet Ella's mind was only focusing on what she would have done had she travelled four years earlier, with her braces on. With horror, she felt a laugh coming up from her insides and had to bow her head to the ground to conceal her face and hoped neither the King nor his friend, a certain Nicholas, would hear her.

It became harder to refrain her urge for laughter when she remembered Iris's large tattoo on her forearm and tried to imagine how she would have justified it to anyone living in 1510. The insidious voice inside her head pointed out that it may very well have been seen as witchcraft. Ella was unsure of when witchcraft trials had started to take place in England but the image of her best friend burned to death was nevertheless enough to calm her down.

She looked up and stared at the expensive gemstones on the King's jacket as they walked on the bridge leading to the palace. She vowed to stay as quiet as possible to not betray herself until the first opportunity to run back to the woods and find her grandmother's ring.

Every single man they met in the palace stopped what they were doing to bow to the King, but not without staring at Ella like the latest, curious, wild addition to a zoo. Most were intrigued, some were amused, others looked scared. They were all clueless about who Ella was and what she was doing there. And so was she. The few women present curtseyed to the King, so low in fact that Ella feared they would collapse to the floor. One of them gasped when she spotted her. It was as if she was no longer wearing a summer dress, but only a pair of knickers.

The King was oblivious. He did not pause for any of them, not even when a man bundled in a red velvety coat walked up to him.

'Not now,' the King said, and the man bowed reverently. Ella heard him whisper his bitterness behind their backs, but the King led the way through a dark corridor and only stopped to give the dog to a good-looking man named Charles.

Ella smiled when she heard the dog's name. Pan. Out of all the names she could have imagined for the pet of the soon-to-be gruesome

Henry VIII, Pan was an outsider. It was cute, and perfect for the youth that the King was. Charles, whatever his last name was, did not say a word to her, but looked awkwardly at her dress before disappearing with the pup in his arms. Ella had to hurry back after the King, who had started to walk again.

It did not matter who they met on the way, they all looked at Ella as if she were insane. She started to panic about what the doctor would think. Her choice of faking amnesia might not have been the cleverest after all. She was only now realising that people had no medical notion of memory loss back in 1510.

Still focusing on the King's glittering jacket to control her breathing, Ella wondered what would be done to her if the doctors diagnosed her as crazy. Three options came to her mind and none of them was ideal. They could lock her up in jail, or kick her out of the palace and let her fend for herself in the streets, which was terrifying, but not as much as them trying to cure her. Ella's eyes started to burn. She would rather die than turn into a guinea pig – covered in leeches or poisoned by mercury.

Deep in her morbid thoughts, Ella did not see the King stop and turn around to face her. She bumped into him, scratching her face. Her legs lost all strength at the idea of having bumped into someone who would at some point in his life develop the habit of cutting off other people's heads. He grabbed her arm instinctively, just in time to prevent her from falling miserably to the floor, and she forced herself to ground her feet and stand up.

'We are deeply sorry.' His tone was assertive, yet infused with a childlike innocence.

'No, I… I am. I didn't see you stop. I feel a little weak,' she told the truth.

'You look very pale indeed. The Queen's physician shall see you at once, for your head and your cheek. We are ashamed to say our doublet drew your blood,' he told her.

Ella touched her cheek and flinched. She was bleeding. The King looked contrite, which she could guess did not happen very often. It was a relief. After all, she was a stranger who had hurt herself while helping *his* dog and whom he had hurt with *his* jacket, all in the same day. With a bit of luck, he would make sure that no more harm would happen to her.

Unless his wife's doctor says you are a witch, the cruel voice inside her head made itself heard.

Ella could have thrown up, but the King entered the next room, demanding with a powerful voice for someone to fetch a Dr Alcaraz. Ella followed him into a large space with a high moulded ceiling, where at least two dozen women curtseyed to the King in a complete silence. They all were then shocked when they saw her. Ella felt very underdressed, finally understanding that she was the only one with a sleeveless dress. She looked for the King and found him talking to a pregnant petite woman wearing a magnificent red gown. Its neckline and the frame of her headgear were both encrusted with rubies and emeralds.

Queen Katherine. Katherine of Aragon, the first of the rhyme – divorced, beheaded, died, divorced, beheaded, survived. Except she was not divorced yet. Lolly had talked about her so many times, praising her courage and her kindness, that Ella felt like she knew her already. She regretted her grandmother's absence more deeply than ever when she thought about just how much she would have loved to meet her.

When the middle-aged Spanish doctor arrived for her consultation, a terrorised Ella thought for a second that she would pee herself. Instead, Dr Alcaraz made her pee in a cup.

Her few minutes with the Queen's personal doctor turned out to be the strangest medical experience of her life. The man did not deem necessary to feel her imaginary bump. He checked her pulse, cleaned the scratch on her cheek with vinegar, then focused on her urine, alternatively staring at it and smelling it. Ella could not hold back a disgusted face when he tasted it.

Dr Alcaraz did not seem to suspect her of being a witch but was at a loss about what to do with her. Ella heard him through the wall explain to the King and the Queen that he believed her ailment to have been caused by her fall, but that he did not have any remedy.

'She is overall in good health. Her skin and teeth are of exceptional quality. Her bodily odour is… distinctive, but acceptable. God willing, time shall cure her,' he said.

Ella did her best to remain emotionless. *Distinctive but acceptable.* She was surrounded by people living in a time that had probably not discovered deodorant yet and the man thought her smell was only just acceptable. She could have laughed.

Maybe it is his way of reassuring his king and queen that I am not a peasant trying to break into the palace, Ella tried to reassure herself.

'Can she be the cause of any harm to herself and the persons around her?' the Queen asked.

'It is not my opinion, Your Grace,' the physician answered.

'Then Mistress Elizabeth is to stay at court. We are much indebted to her. She shall wait upon the Queen and we shall all pray for her recovery,' the King decided.

Ella did not have time to catch her breath nor even comprehend what the King's verdict meant for her. A Spanish woman called Maria, with dark blond hair so long she could have sat on it, took her to another, smaller, room, with walls of dark panelling. Maria was not very happy about her task but helped Ella clean her hands of all the dirt and dry mud, and gave her one of her own dresses.

Below the square neckline, Ella's waist looked slimmer because of the bodice, and the black taffeta skirt was so wide on the floor that it made her feel like a walking hourglass. In truth, it would have not mattered much if Maria had also given her a pair of knickers, but the only thing she had given her was a shift, which was some sort of knee-length underdress made of white linen. And no knickers. Ironically, despite the layers and the long sleeves, Ella had never felt more naked.

She watched, uncomfortably, almost grievously, as Maria took away her clothes. The woman did not give any comment on them, but she did not need to since her face was communicative enough. Maria was both baffled and suspicious, but Ella was not sure which feeling was dominant.

'Are you aware whether or not you are wed?' Maria asked her as if it was the strangest thing she had ever said in her life.

'No,' Ella answered. All she could think about was what would be done with her knickers.

'You shall then keep your hair uncovered, for now. You must comb your hair,' she stated, grabbing a comb from a wooden box behind her. 'Her Grace has requested to talk to you before supper. Do not look at Her Grace in the eyes. Do not talk to Her Grace until Her Grace talks to you first. Do not sit unless Her Grace invites you to,' Maria told her once Ella was done with untangling her hair, and frowned as she saw her try to arrange her breasts, compressed under the close-fitted bodice. It was as if women were supposed to make people forget they had breasts. 'And do not do that. It is unbecoming. Let us join the others, now,' she said, Ella feeling like a little girl caught picking her nose in public.

Ella followed Maria out of the room, hoping the other women would like and trust her better than their colleague. They had to, so she could have the opportunity to escape and find Lolly's ring. She was safe for now, but one mistake, one poor choice of word, could end it all. Besides, she was not without knowing people could die of anything in 1510. Antibiotics were not a thing yet, nor were vaccines or painkillers. Something as little as a cold could send someone to death's door. She had to go back home before that. And, in the meantime, her vaccinations had to pay off.

Considering how high-pitched the King's voice was, Ella thought it funny to hear how low his wife's was. In a strong Spanish accent, the Queen had invited her to sit down and had explained to her that it was not the first time for Pan to get lost in the gardens.

'He is to be scared easily, although he usually comes back upon hearing His Grace sing,' she said.

'This is how I found His Grace,' Ella told her, understanding now why the King had been walking around his gardens singing out loud.

'My husband the King feels very much indebted to you, mistress Elizabeth, and so do I. Pan certainly shares this feeling also,' she said with a smile. 'It amazes me that he let you carry him, as he has so far only allowed few persons to do so.' Ella smiled but said nothing. 'Life at court is beautiful and exciting. However, it may be challenging for young persons. From this day, your behaviour reflects on me. You are expected to behave humbly, piously, virtuously, and honourably, always,' she declared.

'Yes, Your Grace,' Ella replied.

'I am aware that you are familiar with very little here. My husband asked me to appoint a lady to help you settle. Lady Mountjoy shall be that person,' the Queen said as a young woman wearing a conic headdress resembling the Queen's entered the room.

Ella felt light-headed as she followed Lady Mountjoy out. The Queen was as kind as Lolly had always said she was, but seeing the love and devotion in her eyes every time she mentioned her husband was painful, considering England would be reshaped forever by the annulment of their marriage. Both school and Lolly had taught her all about it.

The baby that the Queen was carrying right now would be a boy who would die within weeks. He would only be followed by one healthy sister, making his father panic about having no male heir to succeed him and move Heaven and Earth to be free to remarry and have a son. This would lead to the break with Rome and the Pope, and the English Reformation. The Queen would be repeatedly and publicly humiliated, separated from her daughter, rejected by the love of her life. Her existence would end in misery, away from anyone she loved, but Ella was not supposed to know that and could imagine that warning the Queen about her unenviable future would not be taken that well. She had to bite her tongue and let history follow its course.

3.

THE IMPERTINENT QUESTION 1510

Every single person was talking about her. Getting amnesia and a place in the Queen's household on the same day must not have been very common. Ella couldn't help but think they were all staring at her because they knew she was walking around with no knickers on. The Queen had allowed Lady Mountjoy, whose name was Inez, to have the rest of the day free of duties to show her around court.

Like Maria, Inez was Spanish. Unlike Maria, she was pleased to have someone under her wing. There was a slight condescension, which Ella put on the difference of rank, but there was also a lot of enthusiasm. In less than an hour, Inez had shown her so many people, explaining who they were and how they were related to one another that Ella was completely lost. They all seemed to be related somehow!

At least, the great hall was familiar. The main room of the palace, with its hammerbeam roof, was the same as the one visited so many times with Lolly, with the exception that there were large bright tapestries hung along its walls, gold covering parts of the ceiling, and some odd kind of carpet on the tiled floor. Ella could swear Lolly used to call it rushes.

'Rushes are made of hay,' Inez said after noticing the way she was staring at them. She smiled and hesitated, unsure if more explanation about the most basic aspect of the palace was needed. 'They collect dirt and dust and also help with the odours,' she eventually told her.

Ella nodded. She did not know yet what her impression of the palace was. In some way, it was an explosion of luxury. Ceilings, walls, window frames, everything had been moulded, decorated, carved. Gold had been put literally anywhere possible and rich tapestries were in almost every room.

But, at the same time, it was all dark and almost bare of any furniture. There was so much unoccupied space that any word, any sound, resonated around the room. And, despite the help from the herbs among the rushes, the smell was not for the faint-hearted. Ella was starting to understand why she was not wearing knickers. Earlier, with the King, she had been too preoccupied about the possibility of being burned alive to give much attention to anything else, but she had now no trouble identifying the smell around her: urine. People were relieving their bladders wherever and whenever they needed to.

'Lady Mountjoy, a pleasure,' Ella heard a voice behind her and turned around to see the one with the velvet coat from before. The man with him was older and had the largest forehead Ella had ever seen. 'Please, do introduce us to your new friend,' he asked Inez with a smile that did not reach his small porcine-looking eyes.

'My lord, this is Mistress Elizabeth,' Inez said, but paused. A dash of red came up to her cheeks. The King had forgotten to give Ella a surname. 'Mistress Elizabeth joined the household of Her Grace this morning,' Inez went on, increasingly embarrassed at the further realisation that no one knew in what way "Mistress Elizabeth" had joined the royal household. Ella briefly wondered if the Queen was to make her, the amnesiac girl fallen from the sky, her fool. 'Mistress Elizabeth, you are in the presence of my lord the Duke of Buckingham, and my dear husband, Lord Mountjoy,' she made the presentations.

Ella curtseyed. She was supposed to curtsey to anyone outranking her. Basically, everyone.

'The famous Mistress Elizabeth. The ailment such as yours must be so difficult to bear. I have never heard of such a thing, have you, my lord?' he asked Inez's husband.

Ella was dying to dig a hole in the hay beneath her feet and bury herself underground. Even Mountjoy was uneasy, and Inez's face was now as red as Buckingham's coat. The King's voice, filling the entire room, saved them all from the awkward moment: 'Buckingham, it is our hope you are not troubling these fair ladies!' he laughed.

'Your Grace rests assured, I am not,' Buckingham said, bowing his head to the floor. Ella curtseyed low once again. She was starting to feel a burn in her thigh muscles.

'Good, good. Mistress Elizabeth, we trust you appreciate our palace of Eltham?' the King asked.

'Very much, Your Grace,' Ella replied.

'You are to eat with us and the Queen tonight. We shall like to know more about you,' he declared with a friendly smile. Ella was about to thank him but the King turned to Buckingham, who looked both surprised and insulted at the invitation: 'You wished for your king's ear before. Come, now,' he demanded.

Buckingham followed the King out of the hall after glancing at Ella as if she was a cockroach he had just been forbidden to crush but really wanted to exterminate. She felt chills go down her spine. He despised her. She was sure nobody had ever felt this way about her before.

Mountjoy took his leave from his wife with tenderness in his eye, which turned into a certain mistrust when he politely said goodbye to Ella. He had no clue how to act around her, what to say, or certainly even what to think. Inez took her outside. They walked past the chapel and crossed the bridge, Ella's smile becoming wider as they were getting closer to the crossroads. In front of them was the gatehouse. On their right, further down, the forest and the ring.

Inez turned left. Ella's heart sank. They followed a garden path running through the centre of a series of square beds, in each of which were planted different kinds of flowers and herbs.

'I am afraid the Duke of Buckingham does not appear to be very fond of you,' Inez said.

'I noticed.'

'As the sole duke in the kingdom, it is advisable to not be his enemy, although he has not enjoyed much influence with His Grace lately.'

'Why not?'

'This is a rather impertinent question,' Inez gently scolded her. 'His sister, Lady Anne Hastings, entangled herself with a man. Her husband, Lord Hastings, was not pleased, and her brother even less so. At first, they both thought she was involved with Sir William Compton. There was a fight between him and Buckingham. But, in reality, it was His Grace who had been in Lady Anne's bed… It was all very upsetting!' Inez exclaimed, obviously having enjoyed the so-called upsetting affair as much as Americans did the Super Bowl.

'Where is she now?' Ella asked.

'She has been sent to a convent. I do not know if she is ever to come back to court. To be an unfaithful wife is a dangerous thing, Elizabeth,' Inez warned her.

'I thought the King and the Queen were happily married,' Ella admitted, thinking about all the love she had seen in her eyes, but also in his. Anyone could see that they adored each other. If the affair had been such a scandal, the Queen must have been devastated. Had she been in her royal shoes, Ella would never have been able to forgive him.

'There is much love and happiness. Most husbands find mistresses when their wives are with child, some even when they are not,' Inez said with a sly smile.

Husbands' unfaithfulness to their wives sounded so normalised that Ella had to bite her tongue to avoid being impertinent once more, but could not help but wonder out loud what the Bible said about adultery. Inez's cheeks flushed, shocked to hear her link the King's behaviour with sin.

'I am sorry. It must be the effects of my fall. There are many things I do not remember,' Ella hurriedly explained herself.

Inez relaxed. 'Though usually frowned upon, the Church encourages husbands to bed other women when their wives are with child. Otherwise, the baby could be harmed in the womb. It is also recommended for a man's health to regularly… engage… in the act of procreation. Waiting until the child is born is not advisable.'

Ella found it best to not reply. She felt sorry for the Queen. And for Anne Hastings, and every single woman living in this century. Which now included herself, for a time she hoped to be very limited.

Ella was eating the lamb on her plate in silence, listening to the conversation the King was having with the Queen and Lord Mountjoy, who had been invited to the King's table as well as Inez, about how necessary it was for the wealthy to take account of the needs of the poor. Considering their table of six had been served enough meat to feed the entire kingdom for a month, Ella had to see it as blatant hypocrisy. She was too worried however to really care about it.

She was already giving up on trying to figure out how and why she had time-travelled, like a character of a fantasy novel, because it would only drive her mad. How time travel was possible; who or what had turned the ring into a portal; had Lolly known; why the sixteenth century. There was no sense to any of it, and there were no answers to her questions. It was all out of her grasp. She could not even explain why she understood the people around her so easily, and why they understood her. She was making a conscious effort to form her sentences in a way that followed theirs, but her twenty-first century English and accent had to be different from the speech of an early sixteenth-century royal palace. Or so she had thought. Because, somehow, it was not.

Maybe the ring is helping, which would mean it is here somewhere, she thought.

There are more important things to worry about, the irked voice inside her head reminded her. Ella had to admit it was right. There was a possibility that, hidden behind his friendly invitation to his table, the King was trying to see if she was hiding something. She drunk up her wine, anxious. One could not end up in the middle of the king of England's gardens and expect to be welcomed as a friend into the palace. Her last bite of lamb was tasteless. She stared at her empty gilded plate, wondering if the whole evening were a test, and what would happen to her if she failed it.

'You are not eating, Mistress Elizabeth. Are you indisposed?' the King asked her out of the blue.

'I have eaten very well, Your Grace. I am not hungry anymore,' Ella answered.

'One's mind must be at ease for one to enjoy the pleasure of the table,' the Queen's chaplain said.

'My mind is not at ease, you are correct,' Ella agreed, resisting her strong desire to insult him – what a moron.

'Would you care to share the burden that is on your mind?' the Spanish man insisted on keeping her in the spotlight.

'I do not wish to trouble Her Grace, but thank you,' she retorted, but had to come up with an answer when the King invited her to talk as it would, according to him, not trouble his wife. 'It is upsetting when one knows that one is not at home, but does not know where such home is, or the way to get back to it,' Ella shared a half-truth, her eyes watering at the thought of her tiny London studio flat, which had a toilet and Wi-Fi at least.

'Enquiries are being made,' the King announced. 'If any young lady of good birth has disappeared from her home or convent, we shall soon be made aware.'

'I thank Your Grace,' Ella managed to say. What would be made of her once it would become clear that the search was a dead-end was a mystery that she did not want to see resolved.

'I am familiar with the feeling of being away from home, as I left Spain ten years ago, but home is somewhere we must take with us. We shall keep you in our prayers,' the Queen said.

'I thank Your Grace for such kindness,' Ella replied. She would have loved to tell her that leaving one's home country to become queen of England was not remotely on the same level as travelling by mistake five hundred years to the past.

The Queen's chaplain, who was sitting next to her, firmly put his hand on hers and added to the Queen's words that his confessional was always open. Ella faked a smile and thanked him but freed her hand. Fray Diego Fernandez was young, Spanish, and charming. She had disliked him instantly. There was this air of self-satisfaction on his face and this seductive aura around him, sexual, that was so unexpected for a friar that she did not trust him at all.

Everyone but the King seemed to have noticed how the Queen was drinking every single one of her chaplain's words. If Lolly had not taught her better about the Queen's integrity, Ella would have suspected her of having an affair with him. The Queen laughed whenever Fray Diego laughed and assented with him every time he opened his mouth. When she heartily agreed with him, repeating his words, one look at Inez made Ella understand she shared her opinion on the two. A nervous laugh threatened to escape her throat and she tried to focus on the first thing that met her eyes: her personal spoon, given to her for all her meals. Forks were only for serving, but people took their personal spoons with them everywhere. Unfortunately, thinking about men carrying spoons as if they were swords led to Ella picturing a spoon fight and made her want to laugh even more.

The King provided her with the perfect distraction when he decided that the conversation about her had come to an end and switched to the happier topic of the upcoming birth of his son. Despite the lack of proof, he was convinced the yet unborn baby was a boy, and was ecstatic. Ella forced herself to follow the discussion and forgot about Fray Diego. When it was time to go back to the Queen's apartments, she did her best to avoid looking at him in the eyes, like a Londoner on a busy tube carriage.

Ella was shown to a single bed, surrounded by many others. There were too many people in the Queen's household for everyone to have their own room. As she laid her head down on her tiny pillow, she heard whispers. Some were angry. Although not officially a maid of honour, she had not been designated as a servant either. She was some sort of extra presence in the household, yet she slept among the maids of honour, all of whom were daughters of good families. Their relatives had had to fight to get them a place in the Queen's household. All she had done was find Pan. And she had spent the evening in the King's privy chamber. She wondered whether that was a very maidenly thing to do.

She cried herself to sleep that night. The five nights after that, too. Every morning, she would wake up planning to escape to the gardens, find Lolly's ring and go back to her century. Day after day, she would realise not a minute of her time was spent alone. She would then go to bed without even having made an attempt, paralysed with the fear of getting caught.

Ella was torn between her craving for privacy and her desperate need to talk to someone about what had happened to her. If only someone knew. Even only her real name. She was not Elizabeth! If only someone could empathise with her feelings and appreciate everything she had to get used to. If only they could just understand.

If only it could be a nightmare. If only she could find herself in her bed, her real bed, able to get up to the kitchen counter, pour herself a cup of tea, and go back to bed with a bar of chocolate to spend the day under the covers.

Historical movies had not prepared her – she could not help but be angry at them. They had shown her the beautiful dresses, the curtseys, the court intrigues. Lolly had told her about how people who had lived five hundred years before her birth could be so different and yet so similar to her. No one had ever warned her that she would have to relieve herself in a chamber pot and use washable rags to wipe herself. Or use toothpicks to remove the food stuck in her teeth before rubbing them with a piece of linen. There was no toothpaste. There was no shampoo either. They did not bathe, as warming the water by the fireplace took forever.

If she was to be honest with herself, people did not smell that bad. It was all about dry-rubbing the skin with linen and, according to Inez, changing the shift at least once a day. It was the only piece of clothing that could be washed at all.

Iris used to complain about her parents making her wash her own clothes even though she still lived with them. How Ella would love to complain about that now. Her smile froze. For the first time in almost a week, she wondered if people were looking for her. Iris, or even her boss, must have reported her disappearance. Hope threatened to overwhelm her before reality led to fresh new tears that rolled down her face: no one knew they had to look for a when, not a where.

4.

Wicked Mind and Behaviour
1510

On the sixth night, Ella woke up in complete darkness, her senses in alert. It took about a minute for her brain to understand the situation and send the signal to her body that it had only been asleep. Her muscles relaxed. Her pulse slowed down.

The Lolly she had met in her dream, waiting for her in the gardens of Eltham, accusing her of stealing the ring from her and sending her to prison, was not real.

The other Lolly, standing next to the Queen with her costly gown matching the blue stone of her jewel, was a product of her imagination.

The third Lolly, terrified, running away from danger, the time travelling sapphire on her finger, had never existed.

If Lolly had ever travelled to the past, she would not have kept it from her granddaughter. It was only a nightmare.

Ella lied to Inez's face when she pretended to have a headache so strong that she could not attend mass that morning. When the Queen left with most of her women for the chapel, Ella finally found the courage to run outside. Well, she could not run without raising the suspicion of the yeomen of the guard, but she traversed the courtyard, holding her breath as she walked so close to the chapel, and walked across the bridge without anyone bothering her. She turned right and followed the orderly path until it turned into a leaf-carpeted one. She had reached the edge of the woods.

Her heart pounding in her chest, Ella walked where she had run a week earlier, holding her long hair in a side ponytail and her chin down to the ground. The large trees were stretching upwards with all their might, like guardians of the most valuable secret. It was almost peaceful. It would have been if she had not been so obsessed about finding the diamond.

She did not have time to go very far before she heard her pretend name. She had to repress a couple of swear words. How was she supposed to get out of this century if no one gave her time to look for the ring? She could have murdered her intruder out of frustration. Her legs turned into jelly when she saw who this intruder was; the Duke of Buckingham was observing her from the border of the forest, accompanied by the Countess of Suffolk, one of the Queen's ladies in waiting – the highest ranked women in the household. Ella walked back to them, trying to look as composed as possible and to understand why the man was having a private walk with a woman whose husband was in prison for trying to steal the crown from the King's father.

'Mistress Elizabeth, I hope there are no more dogs for you to save in the gardens,' Buckingham joked with a haughty smile.

'I do not think so, my lord,' Ella replied with a quick curtsey.

'I must confess I am shocked to see you here. Your presence at court is always… irregular, of course, but Lady Suffolk was just assuring me you were unwell today,' he said.

'I am surprised to see you too. We all have reasons to not be at mass this morning. If I may, how is Lady Anne Hastings?' she asked, regretting her affront as soon as the words came out of her mouth.

Buckingham's face turned purple with anger but the countess put her hand on his arm, which made him control himself. Ella curtseyed her way out and went back to the Queen's apartments, where she hid herself under the covers of her bed and cried hysterically. She, a nobody with no family nor money, had provoked the second most powerful man in the kingdom in front of a witness. For someone who had vowed to keep quiet as to stay out of trouble, she had behaved stupidly.

She fell asleep, exhausted by her confrontation with Buckingham and the tears that had followed. She was woken up by Margery, one of the rare maids of honour whom Ella had never caught looking at her like a beast that should have been sent back to where it came from. The daughter of the late Sir Robert Tate, who was once Lord Mayor of London, Margery had lost her only sister in childhood and had been brought up with five brothers. She was seventeen years old and always sympathetic, as if she knew what it was to be the outsider.

'Her Grace is in the King's apartments with some of her ladies, and told me to enquire about your health,' she said, her deep brown eyes staring at her.

'I feel better, thank you. Will you please help me get dressed?' Ella asked, hoping her eyes were not too puffy.

Margery agreed. Soon, Ella was presentable again. She waited in the room next door as the girl needed to empty her bladder, killing time by sniffing the enchanting smell released by her pomander, this hollow scented ball carried around by everyone as a shield against more sickening smells like human waste and rotten food.

'Mistress Elizabeth, it is with great pleasure I see you well rested,' the voice of Fray Diego filled the room.

'Thank you. I feel better and will now join Her Grace,' Ella replied.

'Her Grace's ladies are renowned for their fairness, but you are the fairest of them all. I insist that we might become better acquainted,' he said, walking towards her without even trying to conceal his lusty thoughts.

'I have to go to the Queen,' Ella retorted, chin up, refusing to take a step back.

'I am confident Her Grace shall manage to spare you for a moment. I promise you will not regret it,' he whispered.

Before Ella understood what he meant, he grabbed the neckline of her dress and pulled her towards him with force. She pushed him away, avoiding his lips on hers but feeling them, wet, unwelcome, against her cheek. The friar's hand was still gripping her dress, his fingers down her cleavage. She sunk her nails into it before remembering she had had to cut them short at her arrival in this century. Out of frustration and resentment, she spat to his face. His eyes black with anger, Fray Diego took his hand back to wipe his chin.

'Don't lay your hands on me ever again!' Ella warned him, barely keeping her hatred for him under control.

Fray Diego opened his mouth, but Margery entered the room and asked what the matter was in a trembling voice. She had heard everything and had come to Ella's rescue, taking the friar by surprise. He did not give Ella time to answer Margery's question:

'I do not know who you truly are but I shall see that your wickedness be revealed to Her Grace. One with a righteous mind would not have been punished by the Lord!' he shouted and stormed out of the room.

'Such a depraved, shameful man!' Margery exclaimed when he was gone.

'How can the Queen accept his presence?' Ella cried. Her legs were so weak she had to sit down.

'He conceals his true nature to Her Grace. Elizabeth, you fought for your virtue with an admirable dedication,' Margery complimented her.

I lost my "virtue" at sixteen, I just didn't want to be raped, Ella meant to answer. She kept quiet.

'We must report him immediately. Only the King bears more influence than him on the Queen,' Margery decided.

Ella would have loved to stay on her wooden stool for a little bit longer, as her legs were still shaking, but followed Margery out of the room. Part of her wanted wanted to doubt that the Queen would believe her chaplain when he would tell her that the stray cat she had just taken in had been deprived of her memories by nothing less than God because of her evil soul. But it was 1510. Ella felt sick to her stomach.

'Am I in trouble?' she murmured to Margery as they were walking as fast as decency allowed.

'Virtuous behaviour is very important to the King,' she replied, making Ella feel even worse. The King and Anne Hastings had both cheated on their spouses, yet only one of them was now in a convent.

'Am I going to be believed?' Ella asked, but Margery stopped walking and curtseyed. The King had appeared at the end of the corridor and was approaching them with an older man.

'Mistress Margery, Mistress Elizabeth, we are afraid we have been called by matters of state, but we shall hear you sing tomorrow, as we felt very sorry of your absence today,' the King announced.

Replying it would be an honour to sing for him, Ella moved on to the subject that interested her, terrified the King would think it impossible for a man to take advantage of a woman.

'Your Grace, may I please discuss Her Grace's chaplain, Fray Diego,' she said.

The King agreed, apparently unaware of what the problem could be, but the other man's face fell. Ella knew he knew. The King's jaw tensed and his eyes narrowed when Ella explained what had just happened, deciding to share every detail. Her words were confirmed by Margery, who repeated her admiration for how Ella had "protected her virtue".

The King did not say anything to them but barked at the man to get Fray Diego for a meeting with him in his privy chambers, and left in a hurry.

Margery smiled. 'You did well. Many of us women desired that Fray Diego be punished. Always ravishing married ladies, so they could not tell a soul without suffering the wrath of their husbands… until now.'

Ella did not say anything and focused instead on the view of London that the palace, built high, was offering her through its bay windows. It was more of a small town than the big city of her childhood. Her eyes went from the boats on the Thames to the multitude of church spires; they started to look like a forest of brambles and thorns. Ella had trouble to believe her word would count more than a man's, especially a man of God's. Or that the King cared about women's consent at all. Sixteenth-century men cared less than twenty-first-century men about it, and that was saying something.

She was to be proven wrong. Inez was teaching her a piece on the virginals, which was the closest thing this century had to a piano, when the King and Queen entered the room the following morning. Everyone got up to their feet. The Queen robotically walked to her closet, as if she was doing everything in her power to not fall apart in the middle of the room. Her husband watched her leave, his body present but his mind elsewhere.

'Her Grace's chaplain, Fray Diego Fernandez, is on his way back to Spain. He is never to return to England. The discovery of his wicked mind and behaviour caused great distress in the Queen,' the King came back to his senses once the door had closed behind his wife.

He kept talking but Ella stopped listening. Fray Diego was gone. She was safe. The King had believed her over him. She took her face in her hands, astonished. Inez discreetly tapped on her elbow to remind her that she was not alone. She collected herself. The King asked all the members of his wife's household to return to their various occupations, and sat down next to Ella, both facing the virginals. She played the piece Inez had just taught her.

'It was very agreeable,' he complimented her.

'I thank Your Grace. Also, for...' she meant to mention Fray Diego.

'Fray Diego Fernandez's behaviour was not to be suffered at our court,' he interrupted her. 'We offered you shelter, Mistress Elizabeth. We did so because you were in need of assistance, not to have you insulted within our walls. You shared how you felt to be without a home, but as long as God intends it, you are home at our court,' he said. 'As maid of honour to Her Grace,' he added.

'I am struggling to find the words to thank Your Grace appropriately,' Ella replied, and for once did not have to lie. This man could *not* be the great tyrant of England's History.

'Then we shall stop speaking and teach you instead our favourite piece on the virginals,' he told her.

Ella watched his strong and oddly feminine hands dance on the musical instrument. He was obviously gifted at music and enjoyed playing as much as she did. She smiled. A nineteen-year-old, barely even an adult, historically known for his harsh treatment of his six successive wives, had believed her when she had complained about another man touching her without her consent. He had not accused her of lying. Nor had he assumed she had said or done something misleading. He had believed her and acted on it. Nothing more, nothing less.

Ella was still desperate for the next opportunity to escape to the woods to find Lolly's ring but, for the first time in days, the next breath she took was a breath of hope.

The Duke of Buckingham and the Countess of Suffolk, whom Ella suspected to be lovers, always had an eye on her. Days became weeks. Lolly's ring was still lost somewhere in the woods. It was so frustrating to know it so close to her, yet unattainable, that Ella cried herself to sleep every night.

A lot of her time was spent with the Queen. It was the safest place to be for her now that her chaplain had been replaced. Men at court had many opportunities to exercise, but little else. Boredom often led to drunkenness and the Queen's presence was the only thing reminding them that they were not barbarians and had to behave. Ella would accompany her anywhere she was allowed to and was especially keen to come with her to mass. Whether it was in her personal closet or in the palace chapel, with its altar made of gold and precious stones, Ella was always there, pretending to pray with her for hours on end. She did not believe in God, nor had she been schooled in the liturgy like everyone else, but it was giving her time to think and was relieving her from the pressure and anxiety of saying or doing the wrong thing.

The Queen had had to grieve the loss of Fray Diego and accept the reason behind it. But, day after day, prayer after prayer, Ella could see the

Queen's behaviour change towards her. She would speak to her more often, in English or in Spanish, as Ella had decided her linguistic abilities could be a great way for them to bond. It had delighted both the Queen and Inez, but had only made the other Spanish women in the household more distrustful of her as they disagreed on who she really was.

'The way she speaks is not from Spain,' one of the maids of honour, Isabel de Vargas, said one day. 'Where is she coming from?' Ella overheard.

'The question is, where is she running from?' Maria retorted.

'A convent? Or an unkind husband, maybe,' Isabel's sister Blanche guessed. 'The Queen does enjoy her company.'

'Well, I do not,' Maria put an end to the conversation.

Inez was giving Ella an informal writing lesson. The student was doing her best to ignore the hostile glances and irritated murmurs around her to focus on the shape of her letters. If the ring may have been helping with her pronunciation, it was not with her twenty-first century writing. It did not have a place in the sixteenth century and neither did Ella. Every time she looked up, someone was making sure she did not forget it.

'Mistress Maria and many others do not look pleased with me,' she whispered to Inez.

'It was to be expected. The Queen is taking your advice on dirt. Every time one has to wash one's hands, one knows why,' she replied.

'I find it to be a rule that shall bring good health to us all,' Margery intervened.

Ella had explained to the Queen that she believed dirt to be dangerous for her health and the health of her unborn child, as it could be carrying diseases. The Queen had listened, agreed, and decided that the members of her household would now have to wash their hands with soap every time they needed to touch her or her personal belongings.

'I agree, but Elizabeth must be more sensible. Any mark of favour from Her Grace shall alienate the ladies further from her,' Inez told Margery like a teacher would speak to a pupil's parent at the end of the day.

It was a fact: the closer Ella was getting to the Queen, the less friendly most of the household were to her. Inez and Margery were the only women who liked spending time with her. The experience with Fray Diego had drawn Margery and Ella closer, and although her new friend looked at her as if they had killed a kitten every time the Queen openly regretted the absence of her former chaplain, it was now accepted by the entire household that a decent person would not have been kicked out of England.

Ella had thought life would have been boring. Praying, knitting, singing, dancing, playing music, reading – that was all women were doing at court. In some ways, it was boring. But her mind had never been clearer. There was no phone, no internet, no social media. Nowhere to be, except where she was. Nothing to do, except what she was doing. No stranger to compare herself with.

It was ironic, and even absurd, because she wanted to leave this century and never come back but, for the first time in her life, she was living in the moment. There was no more fear of missing out on the latest exhibition at a London gallery, no more pining for likes every time she posted something on social media.

Sometimes, she wondered if the reason she could really see more clearly was because her hair was finally used to the lack of shampoo but, deep down, she knew this break from the twenty-first century was not all bad.

She changed her mind when she woke up one morning to find some ladies packing. 'What is happening?' she asked Margery.

'The court is moving to Greenwich Palace,' she answered. 'Are you all right?' she quickly asked when her friend grabbed the nearest piece of furniture for support.

'Why… why are we leaving?' Ella stuttered.

'Eltham Palace needs to be cleaned!' Margery said, repressing a laugh because of how obvious the answer was. 'You shall see, Greenwich Palace is very beautiful. It is where His Grace was born.'

Ella nodded quietly. If delaying her search for Lolly's ring to avoid Buckingham's scrutiny was fine, leaving it behind was another story. Animals could steal it. Weather conditions could corrode it. Knowing it could be gone the next time she would come back to Eltham Palace, and also that she had to leave anyway, was harder than anything else she had ever experienced.

The walls started to close in on her. She left the room. Before she knew where she was going, she found herself in the great hall. The large wooden door was open to the outside. Ella walked towards it. She had to get the ring back. It was now or never.

'Mistress Elizabeth!' Maria's voice snapped spitefully behind her. Ella could have slapped her. 'It is the third time I call your name,' she reproached her. Ella apologized. 'You must help for the packing. We are to leave soon,' Maria said abruptly.

There was no choice. The King and the Queen were moving to Greenwich Palace. Elizabeth White had to follow them. Lolly's ring was staying behind.

Elizabeth White. The King himself had picked out this surname for her, weeks after giving her a first name. It was a compliment for being the palest-skinned woman at court. She had always felt self-conscious about her inability to tan in summer but, here, the paler the better.

Greenwich Palace had felt like the cleanest palace that had ever stood when the court had arrived from Eltham Palace and its stench, but by the end of November, it had become so filthy it was impossible to breathe through the nose. Urine was everywhere, excrement was stocked underneath the palace, leftover food was rotting in every corner, walls were covered in soot from the fires. The King had planned the court's move to Richmond Palace for the next morning.

The Queen had given Ella the last day in Greenwich Palace to rest, as, early in the morning, she had forgotten her pomander before heading to mass and thrown up because of the smell. Despite the cold and windy weather, Ella had escaped with Inez to the gardens. She was still not used to how different the palaces of Eltham and Greenwich looked from the outside. When the former was placed high and surrounded by a moat, the latter was a long and low building along the river.

Out of nowhere, Inez told her that she had had words with Maria. 'She believes me to be foolish to trust you, as you may be a French spy, an outlaw, or even both,' she explained.

Ella's first reaction was to laugh. Most courtiers believed her to be running away from a convent. Being an outlawed French spy sounded much more exciting. Inez watched her in silence for a second and Ella realised she had to defend herself.

'If I was an outlaw, why would I run away to court? And I do not speak a word of French,' she exclaimed, although she did have some basics in this language.

'Calm yourself, I do know she is mistaken about you. I am quite certain Maria's animosity towards you is jealousy,' Inez reassured her. 'She is hurt because of how much Her Grace values your company. I have been by the Queen's side for more than ten years and shall serve her faithfully until the day I die, but never have I enjoyed Her Grace's friendship like Maria does and like you do now,' she said.

'I am sorry,' Ella started to say, but Inez shook her head with a smile.

'I appreciate what the Lord has given me, rather than what He has not. Oh, the King,' she said, and they both curtseyed as he walked towards them, wrapped up warm in a furry cloak.

'Lady Mountjoy, Mistress Elizabeth,' he saluted them. 'This rascal lost his way and had to be rescued once again,' he told them, taking Pan from under his cloak and smiling at Ella, clearly remembering how they had first met. Pan stretched his neck towards Ella with a few repeated sniffs, then proceeded to lick the air, as if licking Ella's cheek.

'Pan, you are as cheeky as you are handsome!' she exclaimed, which made the King laugh loudly before asking Inez to go back to the Queen.

'We heard you were unwell today, Mistress Elizabeth,' he said once Inez had left.

'I was, Your Grace, but I am feeling better now. I had forgotten to take my pomander with me.'

'We are much eager to travel in the morrow. Dirt and stench are strong enemies!'

'They are,' Ella sighed, daydreaming about her clean and fresh smelling flat in 2020 and the army of cleaning products under the sink.

'We have been told that you advised the Queen to require clean hands from all her ladies,' the King said, turning Ella's stomach into one big knot of anxiety at the possibility of him being upset.

But the King was known to lead a war against dirt. 'I believe dirt may carry diseases,' she admitted, annoyed that people were unaware of germs and that she could not tell anyone she, a woman, knew better than the physicians.

'We as well. The health of our son and the Queen are of the greatest importance. Can you write?' he asked, and Ella replied that she could. 'You shall write down rules that can improve the cleanliness of our palaces. You shall also be responsible of their respect during the birth of our son,' he declared.

Ella was not sure if she had to jump for joy or cry of despair. She loved the idea of bringing some healthy changes to court, but she did not want to be held responsible for the baby's death when it would happen. Historically, he had died after a few weeks. Ella stayed quiet for a moment and nodded when the King asked her if she was already thinking about her assignment. That was a lie. Telling him she was thinking about the coming death of his unborn child was even worse than breaking the news to him that time travel was possible.

With its white stones, its pinnacles and its turrets surmounted by bell-shaped domes, Richmond Palace looked exactly like the fairytale palaces Ella used to imagine as a little girl. She smiled sadly as she could not help but wonder if Lolly had ever seen it for herself. She was adamant that her grandmother would have never kept it from her, but there were some days the more cynical voice inside her head was bringing second-guesses to the party. Every single time, Ella had to shake them away. There was no point in torturing herself over answers that were out of her reach.

The Queen was about eight months pregnant. With great formalities, she entered her bedchamber, where she was to spend the last weeks of her pregnancy with her ladies in confinement. It had been made dark, warm, and quiet, as to resemble a womb, and no man would be allowed in until the birth of the heir, not even his own father. Ella took the assignment the King had given her very seriously and wrote down a set of rules, hoping he would at least agree with her idea of forbidding men to relieve their bladder in the fireplaces.

Ella turned twenty at the end of December, lonelier than ever. Not a single person knew when her birthday was. The King had given her an identity but not a date of birth. Even her friends never wondered how old she was. The amount of candles that should have been on her birthday cake this year was the one thing that did not draw attention to her, as most of the courtiers were more or less her age.

She was staring at the ceiling one night, listening to Margery's loud breathing and thinking about her life before this madness. She used to be so anxious about turning twenty without her life figured out. Her age was the least of her worries now. In fact, the only thing that mattered was to spend her twenty-first birthday in the twenty-first century. She wanted the son-less Queen Katherine of Aragon to be back in her books about the Tudors, not in the room next door.

Ella sat up. The lack of sons in the King and the Queen's marriage had changed England's history for ever, but it did not mean it was bound to happen again. If the boy was to live, the King would never want to get rid of his wife. All he wanted was a male heir. If he had one, he would never start wondering if his marriage was valid or not. It would not prevent him from falling in love with the infamous Anne Boleyn, but it would prevent him from discarding his wife and marrying her instead. And there would be no break with Rome. No Reformation. England would stay Catholic, at least under the reign of Henry VIII.

Her fingers on her temples, Ella tried to remember what Lolly had told her about the baby's cause of death. Her mind went blank. She sneered. The survival of one baby could change everything, but it was impossible to save him if she had no idea how he had even died in the first place.

Besides, she believed the Reformation to have been a good thing. Only a few weeks at court had been enough for Ella to witness the greed and the lust of several men of the Church. Bishops had mistresses and illegitimate children whilst asking for money from sinners for them to be forgiven and escape Hell. Despite her atheism, she knew something had to be done.

The Reformation has to happen, she thought, lying back on her pillow.

Meddling with the past was too risky and would have consequences on her present. History had to follow its course, which meant this baby had to die once again. Ella closed her eyes.

2011. Emily Buckley had taken her granddaughter on a weekend trip to Peterborough, mainly to visit its cathedral and the tomb of Queen Katherine of Aragon in it. Or Katharine, as the gold letters in front of them spelt her name.

'It says queen of England, darling, but she was buried as Dowager Princess of Wales, as if she was still the widow of her first husband, Prince Arthur. As if her marriage to his brother, Henry VIII, had never happened. He insulted her even in death. He also didn't allow their daughter to attend. The princess was devastated.'

'It's not very kind.'

'No, it's not. There were many abuses within the Catholic Church, which needed to be taken care of, but the way Henry VIII made it happen and what he did to his wife for it was cruel and wrong. She deserved better. So many lives were destroyed for him to have a son and for the Reformation to happen the way he wanted it to happen.'

As Lolly's voice echoed in her head, Ella opened her eyes and sat back up. That baby would be followed in death by thousands of people, including his own mother. The ones refusing to acknowledge the King's remarriage to Anne Boleyn and to recognise him head of the Church of England would lose their heads. Others would be tried for heresy and burned, under his reign but also the reigns of his children.

So many lives were destroyed for him to have a son. And it had all started here and now. The tale of the bloodthirsty tyrant and his six unlucky wives, or the damages a bruised ego could do to a man and a country. The King was kind and probably as cruel as he was faithful to his wife, but God's refusal to give him a son, followed by the Pope's to grant him the annulment of his marriage, would turn him into a bitter and violent man, executing first and thinking later. Ella could change that. Adrenaline coursed through her veins.

She could change history. She just had to find a way to save that baby.

5.

ONE PERFECT BOY
1511

The midwife looked concerned. It was late on New Year's Eve, maybe early on New Year's Day. The Queen was in labour, her face deformed by pain and terror, but she was refusing to push. Her ladies were soothing her with empty words. She was desperately holding on to the relic she had had brought from Westminster Abbey, supposed to be the girdle of the Virgin Mary herself, dropped by her as she was ascending to Heaven.

'Your Grace, the time has come,' the midwife repeated with a soft voice. The Queen kept her eyes closed, her lips mouthing something in Spanish.

Ella could not bear it. She remembered that this baby would be born perfectly healthy and could not understand why the Queen was not pushing. She left Margery's side and walked up to the bed, ignoring the Countess of Suffolk saying her name, twice, unimpressed. She would not let anyone harm this baby. Not even his own mother.

'Your Grace. The healthy, beautiful baby boy inside you needs his mother's help,' she said firmly, putting aside for the time being that she was talking to the queen of England.

'My baby girl was dead,' the Queen replied in a murmur.

Of course. The Queen had given birth to a dead daughter the year before and was terrified now to give birth to a son only to lose him too. Ella swallowed with difficulty when she thought about all the miscarriages and stillbirths her history books said the Queen had suffered and needed to shift her focus back on what really mattered: the baby who had to live to become king of England after his father.

'God took Your Grace's daughter away but sent a son instead. I beg Your Grace to be strong and deliver him into the world!' she exclaimed.

'A boy…' the Queen smiled weakly.

'Yes. A healthy prince.'

'Healthy…'

'Yes, Your Grace. You must deliver him into this world now, and we shall all pray for his good health. I beg Your Grace to let the prince be born! You must help him live!' Ella insisted, trying to walk the thin line between sounding convincing and threatening.

There were some shocked voices in the background. She knew that she was crossing a line. She had no right to speak to the Queen in those terms. But it worked. One hand in Ella's, the other pressing the holy girdle on her chest, the Queen finally started to push.

The midwife grabbed the baby boy by the shoulders and pulled him out of his mother. The Queen dropped her head back, exhausted, her red-gold hair on the pillow giving the illusion of a crown. She laughed when the first cry of her baby filled the room.

'A prince, Your Grace!' the midwife cried.

The Queen, beaming, looked at Ella and repeated the words she had told her before: 'a healthy prince.' Ella laughed and kissed the new mother's hand. He was alive.

Someone opened the door to tell the King's messenger about the birth of the heir. The man was then to run to the King himself. As a few others were reverently washing the baby, the Queen pressed Ella's hand in hers and thanked her. They watched together the baby being swaddled.

The Countess of Suffolk was about to put the baby in his massive cradle when the door was flung open. The King entered, floating on air, his cheeks pink and his smile bigger than his palace.

'A boy! A prince! An heir!' he cried in a loud voice, himself looking like a boy discovering his Christmas presents.

There was so much pride and love in his eyes as he took the Queen's hands in his that Ella would not have believed him capable of ever mistreating her, had she not known better.

Wrapped up tight, the baby boy was sleeping in his cradle under a red and gold fringed cloth. His mother had been moved to the huge bed in her presence chamber as soon as she had felt well enough to sit up and receive people, looking regal in her red mantle, and Ella was trying to figure out a way to convince her that lying in bed for an entire month after childbirth was not as good for her as her midwife thought. The circumstances in which blood clots formed were not common knowledge in this century, but that did not make them any less dangerous. Sooner or later, Ella would have to make the Queen understand that her views on health were better than the ones of the midwives and the physicians, and that would not be an easy task.

The Countess of Suffolk sat down next to Ella and looked at her with contempt. 'You have forgotten your place, Mistress Elizabeth,' she said.

'My lady?' Ella feigned innocence.

'You showed a lack of respect to Her Grace and envisaged the death of His Grace's son and heir should the Queen not "help him." It is high treason,' she reminded her.

'The prince was not born yet when I said that,' Ella retorted.

Mentioning the death of the King, the Queen or their eldest son and heir was high treason. Ella knew that the countess was not making it up. The King chose this moment to enter the room and tell her to follow him. Ella saw the countess's satisfaction as her wobbly legs led her out of the Queen's apartments. She could have sworn Maria was smiling. She had indeed forgotten her place: it was 1510, not 2020. She was going to pay the price.

'We are now the father of a healthy son,' the King declared once in the corridor, walking by her side and followed at a respectable distance by a small group of courtiers.

Ella hated the idea of being told off, or worse, with an audience, especially as the Earl of Wiltshire was part of it. The man was Buckingham's younger brother and had once called her "the King's odd creature" with such disdain that she had believed herself to be, for a minute, a deformed animal.

'May the Lord bless him,' Ella said with a trembling voice.

'Mistress Elizabeth, we had a conversation with the Queen regarding the birth of our son. You are to be rewarded, both financially and with our trust and gratitude,' the King told her, then waited for her to wrap her head around the fact he did not mean to have it cut off.

'Your Grace's trust and gratitude are an honour, but I do not wish for any money.'

'Your help extended to our son and heir, and thus to our kingdom,' he pointed out. 'We are to appoint you as a woman of the prince's bedchamber. You shall stay here with the nursery. The rules we have decided are to be strictly respected as to ensure the good health of the prince,' he declared, forgetting the rules had been decided by her and not him.

To be fair, it did not make much difference. He was at the centre of everything. Of what everyone was doing. Of what everyone was thinking.

The King was trusting her with the welfare of the most precious thing in his life. More than unexpected, it was ironic. Ella had never seen nannying as her calling but it was following her through time. She was offered the opportunity to actively protect the baby from anything that could lead to his early death instead of having to wait for its news. It also meant that the boy's death would, partially at least, be her direct responsibility should it happen once again. It was too much of a gamble.

'Your Grace, this is more honour than I deserve. I am not sure I am the person for this task,' Ella said.

'We are confident with our decision, as we were when we appointed you maid of honour to our wife the Queen. You may renounce these favours if they are against your conscience,' the King replied.

His words bore no animosity but could be easily translated; Ella only had a roof over her head and food on her plate because the King had been kind enough to allow it. He could also take it all away. Someone behind them sniggered. Ella could have sworn it was the Earl of Wiltshire. She bit the inner side of her cheek. The King had saved her in more ways than one, but she now owed him. She was utterly dependent on his goodwill. Saying no to him was not an option.

'Your Grace's trust in my person is all that my conscience needs. I am thankful,' she told him what he wanted to hear.

The King nodded, satisfied, then proceeded in listing all the rules "he" had come up with. If he had said no to opening one window per room each morning, since it was believed diseases were transmitted through the air, he had agreed to hand washing with soap before touching the baby and after each sneeze, but also to the interdiction to leave food around or to come anywhere near the boy with an upset stomach.

Although born in a time when kings of England ruled the country and mattered on a national and international scale, the heir to the throne turned out to have fewer godparents than the one born only a few years before Ella's time travel. The New Year's boy was christened in the church of the Observant Friars five days after his birth in the traditional absence of his parents. The Earl and Countess of Devon, who were the baby's great-uncle and great-aunt, and the archbishop of Canterbury, were chosen as godparents. The king of France and Margaret of Austria, the daughter of the Holy Roman emperor, completed the list as the prince's sponsors.

'I am looking forward to seeing Margaret of Austria,' Ella said before the ceremony. The widow of the Queen's brother John, and the sister to Philip, the dead husband of the Queen's sister Joanna, Margaret of Austria was regent of the Netherlands in the name of her nephew, Philip and Joanna's son Charles. For the first time in months, Ella was going to breathe the same air as a powerful and independent woman.

Maria laughed. Inez gave her a dirty look, then turned to Ella. 'None of the prince's sponsors is to be in attendance, Elizabeth. Crossing the sea would take too much time and would cause much disturbance for them. Two good Englishpersons will stand proxy for them,' she explained, oblivious to Ella's disappointment.

The door and nave had been hung with cloth of gold and beautiful carpets had been laid out all the way to the altar in the sweet-smelling church. It was the first time in this century that Ella had seen carpets laid on the floor, as they were usually used to cover furniture. As for the baby, he wore a robe with a red mantle over it, with a train longer than any twenty-first century bride had ever dreamed of, and was carried to the altar under a canopy of estate surrounded by two dozen unlit torches, followed by two hundred more.

As a *Te Deum* was sung for him, the baby was washed behind a curtained area with a little fire to keep him warm. Ella watched but did not participate. She was only to make sure anyone who touched the prince had clean hands. The ceremony was immediately followed by his confirmation, and once heralds had cried out 'Henry, son and heir to the king of England, Duke of Cornwall!' the Countess of Devon, with the newly christened baby in her arms, led a procession of men carrying now lit torches back to the Queen's chamber.

Ella was still fuming about the truth behind the churching ceremony when time came for the Queen to undertake this mandatory purification. What she had always thought to be a way to bless mothers and give thanks for their survival from childbirth was actually meant to purify their souls and bodies, as delivering a baby through one's vagina was apparently so impure that women were not allowed to go back to a normal life before going through churching.

Soon after, the Queen left with the King and court for Westminster Palace, leaving behind their one-month-old son. Ella waved Inez and Margery goodbye from the window upstairs, her heart in her mouth, as if she was losing Iris all over again. Neither of them could have ever filled the hole created with the temporary loss of her best friend, but they had helped her feel almost safe in this strange and scary world. Now they were gone and Ella was trapped. The survival of the most important baby in the kingdom was her responsibility and the one of her new colleagues.

There was a very nasal woman called Agnes, whose baby had been born on New Year's Eve but had died before seeing the New Year. She was the wet nurse, which meant she was now used as a human breast milk vending machine for another woman's baby. There was also the lady mistress, a thirty-something-year-old woman called Lady Alice Shelley. Her older brother, Sir Edward Belknap, was a friend of the King. Then, there were four rockers to lull the baby to sleep, and the Spanish Dr de Vittoria. Ella promised herself to learn the names of everyone else, but there were too many people. At least, there was Thomas, the baker, who was not against preparing extra treats for the people he got along well with. His home-made marzipan was so good it could make Ella forget about chocolate.

The sky was still dark outside and Ella was staring at her pint of ale, thinking about how she might actually be willing to kill someone for a cup of tea. The water in 1511 was contaminated with sewage and could send the healthiest of horses to death's door. Although she could guess that boiling it would get rid of the bacteria, she was not ready to bet her life on it. Just like everyone else, she drank a low-alcohol ale or wine instead, even for breakfast. She was still not used to the nutty taste first thing in the morning. She looked at her pint, then at her little piece of bread. She wanted avocado on toast. She wanted a fry up. She wanted waffles. She wanted French toast.

Ella stopped making the counterproductive list of everything she wanted to eat when Agnes entered the room to get her own bread with butter and sage and her pint of ale. Even pregnant and breastfeeding women drank ale. Ella used to wonder why so many babies died in the past, but she was now puzzled that any of them made it to adulthood.

Agnes sneezed. 'Bless you,' Ella said out of habit. As the woman was staring at her awkwardly, Ella finished her bread as quickly as possible, washed her hands and escaped the room. She made a face when she realised she had no idea if people had already started to answer to a sneeze by "bless you" in this century but shrugged. Agnes would not be the first nor the last to think she was odd. Ella went to get baby Henry from his bed.

'Good morning, my little Hal,' she whispered. His big blue eyes opened wide and once again melted her heart. He was the most adorable and alert baby she had ever seen.

He was soon to be hungry, though, and started to cry. Alice and Agnes appeared immediately. Ella was about to give the baby to the latter for his suckle when doubt made her change her mind.

'You did sneeze not long ago. Did you clean your hands?' she asked.

'My lord the prince is hungry!' Agnes reminded her.

'I can see. That was not my question,' Ella retorted.

'As the prince's lady mistress, I demand that you let Mistress Agnes feed him,' Alice jumped to Agnes's help.

'Mistress Agnes must clean her hands, using plenty of soap, or another wet nurse will be found. The rules are the rules,' Ella said firmly.

She did not blink when Alice looked at her like the only thing preventing her from strangling her with her bare hands was the royal baby crying in her arms. Agnes gave up and washed her hands. The room fell silent as Hal started suckling, but Alice was still looking at Ella with a clear desire for murder in the eyes.

There were plenty of reasons why a baby could die, especially in this century, and his nurse holding him with hands full of germs was one of them. Ella could not help but roll her eyes when she realised just how many people may have met a violent end because the woman in front of her had sneezed, forgot to wash her hands and then fed the heir to the throne. Lack of personal hygiene may have led to the English Reformation.

'Unbelievable,' she murmured to herself.

'His Grace shall hear about this, Mistress Elizabeth,' Alice threatened her between her teeth.

'I trust you are prepared to face the consequences, my lady,' Ella replied with a provocative smile and exited the room, not because she wanted to take her leave dramatically but because she had started to feel something warm running down her thigh.

The last time Ella had had her period was early September 2020. She had not panicked when it had not come the following months, as she had not had sex since way before Lolly's death. She had even enjoyed it. Her body had been affected by time travel in ways she would never comprehend. It was now recovering and bringing delightful menstrual cramps and blood back into her life. Ella regretted not having been more curious when watching Inez and Margery mixing some herbs together to ease their pain. It was not something she was now likely to find in a book, as the all-powerful Church believed menstruation was some divine punishment for Eve's original sin and forbade the use of painkillers for cramps. Women were expected to obey, however insane it was.

Alice burst into the room as Ella was standing in the middle, legs wide and dress pulled up, looking for blood stains. The woman's anger turned into the kind of compassion only people experiencing menstruation knew and went to get the box with the old rags that they were supposed to put together between their legs during their period, with some kind of underwear to keep them in place. It looked more like a chastity belt than a pair of knickers. Ella sighed. If only they had tampons.

'You look pale,' Alice noticed.

'I need to get used to it again, that is all,' Ella said.

'Have you missed some courses lately?'

'Four.'

'Were you with child?'

'No, and it would be of no concern of yours if I had been,' Ella snapped, always wanting to avoid people being curious about her.

'I apologise if I have offended you.'

'Five minutes ago, you were menacing to complain to the King about me.'

'You must recall you were preventing the prince from being fed!'

'I was protecting His Grace's son and heir against a high risk of disease! I do not doubt of your best intentions, but I was in the right and you were not.'

'Is there a stain?' Alice changed the subject.

'On the shift, yes,' Ella replied.

Alice helped her get undressed despite her anger towards her. The two women proceeded in an irritated silence, putting a clean shift on Ella's back and soaking the stained one in cold water. Alice then gave her two little scented pouches, explaining that they were to be carried around the waist and would help with the smell. Ella thanked her but barely had time to get fully dressed that Alice got a third pouch out, which was scentless.

'You shall bleed less with this,' she declared. 'Inside are the ashes of a burned toad.'

'Pardon?'

'The ashes of a burned toad,' she replied like it was perfectly normal. Ella faked a smile, fighting against the urge to throw the pouch across the room, and took what was left of the poor toad with her. How upset animal rights defenders would be at Henry VIII's court. With the burned toads, the various animal parts used for remedies, the hundreds of pounds of meat eaten every day and the real furs worn in cold weather, the sixteenth century was not for vegans. Or for animals.

The King was visiting his son for the first time since his christening. For a reason he did not share, the Queen did not come with him. Ella was smiling, watching him walk around the room with Hal in his arms.

The King was looking at his son like he was the best thing that had ever happened to him. Ella could tell he loved him, although that may not have been perceived this way in her native century. He loved his son from afar, seeing him for a few minutes every few weeks, but without a doubt would expect him once older to obey him in every aspect of his life because he was his father. If Hal was ever given a ring from his dead grandmother, his father would probably try to take it from him to sell it.

He is not your father, Ella silently reminded herself as the King sat down on his chair, his son still in his arms. He showed her the small stool next to him. Ella sat down, happy to have a chat with someone she would not end up arguing with over hygiene.

'His eyes are blue, like ours. We have never seen a healthier boy, have you, Mistress Elizabeth?' he asked.

'No, Your Grace,' Ella answered, although he may have forgotten his wife's eyes were blue too.

'One perfect boy!' he exclaimed, before asking her if she knew who Sir Thomas Knyvett was.

'Your Grace's master of the horse?' Ella said, picturing a blond man with a long nose and a constant excitement for court entertainment.

'Indeed. You have missed quite the tournament! We were attired in superb purple satin, displaying gold initials of the Queen and us. But common folk doubted that the gold was real!' he cried, his mouth wide open, as if in shock. 'We told them that the king of England wears real gold, and that they could try pulling it off! And they did! And not just! They took everything! We ourselves were down to our doublet and hose, but Sir Thomas had not even his shift anymore!' he burst out laughing, so hard that he had to give his son back to Ella.

Picturing people stripping Sir Thomas Knyvett of all of his clothes was funny, but not as much as the King's communicative laugh. Ella would have gladly laughed with him if only women were allowed to find male nakedness amusing.

The King regained control of himself and, his cheeks slightly red, apologised for talking of trivial things with a "virtuous and honourable woman". Ella kept quiet, waiting for the King to change the subject, but the memory of his friend running away naked in public was too much for him and he grinned, a hand pressed on his mouth. Most kings would have been outraged at this kind of behaviour, but not him: he thought it was hilarious.

'Forgive us.'

'Your Grace did not offend me,' Ella said with a smile. 'I do feel sorry for Sir Thomas,' she added, which made the King laugh even more. Once calmed down, he wiped a tear off the corner of his eye and took his son back in his arms. He kissed him gently on the forehead.

'Our good Dr de Vittoria shared with us that you sometimes quarrel with our son's lady mistress,' he said.

'Rules on cleanliness can sometimes be overlooked, which can upset me,' Ella admitted.

'That is what we heard. We thank you for your dedication. Lady Shelley has been reminded of the importance of the rules and is now to ensure their strict respect,' the King reassured her.

Ella nodded and smiled, happy that she had won over Alice. The woman had clearly been given an ultimatum between following the rules or being replaced. The King did not stay much longer, deciding it was time for him to leave as soon as his son began to cry. He was already gone when Agnes started to feed the baby, with Dr de Vittoria over her shoulder making sure the future king was getting the right quantity of milk.

Ella did not move from her stool for a while. Hal had been on Earth for only a few weeks and had mostly spent them with people that were not his parents. When one could afford it, it was normal in 1511 to send one's child away to be raised by someone else. Ella could not blame anyone, but she had to feel sorry for the baby. His father had decided that less than an hour was enough time with his child for now. His mother had left him behind a month after his birth and had not been back yet. Ella did not know what had kept her away, or how she was coping with being parted from him. All she knew was that this boy had two parents, a grandfather, aunts, uncles, cousins and a large extended family, but not a single one of them was under this roof.

Ella came to wonder if the Queen had even had the chance to see her son again after leaving him to celebrate his birth in the history she had known. It was impossible to tell and was making the prospect of her failure to prevent Hal's death even harder. Ella had to leave the room when a vision of Hal's dead body forced its way into her brain and she realised she was crying. But she blamed her emotional state on her period.

6.

SIMPLE BLISS

1511-1513

Ella's morning routine used to be snoozing her alarm until she found herself late for work. It had now become waking up early to comb her hair with her special lice comb. Pop used to put drops of lavender essential oil behind her ears and in her scarf and hat against lice. Ella was still using this trick to ward off those tiny parasites, but head lice was such a known problem at court and in the nursery that seeing her colleagues scratch their heads was making her paranoid.

She was interrupted by a letter that was brought to her and smiled when she recognised Inez's handwriting. It was now June. It was her fifth letter in five months, again signed with both her name and 'M' for Margery as the latter was one of the many women who had never been taught to read or write. Inez's spelling was sometimes questionable, but knowing that someone regularly took the time to send her a few words always felt like a breath of fresh air.

'From Lady Mountjoy?' Alice guessed.

'Yes. She shares her excitement about this year's summer progress, but also her worries about the plague in London,' Ella told her.

'Praise the Lord, the prince is safe in the pure air of the country. And, considering Her Grace's condition, it is also advisable for all to be away from London,' Alice said.

Ella folded the piece of paper, trying to focus on the Queen's third pregnancy rather than the people dying of the plague in the overcrowded capital. It was Ella's first summer in this century, and ever since Dr de Vittoria had expressed his concern that the most serious outbursts of the plague happened in summer, Ella was terrified to find a rat in the nursery. But even Dr de Vittoria thought this disease was caused by some poison in the air absorbed through the skin, which was the reason why the King wanted to be far from foul-smelling London. It was so frustrating to know more than everyone else without being able to share her knowledge that Ella had started biting her nails; in the meantime, she was constantly looking for smudges along the walls, damages on the furniture, and was listening for any abnormal little squeak.

She was about to leave Alice's side when she froze and unfolded the letter again. The date was there, dark ink on pale paper. The twenty-second day of June.

'He was meant to die after a few weeks', she whispered to herself, a hand over her mouth. And she giggled.

Hal was a sturdy, healthy six-months-old boy. Almost seven months. Ella could not remember the exact day of his historical death, but she would have bet everything, even Lolly's ring, that he had not seen the summer of 1511. Ella laughed harder, ignoring Alice's weird glance. The baby boy sleeping in the room next door was gorgeous and full of life, with two big blue eyes curious about everything and two chubby arms that were trying to pull him up on his feet every chance they got. And a heartbeat. He was alive.

It was absurd to chase an answer to why he had survived this time, but he had. Maybe it was all the rules his father and herself had forced the nursery staff into following. Maybe it was because his original household had been the one responsible for his death. Maybe it was Agnes. Or it was just luck.

Overwhelmed, Ella went to take Hal in her arms. He was still asleep. She hugged him tight against her chest, his red curls tickling her cheek. Happiness, relief, love, pride, Ella did not know which was the strongest. She felt them all at once like a slap on the face. Hal could still die any minute, whether it was from the plague, a fall or even a cold. But, today, he was alive.

History had changed, but also the reason behind Ella's commitment to ensure Hal's survival. In truth, it was no longer about preventing the dark, tumultuous years England would fall into if the King found himself with no male heir, nor was it about saving the lives of people she had never met. Hal's lips formed a smile against Ella's neck and he put a sleepy hand on her chin. She hugged him tighter. It was all about her love for him.

The summer royal progress only came to an end in October. The King and the Queen, but also the King's younger sister, Princess Mary, rode to Surrey to visit the nursery. The King was the first person to enter the room, happiness making his face even more childlike than usual, and swiped his son in the air with a laugh. The Queen followed, her baby bump covered by a gown of blue satin that matched her eyes. She was not the only one expecting, and Ella remembered at the last second that she was supposed to curtsey to the Queen and the princess – she only wanted to run to Inez's arms to congratulate her for her own pregnancy.

As the time Hal usually had a nap was dangerously approaching, Ella forced herself to focus back on him: 'If I may be so bold as to beg Your Graces for a minute of time, my lord the prince's latest prowess deserves to be shown,' she said.

'Let us see, then!' the King replied and gave the baby back to her.

Ella pinched her lips with excitement and put Hal's feet on the floor. She started to walk with him. She only let go of his hand once they were close enough for the crouching King to catch his son if he was to fall. He did not. With his robust legs, Hal had taken his first steps not long ago, just a few days after turning nine months old. Ella's smile did not leave her face as she watched the King grab his son and pirouette with him. The Queen put both hands on her heart. For just a minute, they were not Henry VIII and Katherine of Aragon, but parents witnessing their child reach a milestone.

Inez took the opportunity of this family moment to sit down with Ella by the window. 'You must be displeased with me,' she whispered, taking her hand in hers.

'How could I?' Ella retorted. 'You are to be a mother! It brings me so much joy!' she exclaimed, forgetting to lower her voice.

'Forgive me for not putting you in the confidence. I was with child once before, but it died shortly after it quickened.'

'I did not know. I am sorry.'

'I thank you. My beloved William is father to a girl from a previous marriage. We are praying for a healthy son,' Inez told her.

Ella smiled, happy to see her living her dream. Women of this century had been taught from birth that they were born to give their husbands sons and Inez firmly believed it. Ella had to bite her tongue, knowing that gender equality was not a fight she could win in 1511. To put it as simply as possible, women were owned by their fathers until their wedding, when the ownership would be passed on to the husband. It was their reality. Most women had accepted it like one accepted the sky to be blue and the grass green and Ella did not want to frighten anyone or put her life on the line trying to change something people were not ready for.

The King was now touring the room with his son in his arms, walking so close to the tapestries hung on the walls he seemed to be part of them. As he was telling Hal in a babyish voice how extraordinary his life was going to be, his sister gave an amused look to the Queen. The King either didn't care, or he had forgotten he could be heard.

'You shall rule over England and France. We shall take back what King Henry V won but was unjustly stolen from us by the wickedness of Frenchmen,' he said to his son, freshening up Ella's History lessons.

King Henry V had conquered most of France in the previous century. It had then been lost by his own son, a child king who would in turn become a weak one, eventually deprived of his crown by Hal's great-grandfather, Edward IV. The King, in all his pride, believed he was the greatest king that had ever ruled England and that he would give it back its glory by conquering the lost territories – and more. Ella could not help but think it was a bit hypocritical as he spent a lot less time governing the kingdom than hunting and playing with his friends, like Charles Brandon or William Compton, the man whose weirdly coveted job was to accompany him to the toilets. If one could call toilets a wooden box with a cushion-padded hole at the top and a bowl inside it.

Fifteen-year-old Princess Mary, bored with the talks about France, went to find the lute in the corner of the room and started playing. Her red hair and blue eyes were not the only traits she shared with her brother, as she was also gifted at music. Five minutes later, some ladies were dancing for the Queen. Ella surprised herself to feel a disarmingly simple bliss. She was happy, not because of Hal surviving longer than feared, walking for the first time or laughing at her peekaboo. There was no cause for it. She was just there, dancing and singing, making the most of this random chapter of her life.

When Ella curtseyed to the King and the pregnant Queen at the end of the first dance and saw Hal giggling in the arms of his father, she realised that, although she still wanted to find Lolly's ring and travel back home, it was fine if she couldn't do it right this second.

Before Ella knew it, the year 1512 had flown by without the slightest opportunity for her to get Lolly's ring back. The King was having the hill facing his apartments in Eltham Palace flattened to improve the view from his windows, and was also extending the chapel. It was a no-go zone.

It was a slow life at the nursery, yet Ella often wished she could pause time. Every minute of every day was devoted to Hal. He had not been joined by a sibling after all, as the Queen had delivered a still-born daughter, and was still Ella's one and only priority. Most days, she hoped they would never, ever, have to leave their golden bubble.

Especially now that the King had declared war on France. Ella could not remember whether the King had declared war on the French during the first version of history, or if he was only doing it now that he was the father of a living male heir whom he wanted to be crowned king of France one day. Either way, she was worried. If the King was mortally wounded on the battlefield, or even died of dysentery – a common cause of death for soldiers – like his warrior hero Henry V, his soon-to-be two-year-old was nowhere near ready to sit on the throne. Henry VI had become king aged nine months and had grown up surrounded by self-interested politicians, against whom he had never learned to assert himself. And Edward V, the current King's uncle, had been only twelve when his father had died. He had been deposed and had disappeared alongside his brother in the Tower of London. As of 2020, their bones had still not been found with certainty.

This was not what Ella wanted for Hal. In one of her letters, Inez had told her about the recent death of Sir Thomas Knyvett in France. The King was upset at the loss of a friend. Ella could only hope he would not lose his own life, too.

Ella was sitting with Hal on a sunny day of June, making up stories under the shade of a large hawthorn tree in the gardens of Woodstock Palace, where the nursery had recently moved, when the King showed up unannounced. As usual, he was followed by a few of his retainers, but the men stayed at a distance. Ella was now used to pretend they were not there. The King asked her to stay when she was about to leave father and son some privacy. After a cuddle and a quick talk with his toddler, he laughed as a couple of white petals fell from the tree above their heads on his son's ginger hair.

'Hawthorn trees are much satisfactory to the eye on the blossoming season,' he declared.

'Your Grace is right,' Ella agreed, looking up at the thousands of little white flowers and savouring their sweet aroma.

'It is a sacred tree. It is also one of the badges of the House of England, as the crown of the usurper Richard of Gloucester, then called king, was found under one on the battlefield where he was slain by our late father,' he explained, although it was a story everyone already knew.

'Praise the Lord,' she replied.

'As King, our father faced many challenges and preposterous pretenders, Mistress Elizabeth, but he was blessed to have fathered two healthy sons. When our brother Prince Arthur departed to God, the Crown was not without an heir,' he went on.

The law did not say anything against your sister sitting on the throne, Ella wanted to retort. She held her commentary back and nodded instead.

'We have one healthy son and heir,' the King said.

'I pray the Queen shall be with child again soon,' she told him, understanding what he really meant. He needed not one, but two male heirs to feel safe. In case one died unexpectedly.

Officially, there was no Tudor dynasty. Henry VIII was the second monarch of Tudor blood but considered himself the rightful king: there was no dynasty, there was only the royal House of England. However, there were still men and women with royal Plantagenet blood coursing through their veins. It was unlikely that the King would admit it, but it was a dynastic threat for him. The recent beheading of the Earl of Suffolk was proof that he was not without fear.

The earl, as the nephew of Edward IV and Richard III, had been, at least until the last day of April, the claimant to the throne from the House of York, and had spent the last few years imprisoned in the Tower of London. He was now without a head, taking his widow down with him as the suspicious Countess of Suffolk had ended up without title, lands, or even her former place in the Queen's household.

The King did not let Ella think about the fate of the countess any further: 'the Queen is with child,' he surprised her.

'Please allow me to congratulate Your Grace and the Queen,' Ella answered.

'We thank the Lord for His favour. Mistress Elizabeth, you are to return to your position in the Queen's household,' he said.

'What?' Ella blurted out, forgetting all decency. 'May I ask Your Grace why?' she asked in a more even voice, trying to stay in control.

It only lasted a second, but Ella saw the muscles of the King's jaw tense and his eyebrows sink. He did not like to be challenged. He refused to have to explain himself, ever. But then he looked at her. And he looked at his son. And he sighed.

'You may. It is the fourth time the Queen is with child,' he declared, his eyes locked on their only surviving child. 'The Queen lives in fear and wishes for you to be back in the household. You were of much help during our son's birth and Her Grace believes your presence shall bless us with a spare heir,' he explained.

Ella kept quiet, aware that she could not refuse, as much as she wanted to. The Queen was terrified of losing a third baby and the King wanted his spare heir too much to take any chances. Ella thought the very notion of a spare heir to be vile. It was as if this child would only ever matter if his brother died, and if he was a he. Ella knew how quickly tables could turn, how unexpectedly life could come to an end, and how the Crown was supposed to matter more than anything else. But these children were more than heirs, they were children. Lives. Heartbeats. Feelings. Hearing these two words in their father's mouth – spare heir – sounded like he had forgotten that.

Besides, Ella did not want to leave Hal. It was unfair.

'We are to announce the coming birth of the prince in a fortnight. You are to come back to court before this time,' he demanded.

'Yes, Your Grace,' Ella agreed, staring at the young boy she had raised for the past two and a half years who was about to be taken away from her. She bit her lip. She loved him more than anything else in this world. He had made possible for her to spend an entire day without obsessing about the ring and her unanswered questions, or even thinking about the twenty-first century.

Alice was still, officially, the lady mistress, but even she knew that Hal had made his choice. Ella was his person. She was only a woman in the household, but she was the only woman he turned to when he was upset. Alice was there because the lady mistress had to be of rank. Ella did not have the rank, but she had the boy's love. Her boy. Her sweet, kind, funny, clever boy, whom she loved as if he were her own child, and from whom she was to be separated because one woman was so superstitious that she thought she was to miscarry or deliver a stillborn baby if she was not by her side. Ella burst into tears in front of Hal as soon as his father had gone. Which, of course, made him start crying too.

7.

THE DUTY OF A WIFE 1513

Proper roads were lacking. The wind was blowing dust in her face. Ella was hungry. She was tired. Her bum was hurting on the saddle. Her back, too. She had never learned how to ride a horse in her old life, but it would not have helped anyway. The side-saddle was uncomfortable and felt unnatural. It was her punishment for leaving Hal behind. She was riding to court with the people the King had sent to bring her back: a couple of his retainers, but also some of the Queen's women and Lord Mountjoy, Inez's husband. He was the Queen's new chamberlain.

'Their Graces wish for you to know that you are to be financially rewarded for your excellent services to the Duke of Cornwall. They shall also provide for your dowry when the day comes,' he told her at some point during the ride.

Ella did not reply at the enormity of his words. Any sixteenth-century single woman with no fortune would have been over the moon to hear these words. For Ella, it only meant that the King was considering marrying her off in a world without any reliable birth control.

The most important duty of a wife is to give children to her husband, and so many die trying, the little voice inside her head came back despite having been relatively quiet lately.

'Is Lady Mountjoy well?' she changed the subject. Her friend's letters had been short and dispirited since her miscarriage.

'She is in good health, I thank you,' Mountjoy replied without any other detail.

Ella sighed discreetly. Thinking about Inez waving goodbye to a healthy child brought her back to her own goodbyes to Hal. Over, and over again. It was merciless. His hands around her neck. His red cheeks soaked with tears. His high-pitched voice begging her to stay. It was merciless, but Ella deserved it. She had abandoned him. And she was going to be paid for it. The King had never really left her with a choice, but, seeing the red bricks of Greenwich Palace after hours of riding, Ella hated herself for what she had done.

Heads turned around when she entered the great hall, including Margery's, who had been waiting for her arrival. Ella smiled for the first time since the sun had risen that day.

'My dear friend, I am much pleased to see you!' Margery cried.

'So am I. We have much to talk about,' Ella replied, fighting back tears. She would not break down in front of the girl standing next to her friend.

'This is Mistress Elizabeth Blount, the newest maid of honour to the Queen. Mistress Elizabeth Blount, this is Mistress Elizabeth White,' Margery made the presentations.

'It is lovely to make your acquaintance, Mistress Elizabeth. Are you a relative of Lord Mountjoy?' Ella asked – Mountjoy's name was William Blount.

'I have the honour of being Lord Mountjoy's cousin,' Elizabeth said. 'But my family calls me Bessie, and I hope you will do the same,' she broke the formality.

Ella followed Margery and Bessie to the Queen's lodgings, wondering why the name Bessie Blount was so familiar to her ear when she had never met that girl before. Everyone at court was a lot younger than twenty-first century movies had led her to believe, but Bessie could not have been more than thirteen or fourteen years old.

'Mistress Elizabeth, such a pleasure!' the honeyed voice of Buckingham resonated behind her.

Ella reluctantly curtseyed. She did not have the strength to deal with that man today. Not after so many hours perched on a horse.

'My lord, the pleasure is mine,' she lied.

'It seems that your presence is needed once more for the birth of the King's son…' he said with just enough irony to make her understand he disapproved, but not enough to be heard ridiculing his sovereign's decision. 'How very fortunate for the kingdom to have you,' he added.

'I thank my lord,' Ella replied with a large, dishonest smile. She was about to leave when she felt the need to annoy him as much as he was annoying her. 'It was a surprise for me to hear that I was not to see the Countess of Suffolk in the Queen's household, nor even the Lady Anne Hastings,' she shrugged, faking a sad shock, and quickly curtseyed again.

Buckingham looked down on her with a barely concealed aversion. The word was that his sister, Lady Anne Hastings, was finally done with her forced stay in the convent, but that the Queen had refused to give her back her place as lady in waiting. It must have had enraged him. When Ella got to the end of the corridor, she glanced at him. He was in a conversation with Lord Howard, a wealthy man in his thirties to whom he had just married his fifteen-year-old daughter. Buckingham glared back at her, hatred overflowing his face.

The Queen was so focused on her Spanish work embroidery that she did not hear the newcomers enter the room. For a minute, Ella observed the Queen's dexterous hands. She had once mentioned the black thread embroidery as "blackwork" but had swiftly been corrected by the proud Spaniard Maria. The Queen was creating a thin and precise floral design on the cuffs of a male's shirt. She got up on her feet as soon as she realised who were the new arrivals in her chamber. Ella sunk in a low curtsey.

'Mistress Elizabeth, I trust you had a pleasant journey. How is my son?' she asked.

'His Highness is well and longs to see Your Grace.'

It was a lie. If Hal longed to see anyone, it was the woman who had raised him. The Queen was his mother, but Ella was his beloved Bet. And Bet desperately wanted to see Hal.

Ella had once hoped both her names were similar enough for Hal to call her Ella, but it was Bet that had stuck. It was for the best; it was easier to compartmentalise. Ella was the twenty-first century girl looking for answers. Elizabeth was the sixteenth-century outsider whose only focus was to create a life for herself, a life that was as safe as possible. There were still nights where her unanswered questions were overwhelming, but she knew that investigating a magic ring could sign her death warrant.

The Queen extracted her from her thoughts. 'You must be weary. Have some rest, now.'

Ella curtseyed once more and went to find her bed. She would have gladly ridden all the way back to Woodstock Palace, all these miles away, alone, at night, with no food nor break, if only it meant getting her old job back. She sat on her single bed and stared at the plain panelled wall, wondering what Hal was thinking of her. She could not bear it if he came to believe she did not love him.

For the first time in years, she wondered if this thought had ever crossed her parents' minds. If her father had ever worried that she might feel unworthy of his love because of his behaviour. If her mother had ever feared that her suicide would lead her daughter to feel unworthy of any kind of love.

Ella shook her head. She had disappeared almost three years ago. She could not even say if her father was looking for her. Or missed her. A tear rolled down her cheek when she tried to picture herself in three years. She did not know in which century to picture herself anymore. Which clothes. Which friends. Which home. Which name.

'Oh, Elizabeth…' Inez appeared next to her and took her hand in hers. 'I am aware of your deep attachment to the Duke of Cornwall, but I promise that you shall find happiness here again.'

'Forgive me,' Ella croaked.

'You do not need to be forgiven of anything. You need sleep. Let us go to your bed, as I am afraid your previous one, this one, is now Bessie's,' Inez told her.

'All right.' Ella could not argue with the change of bed. 'Bessie seems agreeable.'

'She is in her youth still, but is very fair and eager to learn.'

'Any other new members of the household I should know about?'

'The Countess of Suffolk has been replaced by Lady Parr. The Queen is very fond of her and is godmother to her first child, a daughter born last year and christened Katherine in Her Grace's honour,' Inez explained, showing her to an unoccupied bed.

Ella sat down and thought for a minute. Katherine, daughter of Lady Parr. Katherine Parr. As the queen of England. The sixth and final wife of Henry VIII. Ella burst out laughing. The King was twenty-two years old and his wife was godmother to a baby who would one day, if history repeated itself, become his wife.

Inez was looking at her as if she had lost her mind, but Ella could not stop laughing. Henry VIII's first wife was godmother to his last; that was something that Lolly had never told her. Ella's breathing became erratic when she suddenly realised that Katherine Parr probably had no say in this marriage. Who would want to marry a man twenty-two years older, who had had two of his previous wives beheaded? Ella could not find the answer by herself. She tried to calm herself down but, exhausted physically and mentally, all she ended up doing was turning on the waterworks.

Ella woke up in the middle of the night, her eyes sticky and her mouth dry. She knew where she had heard the name of Bessie Blount before, and it was not in this century.

> *2014. Emily Buckley looked across the Inner Hall in Hever Castle, the childhood home of Anne Boleyn where she had taken her granddaughter for the day. She spotted the teenager*

admiring a portrait hung next to the fireplace. She walked up to her. 'Mary Boleyn... Fun fact, she was a mistress to the king of France. He once called her the great and infamous whore'.

'What a jerk!'

'Language, Ella,' Emily reminded her. 'But you are right. Historians even wonder if Mary consented to the relationship or not. What we know for sure is that, when she left the French court for the English one, she became a mistress of Henry VIII,' she told her while untangling a lock of her hair from the chain on which her sapphire ring was hanging.

'And he married her sister anyway?' Ella asked, making a disgusted face to her grandmother's nod.

'He at least tried to keep his affairs secret, which is more than the French king could say. King Francis even had an official chief mistress! Besides the Boleyns, only Bessie Blount is known to have been Henry's mistress.'

'Why only her?'

'She is the first woman who gave him a son. Henry Fitzroy. He was so proud to prove to the world that he was capable of fathering healthy sons that he acknowledged him and considered making him his heir instead of his two legitimate daughters.'

'What a jerk!'

'Ella-Grace Buckley!'

Ella smiled and speculated for the hundredth time what her grandmother would have done in her shoes. She had eventually convinced her inner voice that Lolly had never found out about the ring's properties. After all, the time portal had only been activated when Ella had put the ring on her finger. Lolly had always worn it on a chain around her neck.

In her place, there was no denying that Lolly would have behaved differently. More subtly, too. She would not have made a personal enemy of the richest peer in the realm. But, if she had displayed this exemplary behaviour by not intervening during Hal's birth, she might have never ended up in his household and he might have died all over again. Ella tried to keep her lacrimal glands under control when she understood that she could not make sure Hal washed his hands, or that the people attending him did, any more. Among other things. He could die at anytime. He could be dying now. And there was nothing she could do about it.

The court was a silent and monotonous place without the King, who had decided to lead his army himself in the war with France. A large portion of the court was part of this army, and the palace was almost empty. The King's invasion of France had forced his brother-in-law the king of Scots, James IV, to prepare for war, as Scotland was France's ally. The pregnant Queen, regent in her husband's absence, was showing a side of her personality Ella had never seen before. Although terrified her husband would come back to her in a box, if at all, the Queen was knee deep into war preparations, whether it was about soldiers, horses, money, ships, or weapons. The King had left her with advisers, but they were only playing a figurative role. For as long as the King was fighting in France, the kingdom of England was to be ruled by a woman.

Ella put down her pathetic attempt at needlework with a sigh and observed the women around her, making banners and standards for the army with their expert hands. After three years and many hours of practice, she still felt like a young child learning to write. The letters were there, but of different sizes, sometimes written backwards.

She spotted Margery wipe the sweat off her brow. The July weather was too hot for anyone to wear long sleeves but women did not have a choice in the matter. Ella looked up at one of the clerestory windows, floating about twenty feet above the floor, and dared to dream of Hampstead Heath and its ponds where she used to go swimming in the hot summer days. Oh, the dragonflies circling in the air above the swimmers' heads, the picnics that followed, the barbecues in the nearby Waterlow Park. She missed all of it. The long-lost taste of a good summer Pimm's came back to haunt her mouth and she decided to leave her stool.

'Elizabeth?' Margery whispered, frowning.

'Follow me,' she said and walked decidedly towards the door.

'Where are we going?' Margery asked when the door closed behind them. 'We should finish our work!'

'It is too hot to stay inside!' Ella disagreed, leading the way outside through the deserted corridors. The two friends walked passed the orchard trees, the medicinal garden, the fish ponds and the flower beds, only to stop once they were far enough from the palace building. Ella turned to Margery: 'help me untie,' she asked.

'Elizabeth, I would not! I do not think it is wise!' Margery exclaimed.

'Do not be so shocked, I will keep my shift on!' Ella rolled her eyes.

'I hope so!' Margery laughed and capitulated.

Ella's loud relief when her tight-fitted bodice fell to the floor convinced Margery to imitate her. Soon, they were sitting down on the grass in their undergarments, holding their long hair up with their hands to feel the breeze on their necks. Ella closed her eyes, letting the sun kiss the skin of her face.

Breathe in, breathe out. She laid down on the grass, inhaling until her belly seemed about to pop, exhaling until not a bit of air was left in. She could finally breathe.

'I cannot imagine how hot it must be for Inez to be wearing a gable hood by that weather,' she said.

'It shall happen to us soon enough, God willing,' Margery replied – her desire to find a husband was clear.

The later, the better, Ella thought, but smiled instead and rolled up the light sleeves of her shift. Margery copied her, giggling at the realisation that they were doing something forbidden. Ella used to be upset when some men felt entitled to shout unrequited remarks in the street every time she wore a pair of shorts or an over-the-knee summer dress, but she had never thought about how it would make her feel if the law stated that she was not allowed to show her legs or even her arms. She used to have a choice. She had taken it for granted. Now it was gone.

Margery said her name. 'Are you unhappy?' she asked.

'Why this question?'

'I noticed that you looked happier when you were attending to the Duke of Cornwall.'

'My lord the prince brought me more joy than words could say. I think much about what I am missing,' Ella admitted, not sure what she missed the most between Hal and 2020.

'I understand, but you are my friend and your pain saddens me.'

'You are my friend, too.'

'Mistress Margery? Mistress Elizabeth?' a voice broke their bonding moment. The two women jumped on their feet, spontaneously putting their hair behind their red ears.

'My Lady Parr,' Ella said. 'Mistress Margery was close to faint because of the hot weather and I decided to take her outside for some fresh air. I beg you to forgive our appearance.'

'Are you feeling better, Mistress Margery?' Lady Parr asked, a hand resting on her pregnant belly, startled to find them in such scandalous accoutrements. She smiled when Margery nodded.

'Would my lady like to join us? It is very enjoyable in this heat,' Ella offered, hoping it would prevent her from telling on them to the Queen.

To her surprise, Lady Parr shrugged and took her headdress off, revealing long golden hair, and asked for help to remove her pregnancy clothes. Queen Katherine Parr's mother laid down on the grass with the two maids, laughing uncontrollably at her own defiance. When she calmed down, Ella turned her head to examine the woman she had never talked to before, but who was breaking all the rules in her company. Two big hazel eyes were already staring at her.

'I trust you are curious to know how I found you,' Lady Parr murmured. 'Mistress Maria noticed when you left and begged for me to find out your whereabouts,' she told her.

That little cow, Ella internally screamed. 'She did not trust me when I arrived at court. My Lady Mountjoy was kind enough to share with me that Mistress Maria believed me to be a spy or a felon. I must confess I thought she had come to her senses after three years,' she said.

'Oh, but she has not!' Margery intervened.

'The Queen trusts you and I believe Her Grace to be a formidable judge of character,' Lady Parr reassured her.

Ella meant to remind her that this formidable judge of character had trusted with the life of her child a woman who had simply turned up one day, with no name, family or reputation; who had not been claimed by anyone after months of enquiries, so that they had had to be abandoned; who still did not have as little as a date of birth.

Ella wisely kept all this for herself: 'I thank you, my lady,' she said.

'Please, in private, call me Maud.'

Ella was still upset at Maria for putting her under surveillance when, along with Maud and Margery, she decided it was time to go back to the palace. She took the Spaniard aside for an open-hearted conversation. The last thing she wanted was to make an enemy out of her. Maria was one of the Queen's rare true friends and Ella knew how much she meant to her, but she could not be shadowed by every woman who still distrusted her on the day she would be allowed to go back to Eltham Palace and look for Lolly's ring. She could not be certain the ring was still there, but she had to hold onto hope.

'I feel like you do not trust me, after all this time,' Ella said to Maria.

'I do not,' she admitted.

'Why?' Ella asked.

Maria looked at her as if she were joking. 'You fooled the Queen, as she is the kindest of souls, but you shall not fool me. I have agreed to endure your presence because of the love the Queen bears for you. I do not desire your friendship. I do not wish for you to view me as your friend. You might not be foreign, as I once thought, but Mistress Elizabeth White does not exist. I do not believe one can lose all knowledge of one's identity. You are not honest. You have risen far beyond your station. You are a danger for the Queen and I pray for the day you shall be left alone on the streets,' she monologued.

Ella considered negotiating a truce for a moment, but the blonde woman was staring at her with such hostility that she gave up almost instantly. There was no point. Ella walked so close to her that their noses were almost touching.

'Today was the last time you sent anyone after me. I do not tolerate your suspicions and the Queen shan't either. Distrust me if you will, but do so privately, or you shall find yourself having to do so from Spain,' she said without blinking.

'Is this a threat?'

'What do you think?'

'Who are you?'

'Someone who wants the Queen's happiness as much as you. Her Grace would feel much sorrow if you were to follow Fray Diego out of England.'

Maria hesitated for a second, probably contemplating murdering her on the spot, but left the room.

That was low, even for you, the judgmental voice inside Ella's head said. She massaged her eyelids and took deep breaths until her heart rate went back to normal. If a good old threat could get Maria to leave her alone, she did not think she minded having stooped so low. The woman had not given her an alternative. Ella could not let her convince the Queen of her lack of respectability. At least not without putting her position at court in jeopardy, and ultimately her life on the line.

That night, Maria's words echoed in Ella's head. *Who are you?* It was a good question. She was not really Elizabeth White. And yet,

Ella Buckley would have never threatened a woman with deportation only to make her own life easier. The person she had become was prepared to put her menace into practice and Ella was not sure that she liked her very much.

As the King scored a victory in Thérouanne, France, his Scottish brother-in-law decided to attack. The Queen wanted to travel north with the army, where she felt the regent belonged. The archbishop of Canterbury, William Warham, her chief counsellor in the King's absence, was rigorously against the idea and, maybe for the first time in her life, Ella was on the side of the older man rather than of the woman.

Defeated by the Queen's determination, the archbishop left the room. Ella fell on her knees. 'I beg Your Grace to reconsider,' she said, looking down on the floor.

'Mistress Elizabeth?' the Queen's low voice sounded incredulous.

'Your Grace is with child, a healthy prince much beloved already. There is great concern in my heart and soul that travelling north will exhaust Your Grace, and thus His Grace's second heir, too much,' Ella kept talking, still looking down.

You made me abandon Hal for the safe delivery of his sibling and I am not to let you put his health in jeopardy because you love being regent, Ella thought.

The Queen was thinking too. The room was silent. Ella's knees were starting to feel uncomfortable on the floor.

'I beg Your Grace to forgive me for my impertinence,' Ella apologised in advance.

Queen Katherine did not reply, but the Earl of Surrey was sent with his own army to the Scottish border. The Queen decided to stay behind.

The Queen gave such a vigorous and inspiring speech to the royal troops before they marched up north that, for a moment, even Ella wanted to jump on a horse, grab a sword and defend England territory. Inez laughed when Ella shared her thoughts with her.

'Her Grace is the daughter of Queen Isabella, exemplary in all acts of virtue,' Inez replied.

Ella smiled, taken by the immense pride in Inez's eyes. She was proud of her queen, not because she was King Henry's wife, but because she was Queen Isabella's daughter. 'How old were you when you left Spain?' she asked.

'Fourteen. Her Grace was sixteen. It is old enough for the memories made to remain in my heart until my last breath,' Inez said.

Ella, Inez and the other ladies followed the Queen back indoors and the dedicated English soldiers went on to fight furiously for her near Branxton, in Northumberland. It took some time for Ella to realise this battle would in fact also be known as the Battle of Flodden.

Lolly, Pop and Ella had once been invited to a wedding in Bamburgh Castle. The following day, they had driven an extra half hour to visit the Flodden Memorial. Ella had no doubt this high cross overlooking the battlefield would come to be built once more in the future, as over ten thousand men lost their lives within a few hours.

Including the king of Scots himself.

The Queen crossed herself when she received the news of her brother-in-law James's death, but her eyes were so bright that it was impossible to believe she would ever regret him. She had the dead king's bloodstained coat sent to her husband, who won over the French city of Tournai a few days later. But, due to bad weather, the King decided to postpone the conquest of the rest of the kingdom and went with his men to Lille to the court of Margaret of Austria, Hal's sponsor.

As the Scottish threat had been annihilated, the Queen decided she could now spare some time to visit her son. Ella's heart burst in her chest when she saw Hal for the first time in weeks. He had grown so much. And his arms around her neck had become so strong. The heavily pregnant Queen preferred to watch her son from her chair, happy to see that Ella was providing him with the undivided attention he needed.

Ella could not help but eavesdrop as Lady Elizabeth Fitzwalter, who was the sister of both Buckingham and Lady Anne Hastings, mentioned the King's sister Margaret, now widowed: 'I feel for the dowager queen. A widow and a mother to so young a king,' she despaired. The new king of Scots, James V, was only seventeen months old.

'My dear sister is now regent of Scotland,' Princess Mary reminded her.

'Indeed, but the dowager queen is like us of the weaker sex, and the King her brother is at war with her kingdom,' Lady Elizabeth Fitzwalter pointed out.

Although Ella hated to hear women call their own gender weak, Lady Elizabeth was not wrong. The regency in Scotland would have to last until the toddler would be old enough to govern in his own name. Ella did not know anything about Scotland's male egos but, if they were similar to England's, the dowager queen would not last long in power, especially since her own family was responsible for her husband's death. Ella thought about how the woman felt. She had been sold by her father to her future in-laws to strengthen a peace treaty, only for her husband to declare war on her brother's kingdom and be brutally killed on the order of her sister-in-law. And she had had no say in any of it.

'My beloved sister is of strong ability and courage. She shall succeed in protecting her rights and those of her son,' Princess Mary insisted. 'King James is the only soul to blame for his death,' she added after a short silence.

'Yes,' the Queen agreed. 'I asked for his body to be sent to the King my husband, or as little as his head, but found myself be told it was not advisable. The coat stained with his blood was all I could send,' she regretted.

'Blood?' Hal asked Ella, his ginger eyebrows deep in a frown. 'Who bleeded, Bet?'

'A wicked man bled. He is gone now, we are safe,' Ella reassured him. She then changed the subject, before having to explain to a boy of not even three that his parents had had his uncle killed.

8.

A GOOD MATCH 1513

The King came back to England just before the end of October, walking around like a peacock in twenty-first century Holland Park and making sure he was telling his war stories loudly enough to be heard by all. Had Iris been there, Ella would have complained about how patriarchy made winning over two small cities more important than defeating and killing a foreign king in battle.

The court was gathered in Havering, where the Queen had planned a masque and a banquet, among other things, to celebrate her victorious husband. Ella danced the pavane with him, her white skirts contrasting with his bright red doublet.

During the banquet, clearly inhibited, one of the men the King had knighted in France related how the King had tried to marry off his best friend, Charles Brandon, to Margaret of Austria. Ella laughed when the King looked at his wife with the face a little boy would make after breaking something. The drunk knight dropped his pint of ale on the floor as, euphoric, he reminisced how the two people had even exchanged rings as a joke. Charles Brandon had the courtesy to look embarrassed. There was no chance a man of such low birth could pretend to marry the daughter of the Holy Roman emperor.

'Elizabeth, why is the princess looking so little pleased with Lord Lisle?' Margery asked her, barely audible because of how loud the men were in the hall.

'Who is Lord Lisle?' Ella doubled checked.

'Charles Brandon. Have you not heard that he is precontracted with the Viscountess Lisle?' she replied.

What the hell? was almost Ella's answer. Her scandalized face spoke for her. Charles Brandon, approaching thirty years old, had entered a marriage contract with his eight-year-old ward, a little girl who had been born after the death of her father and was, by inheritance, viscountess in her own right. The inheritance of a title by a woman – here, a girl – was such a rare thing that it was not difficult to understand what Charles was after.

What is the worst between marrying one's own foster child and marrying the goddaughter of one's first wife? Ella silently wondered. No wonder those two were best friends.

Thinking about the viscountess made Ella feel sick and she focused on Princess Mary instead. The King's sister was staring at Charles, unhappy, but also bitter and distressed. Ella choked. Princess Mary was heartbroken. Ella had to fight against a persistent cough for the next couple of minutes. Surely, the princess knew that she was not allowed to marry without her brother's approval, and that he would never approve of a match with Charles. Royal women were useful diplomatic tools. The princess was the King's only such asset, as he had no daughter of his own. Ella moaned. She could sometimes think like a proper sixteenth-century person.

Wanting to take his best friend off the unflattering spotlight, the King asked the Duke of Longueville to come near his table. The Frenchman was a hostage living at court with such freedom and luxury that Ella could still not get her head around the fact that he was a prisoner of war.

'Longueville! You saw our army take Thérouanne, you saw it take Tournai! Now you see our wife great with child! God has sent us a son to crown our victory! God has bestowed the kingdom of France upon us! You shall see us crowned at Rheims Cathedral!' he roared, his arms extended up above his head and his chin held high.

Ella grinned. The King could be such a drama queen. His men cheered loudly, forgetting the decency and manners that were required at meal times, and Longueville looked discreetly around for someone to save him from a delicate position. But the King had no animosity towards the French duke and soon let him go back to his food. Ella observed the King for a while. He was so jubilant and excited that his happiness was contagious. She was curious to know if anyone would dare tell him that believing the Queen's pregnancy to be a sign that God wanted him to sit on the throne of France was a bit far-fetched.

Maria had been ignoring Ella ever since she had threatened to have her deported but stared at her like everybody else when the King entered his wife's apartments in Richmond Palace one morning and asked her to come with him. Excited to be told that she was to go back to Hal after the imminent birth of his sibling, Ella happily obeyed. He was accompanied by his personal chaplain, John Colet, a man in his forties who was also the dean of St Paul's. The once brown hair underneath his headgear was turning grey. Ella was surprised he was still in office. The word was that his sermon against war on Good Friday, earlier that year, had been poorly received considering the King was then just about to lead his army into one.

But the King was always full of surprises: John Colet was still very much in favour and was enjoying a considerable amount of influence, and Ella's excitement was to be permanently spoiled.

'It is the Queen's wish for you to stay in the royal household permanently. Regardless of your admirable devotion to our son, you are not to go back to the prince's household after the birth,' he informed her.

'Yes, Your Grace,' Ella said, barely controlling the shake in her voice.

'You are soon to be married. We are to fulfil our promise to pay for your dowry. Your husband and yourself shall have your own lodgings at court,' he announced, making Ella's heart beat frantically under her tight bodice.

Oh, hell, no, Ella despaired internally. 'I thank Your Grace for being so bountiful. To whom am I to be wed?' she asked, terrified of his answer but even more so that she had to ask this question.

'Sir Nicholas Elys. He is delighted. You are to be wed in a fortnight. You shall then take the position of lady of the bedchamber to the Queen,' he told her.

Ella faked a grateful joy. The King was going to spend a lot of money on her marriage and was also promoting her, but all she wanted to do was cry. She curtseyed as beautifully as her weak legs would let her when the King decided their conversation was done and left her behind in the great hall. The life-sized statues of the kings of England were lined up in front of her, each separated by a window. Edward III and his long beard; Arthur Pendragon and Brutus of Troy, as if they were not legendary, fictional, characters but real ancestors whose blood ran in the King's veins; Henry VII and his serious look, forever set in stone.

Ella's head tilted on the left. Her face made a pout. Sir Nicholas Elys also looked continually serious. The King was marrying her off to his father.

She escaped outside despite the cold and sat on the step to the large fountain in the middle of the courtyard. The smell of the fresh rose water cascading into the receptacle distracted her for a while, but her mind was still refusing to accept the news when Pan, always wandering, jumped on her lap.

'Do you even know how lucky you are to be a dog?' she asked him, scratching the thin white line of fur between his kind eyes. 'Dogs do not get married.'

He ran away as fast as he had come when furs were dropped on Ella's shoulders. She looked up. Maud and Inez sat next to her, concerned.

'I am to be married,' she told them.

'Is only this the source of your distress?' Inez asked. She was relieved.

'Is it Francis Bryan?' Maud alarmingly grabbed her hand.

'No,' Ella chuckled. 'I do not want to think about the woman who shall one day become that man's wife,' she said. Francis Bryan was one of the King's friends and the most sex-obsessed person that Ella had ever met. It was not rare to stumble upon him in action with women. 'Sir Nicholas Elys,' she said out loud for the first time.

'He is very respectable. His father has always been loyal to the King's father. Besides, he is highly skilled at jousting,' Maud exclaimed, as if those were good enough reasons for a woman to marry anyone.

'This is a good match, Elizabeth,' Inez agreed. 'He is an honourable man and a personal friend to the King. My husband once told me the King, Charles Brandon and Nicholas Elys were inseparable in their youth. What upsets you so?'

'Marriage leads to being with child, which leads to lying in the grave,' Ella replied, fighting back tears.

One of them slipped from the corner of her eye when she realised what she had said to a woman who had been through two miscarriages and was desperate to conceive again. Inez took her free hand in hers and pressed it but did not say a word.

'Delivering a child into the world is frightening but, God willing, it also leads to motherhood. The pain I felt during childbirth was little compared to the immense joy of holding my children in my arms,' Maud shared. She had given birth to a son two months before, exactly one year after the birth of her daughter.

I do not want to deliver anything through my vagina in this century! Ella wanted to say. Instead, she forced herself to smile and thanked her friend for her kind words.

Maud and Inez started to debate whether Sir Nicholas Elys was the best jouster at court but Ella refused to listen. Ironically, her future husband gave her the means to dodge her friends when he came out of the great hall and walked towards them. Maud and Inez left them alone. Ella would have loved for the fountain and its decorative red dragons to be swallowed by a hole underneath.

'Mistress Elizabeth, may I offer you company?' the man asked in a low, gravelly voice.

Ella nodded. She had never given much thought about him. Besides the King, he was the first man she had ever met in this century, but he had always been so quiet and sober compared to the other courtiers that he had never stood out from the crowd. Unless he was on a horse during a joust, of course. He was often praised by the King himself.

Sir Nicholas Elys was almost as tall as his royal friend but, unlike him, he was closer to his thirties than his twenties. Ella tried to imagine what it would be to have sex with him, then turned her head to the side to have a proper look at him and shivered at the possibility of being raped if she one day refused him marital sex.

'Shall your company always be a silent one?' Ella asked to chase away her traumatizing thoughts.

He smiled and looked at her. She had never noticed it before, but his eyes were of an unusually perfect shade of amber, framed by dark brown hair down to his sharp jaw line. 'I find myself unsure of what to say,' he confessed. 'I trust His Grace told you we are to be wed.'

'Indeed.'

'You do not look much pleased.'

'I am,' Ella lied.

'I am not,' he retorted with so much honesty and so little anger that it made her laugh. 'Have I offended you?' he checked.

'Not at all,' she managed to say before nervously laughing again.

'I tend to offend members of your sex, although it is never my aim,' he told her.

'All is well,' she reassured him. 'May I ask why you are so unenthusiastic with the thought of becoming my husband?'

'You look very fair. I always take much pleasure listening to your singing and your playing on the virginals,' he complimented her. 'My father died on the battlefield for the late king Henry. I have been brought up at court and shall be grateful until my last breath, but I lack powerful kinsmen. It was my hope to find some through marriage,' he explained.

Ella could sympathise. Nicholas Elys and Charles Brandon had the same kind of background, which was why the latter was planning on marrying an eight-year-old in the first place. Although the King usually had good reasons when he decided something, Ella did not understand why he had chosen her for one of his closest friends. The man wanted to marry a rich heiress, not an amnesiac girl with a made-up name. She could not hold it against him.

Sir Nicholas Elys became the owner of Elizabeth White before the end of November. Ella was wearing a new gown of crimson satin that the King had had made for her wedding day and unwillingly vowed she would obey her husband in everything until death took them apart. She was close to raise her hand when the priest summoned anyone who had anything to say against the marriage to declare it. But she did not. And no one else did.

On her wedding night, feeling her husband inside her, all Ella could think about was that she was now his legal property. She was a car. She was a house. Nicholas had full rights over her. He could beat her and cheat on her, but she could not. And she could not own anything without his consent, or even make her own will. Like a five-year-old child. She was stuck with him, until death or time travel do them part.

The King gave the newlyweds a manor house in Kent as a wedding present. Ella smiled when she saw it for the first time. As the architect he once was, Pop used to be annoyed upon hearing his granddaughter describe timber framed houses as "Tudor houses", but Sir Nicholas and Lady Elys's manor house was just that: a typical, black and white, Tudor house. U-shaped, it was of very decent size and Ella would have even called it large had she not been living in royal palaces for the past few years.

Ella and Nicholas spent the first days of their marriage there. It did not feel like a honeymoon. They were uncomfortable with one another.

The first three nights, Nicholas came to her bedroom at night to perform their marital duties and, as any twenty-first century woman knew to be important after intercourse, Ella fled every time to use the chamber pot, only to come back to a deserted room. On the fourth night, Nicholas asked why she needed to relieve herself so quickly after bedding.

To get my urethra rid of bacteria so I do not end up with a urinary tract infection, Ella thought, but realised that her husband would not understand. Whether it was a UTI, a bacteria or a urethra, he would be utterly clueless. 'It helps me be more comfortable to find sleep,' she lied.

'I understand. I wish you a good night,' he said, but then hesitated. 'Would you care for me to stay tonight?' he wondered.

Ella smiled. 'It would make me happy,' she replied. It was not a lie. They were married and had consummated the union, which meant it could not ever be undone. If it could make it less awkward, she wanted to get to know her husband properly.

They both got back in the bed and Ella turned on her side to face him. 'May we speak about your family?' she asked.

'It shall not be a long conversation. They have all died,' he said.

'I do not remember my family. I wish to know more about my husband's,' she insisted.

Nicholas sighed. 'My father, Sir Nicholas Elys, died at the hand of Richard of Gloucester, on the field of Bosworth, in the year 1485,' he told her what she already knew, although the fact that it was Richard III himself who had killed his father was unexpected. 'I was born shortly after. My mother was called Cecily. She was soon to die of melancholy. She loved my father so very much.'

Ella's heart missed a beat. The established idea was that physical and psychological problems came from fluctuations of four bodily fluids and the fact that those four elements were not balanced like they were supposed to be. There was blood, phlegm, yellow bile, black bile. The latter influenced depression, or melancholy. Ella was struggling to believe that the late Lady Elys had died solely from grief. On the other hand, if one added post-partum depression to it, the results could be deadly.

The face of her mother appeared behind Ella's eyes. When an imaginary rope started to slide around Nora's neck, her daughter forced herself to push the image away.

She would not raise the possibility of Cecily's suicide. Self-murder was seen as a crime that deprived the King of one of his subjects, and it was a general belief that people who died by this method would return as ghosts. They were often buried at crossroads with a stake in their heart to prevent it.

'You are silent,' Nicholas noticed.

'Charles Brandon's father also died at the battle of Bosworth,' she said. 'Lord Lisle's father,' she corrected herself.

'True. Charles was but an infant then. My father and his father fell on the same day, within seconds, at the hand of the same man. The bond between us is unbreakable.'

'Of course. And also with the King?'

He did not reply right away. Ella knew why. Inez would have scolded her for her impertinent curiosity. 'Charles and I were raised at court,' he eventually said. 'When Prince Arthur and Queen Elizabeth departed to God, the late king was inconsolable and His Grace, then Prince of Wales, was in dire need of support. Charles and I provided it. A friendship was born from it.'

Ella smiled. She was grateful that Nicholas had agreed to talk about his life, and also that such a brotherhood had come out of something so terrible as the losses of a brother and a mother. Ella and Nicholas slept in the same bed that night, and every night after that, until they were asked to come back to court for the beginning of the Queen's confinement. They now had a private apartment there, which was a lot better than sleeping in a dormitory surrounded by girls, some of whom still believed her to be hiding who she was.

But, to every good side, there was a bad one: as a married woman, Ella was forced to wear an uncomfortable hood to cover the top of her hair, with a black veil attached to it to cover the length in the back. Her honeymoon had not been long enough for Ella to get used to what people called a gable hood. It was a bulky headdress, triangularly and unflatteringly framing the face, that could be embroidered or bejewelled depending on the woman's rank and fancy. Ella hated it more than marriage itself.

The Queen's labour started two days after her twenty-eighth birthday. Out of superstition, she held the holy relic previously held during Hal's birth in one hand and Ella's hand in the other. The birthing chamber was kept so warm that Ella had to regularly wipe up the sweat from her brow.

'Un niño sano, por favor,' the Queen murmured repeatedly, barely taking the time to catch her breath.

A healthy baby boy, please. Ella had known about Hal's gender beforehand but was this time incapable of guessing what the child would be. The King wanted a boy, of course, thus everyone was talking about the unborn child like there was no doubt about it being born with male genitalia. Historically, though, Ella had not forgotten that the only surviving child of Henry VIII and Katherine of Aragon had been Queen Mary I.

'A prince, Your Grace!' the midwife shouted, proving Ella wrong.

The baby cried and his mother laid back on her pillow with tears of relief, happiness and exhaustion running down her cheeks. 'Un niño sano!' she said, beaming.

'Un niño sano!' Ella repeated, but froze and looked at the midwife for reassurance, silently asking her if the niño was, indeed, sano.

'The prince is the healthiest of them all, Your Grace!' the midwife confirmed.

'Where is our son?' the King's voice soon made itself heard from outside the room.

Ella smiled and let go of the Queen's hand to give her and her husband a resemblance of privacy, but found herself in the King's way. The happy father grabbed one of her hands and the opposite side of her waist, making her follow him in a quick and oddly modern dance move that made everyone giggle, including Ella and the Queen.

'God has blessed us with a healthy son, my beloved!' he told his wife and kissed her on the lips.

'What shall be his name?' the Queen asked.

'Arthur, in honour of our beloved late brother. Lady Elys, we want the Duke of Cornwall here at court for his brother's christening. Our son shall be christened in five days time, like his brother before him,' he declared.

'Yes, Your Grace,' Ella replied, more excited about seeing Hal in a few days than the birth of his sibling.

The King was looking at his youngest son as if he had been sent directly from God. For him, a healthy second heir was the holy promise he would succeed in conquering France. For Ella, it was the reassurance that history would not repeat itself. The royal marriage had once crumbled due to its lack of sons but had now two of them. There was no point in trying to understand why one child would die the first time around and live on the second. Ella did not even understand how there could be a second time at all. But the baby prince was there, healthy, in the arms of his father.

There was still the catastrophic possibility that both Hal and his brother would die before the King but, now that the past had changed, Ella could not predict the future. All that she knew was that the Queen had once lost everything because of her so-called failure to give her husband a healthy son, and she had now given him two. She was safe.

Despite his happiness, the King did not stick around for very long. After a few minutes, he gave the baby back to Lady Elizabeth Fitzwalter, recommended his wife to get some rest and took his leave. Ella rushed after him, having finally done the maths. He turned around when he heard the door. 'Lady Elys?' he said.

'May I be so bold as to beg Your Grace to set the day of my birth on the christening day, in honour of Your Grace's son?' she asked, fingers mentally crossed. Her actual birthday was on the twenty-third of December, five days from now.

'Have we not set a date already?' he wondered.

Would I be asking you if you had? she meant to reply. 'I am afraid Your Grace did not,' she said, thinking about the last three years without a birthday to celebrate.

'Very well, then. We reached twenty-two years of age this year. Let it be the same for you,' he decided, ignorant of the fact that Ella would soon be turning twenty-three.

'I thank Your Grace,' Ella cried, sinking into the deepest curtsey of her life.

Watching the white feather on the King's hat go up and down as he walked away, Ella felt a giggle coming up her throat. He had changed her name, he had chosen a husband for her, he had spent three years unbothered that she did not have an age. But, unknowingly, he had now given her birthday back to her and made her one year younger.

The Countess of Salisbury, who was cousin to the King's late mother, and the Archduke Charles of Austria, who happened to be the Queen's nephew, Princess Mary's fiancé and the Holy Roman emperor's grandson all at once, were chosen as Prince Arthur's sponsors, and the bishop of Winchester, the Countess of Devon and young Hal as godparents. Being the monarch's second son, Arthur received the title of Duke of York just like his father before him, and the celebrations melted into the Christmas festivities.

Ella had never liked Christmas very much as it was usually the day her father would find a way to remind her that he was not and would never be her dad. In the sixteenth century, there was no Christmas tree and Santa had not been invented yet, but if there was one thing that she loved more there than in the century she was born into, it was Christmas. The palace had been heavily decorated with holly, mistletoe, ivy, laurel, and anything green that could have been found, and the Yule log was peacefully crackling in the great hall. Presents were only to be exchanged at the New Year, but Christmas day always marked the beginning of twelve days of complete leisure. It was the best time in the year.

For twelve days, there was music, dancing, and laughter, even more that year as people were all merry with the birth of the baby and with England's victories against the French and the Scots. The King's fools, fancy dressed and teamed up with so-called magicians, were so entertaining that Ella had to escape for a minute to relieve her bladder.

'Elizabeth!' she heard Maud's voice whispering behind the door. Being a lady had put a slight strain on Ella's friendship to Margery, whom she now outranked, but Maud was her equal and the person she liked to spend time the most with at court.

'What is it? I need a moment!' Ella replied.

'The Christmas pie! It is now. Do hurry!' Maud pressed her.

The Christmas pie was a turkey, stuffed with a goose, stuffed with a chicken, stuffed with a partridge, stuffed with a pigeon, put in a pastry case, and served with even more meat on the side. Ella was always trying to eat reasonable amounts of meat compared to anyone else at court but, for the fourth year in a row, she was to make an exception for the deliciously hefty pie.

The atmosphere changed drastically a few days after Christmas, when the King woke up with a high fever. When the physicians realised that he was not the only one, the decision was made to stop the festivities and send the princes away as precaution. The palace remained unusually silent for three days, until one evening, Ella and Nicholas overheard panicked voices near their chamber. Jumping on his feet, Nicholas was only gone five minutes before he came back, his face even paler than hers.

'Red plague,' he said grimly.

'Smallpox!?' Ella cried, alarmed – what if he died?

'The red spots on the King's tongue and mouth are easily recognised,' Nicholas told her.

'Do you think the princes may be sick too?' she asked – what if they all died?

'We would have been made aware had the princes developed a fever, do not worry yourself,' he tried to reassure her.

It did not work. As Nicholas began talking to himself, declaring that the King was of strong build and health and that all would be well, Ella fought against the images of Hal's corpse covered with pustules in his little bed. The world was centuries away from a vaccine against smallpox, and Ella, who was no scientist, was utterly powerless. Even the King, as strong and healthy as he was, was not immune to that deadly disease. Ella was not either. She had not been vaccinated against it as it had been eradicated before her birth.

What is the point of coming from the future if I can't help? she silently despaired.

She did not know a thing about smallpox. Lolly may have told her something about Queen Elizabeth I, the King's daughter with Anne Boleyn, getting countless scars because of the disease, but she was not even sure that story was actually about her.

You are useless! she thought.

'May I speak a horrific truth without my wife believing herself to be wed to the most wicked soul in England?' Nicholas asked.

'I will try to reply to your truth with something even more wicked,' she replied.

'The Duke of Buckingham is down with the red plague as well, which I consider to be joyful news,' he whispered.

'I shall then say my wicked truth: my only wish for the duchess is for her to enter widowhood!' Ella exclaimed, forgetting to whisper.

Nicholas quickly put his hand on her mouth. Eavesdropping from other rooms was as easy as it was common.

'It had not come to my attention that my wife shared my feelings about this individual,' he said.

'Is your eyesight troubling you so that you did not notice his distaste towards my person?' Ella joked.

'You must have wronged him,' he frowned. 'Living at court with no earl as a father is deeply offending indeed,' Nicholas added, aware that it applied to the both of them.

'He detests you as well, does he not?' she asked rhetorically.

'Very likely as much as the red plague,' he answered.

Connecting for the first time in over a month of marriage, husband and wife burst out laughing, putting their pillows against their mouths so they would not be heard having such a good time whilst the King might have been dying.

9.

TO THE HORROR OF NOBLEMEN 1514

For days that felt like months, everyone silently thought that the King was not going to make it. Even Ella did. Hal's name was on every mouth. At three years old, the boy could become king of England at any minute. The physicians were updating the Queen three times a day, usually with for only good news that her husband was still breathing.

On the second day of January, they explained that the King's spots had changed into sores and that his face and limbs were covered with a rash. His fever had dropped slightly, but not enough.

On Epiphany Eve, they reported that the sores had become pustules. Five days later, the pustules had begun to form a crust. They promised they should soon start to scab. If the Queen listened to them with a compassionate gravity, Ella needed to fight nausea and disgust. She had never seen the effects of smallpox on anyone before but the physicians did not leave much room to imagination.

Halfway through January, with relief, they shared that the scabs were falling off, but thanks to God's immense love for the King, the skin of his face was so far not left with any scar.

God's love or good moisturiser, Ella thought.

The King was still weak on Candlemas, at the beginning of February, but insisted on celebrating his recovery with a reward ceremony in his presence chamber for the men who had served him well in the war. Among others, the Earl of Surrey became Duke of Norfolk and his son the new earl. And, to the horror of noblemen, the low-born friends of the King, Charles Brandon and Nicholas, were made Duke of Suffolk and Earl of Nottingham, respectively.

Against all odds, three years and a half after her muddy arrival in this century, Ella was now part of the nobility.

Nicholas and Ella's social climbing was commemorated with a present from the King in the form of a new house in Nottinghamshire. Nicholas then made an enormous order of silk material for clothes befitting their new rank and a pearl necklace with a sapphire pendant for Ella. He gave it to her the very day of their elevation to the peerage, surprising her with it in one of the many dark corners around the palace. The blue stone reminded Ella so much about the one on her grandmother's ring that she could not prevent a tear from falling. Nicholas wiped it tenderly.

'I thank you for your generosity,' she said without a smile, her brain attacked by memories of Lolly.

'My dear, do you not like it?' he frowned, worried. Ella realised she was being rude.

'I love it. It is magnificent. I shall wear it with joy,' she reassured him.

'Good,' he smiled. 'The Earl and Countess of Nottingham,' he whispered excitedly, looking at her in the eyes.

'We are our own powerful kinsmen, now,' she told him.

'I feel blessed to have you as a wife. Forgive me for ever thinking otherwise,' he apologised and kissed her on the lips.

Ella smiled but was interrupted in her answer by the voice of the Duke of Buckingham in the corridor, angrily talking with his brother, Henry Stafford, the Earl of Wiltshire. She froze. 'I refuse to ever recognise that country bumpkin as my equal, this is an outrage!' Buckingham barked. 'This is my birth right. Charles Brandon does not deserve anything! His father was a standard bearer! Is the noble blood of this kingdom to be so polluted?' he went on.

He stopped in the middle of the corridor to catch his breath, making Ella and Nicholas hold theirs.

'And Nicholas Elys shan't ever be my equal,' Wiltshire said.

'These lowly men, Duke of Suffolk and Earl of Nottingham? Such indignity! And that… that chancer… picked up from the street, like a dog? A countess? For all we know, she could be a swineherd's bastard!'

Ella put a firm hand on Nicholas's mouth as, enraged to hear his wife being insulted, he was about to jump out of hiding to defend her honour. Her heart was pounding in her chest. She wanted to hear the rest of the conversation. Nicholas looked at her with a furious fire in his eyes but eventually nodded. Ella freed his mouth.

Like many others, the Stafford brothers believed in the social hierarchy. People were born rich or poor because God had wanted it this way and it was unthinkable to even doubt the Lord's will. A rich man would stay rich. A poor man would stay poor. It was accepted that people were not individuals but part of social groups. There was to be no meddling. If one man decided to make a better life for himself, it could threaten the balance of the group, thus the entire society. The King's latest decision was not a popular one among the nobility.

'Thomas Wolsey is poisoning the King's mind. That butcher's son… turned bishop of Lincoln! With his harlot at home and his two bastards! He does not belong in the privy council and he does not belong in the Church!' Buckingham roared.

'I spoke to the abbot of Notley as I went on a pilgrimage to the shrine of Our Lady of Caversham to pray for the King's and your recovery from the red plague,' his brother whispered. 'Out of shame, he admitted that the displayed relic of the holy halter Judas Iscariot used to take his own life is in fact not holy at all. Wolsey himself told him not to blabber and be happy with the riches pilgrims offer to see it.'

'Not here, fool. We should talk more privately,' Buckingham led his brother out of earshot.

Ella's eyes were as wide as her pomander. Nicholas was staring at her as if he had been punched in the stomach. 'Do you think it was the truth?' he wanted to know.

'About Wolsey's family or the holy relic?' she asked, although she knew perfectly well that the bishop had two children with a woman he was forbidden to love.

'Do you believe that holy relic to be fabricated?' Nicholas reformulated.

Duh, the atheist in Ella was close to answering. 'I do not know, but it did not sound like the earl was telling lies,' she said.

'Go back to the Queen and do not say a word about it. We shall talk more this evening,' Nicholas decided, kissed her on the lips and left.

Ella made a face. To her, the idea that men could present fake relics for believers to bring money to their church was not surprising, nor was it even news. Pop used to joke that if the so-called pieces of the True Cross that were on display in Catholic churches around the world were all put together, the result would be at least twice as tall as the Shard. But, for the Catholic that Nicholas was, it had to be a blow.

On her way to the Queen's apartments, Ella spotted Pan. More exactly, Pan spotted Ella and trotted to her. Ella took him in her arms and gently pushed his face away from hers when he tried to lick it.

'Sorry, but God knows where you've been putting this tongue!' she joked. 'Where is your Keeper? You really have a life of your own, do you not?' she asked rhetorically. Pan was looking at her like one would look at a baby talking gibberish.

The Spanish girl Blanche de Vargas interrupted her moment when she appeared with Maria. Blanche curtseyed with the respect a maid of honour was obliged to show a countess, but Maria hesitated. Pan barked at her. Ella had to repress a laugh and smiled provocatively when Maria's knees bent almost against her will.

It was only at the end of the day, as they were all walking back to their private apartments, that Ella found some alone time with Maud and Inez.

'We did tell you the Earl of Nottingham was a good match, but you did not believe us then,' Inez reminded her, with her usual almost motherly look on her face.

Ella knew that, even if she became queen of England, it would not change the fact that she was once under Inez's wing. Inez was only a couple of years older than her but would always behave as if she had helped birthing her into the world. And, in a way, she had.

'In all fairness, the Earl of Nottingham was no earl then,' Maud said. Inez was about to retort something but Maud quickly went on: 'That we did tell you he was a good match is true. I do wonder why the King created Suffolk duke, but Nottingham earl,' she crunched her nose.

Ella shrugged. Duchess or countess, she still outranked the majority of the Queen's household. Besides, the earldom of Nottingham was a mark of high favour. The last person it had been created for was one of the King's royal uncles, the young Richard of Shrewsbury who had disappeared in the Tower alongside his brother.

'If the King should decide one day to create your husband duke, he would be the sixth,' Maud said. Ella mentally made a list; Buckingham, Norfolk and Suffolk were the three non-royal dukes. Hal and Arthur, as Cornwall and York, were the two royal ones.

'It would be interesting to see Buckingham's reaction to it,' Ella grimaced. She would actually love to be his equal, just to annoy him.

'Do not pay heed to this man, dear. There is much bitterness inside his heart. The earl and you deserve the King's favour,' Inez said.

'I thank you. Do you think Margery shares this thought?' Ella asked. 'She has not said a word to me since my husband was elevated.'

Maud shook her head. 'She is your friend, but you are a countess now. She feels unsure of how to behave around you, but she shall come back to her senses,' she reassured her.

'I am sure she will. Do you feel love for the earl? He looks smitten with you,' Inez changed the subject.

'I am content. He is a kind husband,' Ella replied.

'But you do not love him,' Maud guessed.

'You have been wed for two months. Love shall come, do not worry,' Inez promised.

'I am twenty-two years of age and have been married to my husband for six years, but love has still not come,' Maud contradicted her. 'I bear such great love for my children that it does not matter. One's heart is full once one becomes a mother, you shall see,' she smiled.

Ella did not bother to remind her that getting pregnant in this century was her worst nightmare. She wished them both good night when she arrived at her door. As usual, the first thing she did once she closed it back behind her was to take her hood off, feeling the sweet release of its weight on her head. Nicholas was there, the low neckline of his loose-fitting shirt showing his hairy chest, and smiled when he saw her.

'I trust my beloved Countess of Nottingham enjoyed her day,' he said.

'Very much, I thank my lord Earl of Nottingham,' she replied cheekily.

He laughed and came to give her a kiss. Inez was right. After a bit over two months of marriage, Nicholas had developed feelings for his wife. They were not reciprocated yet. Ella knew she could have hardly made any better than him. In all regards, he was a good man and a good husband. Ella was not scared of him, nor did she dislike him, but she was barely starting to consider him as a friend and was still forcing herself into accomplishing her conjugal duty. She was not in love with him. She was good enough at faking it.

'I talked to Charles about what we heard from Wiltshire,' he told her. 'We agreed it was slander to vilify the bishop of Lincoln.'

'Yes, Nicholas,' Ella answered, disappointed. When she locked eyes with him, she realised he did not believe a word of what he had said. She raised an eyebrow. He exhaled loudly.

'Certain facets of the Church are simply... wrong,' he murmured.

'Do you really think so?' Ella asked on the same tone, choosing cautiousness instead of jumping head-first into a heretic conversation.

'I am no heretic,' he claimed as if he had read her mind.

'And I am your wife, forever faithful,' she reassured him.

'It is sometimes in my thoughts that John Wycliffe was not… entirely… in the wrong,' he admitted in a voice so low that Ella barely heard it.

John Wycliffe was a fourteenth-century priest, viewed as a heretic because of his translation of the Bible into Middle English and his attacks against both the Papacy and the immorality of many men of the Church. If the translation of the Bible from Latin to English was not formally and explicitly forbidden, reading or owning a "Wycliffe Bible" could get one to be burned at the stake for heresy. The name which Ella associated with the start of Protestantism was Martin Luther, whom she had learned about at school, but he was only from Germany; John Wycliffe had been arguing for church reform in England over two centuries earlier.

'In what regard?' Ella asked softly.

'The Bible is the true authority. The true guide. The only guide. Not… the Pope, or the clergy,' he declared, walking up and down the room in an anxious state.

'Because clerics feel entitled to hear our sins despite their own immorality,' Ella agreed, sitting down on the edge of the bed, amazed at where the conversation was going.

Nicholas walked up to her and kneeled, taking her hands in his. 'Are they all immoral?' he wondered.

'No…' she conceded, and saw the panic in her husband's eyes ease slightly. 'Yet, I find it difficult to know when one conceals one's immorality. Remember Fray Diego Fernandez, receiving the confession of the Queen's sins, believed by the King and the Queen to be a good man of the Church but leading a depraved life at the very same time,' Ella reminded him. She would not let him forget about the so-called holy man who had assaulted her.

He kept quiet for a moment. 'You agree with the dean of St Paul's,' he let out.

'The dean of St Paul's? The King's chaplain?' Ella repeated. She could not believe her ears.

'He pleads for a change in the living ways of the men of the Church, which he believes to be corrupted by pride and lust for the flesh and riches. He wishes for their minds to be reformed.'

'Reformed?'

'He says that for people to turn to humility and charity… morality… dignity… priests must do it first, so it can then spread throughout Christendom,' he explained.

Ella realised the "reformation" that the dean of St Paul's and Nicholas were talking about was not intended to become the Reformation which she had studied in school. They wanted church reform, but they did not want to replace Catholicism. She did not reply, staring at Nicholas's strong hands still holding hers. She knew that he was attending the lectures that the dean, although quite busy with being the King's chaplain, was holding every week in St Paul's Cathedral. She smiled. They were far from even considering the Reformation to be a possibility, but they were criticising the Church in the state it was now. It was a good start.

But then Ella remembered what Nicholas had said about John Wycliffe. 'I agree with John Wycliffe too. Only God can forgive sinners. God is the only authority and the Bible is the word of God,' she said.

He stared at her. 'It must be translated for all. Many persons have not been taught Latin,' he exclaimed and whispered at the same time, in a confused shock.

There it was. The real issue. Ella caressed the small scar on his left cheek. She wanted to tell him that the people who had not been taught Latin had most likely not been taught to read either. But he was right: the Bible had to be translated officially. People needed to know what they chose to believe in, not what the clerics told them to believe in.

They needed to read or hear the words for themselves, not only other people's interpretations.

There was a faint voice in the back of Ella's head that hoped that every single human being would then come to realise that God was not there. Anywhere. It wanted people to think that, if men of the Church had made them believe certain things for so long only for their own personal gain, maybe none of it was actually real. But Ella also knew that no one was ready yet for this conversation. What mattered, for now, was for men and women to interpret the Bible themselves. They deserved at least that.

Also, what kind of god would let a girl travel between centuries and mess up with the world's timeline, her inner voice could not stop asking.

Ella smiled, wondering what the odds could have been for her to end up forced into marrying one of the only men at court who was ready to question the unquestioned.

'I love you,' she said to him, although she was not feeling love, but pride and thankfulness.

'I love you too,' he found his smile again. 'Do not say a word to anyone about this. My friendship with the King would not save us from the stake,' he warned her.

'The King is not ready yet but, God willing, he shall be one day,' Ella replied, trying to picture Nicholas's face if she told him the Henry VIII from her school books had broken with the Pope and brought the Reformation to England.

Nicholas distractedly nodded. She could sense he had gone somewhere else. They both climbed into bed. Ten minutes went by in a complete silence, until she heard his voice again: 'I trust you have never heard of William Tylesworth?' he asked.

Ella turned around under the covers to face him and murmured that she had not.

'He was burned at the stake some years ago. There was an enquiry into heresy in Amersham. I was sent there, along with two other retainers,' he said. He paused. 'Some men had been involved in prayers and readings conducted in English. Most of them agreed to recant. One man, William Tylesworth, refused. I shall never forget his defiance. He said that he wished to read the Scriptures in English and that he wished every good Christian would,' Nicholas recalled, then moved down in the bed to put his head on Ella's chest. She had never seen him more vulnerable. She put her hand on his head and slid her fingers through his hair.

'Tell me,' Ella encouraged him. There was something he was not saying. Finally, he blurted:

'His daughter Joan was forced by the bishop to light the faggots.'

10.

UNRELIABLE AND UNPRINCIPLED 1514

Arthur was just over three months old when his mother realised that she was pregnant again, for the fifth time in five years. Ella would not have traded places with her for all the jewels in the world. Five pregnancies in five years. Fertility was an indubitable asset for the Queen, who was taking one sweet revenge on history, but seeing her happy and feeling worthy only when she was expecting was uncomfortable for Ella. She took the first opportunity to enjoy the extra freedom her rank allowed her and escaped to the gardens.

Richmond Palace was even more beautiful than usual, surrounded by hundreds of snowdrops whose petals matched the white glow of its stones. Ella sat down on a bench, shivering in her furs despite the early spring. After a while, her mind wandered off. She did not even think about the ring, but she tried to imagine what Iris was up to. Her father, too. It did not happen very often anymore, but she sometimes still wanted to know if he was looking for her. If he had given up. If he had ever tried. He had never been a true parent to her, but at a court where everyone was more or less related, she missed having a blood relative.

'You look very contemplative, Lady Nottingham,' the King pulled her out of her thoughts.

'I was thinking about my father,' Ella replied. You stupid cow, she immediately realised her mistake – so much for having amnesia.

'Your father?' he repeated.

'I am trying to imagine what he could have looked like,' she lied, and only then noticed the red patches around the King's eyes. For as long as she had known him, he had been so confident in his manhood that he had never been ashamed to cry in front of other people. 'Your Grace seems upset,' she remarked.

He sighed. 'You are a humble and learned lady. We shall take this opportunity to ask for your opinion on an important matter,' he announced, his blue eyes half-shut because of the bright daylight. 'Distressing rumours have travelled from Spain. Despite our wish to attack France with Spain's support this year, King Ferdinand of Aragon is now on the side of peace,' he sighed once again.

'Has Your Grace received proofs or rumours?' Ella asked.

'You have sharp wits,' he smiled, paternalistic despite their similar age. 'Mere rumours, so far. The Queen's father shows no sign to prepare Spain for war. Pope Leo encourages peace, although His Holiness's predecessor promised us the title of Most Christian King if we conquered France and defeated King Louis, who currently possesses the title,' he explained bitterly.

'I...' Ella was about to remind him the fate of his good friend Sir Thomas Knyvett, but hesitated.

'Speak freely,' he said, straight in the eyes.

'Two years in the past, Your Grace and King Ferdinand were to attack the French town of Bayonne,' she said, feeling as if she was walking through a minefield with fins at her feet.

'King Ferdinand seized Navarre instead, withdrew from France and abandoned our great army on the battlefield,' the King finished for her the story of his father-in-law double-crossing him.

'Good Englishmen died because of it,' Ella softly pointed out.

'Indeed.' Ella could tell he was reminiscing about his late friend Knyvett. 'It is your conclusion that King Ferdinand must not be trusted by us,' he summed up. There was so much sadness in his voice that Ella would have loved to hold his hand. 'We were seventeen years of age when our father died. King Ferdinand was of invaluable support, both as King and father,' he shared.

'It brings me much sorrow that Your Grace has been deceived by a father,' Ella said, desperate to tell him that she knew exactly how it felt. She did not know the performances of Henry VII as a father, but the King's second father figure was unreliable and unprincipled. She could relate.

'You are very kind,' he thanked her.

'May I ask Your Grace an odd question?' she asked, and he nodded. 'What are Your Grace's fondest memories about the late king Henry? she realised as she spoke that she was out of line. 'I do not remember my father and my husband never met his,' she tried to explain herself.

The King looked at her from the corner of his eyes and smiled. 'Our father was a gracious king but a quiet man,' he told her. 'We were loved dearly by him, as we became his only heir at the tender age of ten. But you asked about our fondest memories of him, and it is the great and pure love he bore our beloved mother,' he said, absently staring at one of the snowdrops.

'How old was Your Grace when the late queen departed to God?'

'Twelve years of age. She was delivered of a daughter, who did not live, and succumbed of childbed fever on her birthday, less than a year after the death of our brother Arthur. We miss her presence still.'

Ella did not answer. They both kept quiet for a while. It was not even uncomfortable. They just let the memories of his late parents and siblings live on their own for a moment. Ella knew that, with his short temper and his future cruelty, his modern reputation had been rightfully earned. The fate of his six wives was certainly not to be envied. Ella glanced quickly at him. The man sitting beside her was only human. He was passionate, sensitive, cultured, and without a doubt the most down-to-Earth monarch that had ever ruled England. He had his flaws. Many of them. He was hypocritical, self-centred, impatient, proud… but he was no tyrant.

Not yet at least. Henry VIII was more than what history books said of him.

'The bishop of Lincoln's advice is to enter an alliance with the French,' the King changed the subject. 'King Louis is in need of a new bride as Queen Anne died two months past. His daughter Princess Renée is of the same age as the prince of Wales,' he told her, clearly interested into marrying both his sister and his eldest son, who had recently received the title of Prince of Wales, into the French royal family.

'It was my belief that Princess Mary was betrothed to Archduke Charles?' Ella wondered. The archduke was King Ferdinand's grandson.

'Not any more. We do not wish to trouble you with diplomacy,' he seemed to realise that talking about his plans to one day have half-French grandchildren to a woman attending his Spanish, anti-French wife, may not have been the best idea. 'We trust you are enjoying being the Countess of Nottingham?' he asked.

'My lord husband and I are very grateful to Your Grace.'

'We have known the earl since our most tender age.'

'My husband bears even more love for Your Grace than for his devoted wife,' Ella said, making the King burst with laughter, a hand pressing his chest.

'Oh, we have not laughed so much since Christmas time!' he exclaimed after he calmed down. He could as well have said 'since the smallpox.'

'I thank God every day for Your Grace's recovery,' Ella lied.

'We went on a pilgrimage to Our Lady of Walsingham to give thanks and shall be forever grateful our sons were spared,' he said. Ella wondered to which fake holy relic he had done his offering. 'We must part now,' he decided when they spotted Thomas Wolsey, the bishop of Lincoln, walking towards them.

Ella got up and curtseyed low. 'The late Countess of Essex, formerly lady in waiting to the Queen, has not yet been replaced. You are to take her place,' the King told her, but did not give her time to thank him for the promotion before thanking her himself: 'we thank you for your time, Lady Nottingham. The earl is in luck to have you for a wife and we feel as such to be your friend.'

He left the gardens, soon followed by Ella. Walking back to the Queen's lodgings, the King's words echoed in her head. He considered himself lucky to have her as a friend.

He does not have any female friends, though, she said to herself. Besides the Queen, the women in his life could be put into two different categories: the ones he was related to and tried to marry off to important people, and the ones he found attractive and tried to put in his bed. He was always discreet, but word at court travelled fast nonetheless. At the moment, his bed was supposed to be regularly occupied by the very young Bessie Blount.

Ella had never seen him lack courtesy with the women who failed to be of his taste, but she had not seen him build any friendship with them either. Somehow, she was different. He had not been ambiguous with her at all. He had never showed her any romantic or sexual interest, had matched her with one of his best friends, and had trusted her with his problems. Ella chuckled.

She had been friend-zoned by Henry VIII.

When Ella eventually reached the Queen's apartments, she found Queen Katherine standing in the middle of her bedchamber, her skirts halfway up, staring at the little puddle of blood on the floor with tears on her face.

Five conceptions, three lost babies.

The Queen was still grieving the loss of her unborn child when her husband announced the peace with France and the double betrothals: his sister was to be crowned queen of France and her brand-new stepdaughter would become princess of Wales. Far from being pleased, but too good a wife to confront her husband about his decision, the Queen took it out on Jane Popincourt, a maid of honour older than Ella who had for her only flaw to be French.

'She is also bedding the Duke of Longueville,' Margery told her with a grimace once Ella had shared her thoughts out loud.

Ella smiled. Little by little, she was succeeding in convincing Margery to remember that she was not only the Countess of Nottingham, but also her friend. 'Her Grace is not supposed to know that,' she pointed out.

'Being French is enough to be displeasing,' Inez said bluntly, making everyone around them giggle.

It was no secret that the French were the old arch-enemies of the English, but their relationship was no better with Spain. The kingdoms seemed destined to fight each other, if only to prove to the world which had the most influence over other countries, especially Italy. Ella always had to remind herself that Italy was not like she remembered – it was divided into several different states with no central government. There was also bickering around the kingdom of Navarre, so small compared to France and Spain that the argument sometimes exasperated Ella; but the Queen's hatred for France was so deeply entrenched that Ella had a hard time believing it was only rooted in politics.

The fact that her father's second wife is French may have something to do with it, she thought. 'I do feel for Princess Renée, if the Queen detests the French so much,' Ella whispered.

'Every sane person detests the French,' Inez replied. 'My son shall never marry a Frenchwoman,' she added mischievously, putting a hand on her belly, which she had been hiding from view but was growing underneath her gown for the third time.

In the great hall of Greenwich Palace, Princess Mary became queen of France. She looked sumptuous in her purple gown and her cap of cloth of gold, but too hot in the mid-August heat as she said her wedding vows. Her husband was absent. The Duke of Longueville stood proxy for him – or the Duke of Longue-*vile*, as Margery now called him.

The court bid the new queen farewell about a month later in Dover, where she embarked for France with Longueville and at least a dozen ships. Ella was doing her best to ignore her menstrual cramps and was instead focusing on Jane Popincourt, who was sobbing because the king of France had denied her request to return to her home country – he had heard rumours of her affair with the married duke. Ella was brought back to reality when the new queen cleared her throat.

'My dearest and most beloved brother, I beg of you to remember the promise regarding my future,' she said.

'Very well,' the King replied, a certain uneasiness on his face that barely lasted a couple of seconds before he regained control of himself. His sister did not seem to notice anything and curtseyed one last time before getting on the ship.

It is only in the evening that Ella finally found herself alone with Nicholas. She had sent him on a quest for marzipan and smiled when he opened the door to their bedroom, proudly showing her the three large chunks of the luxurious sugary treat he had smuggled out of the kitchens for his menstruating wife. Ella kissed him and grabbed her due.

'Will you not leave one for me?' he asked. Her mouth full with her first bite, Ella reluctantly gave some back to Nicholas. He laughed. 'It was but a tease. Please do keep it all.'

Ella sighed of relief. 'You are a blessing. Thank you,' she said. 'Do you happen to know about the promise the King has made to the queen of France?' she asked.

'You shan't ever tell a soul. Not even Lady Mountjoy or Lady Parr,' Nicholas warned her.

'You have my word,' she promised.

'Louis XII is old,' he stated.

'I am aware. He is over fifty, and his wife is only eighteen!' Ella exclaimed but apologised when Nicholas looked unhappy about having been interrupted.

'The King's sister desires to marry for love next, after a respectful period of widowhood,' he said.

'Is King Louis's health so frail?' Ella could not help but ask.

'Elizabeth.'

'Forgive me. I shall keep quiet.'

'His Grace promised Queen Mary that, if she was to become queen dowager without having been impregnated with the heir to the throne, her next husband would be one of her choosing,' he told her, then paused. 'It was not the truth. His Grace is aware of her attachment to Charles… and that Charles reciprocates it,' he explained in a low voice.

Ella's eyes widened as a memory from Lolly and Pop came back like a kick in the teeth.

2015. Paul Buckley was visiting Sudeley Castle with his granddaughter for the first time and let his wife – or self-proclaimed guide – tell them all about the sixth wife of Henry VIII who had lived, died, and been buried in this castle. When they reached the room where stood the seven wax figures of the infamous king and his wives, Ella made a joke on how his shoes looked like pastries.

'They do. And he has a lot of wives,' Paul commented.

'Believe it or not, there could have been seven of them,' Emily retorted.

'Oh, I believe! What was supposed to happen to that one, then?' Paul asked, looking at the waxwork of Katherine Parr wearing a gold dress and cross-shaped earrings.

'The King sent for her arrest because of her religious views but she made him change his mind. She was a clever woman, probably the cleverest of his wives. The King thought about marrying the daughter of his first wife's best friend, who was also the widow of his own best friend and former brother-in-law, but he died before that.'

'Wait, what? The widow of his… brother-in-law?' Ella made a disgusted face.

'His name was Charles. He was quite the character. He married the King's sister behind his back, right after

promising he would not. He went close to losing his head for that,' Emily said. 'It was a love match for both of them, so I am glad he did not lose any body part,' she distractedly stroked the blue sapphire of the ring around her neck.

Charles Brandon was engaged to be married to a nine-year-old and the woman he loved was married to the king of France but, somehow, somewhere in time, they had ended up together. Ella battled against her Renaissance brain, which was slowly but surely making her forget her former life as to replace the space with the new information she needed to survive in this one, and tried to dig up whether or not the King's sister had become queen of France in her old history books too.

Maybe my presence here has changed more things than I thought, she panicked when she could not find her answer. And who on Earth was going to be Charles Brandon's widow? *The daughter of the Queen's best friend.* Ella pressed her fists against her eyes when Maria's face appeared in her brain. She shook her head to make it disappear. Nicholas took her hands in his.

'Sweet Elizabeth, do not upset yourself. The matter would only be delicate if King Louis were to die before Charles's betrothed was to reach a marriageable age,' he told her.

'She is nine!' Ella reminded him sharply.

'We must then pray the Lord that King Louis shall live five more years. His Grace needs Queen Mary's hand for future diplomatic negotiations and shall not suffer for her to be wed to Charles,' he whispered.

'They are in love…' Ella said, unconvinced this point would weigh at all in the matter.

'We were not when we married but we are now. The same shall happen for them, but not together. Elizabeth, a princess of the blood royal cannot marry for love. Queen Mary shall understand.'

Ella bit her tongue so hard she made herself bleed. Swallowing the blood in her mouth, she fought against the urge to grab her husband by the shoulders and put in plain English how hypocritical his royal friend was. She would have given anything to tell him that, in 2020, he was remembered for turning the entire kingdom upside down, discarding his queen, cutting people's heads off and breaking with the Pope so that he could marry the one he loved and have sons by her.

But it was apparently unthinkable for his sister to marry the one *she* loved.

11.

THE WEIGHT OF THE WORLD
1514

With November came the letter announcing the birth of Inez's daughter and requesting a visit from Ella, which the King agreed to. Riding to the Mountjoys' country house with Nicholas, Ella was beaming. After two miscarriages, Inez's dearest wish had come true.

'You look pleased!' Nicholas noticed.

'I am! Inez shall be a wonderful mother!' Ella said. 'Do you believe the poor child shall have her father's forehead?' she asked playfully.

Nicholas cracked up so loudly he scared his horse and was almost thrown from it. Ella's laugh resonated in the empty countryside. She took a deep breath. It was a glorious day. The sky was grey, the weather was cold and forever windy, but it was glorious. Today, she was not bothered that she was living in the wrong century, nor by thoughts of the precious ring still lost somewhere in the woods of Eltham. Ella's focus was entirely on Inez and her newborn baby girl.

After a few hours of travel, the Nottinghams arrived at their destination and Ella let Nicholas wait for Lord Mountjoy alone in the hall, going up the spiral staircase to see her friend as fast as her gown would let her. Inez was in a large bed, her cheeks red and her hair stuck to her brow but her smile wide. 'Elizabeth!' she cried.

'Inez, how pleased I am to see you! How are you feeling?' Ella asked and grabbed her hand.

'I am well, I thank you. God has sent me a daughter,' Inez told her. 'God has sent me a beautiful baby. I am a mother!' she corrected herself with a tired smile.

'You are. And do not worry yourself, boys shall follow. Does she have a name?'

'Lora, in honour of William's late mother.'

'This is a lovely name.'

'You may hold her if you wish,' Inez said, closing her eyes peacefully.

Ella was almost skipping as she headed to the cradle but froze when she saw the tiny little baby girl wrapped up tight in a pale coloured cloth. The tiny little baby girl with the grey face. Ella tried to take the baby's pulse, pretending to caress her head.

Please, God, let her live, she prayed for the first time in her life.

But there was nothing to be done. Lora Blount was already dead. Ella cleared her throat, trying to find the right words to announce such tragic news to her friend, but Inez was fast asleep. Ella shamefully sighed of relief. She was not ready to have this conversation. She covered the baby's face with a piece of cloth. The maid standing by the window at the opposite side of the room, horrified, put a hand in front of her mouth.

'Fetch my Lord Mountjoy,' Ella demanded.

'Yes, my lady,' the maid curtseyed and hurried out of the room.

Ella looked at Inez and shed a tear. She had been dreaming of becoming a mother for so long and now her baby was dead. If a confirmation was needed that God was nowhere to be found, in anyone's life, it was it. Inez did not deserve this pain. Not after two miscarriages. Not ever. Ella wondered if her friend had even had the chance to hold her little girl in her arms.

'My lady,' the voice of Lord Mountjoy made her turn around. 'Is my wife asleep?' he checked. Ella nodded. 'I thank you for your visit, although it was our hope to receive you and my Lord Nottingham in more joyful circumstances. My wife is unaware of the situation. I found out not long ago but kept it from the maid as she would not have been able to hide it from my wife,' he explained.

'Why did you wish to keep it a secret?' Ella asked.

'A wicked motivation, I am afraid. I cannot face her distress once more, my lady, and I beg of you to be the one to tell her about the death of our child,' Mountjoy said.

Ella stared at him in shock for a second. It was his job to be there for his wife for better or for worse, but she could not tell him that. He was not yet forty years old but looked at least sixty. There was no anger or denial in his eyes. Just sadness. So much that one could have drown in it.

Ella nodded again and looked at her friend as if the weight of the world had just been forcibly dropped on her shoulders. Inez had no idea that the most beautiful day of her life was about to become the most dreadful.

A detail Ella had not noticed before made her frown. 'When was the birth?' she asked Mountjoy.

'Several hours ago. She was christened immediately as she looked so frail,' he explained.

'Inez's brow is wet,' Ella ignored the remark about the baby, feeling deep in her core that something was wrong. Inez had been recovering in her bed for hours but her brow was still sweaty and her cheeks as flushed as if she had just ran the London marathon.

Mountjoy reached his wife's bedside only a second after Ella did. Inez was breathing, but when Ella put a hand on her face to check her temperature, she did not need to have a thermometer to know it was way over the normal thirty-seven degrees Celsius. She was burning.

'Her fever is high, she needs to see a physician,' Ella said. Nicholas rushed out of the room.

'Childbed fever...' Mountjoy whispered.

'No,' she retorted, more for herself than for him.

'My first wife departed to God after three days of fever and pain in the body and head following the delivery of our daughter,' he told her, looking like he had already started to grieve his second wife.

Ella sent him out of the room to get some clean cloth and cold water. Her mind was racing. She had been told about the symptoms of childbed fever. Every person attending the Queen was expected to know about them. High fever. Chills. Headache. Distended abdomen. Foul vaginal discharge. As soon as she was left alone with Inez in the room, she uncovered her to check on the last two symptoms on the list, confirmed them, and put the covers back when Inez opened her eyes. Ella faked a smile and took her hand.

'Forgive me for not being the most welcoming, I am much tired it makes my head aches,' Inez said softly.

Ella pressed her hand, but words stayed stuck in her throat. She knew the symptoms, and it had taken her a good quarter of an hour to realise her friend was feverish. Childbed fever was said to kill more women than anything else in this world. Every single person knew at the very least one woman who had died from it, whether it was a mother, a daughter, or a friend. Even the King had lost his mother to it. Maud, too. The Queen had lost one of her sisters to it. Margery, her aunt. And Ella was now losing her friend.

When Nicholas came back with a physician, Ella knew he would be powerless. What Inez needed had not been invented yet: antibiotics.

Inez was waking up three to four times each hour that passed. She had been bled and her urine had been examined, but Ella had not bothered to listen to the physician's diagnosis. He was useless and so was she. Whenever Inez was awake, she looked so weak and exhausted that no one dared to tell her anything about the now empty cradle in the corner of the room.

Deep into the night, the physician was replaced with a confessor and the maid was sent to bed. Inez was given the last rites as Nicholas was falling asleep fully clothed on the floor against the tapestry. Ella could not have even tried to sleep. She could barely think. She was mechanically putting a cold clean cloth on her friend's brow every time the previous one had turned warm. She did not talk. She could not. Inez was still there, somewhere between life and death, burning with a fever that would not drop. She was fading away in front of her eyes and all she could do was watch.

'I am sorry,' Ella murmured, fighting tears of guilt. She should not have let fifteen minutes go by without noticing something was wrong. She should have found a way to help her without modern medicine. She should have saved her. She didn't.

'It is God's will. You helped her the best of your abilities, my lady, and I am deeply grateful,' Mountjoy told her.

This God thing again, Ella thought bitterly. 'Please, call me Elizabeth,' she replied.

'And I William. You were highly esteemed by my wife. You are. Forgive me, I am unsure how to…' he started to say, but his voice broke and he decided to cut his sentence short.

'Why does Your Grace look so sad?' Inez asked weakly, mistaking Ella for the Queen. 'The birth of my child shall make Your Grace smile again. It should not be long now. Oh, Your Grace, how I have longed for a child. I cannot wait for my baby to be born,' Inez declared, beaming at the ceiling and lovingly caressing her empty bump.

Ella meant to say something. No sound came out. 'How shall we call our child?' William intervened.

'William, if it is a boy. Lora, if it is a girl. My husband and I hesitated with Isabella, in the honour of Her Grace's mother. But… but it is a boy. It is a healthy boy. *Un niño sano!* I am so pleased! I gave my husband a son. Prince Arthur and my dear William shall be friends,' Inez closed her eyes and tried to laugh, but her weak body did not let her, and she went back to sleep. Her husband and her friend shared a look full of gloom and sorrow. The room fell back into a painful silence.

As the sun started to rise that morning, death crept closer. Inez's breath became less regular. Deep dark circles had formed under her once bright blue eyes and the red in her cheeks that had been so alarming earlier was now gone, replaced by a ghostly grey. As if a voice had warned them all it was the end, Ella took her friend's hand in hers and William kissed his wife on the forehead, holding her other hand. Ella felt Nicholas's presence next to her and was surprised to find comfort in it as Inez slipped away to the darkness.

The King and the Queen both made the journey to attend the burial. It was unusual, but William had been the King's tutor and close friend before he even sat on the throne, and was also the Queen's chamberlain. Although the ladies who had come with the Queen mourned Inez de Venegas, Ella knew the royal couple was only attending the burial of Lady Mountjoy. Wearing black from head to toe, she stared at Inez's coffin until the last second. Her body was present, but her mind was replaying her friend drawing her last breath over and over again.

On their first night back at court, Nicholas laid down in bed with his wife, taking her in his arms without expecting anything more. Ella's mind was in such a fog that he could have done whatever he wanted to her and she would barely have noticed on the moment. But he respected her grief, her silence, and her integrity.

'Nic?' she said on the second night back.

'Yes?'

'Do you really believe in Purgatory?'

'It is best to not discuss this.'

'I often see your face when it is mentioned.'

'Elizabeth…' Nicholas sighed. 'I sometimes have doubts, but yes, I believe. You are mourning. Do find comfort in the thought that Inez made a good death. Let us sleep, now,' he decided, stubbornly keeping his eyes closed when Ella asked him if he genuinely thought money could release a soul from Purgatory more quickly.

She let go of his embrace and stared at the dark wood beams on the ceiling for a while. It was frustrating to know in her heart that the part of Nicholas that did not believe in Purgatory was bigger than the one that did, and yet be unable to have a conversation about it with him. Ella now lived in a world where death was such a great part of life that men and women were more interested in properly preparing for it than escaping it at all costs like most twenty-first century people. They did not fear death, they feared dying unprepared. Preparation was what made a death good or bad.

People all believed in a place filled with fire, pain, and punishment, which was not Hell yet but felt a lot like it: Purgatory. They were convinced that their souls would one day have to go through this terrible place to eventually have the doors of Heaven opened to them. Pop had one day compared it to Londoners suffering willingly in the overcrowded trains to Brighton on a hot and sunny weekend to be able, at some point, to enjoy the beach. Except, here, the aim was not to tan in the sun and swim in the fresh waters, but to avoid burning in Hell for all eternity.

As far as Ella understood it, each soul could achieve some kind of equilibrium. Committing sins in the first place tilted the balance in favour of eternal damnation, but confessing them and paying a fine more or less made up for it. Purgatory was then the place where that balance would be extracted at long last, and again, it was believed this purifying and difficult time for one's soul could be shortened if money was donated to the Church for masses to be heard for the deceased. Those taken by surprise by death had no time to confess their sins and receive absolution before their last breath and were, in short, in a bit more trouble depending on the gravity of their sins.

Money ruled both Ella's birth world and current world. The reasons were different, but the root of the problem was the same. It was always money. Ella sometimes wished she believed in God. Life would then be much easier. But even if she did, the amount of money the fear of Purgatory and Hell brought to the Catholic Church was enough to convince her that Inez's soul had deserted every conceivable existence at the same time it had deserted her body.

The next few weeks were complicated for Ella, who had trouble processing the death of a woman still in her twenties at the same pace as everyone else. An early death was common, even more for women. To most, and although she had been no firefighter or police officer, Inez had died doing her duty. Even her widower, William, had moved on and was looking for his third wife. Only Hal ever managed to take Ella's mind off death and its inevitability. Her boy-prince had arrived at court with his brother on Christmas day and was brightening her mood considerably. He always seemed happier to see her than anyone else. He was about to turn four and was a lot taller than any four-year-old Ella had ever met, but also so much smarter he sometimes made her feel like she was chatting with a ten-year-old.

The morning before the New Year, the Countess of Surrey angrily burst into the room, followed by a clearly irritated Maria, and almost demanded that they both attend a private discussion with the Queen and Ella.

'What did I do now', Ella whispered to herself as the other ladies left the room.

Maud locked eyes with her on her way out and formed a grimace that made her smile, but the fact that Maria was a part of this was enough to make Ella wish to be anywhere else. Worse, and even though she had always been nice to her, the countess was Buckingham's eldest daughter.

'Lady Surrey, what seems to be the matter?' the Queen asked.

'I have heard wicked words about the Countess of Nottingham in Mistress Maria's mouth, so appalling I find myself ashamed to tell Your Grace of them!'

Ella needed a second to understand that Elizabeth Stafford was defending her and accusing Maria of something. The Queen delicately flattened the rich purple fabric of her dress on her lap.

'It is my desire to hear it,' she said.

'Mistress Maria wished aloud to see the late Lady Mountjoy alive once more, her life traded for the life of the countess,' she spat out. 'Lady Nottingham is of noble rank and position, which is like mine and much above Mistress Maria's!' she added, fuming.

The Queen thanked the Countess of Surrey and asked her to leave. Ella was trying to handle her conflicted feelings. Somehow, she was both indignant and detached, both amused and heavy-hearted. Maria had shared out loud that she wanted her dead, which was a step beyond her usual antipathy, but Ella also knew there was very little she could do to harm her. The countess's reaction was proof of it. Of course, Elizabeth Stafford was not defending Elizabeth White. It was the Countess of Surrey who was defending the Countess of Nottingham. It was all about rank and the hierarchical respect attached to it. Ella would have smiled had it not been so sad. The mention of Inez's passing was not making things any easier to digest.

'Mistress Maria?' the Queen asked her long-time friend.

'Your Grace is aware of my dislike for the Countess of Nottingham,' Maria replied as if Ella was not even in the room.

'You have been told repeatedly to regard this dislike as misplaced. You have offended the Countess of Nottingham but also the Countess of Surrey, and your Queen.'

'I beg Your Grace to forgive me,' Maria fell to the floor. Ella looked at the top of her blond head from above, guessing she craved forgiveness from the Queen but not from her. 'My only aim is to protect Your Grace from pretenders,' she said.

That woman is one stubborn cookie! Ella thought, rolling her eyes.

'Enough. I shall like for you to apologise to the countess immediately,' the Queen demanded, but Maria was interrupted by the King opening the door behind them.

Ella curtseyed and the Queen told her husband what had caused this little reunion. Maria was holding her breath. Ella was focusing on the tapestry behind the Queen, hoping to detach herself as much as possible from the situation. Countess or not, Maria was still highly suspicious of her. Ella did not know how the woman would be punished for her offence. The King and Queen were firmly against rudeness and disrespect. Rank or friendship could not prevent one from being told off if one crossed a line.

There were so many figures stuffed into the tapestry scene that Ella started counting them, at least until she realised just how heavy the silence around her was. She turned her head to the King. He was looking at Maria with such shame in his freezing blue eyes that Ella would have wet herself had this stare been destined to her.

'Lady Nottingham, it is our wish for you to decide retribution for this offence,' the King surprisingly declared.

Ella smiled, even more surprised at the evident answer that popped up in her mind: 'I have decided to forgive Mistress Maria.'

'Are you certain?'

'The death of Lady Mountjoy was a struggle for us all. I forgive her and humbly beseech Your Grace to forgive her too.'

'We are blessed to have such a kind and gracious lady at our court. Your Grace?'

'I agree with my beloved husband and I thank my dear countess for her benevolence,' Queen Katherine said, relief in her eyes as she realised her friend was not going to be sent away.

Ella curtseyed when the royal couple left the room. Maria watched her rise sceptically. Ella smirked. She had to explain why she had not ordered her immediate return to Spain and she knew it but, in all her pettiness, she took the time to fix her veil first.

'You owe me,' she then stated. And left the room.

The Countess of Surrey was waiting for her, chatting with Maud, and promptly asked for them to go for a walk. She was only seventeen years old and was even more petite in stature than the Queen, but she walked with such confidence that all that one could see in her was her father. Maud and she were startled when Ella told them about her decision to officially forgive Maria.

'I would have had her sent back to Spain. She may be from a noble family there, but in England, she is just a maid of honour. You, my lady, are married to an earl.'

'Please, do call me Elizabeth.'

'And I Elsie.'

'I have no sympathy for Mistress Maria, but she is now bound to return me the kindness.'

'This was clever thinking indeed. If my lord father had not such distaste for your person, you would have been great friends,' Elsie laughed.

'I must confess that I do not have a strong liking for your father either,' Ella admitted.

'Neither do I. Let us be friends, then. Lady Parr, as well? Maud?' Elsie offered, and both Ella and Maud accepted. Elsie was most definitely an interesting woman and was both the wife and the daughter of two of the most powerful men at court. She was not the kind of person to have as an enemy.

12.

THE KIND OF LOVE HE DESERVED

1515

History seemed about to repeat itself when King Louis of France died early in January and, a month later, Charles Brandon was sent to escort the non-pregnant, widowed queen back to England. Ella had every reason to think that Charles would still secretly marry his friend's sister, but kept it to herself. Her silence meant that the eighteen-year-old queen of France would be given some freedom of choice, and that the even younger Viscountess Lisle could be freed from her pre-contract with a man old enough to be her father.

She only opened her thoughts to her husband once his friend was already halfway across the Channel: 'Nic, surely, you must foresee what is to happen between Charles and the King's sister.'

'The King made Charles promise he would not propose. He shall be loyal.'

'They are in love.'

'Charles shall not deceive His Grace,' Nicholas insisted.

Ella shrugged but did not say anything else. The King was far from being an idiot but, this time, it certainly looked like it. He had falsely and outrageously promised his sister that she would be allowed to marry whoever she wanted once widowed and had sent the one man he knew she was in love with and loved by to bring her back, giving them the perfect opportunity for an intimacy he so firmly rejected.

'What is it?' Ella asked Nicholas, who was staring at her intensely.

'You think he is to propose?'

'I am not saying he is to propose. I am saying that I shall not be surprised if he does.'

'The King sent Charles to test his loyalty,' Nicholas retorted, his eyes now screaming that he was realising how naive this was. He put his hands behind his neck and his face disappeared between his elbows. He moaned, then joined Ella on the bed to rest his head on her breasts. There was nothing either of them could do about Charles. It was up to him. Ella could not wait to see how all this unfolded.

The King's screams could be heard from miles around Greenwich Palace when news came from France that its young dowager queen and Charles Brandon had tied the knot in a secret ceremony. Nicholas and Ella were in the great hall when they heard enough words to understand what the King was furious about. Nicholas grabbed his wife's arm.

'Do not tell anyone that we expected this to happen. Anyone, Elizabeth.'

'I promise. Do not trouble yourself too much about Charles, I am certain everything shall be fine.'

'This is a serious matter. Marrying a princess of royal blood without the King's consent is treason. Charles might lose his head.'

'His Grace would not sentence one loved as a brother to death,' Ella tried to reassure her husband, choosing to ignore the fate of Anne Boleyn.

If, in the history she had known, the King had sentenced the mother of his own child to have her head cut off, his best friend's life could well be in danger. But Lolly had told her that Charles had lived long enough to marry again after the death of the King's sister. Ella knew his neck would not be harmed.

'It is not about love, it is about honour,' Nicholas interrupted her thoughts. 'I must go to the King now and try to save Charles's life. If someone like Buckingham talks to the King first, he can bid his head farewell,' he exclaimed and left in a hurry.

Ella made a face. Buckingham and a large part of the nobility were desperate for an opportunity to destroy the upstart that was Charles. He had as good as given them his head on a silver platter. Ella started to think Lolly may have had her facts wrong. The King was outraged and the nobles would never let Charles be his brother-in-law without a fight. Ella's eyes laid on the young Viscountess Lisle, walking towards the Queen's apartments with the King's maternal aunt. She smiled. The girl smiled back. Being abandoned by the man she was precontracted with was an insult to her name, but the child looked happier than ever.

Ella hoped Charles would get to keep his head on his shoulders for another few decades but, if he did not, that smile was enough to remind her why she had kept quiet about his intentions.

The King refused to listen to Nicholas pleading for Charles's life, but also ignored Buckingham's demands that Charles be tried for treason. He stayed out of sight for a few days. The next time Ella saw him, he was returning from what looked like a hunting trip. She guessed he had been staying in Wanstead Hall, the secondary house to Greenwich Palace where he could hide from view whenever he needed more privacy than he could normally find in a royal palace.

Ella was sitting on the stone bench near the wonky chestnut tree with Maud and Elsie, gossiping about William's remarriage only a few months after Inez's death.

'Elsie, let us go back to the Queen,' Maud said when the King smiled to them from afar.

'Yes. Elizabeth, you must tell us everything later today. My father and my husband wish for the Duke of Suffolk to be tried and condemned. Naturally, I pray for his neck to be saved!' Elsie joked before leaving, not ever wasting an opportunity to remind her friends that she disliked the two most important men in her life.

It was now more or less widely known at court that the King enjoyed his talks with Ella. They were always platonic, and rather short, but happened several times a week. The King was constantly followed, at a discreet distance, by a few courtiers, but Ella had come to enjoy their talks so much that she sometimes woke up in the morning hoping to have a moment with him, however brief.

Not a single person at court had ever suspected her to be a royal mistress. Not even her own husband, or even the Queen. Ella was not sure if she should have felt relieved or offended. She had never thought about ending up in the King's bed, but the fact that no one deemed it remotely possible nor believable was slightly hurtful.

Far from guessing her thoughts, the King took place next to her. He complimented her on the emerald and diamond brooch that was pinned on her bodice, Nicholas's latest gift to her, and checked she was not cold from the wind before staring at his red-bricked palace in silence.

'Your Grace is upset,' Ella said.

'Indeed. We have given much thought on the matter regarding our sister. We are torn.'

'I am not so bold as to pretend I am able to provide Your Grace with advice but am willing to share my views if Your Grace requests it.'

'We do. It is the wish of many men at our court to see the Duke of Suffolk severely punished, although the archbishop of York advises against it,' he told her, mentioning the recently promoted Thomas Wolsey. 'The duke and our sister are much beloved by us, but their behaviour was treacherous,' he went on.

Ella meant to push him towards mercy, as Nicholas had asked her to do if they ever came to talk about it privately, but she paused for a moment. The King believed he was who he was because God had decided it. It was the whole foundation of his education and his being. He believed it so genuinely, so candidly, that he did not imagine for a second that his subjects could do anything that displeased him, except of course the naturally wicked ones.

And now his own best friend had deceived him. He had broken his promise deliberately. When the King looked at her, Ella realised it was not his feelings as king that had been hurt but as friend.

'The Duke of Suffolk behaved shamefully,' she said.

'This is surprising to hear from you. Your husband begged for mercy.'

'And I shall do that too, but it is my duty, as Your Grace's loyal subject and friend, to concede that the duke made a mistake. Concealing the truth and breaking a promise is disgraceful.'

The King had the decency to briefly look down on his hands. Charles had not been the only one to lie and break a promise. The King himself had never planned to let his sister marry anyone but a foreign prince in the first place. Ella kept quiet for a minute, giving the King the time and space to confess about his own deceiving mistake, but it soon became clear he would not.

'I would be very sorry to see the duke on the scaffold and I dare to believe Your Grace would be too.'

'We have known him for all our years. He is a good companion.'

'That is what my husband thinks of him as well.'

'You forgave Mistress Maria for her offence. Why?' the King asked.

'Her departure from court would have hurt the Queen. Mistress Maria is but a person, which means she sometimes makes ill-advised judgements and decisions. I am, too,' she told him.

'The Duke of Suffolk, also,' he guessed where she was going with her answer, but did not include himself on the list. 'You believe we should forgive him. It shall displease many persons.'

'But it is to please the dowager queen. Shall it also please Your Grace?'

The King chuckled and nodded. Ella smiled. Despite his behaviour, it was not a secret that the King loved his younger sister, probably even more than he loved his wife. He just needed to be reminded of it. Charles's neck was safe. When Ella and the King walked back to the palace and entered the great hall together, Ella looked for Nicholas and winked at him. He crossed himself out of relief, but the nearby Buckingham gave her the death stare and left, stomping his feet on the ground.

The King followed Ella's advice to forgive the newly-weds, but not without fining them over twenty thousand pounds. It would have been the equivalent to at least ten million pounds in the twenty-first century. Nicholas did not believe that his friend and his new wife could ever afford to pay it all back, but was so in awe of Ella saving Charles's life that, for an entire month, he showered her with gifts and seized any opportunity to please her. It was mostly by mentioning in front of Buckingham how happy Charles and the King's sister were, honeymooning in France, and then imitating his infuriated reaction in front of Ella in the privacy of their apartment. One evening, face deformed by anger, legs wide and fists clenched on his waist, he did it so well that she almost peed herself in the bed.

Proud of himself for making her laugh so much, Nicholas jumped on the bed next to her and waited for her to calm down, an amused and loving tenderness in the eyes. Ella looked back at him, desperate to feel the kind of love he deserved.

Nothing. She had a lot of affection for him, she supported him, she wanted the best for him, but she did not love him. She loved how he threw his entire body into his laughs, how he listened to what she had to say and remembered it. She loved the dimples on his cheeks, the star shaped scar below his left collarbone. She loved that he could pick up things on the floor with his toes. She loved his hair brushing her face when he kissed her. But she did not love him, and she was starting to hate herself for it.

'I had words with Surrey today,' he said, unaware of the dimness of her thoughts.

'Because of Charles?'

'If it was even possible, the ones who loathed him so for his elevation to the dukedom of Suffolk do even more now that he has become the King's brother-in-law. They want his head on a spike,' he told her.

The disturbing image of Buckingham along with his son-in-law Surrey taking a selfie in front of Charles's severed head popped in Ella's mind. 'I wonder what shall happen once Charles is back to court.'

'I do not think he is to spend much time at court any more but he shall live with his head on his shoulders, and we have you to thank for it.' Ella smiled. 'I love you,' he said.

'I love you too,' she lied.

A few days passed before it occurred to Ella just how much the death of the king of France had shattered the world of the king of England. It was not because it had left his sister widowed or because it could cripple the alliance between the two kingdoms, but simply because the old king's successor, Francis I, was said to rival him in looks and was three years younger. The King had always relished being the youngest and handsomest monarch in Europe, admired by all, and was now so jealous that he organised the greatest May Day pageant in England's history to blow the French ambassador's mind. He wanted him to be so impressed that he would have to invent new words to tell his king how fabulous the English court was.

On May Day, the ambassadors escorted the Queen and her ladies to the woods, where the King, entirely dressed in green velvet, was waiting for them on his horse. Ella herself was on a white horse, feeling regal in her gold and white gown, and watched the two hundred archers in their green livery participate in a contest. She could see the King glancing at the Frenchman to make sure he was as captivated as he was supposed to be.

After the contest, a man dressed as Robin Hood made the ambassador laugh when he came up to the Queen and dared her to enter the woods to see how the outlaws lived. Trumpets played loudly as she gave her hand to her husband to lead her through the labyrinths created for the occasion. There were no dangerous outlaws, but thousands of flowers everywhere and tables set for breakfast in the middle of the woods. The May sun glittering through the tall trees was giving the place a golden atmosphere, making Ella forget just for a moment that she was there and not watching a movie.

The more the French ambassador marvelled at what was around him, the merrier the King was. It was contagious. Ella was happy to see him happy. He deserved it. He had put his dreams of conquering France on hold, had been let down by his father-in-law, betrayed by his best friend, and was now dealing with an intense jealousy, which was not a feeling he was accustomed to. It was nice to see him so completely and unproblematically joyous.

Quite suddenly, the King got up from his chair, prompting every single guest to hastily get up as well. He told everyone to sit back down and looked at the French ambassador with a sly smile. 'Le roi de France, est-il aussi grand que moi?' he asked in a perfect French – *is the king of France as tall as me?*

'Il n'y a que peu de différence,' the ambassador replied – *there it but little difference.*

'Est-il aussi large?' the King continued his interrogation – *is he as strong?*

'Non, il ne l'est pas,' the Frenchman conceded, cheeks flushed with unease – *no, he is not.*

'Quel genre de jambes a-t-il?' the King went on, oblivious to his interlocutor's embarrassment – *what kind of legs does he have?*

'Fines, Votre Altesse,' was the answer – *thin, Your Grace.*

Ella was already biting her lower lip due to the oddity of the conversation between the two men, but had to fight off a laugh when the King pulled aside the skirt of his green doublet to slap a hand on his muscular thigh. 'Regardez donc! Et j'ai aussi un très bon mollet!' he shouted – *Look! And I also have a very fine calf!*

His smile was so radiant it lit up the entire wood. There was so much vanity in his words, but Ella could not find it in her to frown upon it. He was like a child, thrilled to be taller than everyone else at school, or proud to be the best at physical exercise. The way he managed to be the most sophisticated and learned man at court, and at the same time the most childish and gullible, would never cease to amaze her.

The rest of the day was mostly spent jousting. Ella had never enjoyed watching jousts, but her enmity for it increased each time she had to witness her husband risk his life for fun. Because that is what it was, and that is what he was doing. It was entertainment, but the participants often ended up hurt, or worse. Whenever Ella saw the King and Nicholas participate in a joust, galloping in full armour on their horses to try to stab their opponent across the palisade, she wondered if it would end up with Hal sitting on the throne or herself becoming a widow. It was like watching a car drive straight into a brick wall at one hundred and ten miles per hour.

Despite the heavy armour protecting her husband, Ella held her breath when he fought against his friends: Francis Bryan first, then Henry Guildford, William FitzWilliam and Nicholas Carew. He won them all, always bowing to the Queen as he did so, but also to his wife. Ella was beaming. To the King, being a successful jouster was as important as being a great soldier. Nicholas distinguishing himself at such an important occasion was good for his career.

Ella was surprised when Nicholas fought against the Earl of Surrey. Elsie's husband was known to be a fantastic soldier but only rarely participated in jousts. Ella smiled, confident in her husband's abilities and even enthusiastic at the thought of Surrey being beaten in front of his father-in-law by a man whom they both viewed as an upstart. But the first blow was of unprecedented violence.

Jousting was always violent, but not like that. The opponents' aim was supposed to be scoring points, not killing each other. The audience went silent. The atmosphere was tense. On the second blow, Ella clenched her jaw so hard she thought for a moment she had broken a tooth. Sitting next to her, Elsie silently took her hand in hers. One look at her friend made her realise she was not the only one startled by the brutality of their husbands' joust.

On the third blow, Surrey fell heavily on the ground and people cheered loudly. Ella's relief was so great she would have loved to unlace her bodice. Six men were needed to carry the unconscious earl away, the armour being heavy as a dead donkey. Ella looked for Buckingham in the hope to see anger and frustration on his face, but Elsie gasped. Nicholas had taken his helmet off. Half his face was covered with blood.

13.

A GOOD MAN
1515

Ella could hear her husband scream inside the tent. Thomas Wolsey, the archbishop of York, tried to tell her that she should at least wait for the physician to be done, but she looked at him with such poorly concealed irritation that he bowed to her and accompanied her in.

Nicholas was standing in the middle of the large square space, out of breath and still in his armour. Despite the impressive amount of blood that he appeared to have lost, he was not screaming in pain: he was yelling at the physician that he did not need treatment. He walked up to Ella when he saw her, his armour clinking and clattering furiously.

'Elizabeth, dearest, it is nothing,' he said.

'Your face is covered with blood!' she shouted, making the archbishop raise an eyebrow. 'You see me quite upset, I beg you to forgive my emotion,' she corrected herself.

'Surrey's spear penetrated my eye slot but no splinter has pierced my eye. It does look more worrying than it is,' he reassured her. 'I shall clean myself up and get back to the joust.'

'It is an open wound and needs appropriate care. I do not wish to enter widowhood so soon in our marriage.'

'I agree with my lady,' the physician said, but Nicholas growled at him to stay quiet.

'We agree with Lady Nottingham as well,' the King's voice made itself heard behind Ella's back.

Ella had won the argument now that the King was on her side. Having participated in the joust as well, he was still wearing his armour and was followed by a teenage boy carrying his helmet.

'The Earl of Surrey has awakened,' the King declared. 'You fought well, friend. Your wound now needs treatment and you need rest,' he told Nicholas.

'Yes, Your Grace,' Nicholas replied, trembling.

Although Ella could see in his eyes that Nicholas wanted nothing more than to bellow at everybody around him, his wife included, he controlled himself and complied to the physician's requirements. The King ordered everyone to leave the tent, except for Ella and the physician.

She oversaw everything, from hand washing with soap to wound disinfection with vinegar, and honey for antiseptic. The wound went from the outside corner of Nicholas's eye towards his eyebrow and, though it turned out to be neither as wide or deep as she had feared, it was wide and deep enough to soak the padded gambeson underneath the armour with a thick and dark blood. He had been at just a hair's breadth from losing his left eye.

Ella did not know if the available medicine would manage to prevent an infection or if the blow had given him a brain injury and was anxious at the thought of losing him. A woman in this century was never as safe as when she was married. If he died, who knew what would happen of her. Who knew who the King would marry her off to next.

It proved impossible for Ella to close her eyes that night, too worried to end up in the morning with a dead body by her side. When Nicholas woke up after eight hours of a peaceful sleep, he yawned, sat up, wiped off the sleep out of his right eye and put his hair back behind his ears, grimacing as his hand brushed his bandage.

'Good morning, wife,' he said.

'Morning. How are you feeling? Does your head hurt? Are you queasy? Are you tired? Are you dizzy? What about your sight? And your hearing? Did you sleep well?' Ella listed the potential symptoms she could remember of any brain injury, determined to not miss any and prevent any deadly consequence.

Nicholas grabbed her hands. 'I feel well. I am blessed to be married to such a caring soul.'

'Are you certain you are in no need to gag?'

'Elizabeth. I feel as if nothing has happened. It is not the first wound in my flesh,' he reminded her.

He delicately put his hand on the forever swollen scar on the back of his right hand, the long and thin one higher up on his arm, the star-shaped one under his collarbone and, stark naked, continued with the one on his torso, then on his lower body. Ella kissed him on the lips and, for the first time in a year and a half of marriage, found pleasure in having sex with her husband.

As the King and the Queen had both given them the day to rest and recover from the joust, Ella allowed herself to fall asleep. When she woke up, Nicholas was eating in bed, still naked.

'What is a lolly?' he asked when he noticed she was awake. Ella's heart tried to escape her body through her mouth.

'I do not understand what you mean,' she said.

'You were talking about a lolly as you slept but I did not grasp the meaning of anything you said,' he told her. She shrugged, incapable of finding words that would make any sense. 'It is maybe a reminiscence of your life before.'

'Maybe.'

'It is so distressing that time has not cured you yet. How long has it been now?'

'Five years in September,' she said, increasingly uncomfortable. 'Nic, what would have happened to me if you had been mortally wounded yesterday?' she changed the subject.

'I am bequeathing everything to you in my will. You would be the Dowager Countess of Nottingham, with an annual income and the ownership of our houses. I made sure that you would have nothing to worry about.'

'Thank you.'

'Would you wish to remarry if I died?' he asked as if she had a choice. Ella frowned. 'The law states that a widow cannot be forced to remarry,' he told her.

'Then my answer is no. You are to be my only husband. What about you?'

'I would not want to. I would only remarry if we did not come to have sons,' he admitted, then kept quiet for a moment. Ella would have preferred to avoid the conceiving topic and was thinking about another subject to talk about, but it is Nicholas who found it himself. 'If I had died yesterday, where do you believe my soul would be today?'

Ella did not expect that. Nicholas had always refused to challenge out loud the existence of Purgatory or debate about the afterlife. Until today. 'What do *you* think?' she asked.

'I have not committed a sin without confessing it and repenting afterwards, but I sometimes lay awake at night, questioning what I have always thought to be an indisputable truth.' He paused, and Ella gave him the time to put his thoughts in order. 'Men of the Church do not have authority over the absolution of our sins. We mortals' salvation must be only up to the Lord, which must mean that the sale of indulgences is…'

A lie? Abuse? Extortion? Bullying? Ella thought as he hesitated.

She was still bewildered at the amount of money the Church was gaining from the believers' sins and fears. Earthly money to reduce divine punishment was pure nonsense to her.

'… wrong,' he eventually whispered, looking like he was coming clean to a crime.

'I have shared this opinion for a long time,' she said, quieting the part of her that wanted to tell him she did not believe God existed at all.

What Nicholas had just told her was as dangerous a revelation as it was disturbing for him. He had always been taught to believe in certain things in a certain way, which did not leave room for much interpretation. Catholicism in 1515 was what it was and people could not ask for answers to their doubts because they were not allowed to have any. Not blindly accepting the teachings of the Church was heresy. Ella's eyes tingled when she realised Nicholas had just proved her how much he trusted her. He trusted her with his own life.

'Do you believe in Purgatory?' he asked.

'No,' she admitted. 'God recognises the purity or wickedness of a soul.' She told a fable.

'I have killed men on the battlefield. I have killed, Elizabeth,' he told her with such a panic in his voice that Ella moved up to him on the bed and took his face in her hands.

Eyes in eyes, green in amber, she did her best to sound unafraid and confident: 'God knows that you are a good man, Nicholas Elys. I am not to let you believe your soul does not belong in Heaven. You are one of the best men I have ever met. You killed for your king and for England. You are virtuous, faithful, honest, and being your wife is the greatest honour of my life.'

Nicholas smiled. It was so pure that Ella did not regret for a second lying to his face. She did not have it in her heart to tell him what she thought. For his peace of mind, he had to have faith in his afterlife in Heaven. She could not tell him she believed life on Earth was only momentary, and that death marked both the end of a person's existence and the start of their non-existence.

If May had started in blood and violence, it turned out to be the month of weddings. The ten-year-old Viscountess Lisle was married off to the seventeen-year-old Henry Courtenay, the King's maternal first cousin. Charles did not attend the wedding but came back to court a couple of days later with his wife, who was now to be called the French Queen as to not confuse her with the actual Queen. She was technically the Duchess of Suffolk but would forever remain the dowager queen of France, which was a much more prestigious title.

The King made the court attend his sister's wedding, although she had already tied the knot in France in the presence of King Francis himself. The King could not come to terms with the thought of his rival attending the wedding when he had not. Wearing her favourite gown of green satin, Ella got to play the game of who-is-the-most-upset-in-attendance as the proud nineteen-year-old married the love of her life.

Buckingham was clearly enraged and his brother Wiltshire looked scandalised.

Norfolk was unhappy as well, although he was a lot more skilled at hiding his true feelings, as was his son Surrey, who was still limping from his joust with Nicholas.

The Earl of Northumberland and the Marquess of Dorset were making a point of pretending to be bored by the spectacle, but would have been the first ones to jump on Charles's throat had the King changed his mind about him.

Weddings were soon followed by pregnancies. Fortunately not for the young viscountess, who was deemed too young to consummate her marriage, but out of nowhere everyone around Ella was pregnant; the Queen, Maud and the French Queen announced their pregnancies within the same week.

'It is with great relief I have welcomed my courses this morning,' Elsie told Ella shortly after during a walk in the garden, summing up her thoughts.

'I very much agree!'

'Why would you not wish to conceive?'

'Childbirth has always scared me, but even more so since I was the witness of the ravages caused by childbed fever.'

'The late Lady Mountjoy, yes, of course. I find it admirable that you held her hand until her last breath,' she said.

Ella faked a smile. At first, she had relied on luck to avoid pregnancy. Ever since Inez's death, though, she was writing down each month when her period came and was calculating her ovulation window as to know when to dodge any attempt Nicholas made to have sex with her. Not many wives could say the same, but her husband had never tried to force himself into her. It had so far worked well.

Unless one of them was suffering from infertility problems they did not know about, Ella's knowledge on the female reproductive cycle was more reliable and less chilling than the contraceptive ways of the time. Birth control was viewed as a way of interfering with nature, which was both witchcraft and forbidden, but women had their ways to try to prevent conception. Ella had one day overheard a conversation between three women, each with their own technique; one was inserting small knots of wool soaked in vinegar as a kind of diaphragm, the other one was wearing the dried liver of a black cat around her neck as an amulet against pregnancy, and the third one was shoving wood blocks up there as a barrier against sperm.

Wood blocks.

'Why do you rejoice in not being with child?' Ella asked.

'My husband rarely shows kindness towards my person. I am afraid for a son to be the same. As for a daughter, I am afraid for her to be shown the same treatment as her mother,' Elsie explained. Ella stopped walking. 'My Lord Surrey is rather short-tempered, but he shall one day make me a duchess, which is a great blessing,' her friend said with a forced smile.

Ella did not answer right away and took Elsie in her arms. In a world where women were legally owned by their husbands, there was nothing to be done about domestic violence. Surrey had full rights over his wife and was allowed to do anything he wanted to her or with her. Elsie could not retaliate or even complain without risking her husband's displeasure. There was no law against a husband's violence towards his wife. He was guilty of terrible wrong, but not of any kind of illegality. Elsie could not even run away, as she would find herself deprived of any assistance or money. She was stuck.

'I wish your husband had been hurt more badly by mine last May Day,' Ella murmured.

'I too. Elizabeth, I must tell you something. I feel much shame for not doing it earlier. It is to displease you.'

'You are my friend and you can tell me. I shall never be upset at you, I promise.'

'My husband's ambition was to severely injure yours during the joust, worse if possible, as a message that he and the Duke of Suffolk are to never be considered members of the nobility. I beg you to forgive me. I was too scared to confront him about it. I felt much relief when it became clear that your husband was well.'

'I do not think you are responsible for your husband's actions and I thank you for being so brave as to tell me,' Ella said, her closed fists trembling under the cover of her bell-shaped sleeves.

For once, she hoped that afterlife was real and that Surrey would burn in Hell for all eternity. Despite his dislike for the so-called parvenus that were Nicholas, Charles and Wolsey, she had always thought him to be more reasonable and respectable than his father-in-law, but he turned out to be as much as an imbecile than him. Or a *fopdoodle*, as Nicholas would say.

Ella chose to keep the truth away from Nicholas, worried that he would confront Elsie's husband and put her in danger, but she did not get much sleep that night. She had to think of a way to send the man a message as well, without being so obvious that he would take it out on his wife. Nicholas was every bit of an earl as he was and Ella was fuming someone had dared to make an attempt on his life for it.

The next day, as she was heading outside to put her thoughts in order, Pan decided to accompany her. He was followed by the King himself. Ella congratulated him on his wife's pregnancy and took the beagle in her arms.

The Queen had suffered devastating losses on her first, third and fifth pregnancies, but her second and fourth had resulted in healthy sons. With a bit of luck, the pattern would be respected and this sixth pregnancy would end in a third little prince.

'We are the father of two healthy sons. If it pleases God to grant us a daughter, we would gladly submit,' the King admitted.

Because your sister is off the market and you need a daughter to be married off to some foreign prince without her consent, Ella thought, stroking Pan's head distractedly. 'I pray for Her Grace to be safely delivered with a daughter,' she replied instead.

Her eyes were drawn to the impressive jewel that was pinned on the King's doublet. He was always wearing the shiniest of gems, like an extravagant rainbow, but this one was particular. Black as coal, but glistening under the sun, the diamond was framed with gold and was as wide as at least four of Ella's fingers. A heavy-looking white pearl, tear-shaped, was hanging from it, making the jewel as long as her hand from middle fingernail to wrist. She had seen many jewels in her years at the King's court, including St Edward's Crown – the original one, not the replica from after the Civil War in the seventeenth century. She had seen invaluable treasures, but this diamond was monumental.

The King looked down on his chest to understand what she was staring at. 'It is called the Mirror of Naples,' he said.

'It is magnificent.'

'Indeed. The late King Louis offered it to our sister as a wedding gift. After his death, she sent it to us as a token of her love,' he explained. Ella smiled. The French Queen had most likely sent it as a peace offering to save her husband's neck but, in her brother's mind, it was always about him. 'King Francis now claims this diamond is one of the crown jewels of France and demands its return,' he told her.

'But Your Grace said it was a personal wedding gift?'

'Precisely! This was our answer also. King Francis is attempting a purchase but is refusing to match the diamond's value. We have returned other small jewels our sister brought with her from France, but the Mirror of Naples shall stay in England.'

Ella began to imagine the young widowed queen smuggling jewels belonging to the French royals out of their own kingdom to give to her brother and could not help but chuckle. The King told her how Thomas Wolsey, who had always argued for a good relationship between France and his master, may now have a diplomatic crisis on his hands because of this particular diamond. They both laughed nervously. Pan barked, hoping to share the excitement.

Once the King calmed down, he changed the subject: 'Allow us to enquire about your husband's health. We have not spent much time with him since the joust on May Day.'

'My husband is well, I thank Your Grace. He gave me a fright but all is well.'

'Good, good. It was a brutal fight. The Earl of Surrey's leg is still aching from his fall,' he said with a certain amusement in the eye, as if he was talking of how his fool had hurt himself falling from a table.

'May I share a sentiment with Your Grace?'

'Speak your mind.'

'Lord Surrey was too violent for my taste. My husband could have been badly hurt despite his exceptional skills. That ferocity was unnecessary for a friendly joust,' Ella said, hoping for the King to understand what she knew of Surrey's intentions without having to tell him.

'We did think the same that day,' he replied.

Why did you not do anything, then? Ella was desperate to ask, but kept quiet.

'The Duke of Suffolk and the Earl of Nottingham are not much liked by some courtiers,' he declared.

'I find it very upsetting, as both men are well deserving of their honours,' Ella said.

'Your loyalty for your husband is admirable. And we agree.' He paused, and sighed. But he then gave her a smug look and said: 'We are to bestow a dukedom on your husband.'

Ella's eyes widened. She could have kissed his royal lips. For as long as Surrey's father would live, the man would have to publicly bow to Nicholas as he would be outranked by him. That was her revenge. That was her message. Surrey would never be confronted about what he had attempted to do, but watching him bow to her husband and herself as the acceptance that they were of higher rank would be sweet enough.

When Ella realised Nicholas was to be Buckingham's equal, her smile got so wide that her cheeks hurt. She barely even noticed when the King told her the court was to return to Eltham Palace in a fortnight, as the works there were done.

14.

IF EYES COULD KILL 1515-1517

Five years ago, Ella had left Eltham Palace as a maid of honour and at the heart of court gossip. She was now back, still the victim of regular gossip, but as the Duchess of Exeter, one of the highest ranked and richest women in the kingdom.

She entered the great hall. The colours of a rainbow were floating around the room as the sun was shining through the stained glass windows. A peaceful, nostalgic smile appeared on her face when the memory of Lolly dancing in the middle of this hall, a lifetime ago but five hundred years in the future, came back to her mind. It did not bring a lump to her throat any more. She had grieved her grandmother like she had grieved the twenty-first century. She had come to terms with it because nothing could change it.

Except the ring could still be there somewhere. Ella did not have much hope. It had been five years. If it had not been found by one of the builders working on the palace, it might have been damaged by an animal. If it had not been damaged by an animal, it would have been worn down by the weather. England was colder and windier now than it was in 2020. There was very little chance the ring was still where she had dropped it, and it was easier this way.

After five years, the physical impossibility of escaping had led Ella to accept that making the most of her life here was her only option. In some ways, she was happy. Life in this century was not simple, especially for women and the poor. It was misogynistic. It was brutal. It was dangerous. Ella did not have access to antibiotics, vaccines, or contraception. Or drinkable water. She missed her independence. Freedom of speech and freedom of religion. Freedom, in all its forms.

But, as she walked by herself to the woods for the first time in five years, looking for Lolly's ring, she made the list of what was waiting for her in the twenty-first century. A father who had never cared enough about her to raise her. Grandparents who were not there to love her any more because they were dead. A best friend who had probably given up on her being still alive. Standing in a chestnut-coloured gown embellished with gold threads and a jewel-encrusted collar, in the middle of the woods, Ella thought about what she did have here and now. A loving husband. Supportive friends. Two young boys she loved as if they were her own. She did not feel alone anymore. Ella caressed the soft fabric of her gown. She had money, too. Influence. Title. She was someone. Elizabeth White, Duchess of Exeter. People bowed or curtseyed to her as she walked past. She was important.

'What if you could see what the future was made of, though?' she whispered. 'What if you could travel back and find out what Hal's survival brought to England? Would it not be glorious to know that you were the one to thank for it?' she kept talking to herself, sitting down on a log. 'But you could not tell a soul about it. And where would you go? Where would you live? How would you explain a five-year absence? Would you even exist in a world where Hal had succeeded to the throne?'

Giving up the life she had built for herself for freedom and comfort, or not? The crystal-clear answer from five years ago was not so clear anymore, and Ella ended up walking back to the palace empty-handed. Elsie's husband Surrey and his father, the Duke of Norfolk, were standing by the door, in the middle of a conversation. As usual,

Surrey's jaw clenched upon realising he would have to uncover himself and bow to her if they came face to face.

'Lord Norfolk, Lord Surrey,' Ella said with a smile.

Surrey's long nose creased in a frown, almost imperceptibly. Almost. Ella stopped walking, and waited on purpose. The old duke – about seventy years old, which was a bit of a record at court – did not let any emotion show on his face, which was framed with grey hair down to his collarbones, but made a point to remove his own black flat cap. His son reluctantly imitated him, looking like it was killing him inside.

Norfolk paid her the usual, empty compliments that one was supposed to pay a noblewoman, but Ella only pretended to listen; she could see Buckingham staring at her from behind the two men. If eyes could kill, Ella's head would have ended up far from her body.

Neither Buckingham nor Surrey would ever accept her new status.

The court came back to Eltham Palace five times between summer 1515 and winter 1516, staying about two to three weeks each time. Ella took almost every opportunity to go looking for her grandmother's ring. Discovering the answer to her great question was impossible unless she had the actual means to travel back, but the ring was nowhere to be found. It was like a needle in a haystack. After over a year, wrapped up in her sable furs, she started to think it may not have been worth all this trouble.

Maud, the French Queen and the Queen went into labour early in 1516. The first one called her daughter Elizabeth, in honour of Ella. The second one called her son Henry, in honour of her brother. The third one saw her little girl, Mary, buried two days before the time of her churching. Ella could not explain what had happened to the baby, other than the fact that it had been born in the sixteenth century – and that Bloody Mary would never be.

The princess was soon followed in death by her grandfather, King Ferdinand of Aragon, which threw the Queen in such desperation that it became unbearable to stay in her lodgings. By May, the Queen was spending so much time in her closet, forbidding her ladies to play, dance or sing as to not intrude on her prayers, that all was left to do was fix her gowns. She had lost so much weight that they were all too big for her.

Ella dared to enter the Queen's closet one morning, bringing eggs, bread and butter, along with some ale. The Queen had not eaten in the last forty-eight hours. She did not even open an eye. She was on her knees, on the cold, hard floor. Ella was not sure what she was praying for. The strength to grieve the losses of her father and her babies, or maybe the blessing of more than only two healthy children. She looked exhausted, drained. As queen, she had given two heirs to the crown. As a woman, four babies had been taken from her.

Ella could now catch a glimpse of what the life of Katherine of Aragon – the one from her old history books – had been like. Losing her babies, one after the other.

'What is it about?' the Queen said, her eyes still closed.

'I bring Your Grace some sustenance.'

'This is not necessary. I thank you. Please have it brought back to the kitchen.'

'Your Grace, it has been two days…' Ella tried to insist. She had to eat something.

'It is not my earthly body that I wish to nourish at this moment. Lady Exeter, you are a dear friend. I am aware you feel the need to help. I only wish to pray. Please, do leave me alone,' the Queen told her.

The voice was kind. The tone was firm. Ella curtseyed and left her alone to her prayers.

The visit of the King's older sister Margaret, who was queen dowager of Scotland, was thought to be timed perfectly to distract the Queen. The King had planned many tournaments to welcome his sister. But, when the widowed queen entered the palace with her ladies, one of whom was holding a red-haired and blue-eyed baby girl in her arms, it became clear that nothing could have made the Queen feel worse.

Dowager Queen Margaret, once regent of Scotland during the minority of her son, had recently been expelled from her kingdom. Her late husband's first cousin, the Duke of Albany, had stolen the regency from her. The baby girl was her daughter from her second marriage to the Earl of Angus.

'Queen Margaret must miss her son terribly,' Maud regretted as she shared a meal with Ella and Elsie a few days later in the presence chamber.

The richly decorated space was mostly used as a throne room. The chair of estate, which was on a dais and surmounted by a canopy, was standing proudly there, facing the door. Every courtier, however rich or influential, had to uncover oneself and bow in front of it, even if the chair was empty. When the room was not used by the King, members of the nobility would dine there. Ella loved how delicately carved the panelling was in this room. With its intricate garlands and fanciful figures of people or animals, it came straight out of a fairytale.

'Indeed. She also seems to feel great pain in her body,' Elsie said.

Ella agreed. The King's sister clearly suffered in her back and legs with every step that she took. Sciatica was Ella's best guess. 'I must say, though, that Queen Margaret appears more spirited than Her Grace,' she said in a low voice. 'I pray the Lord every day for Her Grace to recover from the recent tragedies,' she quickly added, too scared for anyone to overhear and think she was speaking ill of the Queen.

'This year brought Her Grace much sorrow,' Elsie cried.

And it is only May, Ella wanted to add.

'I wish Maria... sorry, Lady Willoughby, had not left for Lincolnshire. I am aware that she has never been your friend, Elizabeth, but she was a great support for Her Grace. She is missed,' Maud said.

'It is my hope Lady Willoughby shall visit court soon,' Ella lied. She had no desire to see Maria again. The Spanish woman had been asked in marriage by the handsome Lord Willoughby de Eresby and had left with him for his Lincolnshire castle. He aspired to a luxurious but peaceful life away from court, which deprived the Queen of her best friend. The year 1516 was not her best.

At the very least, Ella was relieved of a thorn in her side. Maria had been perfectly quiet since Ella had saved her place at court, knowing she owed her a favour, but her presence had always made her feel watched. In the Queen's household, Maria had been the anchor to the ladies' distrust towards Ella. Now that she was gone, so were the faint whispers behind her back.

At the beginning of 1517, the now-cardinal Thomas Wolsey invited the King, the Queen and the high nobility to the medieval manor that he had started renovating a few years back: Hampton Court. When Ella stepped foot on land after travelling from Greenwich Palace by the river, memories from her old life came back brusquely.

> *2010. When Emily arrived at Hampton Court Palace with Paul and Ella, women wearing period dresses from the sixteenth century were singing a Christmas carol in front of the decorated tree. The blue Christmas lights mirroring the precious stone peaking through her scarf, she listened with her family as long as their toes endured the low temperature. Once inside, walking past one of the most famous portraits of Henry VIII that showed him bearded, standing and wearing an imposing coat, ten-year-old Ella stopped.*
>
> *'He built this castle, right?'*
>
> *'The palace, yes. Although it was first bought by a cardinal, who was like his Prime Minister. He was very rich and he liked dazzling things, so he bought a house in the country and transformed it into a palace that people said to be fit for a king,' Emily said.*
>
> *'So fit that it actually ended up being the King's!' Paul joked.*
>
> *'Why did he give it to him?' Ella asked.*
>
> *'He did not have much choice, darling. He was failing to do what the King wanted him to do and had many*

enemies at court. He gave the palace to the King as an attempt to save himself but fell out of favour anyway. He died soon after,' Emily explained.

'You were only loved by that man when you were useful to him,' her husband said, pointing at the painting.

'That is a gross exaggeration, but not wrong,' Emily admitted and led the way to the non-carpeted adjoining room, where the block heels of her boots resonated on the creaky old floor. 'This sound makes me feel like I am back in time! I feel like a princess!' she told her husband and granddaughter, who burst with laughter and were told off by one of the staff members.

The cardinal gave everyone in the royal party a tour of his new residence. It was still a work in progress, but Ella could not believe her eyes. The lord chancellor, as Wolsey also held this office of state, did not do things halfway. Every time Ella locked eyes with Nicholas, Elsie, or even the French Queen, she knew that they were all thinking the exact same thing – *what the hell.*

Although still under construction, the red-bricked building was astonishing. Gold was everywhere, as were the cardinal's initials but also his coat of arms – four azure leopards, a red lion, two black birds and a traditional Tudor rose. His motto was in every room, too. *Manus Haec Inimica Tyrannis,* which pretty much meant "this hand is hostile to tyrants". It was as if he dared anyone to still think of him as a butcher's son. Hampton Court was nothing less than a provocation. It was the cardinal's message to his enemies that he was wealthier than them, but also more powerful, and that he would not let anyone bully him about his lower birth anymore.

As she danced that evening, the sound of Ella's shoes on the wooden floor of the great hall was making her smile, remembering her grandmother's cheeky green eyes as she said it made her *feel like a princess.* Ella was certainly feeling like one, in her newest gown of blue velvet, a multitude of pearls and diamonds sewn on its neckline and framing her gable hood.

The gowns she was wearing these days were much heavier and a lot less practical than the ones that used to be hers as a maid of honour, but she would not have traded those days only for comfort. She loved being a duchess. She had people attending her every need and more money that she could ever spend in a lifetime. She and Nicholas often donated to the poor, but could not be seen to be more generous than the King and Queen themselves and thus had to limit their almsgiving. It was not the thing she was the proudest about herself, but now that she had tasted it, Ella adored anything that money could buy.

The entire evening at Hampton Court was so delightful that, good wine helping, people even came to forget that they were not being entertained by the King in a royal palace but by one of his subjects. But, when Nicholas and Ella found themselves in the privacy of the rooms allocated to them for the night, he gave her a scandalised look with a spark of laughter in his eyes, and this grotesque smile of his that he had sometimes – with the corners of his mouth lifted and his teeth sunk into his lower lip.

'I know,' Ella said, taking her hood off.

'Tonight was enchanting and you were the most beautiful creature in attendance, but… such opulence! I do not believe any Englishman should be the King's rival when it comes to his residence. It is offensive.'

'I agree, although I thoroughly enjoyed the effect it had on the Duke of Buckingham's mood.'

'He hid it well, but he was beside himself! The butcher's son, owner of a palace worthy of a king!'

'I find the cardinal's ego too great for his character to be likeable. It is a shame, as I do appreciate how far he has come.'

'True indeed. Let me help with that,' Nicholas said when he noticed his wife unsuccessfully trying to take off the costly necklace he had given her two years before. 'The cardinal is very powerful… the King trusts him and relies on him on all matters.'

'His Grace was the only guest who did not seem irritated by the magnificence tonight,' Ella shared, wondering why. The King did not like to share the spotlight and, in the history she had grown up learning, he had taken the place for himself, which must mean he had wanted it.

'I can only suppose that the cardinal is to hold embassies here in the King's name in the future.'

The splendour of the King's minister's home would reflect directly on the King himself, Ella replied in her mind. What was seen as a possible affront by most courtiers was in fact a source of royal pride.

'Do you think he could ever fall from the King's favour?' Ella asked.

'It is very unlikely. His abilities are recognised and appreciated by the King. We must both do what is required to stay in his favour,' he said, prompting his wife to nod approvingly.

Another version of Cardinal Wolsey had once failed to negotiate with the Pope to provide the King with an annulment of his marriage, which had provoked his downfall. The King was now thousands of miles away from even beginning to question the validity of his marriage and nothing could foresee the cardinal falling from favour. Nicholas was right. Ella had to stay in the good graces of Thomas Wolsey.

15.

THE INVISIBLE HAND
1517

'Pack in all haste! We are leaving!' the King shouted one morning, his blue eyes threatening to escape from their orbits. 'The sweat! It is back!' he briefly explained and disappeared out of the room as fast as he had arrived.

Every single one of Ella's organs dropped down to her feet. The Queen crossed herself and gave orders as calmly as she could. Soon, the court was ready to leave Baynard's Castle for Richmond and travelled by water in a petrified silence. Ella had never seen the King so frightened. He had always been afraid of illness. If he could have transferred a disease affecting him to his own wife, he would have most likely done it without hesitation. It was his weakness.

A blue piece of cloth fastened around his mouth, hoping the holy colour of his face mask would ward off the disease, he was restless, constantly looking around to make sure no one was too close to him – close enough to infect him.

The sweating sickness. Lolly had mentioned it once during the first lockdown which had resulted from the Covid-19 pandemic, barely six months before Ella's travel. 'If it was the sweat or the plague, trust me, people would be wearing their stupid face masks!' Ella could still hear her grumble in front of her television screen.

It was Nicholas who had taken the time to explain exactly what made the sweat so feared once he had realised the last outbreak had happened before she had "lost her memories". A chill had gone down Ella's spine when he had said that no one, not even the physicians, knew what it was. The sweat could kill the healthiest of all persons in a couple of hours and only those who made it through the first twenty-four would live.

'Without a warning, one feels as cold as death, then sweats much and dies,' he had then summed up the symptoms.

The physicians were already pretty useless on a normal day, but were powerless once someone had started showing symptoms. Some believed a good bleeding could help release the poisons from the body, others prescribed natural remedies of some herbs infused together but, ultimately, the only thing to do was watch the patient either pull through or perish. As simple as that.

Once at Richmond Palace, the King barricaded himself in his apartments, located in a moated tower separated from the great hall. Looking at the six-year-old and three-year-old red-headed princes, Ella could not shake the feeling that regrouping the King and his heirs in the same palace, however large it was, was the worst idea anyone could have ever had. The twenty-first century side of her understood why parents would want to have their children with them in a time like this, but the sixteenth century one judged them for putting the Crown at risk. Ella tried to think about who would become king if father and sons died. Theories of a dynastic war with Scotland, or yet another civil one between Plantagenet descendants, came crashing into her brain but, exhausted, she fell asleep in Nicholas' arms.

Ella woke up the next morning, her body more rested than her mind. She could not explain why, but something was wrong. She felt it in her core, in her bones. Something terrible had happened or was about to.

'Nic… I know one is not allowed to say it, but…' she started to say after sending away the maid who had helped her get dressed.

'The King is well. The princes also. Please, do not trouble yourself so much,' Nicholas told her, reading her mind without difficulty.

Ella forced a smile, unconvinced. Something was not right. She closed her eyes, hoping to knock some sense back into her. Fearing a disease was pointless. She was fine. Hal was fine. The King was fine. Nicholas was fine. It was all fine! When she opened her eyes, Nicholas was standing in front of her, holding in his hands a gold and sapphire brooch with three pearls pendants.

'A gift. Sapphires bring protection and good fortune to the faithful. They also symbolise virtue, strength, wisdom, and kindness, words that cannot apply to anyone better than they do to you.'

Ella thanked her husband and let him pin the brooch on her bodice, then surprised herself by hugging him tight. How can you still not be in love with such a perfect man? she wondered, holding Nicholas firmly.

Later on, Ella was playing a piece written by the King on the virginals, accompanied by the composer himself on the lute. Her constant anguish was making her head ache and music was the only thing that could take her mind off the threat of the sweat. But, as the Queen demanded for them to play it one more time, Ella's head began to feel too heavy for her neck to hold it up. She wanted nothing more than excusing herself to bed and taking her bulky hood off, but tried to finish the part. She soon realised she was out of tune, though, and stopped playing to feel her brow. It was not feverish.

'Lady Exeter, what is the matter?' the King asked.

'I beg Your Grace to forgive me,' she said, asking herself the same question. When he put his lute down and walked up to her, reality hit. 'No!' she shouted, getting up on her feet and waving her hand to put some distance between them.

Dizzy, she would have fallen to the ground without the desk nearby. Holding on to it with one hand, she pushed the King away a second time with the other as he naively came to her help.

'Leave the room! All of you! And someone gets Alcaraz and Exeter!' he yelled as he finally understood as well.

Ella did not see him escape to the other side of the room, hurriedly covering his mouth and nose with a cloth. Out of nowhere, cold penetrated every bone in her body and she shivered so intensely she did not even try to stay on her feet. She fell on the ground, surrounded by her silken skirts, as cold as if she was buried under a frozen lake in Norway. When Dr Alcaraz entered the room, her heart was pounding so loudly in her ears that she did not understand what he told the King. She heard herself beg for Hal to be taken far away from Richmond. This effort took so much of her strength that she found herself lying down, her cold cheek against the rough floor. She had never been so terrified in her life. She would have needed a good cry, but her body had barely enough stamina to keep breathing.

She was going to die. She was going to die of a disease that no one understood. She was going to die and be forgotten for ever. But Hal had to live. Hal had to live, or the last seven years would have been for nothing. Hal had to live.

The court and the royal family had already left when Ella's body went from freezing to being so hot her bed was soaked with her sweat. Breathing heavily, she endlessly went back and forth between some sort of blurry consciousness and total blackout. It was a cycle. She would wake up, half aware of her surroundings, her body wet and burning, her heartbeat bursting through the roof. And she would fall back into the shadows, sinking a bit further each time, convinced she would never see the light of day again.

But she did. She opened her eyes. Her vision was clear and her head did not feel as if it was imploding. She was exhausted. She was alive. Slowly and carefully, she tried to sit down on her bed. Her arms refused to help. Her body was nothing more than a dead weight.

'I would not advise to move so soon, my Lady Exeter,' the voice of Dr Alcaraz found its way to her ears through the remnants of fog around her head.

Ella turned her head to the left and smiled weakly. 'It is good to see you, doctor,' she said.

'I am very pleased to see you well,' the physician replied. 'The King and Queen shall be thrilled. Your fever was high for longer than normal and everyone feared you would not survive.'

'How long?'

'The last thirty-six hours. The court has moved to Greenwich but the King has requested that I stay with you.'

'How kind. Is His Grace in good health?' Ella murmured, drained by the effort talking demanded.

'Yes. My lady, do have some rest now. I shall bring you an infusion the King has asked me to give you upon your recovery. It will prevent you from falling ill again. Sage, elder leaves and herb of grace. I shall be back soon with it.'

'Thank you. But do tell me, is my husband with the court?' she asked. An invisible hand closed on her heart as Dr Alcaraz's face fell. And crushed it when he opened his mouth.

It took three days and three nights for Ella to find the strength to get up from her bed and walk as far as the window. The weather did not reflect her mood. The cloudless sky and the radiant sun were reminding her that she was alive. She had survived. She had fought death, drenched in her own sweat, and she had won.

Nicholas and his amber eyes appeared in her head and she sat down on the floor. For three days, she had tried to recover both physically and emotionally. To even begin to process the death of her husband. The hows and the whys. She had not cried. She had just tried to understand. How the same disease had lost against her but won against him. Why a liar and a perjurer had been spared but a good and honest man had succumbed. How people could still believe in God after something like this. Why she had never been able to love her husband as much as he deserved.

Ella rested the back of her head against the wall and her eyes finally filled with tears. Gasping for air, she clasped her hands on her breasts and let out a long howl.

Nicholas was dead.

Ella was crying hysterically when Maud found her. It took fifteen minutes for her to calm down and fifteen more went by before she came to wonder why her friend was there at all.

'Why are you here?' she croaked.

'I was about to leave with the court for Greenwich when I found myself also infected with the sweat,' Maud told her. Her eyes were circled with black, mirroring Ella's.

'I am glad you survived it. I would have kept you company had I known.'

'No, no. Dr Alcaraz advised me to let you rest. I only came when I heard your scream. Elizabeth, words cannot express how sorry I am. Do you wish to share with me the weight which is on your heart?' Maud asked, but Ella shook her head left to right. 'I am willing to listen if you change your mind. Let us put you back to bed,' she decided.

'There is so much guilt inside me, Maud,' Ella said, which prompted the return of her tears.

'Oh, dear, why?'

'He is dead…'

'There is not a thing you could have done. He is with the Lord, he is at peace.'

'He loved me…'

'He adored you.'

'Why didn't I love him back?'

'My sweet friend, there are very little opportunities for women to love the men they were told to marry. It only happens to the luckiest of us.'

'But he was kind, and he made me laugh, and he made me feel safe… we rose together, we were… we were happy…' Ella sobbed.

'But he was never your choice,' Maud pointed out.

'I do not want him to be dead.'

Ella fell into Maud's arms, bawling her eyes out. Maud kept quiet for a while and let her, true to her word. Ella had never wanted to have Nicholas for husband, but now that he was gone, she wanted him by her side. She wanted him back. She wanted to fall in love with him. She wanted to lie in bed with him, his head on her breasts as he liked to do when he was upset. She wanted him for their fourth wedding anniversary at the end of the year. She wanted a second chance to fall in love with him. She would even have born him children if only it meant he would come back to her.

'Oh, Elizabeth…' she heard Maud say and realised she had said that last sentence out loud.

'I have been obsessed with avoiding physical pain. And death. And now, it is Nicholas who is dead! Why? Why him? And why did I not give him children? If I have to die here too, should it not at least whilst giving life?'

'What do you mean, if you have to die here?'

'Are we still in Richmond?' Ella changed the subject, erratic in both thinking and breathing.

'Yes. The King decided that the members of the court suffering from the sweat were to stay here. Most of us were too weak to be moved. The King then agreed that we both should stay in the palace until we were well enough to travel,' she told her. Ella meant to smile, grateful for the King's unusual decision, but realised what Maud had said. *We both.* 'Over twenty persons contracted the sweat at the same time we did, courtiers and servants alike. Only we survived,' she confirmed.

After seven years of pretending a devout Catholicism, Ella's automatic reaction was to cross herself. Maud imitated her, her kind eyes full of sorrow.

Over the next few months, the sweating sickness killed more people than the plague had in the previous summer. Maud lost her husband

and the father of her three young children in July. Cardinal Wolsey became severely ill in August, but recovered. The old Duke of Norfolk did not. Neither did the young Viscountess Lisle, who died before being old enough to consummate her marriage. The King, along with his wife, sons, sister and brother-in-law, retrenched himself to Windsor Castle, whilst Maud and Ella escaped with the three Parr children to the countryside, near Exeter, spending the early weeks of their widowhood together in the castle that the King had granted Nicholas to celebrate his elevation to the dukedom two years before.

Everywhere in the kingdom, it was as if time had stopped. People were either dead, grieving, or praying God to spare them.

16.

BITTERSWEET 1517-1518

Maud and her children – Katherine, William and Elizabeth – stayed with Ella until the sweat died down enough for court life to resume. They rode back to court at the end of October. Wearing the same gown of black silk and damask she had been wearing for months, it is only when the red bricks of the royal palace appeared that Ella realised she was coming back as the *Dowager* Duchess of Exeter. She was back at court. Nicholas was not.

Ella fought off the tears gathering up in her eyes. Nicholas had been dead for four months. It was time to move on. She walked up to her apartments with her head held as high as her position of demure grieving widow allowed her and stumbled upon Charles Brandon, who had welcomed a girl with his wife in the sweating sickness outbreak. It was a welcome change to see another person than the Parrs or her servants.

'Lord Suffolk, it is a pleasure to see you. Please receive my good wishes following the birth of your daughter,' Ella said.

'Lady Exeter, I thank you,' he replied. His clean-shaven jaw tensed. He shifted his weight from one leg to another. 'My wife and I were deeply saddened to hear about the passing of your husband. Nicholas was a very dear friend of mine. I am sorry. You must tell me whenever I may be of any assistance to you. Whatever your requirement, I shall be honoured and delighted to help.'

Ella smiled but the words she attempted to let out remained stuck in her throat. Charles observed her with sympathy. They had never been close, but he too had lost someone he cared about. Nicholas and Charles were brothers from another mother. They used to be, at least.

'The King is in the garden with my lords Prince Henry and Prince Arthur. The prince of Wales has longed for your return. If you allow me, I shall accompany you,' he offered.

They walked towards the garden without saying anything more, silence only broken by the sound of her skirts brushing the floor.

'Bet!' they both heard Hal's voice resonate in the garden as soon as they were close enough to be recognised.

The King's laugh filled the space as the red-headed whirlwind he had for a son ran across the lawn and hugged Ella, so tight that Charles had to give a helping hand to prevent an embarrassing fall. Ella closed her eyes even tighter, enjoying the sweet smell of her boy's hair. Her boy from another mother, for as long as she would breathe. Hal's round nose was against her neck and, for a second, just for a second, he was no heir to the throne and she was no widow. They were just Hal and Bet again.

'How I have missed you, my dear Bet,' he said in her ear.

'I have missed you more. I am happy to see you well,' she replied, gently letting go of the embrace.

'I am sorry that Nicholas died. Father...' he started to say. 'My lord father the King was also very upset about the passing of the Duke of Exeter,' he corrected himself, remembering the formality he was expected to express himself with in public.

So much in Ella's life had changed because of the sweat, but not Hal. The same rebellious red hair falling in his smart blue eyes and the same freckles on his nose. Ella noticed the thick glove on his left hand.

'Are you practising archery?' she asked.

'Indeed! Do come!' he exclaimed.

Three-year-old Arthur and his cousin Margaret were playing nearby in the grass with their lady mistress. Little Margaret had been left in England by her mother, the dowager queen of Scotland, for her own safety whilst she was trying to recover her son's regency. The girl was now attempting to participate in some version of a bowl game with all the dexterity of a two-year-old, much to Arthur's frustration. Ella smiled at the normality of the scene.

And then her eyes locked with the King's. Somehow, seeing both Hal and his father was making the task of breathing easier on her lungs. He was patiently waiting, his son's bow in his gloved hand, his smile getting wider as they were getting closer. He did not let Ella stay low in her curtsey for more than a second before rising her up. There was so much friendliness and happiness, both on his face and in his eyes that it lifted all burdens that had been weighing on her shoulders. The King represented her return to a life she had come to label as normal. She could have hugged him.

'Father, may I show Bet what I have learned?' Hal asked, his excitement stronger than his manners.

Far from being irritated, the King laughed again and agreed. For half an hour, Ella watched her favourite human being show off his prowess with the bow under the proud guidance of his father, who had always made it clear that no man but him would ever teach his sons archery. He thought it a skill a boy had to learn from his father, and Ella loved to see them share the same eagerness for it. She clapped at Hal's every shot and enthusiastically congratulated him when it was time for him to leave.

'Lady Exeter, if you are not too weary of your journey, we shall like to walk with you,' the King told her.

'Yes, Your Grace,' Ella agreed. She was not looking forward to sit alone in her empty apartment.

'We arrived two evenings past from a pilgrimage to Our Lady of Walsingham, where we gave thanks for the health of our sons at the close of this deadly summer,' he said. Ella found it slightly insensitive considering she had herself lost her husband.

'It is my deepest joy to see the princes so well,' she replied, sick to her stomach at the realisation that if any god had made her choose between the survival of Nicholas or Hal, she would have chosen the latter in a heartbeat.

'Indeed. We have also arranged for masses to be heard for the Duke of Exeter immediately after his passing, as your health was then very frail.'

He did not really believe in Purgatory, Ella thought. 'Your Grace is very kind,' she said instead.

Despite her husband's doubts about what the Church promised would happen to his soul, she had done what was expected of her and paid for masses to be heard in his memory. Maud had done the same for her husband. Whether or not Nicholas had changed his mind about Purgatory at the moment of his death, Ella's reputation would have fractured had she not done it. It was touching to hear that the King had done it too. It was yet another proof of his genuine affection for his childhood friend.

'Are you well?' the King asked after a moment of silence.

'I have fully recovered.'

'You spent the summer with Lady Parr and her children, did you not?'

'The children distracted us both from our grief,' she replied, wondering what would be his reaction if she told him one of those children would, in what she had to think of as a parallel reality, become his sixth wife.

'Yes, yes. Your presence would have been much appreciated at Windsor, praying for the sweat to pass,' he admitted, his sensitive pale skin blushing slightly.

'I thank Your Grace for this compliment, but I feel blessed to have spent the beginning of my widowhood with someone experiencing the same ordeal by my side. The great burden of solitude was lighter as a result of Lady Parr's presence.'

The King did not answer. Ella shivered when she remembered the long evenings by the fire, her friend lamenting about being a single mother to three young children, and herself about the loss of a man she had never deserved.

'I trust you enjoyed staying at Richmond for your recovery,' he said, switching personal pronouns for the first time since they had met.

'Enjoyed!?' Ella blurted out. It was her time to blush when she realised her rudeness.

'It is my hope you found some comfort in being there at such a troublesome time. I remembered it being your favourite palace, and insisted on extending your stay for as long as was necessary.'

'Your Grace sees me chagrined. I did not mean to cause any trouble.'

'Nonsense. It was my pleasure,' he said. He then reminded himself out loud that she had to be weary from her journey and urged her to go to her apartment to get some rest. He left, almost in a hurry, abandoning Ella behind.

As she walked back inside, the King's words echoed in Ella's head. *I remembered it being your favourite palace and insisted on extending your stay for as long as was necessary*. She did not recall ever telling him about this preference of hers, even though it was true. Richmond was the palace of her childhood princess stories, and the fact that she could now live in a palace that was to be destroyed long before the year of her birth was making it even more whimsical.

But why would he keep a palace running for only two women, with a physician, some maids and a cook, when he could have demanded for us to travel as soon as we could even sit up? Ella asked herself. The conspiratorial little voice inside her head came back running when she pushed the door of her apartment: there was a pandemic, but he made his wife's personal physician attend to you; he was away with his court, but he paid people to take care of you in your favourite palace; he sent the physician a special concoction to protect you from a second illness, it said.

Ella stopped, the door still open. One foot in, one foot out. She could still see him. The length of his body exceeding the one of the marital bed, his feet sticking out. The muscles of his buttocks as he walked naked around the room. And she could still smell him. The unique, singular smell of his sweat, mixed with the lavender Ella was always hanging with their clothes and putting under their pillows. She could still hear him, too. His laughs. His secrets. His war stories and adventures. She shut the door behind her. The room was so silent she wanted to scream to fill the space. The silence was deafening. She wanted to press her fists against her ears.

Her husband was dead.

And the husband of another woman could very possibly be in love with her.

A few uneventful months following her return to court, John Colet came to find Ella. There was a real intelligence behind the kindness of the King's chaplain's brown eyes. As a scholar, his reputation was international and, as an Englishman, he was loved by the King. He had also been respected and listened to by Nicholas, but he had always been non-existent as a person in Ella's life. She observed the short and slender man approaching her, clueless on what he could have come to tell her.

He did not talk. Not before handing her a folded piece of paper, at least. 'My Lady Exeter,' he said.

'Master Colet.'

'It is my belief that the late Duke of Exeter would have been interested in this letter's contents. He once confessed certain concerns to me, which lead me to believe that you share his interest. I must beg that you read it in a safe place.'

He barely even paused before bowing his head to her and left her as ignorant as when he had first opened his mouth.

Ella hid the paper up her sleeve and went back to her apartment. She had time – the Queen was praying and had requested that she be left alone for the rest of the day. Discovering what the inked words were was such a shock that she found herself sitting down.

The name was there, at the top. *Martino Lutther*. Martin Luther. Ella gasped and giggled all at once, putting one hand over her mouth as the other was holding the famous ninety-five theses. They were not famous yet, of course, but they would be eventually. She had studied them at school in the twenty-first century. Although Martin Luther, a German monk, was probably not expecting Lutheranism to ever be established, his ninety-five theses that Ella was holding in her hand were the turning point. They were one of the reasons why the country she was born in and the country she was living in, although the same, were of different religion.

Ella read one these after the other. They were not written in English but it did not matter. She was completely fluent in Latin now. School had already taught her what the theses were about, but reading Martin Luther's own words, so soon after he had written them himself, was exhilarating. It had to be forbidden, too: Martin Luther's tone was academic and, although he was only inviting debate, his work was pure heresy.

He was challenging the Pope's authority and power over Purgatory and the fate of the souls in it, because the afterlife was only God's jurisdiction.

He was reminding people of the meaning of repentance and that it was worthless if it was only coming from the wallet and not from remorse and spiritual work.

He was raising the issue of the sale of indulgences, arguing that attaching a monetary value to redemption encouraged greed and corruption.

Ella had not finished reading yet that she knew she wanted to start again from the beginning, but she paused. Martin Luther had a lot to say about the sale of indulgences. After all, his theses were called "disputation on the power and efficacy of indulgences." According to him, the sale of indulgences was only a false promise, because the sellers could not guarantee salvation – only God would ultimately decide to grant it. He also mentioned how damaging to the Church's reputation it was. The money gained from sales was currently used to build St Peter's Basilica in Rome. People were starting to wonder why, with all its wealth, the Church needed their money to build it.

Ella could remember when she had travelled to Rome with Iris, a couple of years before she had travelled in time. They had visited the Vatican and had climbed the stairs all the way to the dome of the famous church. The view from up there had been so wonderful it had won Ella many likes on Instagram. She had never been interested to know when or how the religious landmark had been erected, but finding out it was, at this very moment, in the process of being built with the money of people hoping to save themselves from Purgatory felt bittersweet.

Ella read the theses again. Martin Luther wanted to debate about the lies that the Church fed its believers every day. What he hoped seemed clear: that people would remember that money was not the answer to everything. It was a truth that many had still not accepted in the twenty-first century.

It was uncertain how John Colet had come to have the theses in his hands. Ella went to find him. He was in the company of Sir Francis Bryan, a friend of Nicholas whom she was doing her best to avoid. The fact that she was in mourning was not holding the man back in his courtship and she had already had to return a precious necklace to him. Ella waited for the man to leave, and Colet, who had spotted her, approached her.

'I trust my lady has now read the news from Germany,' he declared.

'If I may, how did this come to your attention?' Ella asked. News from Germany could take a long while to travel to England. The theses were only three months old.

There was a glint of mischief in Colet's eyes when he smiled at her. 'I am a well-connected man, my lady,' he replied.

'Does His Grace know?

'Not yet, but I shall make sure it is soon the case.' Ella accepted the answer. As his personal chaplain, Colet could approach the King in a way that no one else could. 'The lord chancellor has chosen to regard this matter as the sole responsibility of the Holy Roman emperor,' Colet added.

Ella could not help but pout. If Cardinal Wolsey – the lord chancellor – was unbothered, it was likely that the King would follow his example. Religious turmoil was only happening in Germany. It had not travelled yet. It was not on everyone's lips, in everyone's minds. Ella knew it would come to be so in the future, if this timeline was to follow the timeline of her birth world. She attempted to recover from her memories exactly when Martin Luther had started to annoy the highest spheres of the kingdom of England, but ended up sighing in frustration. She did not have the patience to wait around for Martin Luther to slowly build popularity up, or not, in England.

'How many copies are in your possession?' she asked.

'Only a few.'

'More need to be made. They must be placed in every room of the palace. My desire is for all courtiers to read them.'

Colet looked at her with a new spark of interest. 'My lady is dauntless.'

'Londoners, also. I want the theses on every door in the capital. You may rely on my financial help.'

The King's chaplain did not reply, but the mischief in his eyes had now reached every one of his face muscles. He uncovered himself, bowed and left without another word, looking like he knew exactly how to manage this.

As twenty-first century Twitter would have said, the devil worked hard, but John Colet worked harder. Ella was unaware of how many copies had been made with the money she had provided, but it was soon impossible to enter a room in Greenwich Palace without stumbling on the ninety-five theses, either pinned on a door, left on a stool or even on the floor among the rushes. When one was discovered on the chair of estate, the King demanded that Cardinal Wolsey find the one responsible – it was prohibited to touch the chair of estate or even stand underneath the canopy.

'It was unwise,' Ella told Colet the morning after. 'Who placed it there?' she asked.

'The person has been disciplined,' he replied.

'That was not my question,' she insisted.

'The cardinal has many spies. Caution is needed,' Colet ignored her.

'Cease all activity,' Ella decided. 'It is too perilous to continue for now. Let us speak again in a few weeks.'

Colet agreed. Immediately after, new copies stopped to appear. Martin Luther's introduction to the court of Henry VIII had been short-lived but, Ella hoped, intense enough to have lasting effects. She was thinking about how she would have loved to discuss the subject with her husband when she was joined by Hal. Seven years old now, the boy had never visited court so much since Ella had been back from her near-death experience. It was his last moments of freedom before the start of his formal education with Dr Linacre, one of the King's physicians, as a tutor.

'What are you doing, my dear Bet?' he asked, smoothing his sleeves. The spitting image of his father, he was wearing a black hat encrusted with a ruby. A white feather was pointing softly to the ceiling.

'Thinking. Should you be wandering around the palace alone?' she said. It was unusual. The thought that he may have ditched his company on purpose crossed Ella's mind.

'I am not alone, I am with you,' he retorted, looking at her from the corner of his eye just like his father did sometimes. 'Are you thinking about Martin Luther?' he whispered.

'Why, are you thinking about Martin Luther?'

'Father says that the man's soul shall burn in Hell.'

Ella fought off a smile. John Colet had worked hard enough for Martin Luther to reach Hal's ears. 'What are your thoughts about him?' she asked.

He looked around, then shrugged. 'I do not find his writing so upsetting.'

'Why do you think other people do?'

'I am unsure,' he admitted. 'I should not have been prying, but I heard the lord chancellor say that men should not read the theses not only because there are heresy, but also because there are too many questions in it also. He said that men shall try to find their own answers. Why should it be wrong?'

'Hal, you are old enough to be aware of how delicate it is to question the teachings of the Church,' Ella told him, making sure first that no one could hear them.

'Yes, but it is important to me to have answers to my interrogations. Others must feel the same. And, if what the priest says is true, if what one does is wrong, one should be corrected and then do what is right. Bet, does this mean I am a heretic?' he asked, anxious.

'Not to me,' she kissed the top of his hand. 'But, for many, yes.'

'Am I to go to Hell?'

'No. You are good, humble, and kind. I shall always listen to you and do my best to provide you with the answers you seek, but you must promise me to never speak to anyone else about this matter.'

'I promise. I know we are not supposed to talk about it.'

'Thank you. Listen, it is my thinking that Martin Luther was merely intending to debate, that is all. However, one is not allowed to debate on such things. What you must understand is that what is forbidden is not always what is wrong.'

'I know. Are you a heretic?'

'I believe one should be permitted to share one's beliefs without being in mortal danger.'

'Does being a heretic mean disagreeing with the Pope? Or disagreeing with Father?' Hal wondered, still whispering.

'Both, when it comes to religious matters,' Ella answered, double – and triple – checking that no one was around.

Whether or not he had feelings for her, the King would send her to her death for this.

Time for supper came and put an end to their secret conversation. Ella kept quiet during the meal and her mourning gown helped to prevent others from trying to engage. She had a lot to think about. The heir to the throne of England was questioning his own parents. Ella did not know yet what Hal thought about Martin Luther's arguments but, at seven years old, he was asking the right questions.

And he wanted answers.

And he wanted other people to have answers to their questions.

Whether or not he would turn his back on the Catholic faith was out of Ella's hands, but he refused to believe what the Church was requiring him to believe without bothering to hear his concerns. It was mind-blowing.

Ella put more leeks on her plate. She had eaten so much meat lately, finding comfort in its rich taste and the thickness of its sauce, that her body was finding it tricky to digest. She stared at her greens, smiling at the memory of Hal discovering leek potage for the first time as a toddler and loving it more than anything else in the world. She froze.

His faith did not have to be out of her hands. He loved her. She was his Bet, he was her Hal. He trusted her.

What if this trust is the key which opens the door for the Reformation to happen after all? she wondered. Ella emptied her glass of wine. In the King's mind, his marriage had been blessed by God because of the two healthy male heirs it had produced. The Crown was safe. He had no reason to discard his wife. Nothing would ever be powerful enough to make him risk excommunication. He would never challenge the Pope's authority. He would never break with Rome.

Hal could do it, though. He could be the example that English people needed to start thinking by themselves. To start denouncing the abuses. To start claiming the truth. And to start, maybe one day, realising that God was only a creation of men – a symbol responsible for an incalculable number of deaths and broken lives. The only thing Ella had to do was to make sure Hal saw how greedy and hypocritical the Church could be.

Ella's hand was shaking as she emptied a second glass of wine. She had been battling for months with the guilt of being alive. She could not figure out why she was breathing when Nicholas was not. Part of her knew that not everything had an explanation, but another part of her wanted and needed her life to have a deeper meaning. Maybe she had found it. Henry VIII had once turned his kingdom upside down for the love of a woman and the need of a son. Maybe, the Reformation was still meant to happen, but for the right reasons this time. Maybe, it was Ella's job to make sure it did.

17.

Needed Change
1518

As terrifying as the thought was, with the death of her husband, Ella had become the most coveted woman in the kingdom. Widows were legally left with a third of their deceased husband's lands, but Nicholas had stated in his will that he was transferring the ownership of everything to her. Their properties were hers. Every single farthing of their fortune was hers. Her wealth was colossal, and it was exclusively hers.

She was no longer the wife of a wealthy husband, she was her own wealthy husband.

Every time she said it to herself, she had to chuckle. She was relieved, as life in Tudor England was difficult enough as it was to be without money, but it mostly felt like a true victory in this man's world. It also meant every unmarried man wanted her as a wife.

'My husband shared that the Marquess of Dorset says himself very sorry to be married, as he would have much rather taken you for a wife!' Elsie told her one day, laughing.

'I am afraid I would not have accepted him either way.'

'But his father was half-brother to the King's mother!' Maud retorted.

'But he is a marquess! Elizabeth is right, why would she accept a marquess when she is a duchess? If my husband were to die, I would not remarry below my rank,' Elsie said. When the sweating sickness had killed his father, Elsie's husband had become Duke of Norfolk. Elsie's facial expression was making clear that his death would the best thing that could happen to her.

'That is true, but I do believe your hand shall be asked multiple times as soon as you leave your mourning clothes,' Maud reminded Ella.

'Well, I plan to stay unmarried.'

'I too. I do not wish to jeopardise the inheritance my husband left for our children with the gambling and drinking of another!'

'Amen!' Ella gushed without thinking, raising her glass of wine in the air. Maud looked at her awkwardly but Elsie put her hand on Ella's arm, pressed it, and burst out with laughter.

To make their lives easier, Maud and Ella did not come out of their mourning gowns until summer. The custom was blurry when it came to how long a widow was supposed to mourn her husband. Women had been seen wearing colours again from as little as a month after the burial whilst others kept black for years. It was the only aspect in women's lives that was up to them, although that choice would have an effect on their reputation and respectability, especially if one decided to remarry what was deemed too soon.

Wearing black for a year should have given Ella enough time to evaluate the King's feelings towards her, but she was so busy avoiding Cardinal Wolsey's spies to meet in secret with John Colet that though time passed, answers to her questions refused to come. The King was always, with no exception, respectful and unambiguous with her. He was as friendly as ever and their conversations were always platonic. Yet, there were days when she could feel his eyes on her when she looked away. When he blushed while talking to her. When he laughed a bit too loud. When she caught him searching for her in a crowded room and smile as soon as he found her.

The worst part was that it was not just him. Under the black silk of her gown, every single one of the King's looks gave her the collywobbles. She would wake up each morning, dreading to talk to him but dreading even more to not talk to him. She would then go to sleep at night, fidgety and fearful, wondering if anyone had noticed the shake in her hands and the red on her cheeks every time she heard her name in his mouth. Some nights, her dreams about him were so vivid she could not bring herself to look at him in the eyes the following day.

The game Ella's body was playing was a dangerous one. The King might never make anything plain about how he felt, but her life would never be the same if he decided to and if she accepted him. At least, the King was an adept of courtly love and could even sometimes be a bit of a prude, which meant that he would never dare to force himself into her if she rejected him.

The real question is not about his reaction but yours, the voice inside her head reminded her. As usual, Ella pushed it away. Thinking about either forever repressing the physical urge she felt in his presence or betraying a woman she respected was too difficult.

On the eve of the King's twenty-seventh birthday, Ella invited Maud and Elsie for a glass of wine in her apartment. Nicholas had been dead for three-hundred-and-sixty-five days but his widow was still not used to the sharp claws of loneliness. Her rooms were too silent and her bed was too big without him in it. Silence used to feel like an escape from her life, but she now needed an escape from it.

All she could hear was her own voice, her own thoughts. Her survivor's guilt. Her newfound terror of any disease, especially now that the temperatures had risen and that the plague was just around the corner. Her conflicted feelings for the King. Her procrastination in looking for Lolly's ring the last time the court had stayed at Eltham Palace. Her culpability when time had come to leave without her trying even once. Her disturbing sentiment that she had lost her youth at the same time she had her husband, as if the young and pretty duchess and her gorgeous gowns had overnight become an old hag with a "widow" label on her wrinkled forehead. It was all too loud.

'It is very odd to think you both were fighting for your lives exactly one year ago,' Elsie said.

'I do not recommend the experience,' Ella replied.

'How does it feel like? The sweat?'

'Sweaty.'

Elsie laughed loudly.

'I genuinely thought I was going to drown in my sweat. Even childbirth had not frightened me so,' Maud recalled.

'Let us speak of more joyful matters,' Ella decided. Mentioning her battle with the sweating sickness always gave her the creeps. 'I plan to leave my mourning clothes in the morrow and I must show you something,' she said, walking to where she was keeping her headdresses.

When she had moved on from her last boyfriend, Ella had briefly dyed her hair blond. The time before, she had cut her hair short. Women of this century used urine to dye their hair, which was a bridge she was not willing to cross, and she remembered too deeply the instant regret she had felt after cutting her hair to renew the experience. Maud and Elsie gasped when she came back with a French hood in her hands.

If the gable hood was conic and bulky, the French one was round and light, and where the former covered every single bit of hair, the latter revealed a portion of it at the front. Both had a black veil attached to it at the back. The French Queen had tried to introduce them to England at her return from France but she had since then spent so little time at her brother's court that she had not managed to make them popular, especially considering Queen Katherine hated them.

'Surely you must know that Her Grace finds it very unbecoming!' Maud echoed her thoughts.

'Yes, but I do not share this opinion. I have had three of them made. I have much fondness for this one,' Ella said, putting in her friend's hands the hood, made of green velvet and lined with pearls.

'I had one made shortly after the French Queen's marriage to the Duke of Suffolk but I changed my mind when Her Grace reprimanded Jane Popincourt for wearing one,' Elsie revealed.

'This one is beautiful work,' Maud admitted. 'Are you not afraid of displeasing the Queen?'

'My marriage is over and my mourning too. I cannot explain why, but I feel this change in my appearance is needed,' Ella replied.

'My marriage is not over but I shall accompany you with this change in the morrow,' Elsie took the hood from Maud's hands and went to put it on Ella's head. 'You shall look magnificent!' she exclaimed, her eyes full of admiration.

'We both shall. Maud?'

'No. Francis Bryan is courting me. I intend to stay in mourning until he tires of me.'

'He is courting me too!' Ella said.

'I am aware. He is a wanton. I would rather die than making him the father of my children!' Maud cried.

'You can refuse him, even if he asks for your hand in marriage,' Elsie reminded her.

'He is a close friend of the King. Whatever the law says, if the King insists on the match, I shall not have a choice. I am willing to stay in mourning until I am past my child-bearing years and my three children are married if it is what it takes to protect their future.'

'I have never understood why that man was a friend of the King and Nicholas,' Ella said.

'If one is not a woman protecting her virtue, he must be of the most entertaining company,' Elsie commented with a shrug.

The following morning, when Ella and Elsie entered the Queen's apartments, they were surprised to see the entire royal family gathered there. The Queen looked unimpressed with their hoods, and more precisely the quarter of an inch of uncovered hair above their brows, but her young niece Margaret declared that they both looked very pretty.

Ella had not felt so good-looking in a while. As bizarre as it was for a woman born in the year 2000, she was finally feeling like herself again thanks to her headgear matching her imposing gown of green velvet. She had had over two hundred pearls sewn onto the gown and was wearing one of the brooches Nicholas had gifted her during their marriage. After a year of wearing black and leaving her jewels in their box, she felt wonderful.

'Lady Exeter, you are not in mourning anymore,' the Queen said kindly, focusing on what she could praise rather than what she disagreed with.

'I am not, Your Grace,' Ella replied and curtseyed to husband and wife.

'Green becomes you, Lady Exeter. So does the French hood,' the King complimented her. 'It suits both of you,' he added in a hurry at Elsie's intention.

Ella was so uneasy that the blush on her cheeks mirrored his. After another curtsey, she went to ask Maud if she needed any help with her embroidery project.

Since the dowager Duchess of Norfolk, the French Queen and the Duchess of Buckingham all lived away from court, Ella and Elsie were the only duchesses to attend the Queen and succeeded where her sister-in-law had failed: they started off a small fashion revolution. Before as little as a week, over a dozen ladies were wearing a French hood. It was as if they had all kept one safe at home until it would be deemed acceptable to wear it at court. The Queen was not thrilled, but Ella was wondering if her name would one day be remembered for bringing this change to England.

As expected, Francis Bryan jumped on the first occasion to ask for Ella's hand. She rejected him, and the seven other men who dared to do so over the following days. She escaped to the gardens after turning down one of Elsie's brothers-in-law and sat as far as she could from the palace, hoping no one would find her there.

Someone did.

A tight knot formed in her stomach when she spotted the King galloping back from a hunt. Leaving his horse in the care of one of his servants, he came to offer her some company.

'God's grace has been kind on today's hunt,' he said.

'Your Grace was successful, then?'

'Of course. There shall be plenty for supper. Sir Francis Bryan did well, too.'

'I am glad,' Ella replied as Maud's words came back to her mind. *Whatever the law says, if the King insists on the match, I shall not have a choice*. Please don't make me marry another one of your friends, she silently begged.

The King laughed. 'It is as if I could hear you think. I trust you know you shall always be free to speak your mind with me,' he told her, looking at her from the corner of his eyes.

'I worry that Your Grace may insist on a union with Sir Francis despite my refusal,' she admitted.

'Fear not. Sir Francis is a valued friend, but you may remarry whom you please. You are certainly in demand,' he commented.

Ella held her breath when she noticed that his hand was not on his lap anymore, but on the bench. If she could shift, somehow, just three of four inches towards his hand... Ella discreetly sighed when he got up. The small group of courtiers that accompanied the King everywhere had been standing at a respectable distance, out of earshot, but, in his red outfit, Thomas Wolsey was now walking towards them. Ella was about to curse him in her head for interrupting their moment when the King raised his hand, palm towards the cardinal, which made him stop.

Both Ella and Wolsey ended up standing aimlessly, waiting for the King to say or do something that would explain his sign, but he did not. Ella found herself staring at him for much longer than was acceptable. The longer she stared, the more difficult it was to resist the urge to get on her toes and kiss him.

'The cardinal seems to have a pressing matter to discuss with Your Grace,' she said with a hoarse voice.

'I lied to you, this year past,' he ignored her remark. 'After the sweat, I went on a pilgrimage to Our Lady of Walsingham, but not to give thanks for the survival of my sons,' he explained, now looking like a boy lost in sumptuous clothes.

'What did Your Grace give thanks for?'

'Not taking you away from me.' He paused. Smiled briefly. Exhaled sharply. 'I could not eat, nor sleep, for as long as you were sick. I was not myself. You have been haunting my days and my nights for long before, but knowing you were suffering so greatly was unbearable. As a life without you would be. No, I am begging you to not say a word to this,' he pleaded, blushing violently as Ella opened her mouth. 'Years in the past, you forgot the person that you were. You lost more that day than any soul should ever lose, and I am ashamed to say that the blame lies partly on my own self. Chivalry demands that I should not have expressed my feelings towards you. Forgive me.'

To this, he left her there. Shaking and out of breath, Ella sat back down on the bench, her mind blank, and watched as the cardinal and the King walked away, one bright with red silks and the other glittering in all his jewels.

18.

I AM ELIZABETH
1518

'Chivalry demands that I should not have expressed my feelings towards you,' Ella repeated out loud, stunned.

She took her face in her hands and massaged her eyelids. Hundreds of questions were attacking her brain and she was struggling to separate them. She took a deep breath and had to laugh when she realised that, all those years ago, the King had not taken her in to thank her for finding Pan, or even out of the goodness of his heart. He had taken her in because he had not been able to control his pet and had indirectly, or so he thought, caused her harm. He felt guilty for the loss of her memories.

The diamond necklace Nicholas had given her for their second wedding anniversary was weighing against Ella's skin, at the top of her sternum.

Did he force Nic to marry me instead of a rich heiress so I could be taken care of by someone he trusted and loved? she wondered. She shook her head, refusing to believe he had played with his childhood friend's life for a woman he barely knew anything of. But what had not made any sense then made all the sense in the world now. Ella knew what the answer was. Just like she knew that his guilt surrounding her pretend amnesia was the reason why he had never tried to put her in his bed.

That night, Ella did not sleep. Although the King had asked her to say nothing to his declaration of love, there was a decision to make and this decision would shape her future. In her nightshirt, she went to grab a quill and some ink. Sitting by the stone fireplace, she listed the pros about becoming the King's mistress.

Satisfying her lust and feelings. Ending her loneliness. Increasing her influence.

Then, the cons.

Betraying another woman. Losing her respectability. Risking pregnancies and sexually transmitted diseases.

She sighed and listed the cons about not becoming the King's mistress.

Hurting the King's feelings. Jeopardizing their friendship and her influence. Creating frustration that would lead to an increase of her loneliness.

Ella bit her upper lip, her quill suspended in the air, thinking about what the pros of refusing the King were. Staying loyal to the Queen was the only one she could find, until she remembered a lost version of the King: married six times and responsible for the decapitation of two of his wives.

2007. Emily and Paul waited for the storyteller at Windsor Castle to release her group of captivated children, which included their granddaughter, before taking her to St George's Chapel to finish their tour.

'What did you like the most about the story, love?' Paul asked.

'When she said that the future King Henry had a tantrum when his sister became queen of Scotland and she had to walk in front of him because she was more important than him!' Ella replied with a giggle.

'He was twelve years old, then. It is true that it is a bit old to have tantrums in public!' Emily conceded and, whilst her husband was chatting with the girl on the way to the chapel, busied herself with sliding, left to right and

right to left, the sapphire ring on her chain. 'Look, he is buried here, in the crypt. Queen Jane Seymour, the mother of his son, King Edward VI, is buried with him,' she pointed at the black marble slab on the floor.

'I'll never keep a straight face to this!' a visitor said loudly to her friend. 'His ego was so big, but now we get to walk all over him. That should teach him for his cruelty!' she said, stepping on the slab with obvious pleasure.

'Many people are quick to judge his actions by our standards, forgetting that he was born in a different world than them,' Emily told her granddaughter.

'Emily, I think she is too young for that man's horror stories,' Paul stepped in.

'Ella, darling, Henry VIII did some very bad things, but doing bad things does not make you a bad person, and it did not make him a bad person either,' Emily ignored her husband.

'Why did he do so many bad things?' Ella asked.

'I think that his problem was that he never stopped throwing tantrums. He was a very clever person, and believe me or not, he was also very kind, but he never learned how to control his temper or to cope with the frustration of being told no.'

'Which is no excuse for murdering two of your wives! Who are you and what have you done to my wife? She always defends this guy's poor queens!' Paul exclaimed.

'I defend whoever needs to be defended. Rules were not the same back then. They thought differently. It is easy to judge from the comfort of 2007. Life was different five hundred years ago.'

Ella smiled as she remembered the bickering that had followed that day. It had lasted for the entire journey back to London. Lolly would repeat that judging people from another era by the standards of today was unfair; Pop would remind her that even the King's contemporaries did not finish the grand tomb he had planned for himself, which had to mean something regarding their understanding of his actions; Lolly would bark that the tomb had never been finished only because of financial problems; Pop would retort the King's ego was such that he would have bankrupted his kingdom just to finance his tomb; Lolly would shrug and say how much of an imbecile she was married to.

Ella threw her diagrams in the fireplace and watched as they burned slowly.

Overnight, the King decided to go back on a hunting trip. Taking a dozen of friends with him, he was gone before sunrise. The Queen hid her surprise and sorrow well but admitted to her ladies that her heart ached that he had not said goodbye to her. Ella's broke. As widely known as his love for hunting was, she knew he had left the palace in order to avoid her.

Queen Katherine was thirty-two but looked so worn out by life that not a soul could have guessed her age correctly. Her blue eyes had lost their sparkle and her body had shed any ounce of fat it had ever had on. Ella had seen with her own eyes that, under her conservative gable hood, her hair had already started to turn grey. Suddenly, her intention of becoming the mistress of that woman's husband felt like kicking someone already down. She left the room to try to catch her breath under her tight bodice.

You are a terrible person, she told herself. Over the years, the Queen had learned to look away from her husband's affairs. She always seemed to know who at court was sleeping with him but never reproached anyone about anything. Letting one's husband have sex with other women, even teenagers, was the duty of a good queen.

You are her friend, the voice inside her head reminded her sharply. She could have never bonded with the Queen like she had with Maud,

Elsie or Inez, because of the difference of rank. But she had held her hand during the births of her children. She had comforted her when she needed it. She had wiped her tears after the death of the newborn princess. She had prayed with her in her closet, or at least pretended to, for hours on end. She had played on the virginals for her, sung for her, danced with her. The Queen had been a constant presence in her life for years, and was as intelligent and kind as Lolly had ever said she was.

Ella rested her forehead on the wall. Her eyes caught the sight of the devotional gold enamelled book hanging at the end of her girdle. It was minuscule but so precious she was wearing it more as a display of wealth than a proof of her piety. The Queen herself had gifted it to her for the New Year. Ella closed her eyes, wondering what had happened to her life for her to aspire to be a home-wrecker.

There is no more home to wreck, she is already a cuckquean, she thought. The King had already cheated on her with Lady Anne Hastings, then with Elizabeth Bryan, the young sister of Sir Francis, then had a brief fling with the French maid of honour Jane Popincourt, and was currently sleeping with Bessie Blount. Ella sighed and mentally listed her options.

They were pretty limited. Spending the rest of her life as a widow, protecting her wealth against male suitors and sleeping alone in her empty bed until the day she died. Or, marrying a rich man who could increase her wealth, but risking being given less than half the freedom and gentleness she was given in her first marriage. Ella shivered when the image of the abusive Norfolk popped up in her head. She could only imagine what Elsie was going through on a daily basis.

It is easy to judge from the comfort of 2007, but life was different five hundred years ago, Ella heard Lolly's voice in her head.

The King stayed away for an entire month. Ella missed him. Taking advantage of his absence, she and Colet made Martin Luther's theses circulate again. A translation in English was also in the works. Every courtier had an opinion to give, but the only opinion Ella would have loved to hear about was the King's, even if it had been anger. As laughable as it was, she just wanted to see him.

He came back to court mid-August to celebrate the Assumption of the Virgin Mary. The day was split between praying and eating, and when Ella found herself alone once more in her apartment at night, she realised he had spent the day avoiding any interaction with her. It was so infuriating. She had to be the only woman that man had ever had feelings for and yet refused to sleep with. She had to be the only woman in the entire century being denied intercourse because of an integrity matter!

Ella decidedly walked to the door but, her hand resting on the handle, she cursed. It was a Feast Day. Even if she managed to convince him she was not a damsel in distress anymore, it would not change the fact that sex was forbidden on Feast Days. The King was not one to disobey the Church.

The frustration of having to spend yet another night alone made Ella forget all about her internal debate. For once, both her brain and her body were agreeing on what they wanted to do. The following evening, she was wandering in the corridor, realising as seconds went by that she had no way of knowing if the King was alone or not. He could be with Bessie. He could even be with the Queen. Besides, one could not barge in his apartments without invitation.

'Who is it? Lady Exeter, is that you?' a voice behind her made her jump, but she relaxed when she recognised Charles Brandon.

'Lord Suffolk. I thought you back in the countryside?'

'I leave in the morrow. I had unfinished business here today. Are things all right?'

'Did you mean it when you offered your assistance to me, whatever my requirement be?'

'Yes. I am a man of my word,' he reminded her. The corners of Ella's mouth had to rise up when she remembered what had happened the last time he had given his word to the King.

'I need to see the King,' she declared.

'Follow me,' he said without asking more questions.

Ella had never thought about the possibility of the King telling his best friend about his extra-matrimonial feelings for their common friend's widow, but one look at him was enough to understand that he knew. As a gentleman, Charles led the way in a respectful silence to the King's private chambers, using a discreet set of doors. He knocked twice on a large dark wooden double-door. The King's voice allowed them to enter and Ella took a deep breath, praying he would not reject her and leave her alone again.

The King jumped out of his chair when he realised Charles was not alone and did not even seem to notice when his friend left the room. Ella swallowed with difficulty. He usually looked a lot less impressive without his hat or his doublet, always so heavily encrusted with jewels one could barely see the fabric, but seeing him tonight, in the intimacy of his bedroom, his shirt not even tucked in his hose, was not like watching him play tennis or run at the ring. She had never been more attracted to him.

They stared at each other in silence. For a moment, the floor creaking in the room above and the wood burning in the fireplace was all that could be heard. And, it seemed, Ella's pounding heart.

After all this time questioning and blaming herself, Ella could not find it in her to regret the decision that had led her to the King's bedroom. Looking at his pale skin reddened by the heat of the fire, she knew she wanted him.

'You should not be here,' he said, when his eyes screamed the opposite.

'Your Grace should not believe I have lost all knowledge of who I am.'

'Why ever not?'

'I know who I am.'

'Tell me,' he demanded.

He stood still as she walked up to him. He was staring at her so intensely she felt as if she were naked, but did not mind it at all. The fire was turning his red hair into gold and he had never looked more handsome.

Ella got so close she could smell his breath. 'My name is the one you gave me,' she murmured.

'It is not…' he started to say, but paused when she reached for the drawstring of his shirt. She twirled it around her finger in silence. When she looked up, his gaze was on her, his mouth slightly open. She could see the battle in his eyes. Between right and wrong. Between reason and desire.

'I am Elizabeth. And I am yours,' she told him.

He stopped hesitating. His arms brusquely pulled her to him and his lips came crashing onto hers, as the fire escaped the fireplace to lodge itself into Ella's body. She kissed him back with a passion she had never felt before, grabbing his face, running her fingers through his hair, welcoming the taste of his tongue. It was not the idealistic first kiss from modern day movies. It was not gentle. Not romantic. It was two adults, embracing their lust and thirst, satisfying their urge after hopelessly fighting it.

They did not take time to remove their clothes. Ella only had to help him lift her skirts up to feel him inside her. But one time was not enough, and their clothes ended up scattered all over the bedroom floor.

Lying naked in his arms in the middle of the night, her head resting on his smooth chest, Ella smiled. For the first time in this century, she had slept with a husband who was not hers, but for the first time, it had felt right. They had both wanted it. They had both chosen to. Nothing but their own feelings had made them do it.

'Did I hurt you?' he asked, his fingers playing with her hair. Her smile got wider.

'No…' she replied, but hesitated on how to address him.

His chest jumped up as he chortled. 'Henry. In private.'

'Henry.'

'I did not foresee you coming,' he admitted.

'Are you displeased?'

There was a moment of silence during which Ella started to panic he was going to resent her for making him give up on his principles. But the King – Henry! – turned on his side, now lying face to her, and caressed her cheek.

'Far from it. I shall never be. I concealed my feelings for you for so long that it is difficult to remember when they first occurred to me. The only certainty is, from the time we met, your presence has always brought me joy and comfort. It was soon to become a much-needed delight. I abhor the days our talks cannot be arranged. Elizabeth, I am yours, body and soul,' he said, locking eyes with her and refusing to let her look away.

Ella reached for his lips so he would not see the tears in her eyes. Her heart had exploded in her chest. No one had ever felt this way about her. No one had ever made her feel so wanted.

19.

DANGEROUS WATERS

1518

Ella was woken up a couple of weeks later by Henry kissing her softly on her shoulder. She turned around under the silk covers. He kissed her on the forehead, then on the nose and on the lips, and she wished they would never leave the room. When she opened her eyes, his were gazing at her with all the tenderness in the world.

For two weeks now, he had spent almost every night with her. Bessie was openly complaining that he had deserted her bed without explanation and everyone at court was speculating in whispers about the identity of the new royal mistress. Their relationship had been kept mostly hidden from the courtiers. Only Henry's closest friends were aware, and some strategic servants to them both, in order to make their nightly meetings possible. They had all sworn to keep it a secret. It was a bubble of happiness that Ella wished would never pop. The only thing she felt guilty about was keeping her friends in the dark, more in fact than betraying the Queen.

'What are your thoughts, my darling?' Henry wondered.

'I shall like to tell the Duchess of Norfolk, Lady Parr and Mistress Margery Tate about us, if you do not object,' she said.

'Of course. You trust them to keep away from gossip and thus I do too.'

'I thank you. Maybe Bessie should be put in the confidence as well.'

He frowned. 'I have not shared her bed in a fortnight. Is she a close friend of yours?'

'No, but she is upset about you leaving her bed.'

'It was to be expected. My darling, she was merely a way for my thoughts to keep away from you.'

She kissed him. Her heart was full, yet it was impossible to ignore the images of them together. Bessie's lips against his skin. His member inside of her. Ella's body tensed. It was as uncontrollable as it was pointless. Henry was bound to sleep with at least one other woman – the Queen. Jealousy would not change that. Heirs had to be produced, duty had to be completed and appearances had to be saved.

But Ella could not control herself.

'I am concerned for her, Henry,' she lied. 'It is common knowledge that she is no longer chaste. I am afraid she will not find a good husband.'

'Is this what agitates your mind?' he asked. Ella lied again when she nodded; if it was a concern for Bessie, it was not one for her. Henry looked at her as if she was an angel descended from Heaven. 'You have a pure soul and a heart of gold,' he said, then thought for a moment. 'I shall not rest knowing you unhappy. It is known that Lord Clifford's heir is looking for a second wife. I will arrange for him to wed Bessie. She shall be Lady Clifford at the death of the old man. The family seat is in Yorkshire and they rarely come to court. Does this please you?'

'Immensely. Thank you, Henry,' she kissed him.

It was adorable to see him so worried his solution would not make her happy. Ella hoped he would never realise she had manipulated him.

She was still struggling to accept that the man surrounding her with so much love and the cruel tyrant of her twenty-first century memories were the same person. The man kissing her with so much devotion was the man who had ordered the executions of thousands of people. Maybe, he had it in him already. He was hot-blooded and passionate, which often meant angry and frustrated, but Ella could not read cruelty in him.

If he did have it, nothing had made him unleash it yet. His wife had given him heirs to succeed him and he was fit and healthy. Lolly had told her one day how he had once hurt his leg so badly during a joust that it had never healed. The never-ending pain had forced him to give up on what he loved the most: exercise. Jousting, wrestling, running, hunting, playing tennis, anything that could get his heart rate up and an endorphin release. Ella knew him enough now to understand just how traumatic it must have been. She knew how important it was for him to best other men at sports. And, as she happened to know a thing or two about his appetite, it was no wonder why he had died obese.

Bessie left for Yorkshire in tears. Ella had underestimated the authenticity of her love for Henry but buried her guilt as far down as she could. Henry was hers. She would not let anyone but the Queen in his bed.

She could not do anything else, now that her virtue had been compromised and that even Cardinal Wolsey was aware of it. Henry never hid anything from him. Besides, Ella knew that her heart would never heal if he was to choose Bessie over her. Lolly's words came back to her mind: '*Bessie Blount is the first woman who gave him a son. Henry Fitzroy.*' Ella smiled as she watched Bessie's carriage leave the palace grounds. Henry Fitzroy would never be born.

'You seem pleased to see her go,' Elsie's voice pulled Ella from her thoughts.

Maud was there too. Grabbing them both by the arm, she led them to the gardens. Margery was not with them, but the urge to share her secret was too strong to wait. Leading the way around the raised flower beds and the hawthorn hedges separating the different plants and areas into neat geometrical shapes, Ella second guessed herself. Maud and Elsie were her closest friends, but they were also friends with the Queen. If Ella was to lose their friendship for her betrayal, she would find herself even lonelier than during her first year of widowhood.

'Elizabeth, what is the matter?' Maud asked.

'I wish to confide in you, but I am fearful that what I will tell you will make you withdraw your friendship,' Ella told the truth, for once.

'This can never be!' Elsie exclaimed, taking her hand in hers.

'I agree. Your friendship is worth much to us,' Maud said.

'I have found love', Ella blurted out.

'Oh…' Elsie started to say, then took her hand back to rest it on her slightly round belly. More than once, she had shared how scared she was to conceive a child with her abusive husband, but it was now reality. Ella knew she would have given anything to be in love with the father of her baby. 'We must congratulate you!' Elsie said.

'Indeed! Do tell us more. Who is it? And why would you dread our reaction?' Maud asked.

Ella did not answer right away, unsure of how to break the news. Maud stopped walking. Her smile became a frown. Her chin and lower lip dropped down. She was looking at the fish pond at her feet without seeing it.

If they could not have been seen by anyone, Ella would have fallen onto her knees. Living in the sixteenth century had made her rather dramatic. Instead, she took Maud's hands in hers, real tears in her eyes.

'The King?' Maud whispered.

'My wish has always been and still is to serve the Queen faithfully. It was never my intention to be any source of pain. I did not foresee these feelings,' Ella tried to explain herself.

'Is that why Bessie was sent away?' Elsie wondered, her eyes rounder than her bump.

'Yes. I asked for her to be wed.'

'It is good that you did so, my friend. With her reputation, I do not think she could have pretended to such a good match otherwise,' Maud said.

'Am I your friend still?'

'How can you even doubt it! Elizabeth, it is not my place to have an opinion on whom the King chooses to share his bed.'

'One cannot decide where one's heart goes to,' Elsie added.

'My dear, are in you in love with His Grace? Truly?' Maud asked.

'I... am.'

'I know you never felt this way for your late husband, God rest his soul. I am delighted for you,' she pressed Ella's hand in hers.

Elsie, quite surprisingly, hugged her. Ella had to fight against tears of relief. She would have never expected to build such strong friendships with women born and raised five hundred years before her, but could not imagine her life without them. And Maud was right. In almost four years of marriage, Ella had never felt for Nicholas the passion she felt now for Henry. For the next half hour, she told her friends all about her relationship with him, forgetting all decency. Five centuries had not changed much when it came to friends chatting to each other about sex.

Ella was dressed before dawn. Looking down at the Thames through one of the bay windows of Baynard's Castle that October morning, she was struggling to keep her eyes open. She wished she could have slept, but her mind kept wandering back to the Queen, with whom Henry had spent the night. At first, she had suspected jealousy to be keeping her awake, but it had become clear that it was guilt. Henry had gifted this castle to his wife the day before their marriage. It was owned by her. Last night was the first time Ella had occupied a room in it since she had become Henry's mistress.

For years, she had watched movies and read books about married men betraying their wives and had always loathed both husbands and mistresses. Tables had turned and she was now the other woman. For as long as she was in Henry's company, Ella was in high spirits, but as soon as he left the room, it was as if a hand was slowly crushing her soul. She often spent hours trying to put a word on how she saw herself – it was never a praise.

'Lady Exeter, why this sorrow on such an exciting day?' the high-pitched voice of the French Queen resonated in the dark corridor.

'Your Grace,' Ella curtseyed to Queen Mary. 'I see we both have trouble sleeping.'

'Indeed. This child shall have as much stamina as my beloved brother!' she joked. At twenty-two, she was already expecting her third child with Charles.

'You have my compassion,' Ella returned the joke, making the French Queen laugh.

'I am afraid we do not have much time before the castle finds its liveliness for the day. My lady, I have found you uncomfortable in my presence the day past. Although I have known the Queen for most of my years and love her as a sister, I cannot be upset at the nature of your relationship with my brother. You bring him too much joy for me to ever resent you.'

Ella had not expected her to go so quickly to the point. She chuckled gawkily.

'It is the truth. It seems like you have been loved from afar for a long time. My brother was in the greatest distress during the summer of the past year. I should have known it was about a woman. I am very thankful that you have been spared from this disease.'

'I thank you,' Ella replied.

'Forgive me for reminding you of your late husband.'

'The Duke of Exeter was a kind man and I am blessed to have been his wife, however limited this time was'.

'My first husband was kind to me, too. I did not love him but I was saddened when he died. For a Frenchman, he was intelligent and wise,' the French Queen said.

Hearing her talk so highly of the late Louis XII was surprising to Ella. She had only been married to him for a few months and he had been almost thrice her age.

The women watched in silence the sky change its colours above the London skyline. Tower Bridge, the Elizabeth Tower and most buildings that made London the city of Ella's childhood had not been built yet, but the sun rising above the hundreds of church spires was making the city every bit as magical as it was in her memories.

London was preparing for a new day, which would see Hal's betrothal to the Princess Renée broken. As the daughter of Louis XII, she had lost much of her value at his death. The new king of France, who was the late king's cousin, wanted his own daughter on the throne of England: Princess Charlotte, aged two. Wolsey had negotiated a new treaty with the French over the summer to make it happen. It was to be signed today.

'May I share a thought that ought to stay private?' the French Queen asked.

'Of course.'

'The reason why my beloved brother chose the only man I wished to marry to escort me back from France, out of the many other men available then, is still out of my understanding,' she admitted, trying to stay serious.

Ella laughed, and the French Queen put a hand in front of her mouth to accompany her.

Ella had to make a conscious effort to remember the St Paul's Cathedral she had known for the first twenty years of her life when she arrived at the St Paul's of Henry's time for the signing of the treaty. Every time she was in London, she smiled at the thought that this St Paul's Cathedral looked more like Westminster Abbey than St Paul's Cathedral. It was on the exact site of the future one, but built in the same Gothic style as the abbey. The dome which Ella had known had now been replaced by the tallest spire she had ever seen. Even after so many years, she had to correct herself: it was the dome that would replace the spire after the infamous Great Fire of 1666, if it was going to happen again.

Ella watched the ceremony from the upper level, in the interior gallery. The Queen was reminiscing about the day when she had married there Henry's brother, Prince Arthur, about seventeen years before, but was upset to see her husband betroth their son to yet another French girl.

With this new treaty, the toddler-princess had her entire future decided. Of course, if she happened to die before her wedding day, Hal would marry any hypothetical sister she might have by then. If Hal was to die first, she would marry Arthur instead. The most shocking in that kind of clause was that it did not even shock Ella anymore. The crown was bigger than the individual. It was the only thing that mattered. It was why Henry had battled so much to have a son in the history she was the only one to remember.

There were rejoicings and tournaments to celebrate the new treaty, but Hal and Ella managed to find their way to the gardens at the end of the day. They walked underneath the wooden pergola, leaving behind the music and the noise. Hal was silent. At seven years old, he was getting more serious every time Ella saw him and this new treaty was not making things easier for him to remember that he was, after all, just a child.

'I had to profess my love for Princess Charlotte to the French ambassador today. Bet, I lied. I do not love her,' he confessed, blushing.

'Of course not. You have never met her, and let me remind you she is two years of age!'

'Mother says she loved Father deeply even before their marriage.'

'They had known each other for many years before they were wed,' Ella pointed out. Considering what she was doing to his parents' marriage, she would have loved to talk about anything else, but realised Hal had worries that no one ever took the time to listen to.

'Yes. Mother was wed to my uncle first. Bet, do you think the princess will love me once we are married?'

'She would be a fool not to.'

He laughed but soon regained seriousness. 'Did you love Nicholas when you married him?'

'No. It came later,' Ella lied. She did not have to tell him that it had never happened. It was best to keep him motivated. Henry had decided his son would marry a French princess and it would happen, whether the groom and bride wanted it or not.

'It is my hope the same shall happen to the princess and myself, then,' he said. 'I have been thinking about Martin Luther,' he changed the subject, lowering his voice.

'What about him?'

'Well, mostly about the translation of the theses into English. I found a copy between the pages of a book during my Greek lesson.'

Ella raised an eyebrow. 'What did Dr Linacre say about it?' she asked. If Hal's tutor was a good friend to John Colet, he had so far never been heard commenting on Luther.

'He asked me to fold it away and concentrate on my lesson,' Hal explained. 'Who do you think placed the theses there? There used to be many of them everywhere in the palace, too. Father and the cardinal are not very pleased about that person.'

Ella pressed her lips against one another. 'I do not know,' she lied. 'Did you enjoy your lesson?' she changed the subject.

'Very much. I am very fortunate to learn Greek. Many men do not know Greek.'

'I do not know Greek either.'

Hal acquiesced. 'And many men do not know Latin,' he added in a murmur. 'It shall be beneficial for them to have the theses translated.'

Ella hesitated. She looked around, making sure they were out of earshot. 'Are your thoughts similar regarding other works?' she asked.

'What do you mean?' he wondered, but Ella let him think by himself. 'The Bible,' he understood. He remained quiet for a minute. 'Men who have not been taught Latin should have the opportunity to read the Bible still,' he came to his own conclusion.

His eyes were so round they were eclipsing half of his face. He looked at Ella as if he had verbalised the most horrifying insult, the most sickening slander that the world had ever seen.

Ella took his hand in hers. 'I agree with this statement,' she reassured him softly and observed him as his tensed muscles relaxed one after the other.

'The Bible is the word of God. They say translating it is heresy as they want to prevent errors in the translation,' he reminded her.

'They also reject Martin Luther's theses, although his message is for us to remember the importance of the Scriptures over earthly money,' Ella retorted.

Hal opened his mouth but no sound came out. There was this wrinkle between his eyebrows, much too deep for so young a child, but this opportunity was too life-changing to be wasted. Ella may have been watching history in the making.

'Why...' Hal started to say, but was visibly struggling to form a sentence that made sense.

'Why do they condemn the translation in English?' she did it for him. He nodded. 'The fear is that common people would realise that some men of the Church do not behave as they are supposed to. It is my thinking on the matter. Greed is powerful,' she explained.

'Why does Father ignore it?' Hal asked, dismayed.

'You are finding difficult to question what you have been taught for seven years, but your father has been taught the same for twenty-seven years. We must be compassionate.'

Hal agreed but still looked confused when he was called back to the party. Ella was grinning internally. She would have given everything she owned for Nicholas to hear the conversation she just had had. He had died before seeing his wish of an officially translated Bible fulfilled. There was very little hope Henry would ever accept the idea, but Hal would. Ella would make sure of it.

'My Lady Exeter,' the voice of John Colet interrupted her thoughts.

'Master Colet,' she replied. 'I was just discussing our friend with my lord the prince of Wales,' she declared, insisting on the word "friend."

John Colet was never easy to read. As the King's chaplain and a reputed scholar, he had to maintain, at all times, a certain control over his facial muscles. But the silent mention of Martin Luther's name in the same sentence as Hal's was so unexpectedly grave, and could have such far-reaching consequences, that his lips parted from one another and his eyebrows jumped up to the middle of his forehead.

'May I sit with my lady?' he asked once he regained countenance.

'Of course.'

'I trust that my lady is aware that the road she has taken may lead to dangerous waters.'

'It is the prince who came to me with questions. I only answered them,' Ella retorted, defensive. 'A copy of the translated theses has been found by the prince in a book during his Greek lesson.'

'It was my doing,' he surprised her. 'Thomas Linacre has been a friend to me for many years. I had but little doubt that he would let my lord the prince keep it.'

'What are Dr Linacre's thoughts on it?'

'He does not wish to involve himself in theological debates but sees no harm in others doing so.'

'The prince appears to question the unquestioned,' Ella simply said.

A smile brought light to Colet's somewhat tired eyes. He did not reply and did not have to. King Henry IX was going to be the first king of England to allow his subjects to read the Holy Book in English without fearing for their lives. Ella had decided it.

20.

HER MOST INFLUENTIAL SELF
1518

Princess Charlotte was absent when she was formally betrothed to Hal, a few days after the signature of the treaty. Ella turned a blind eye on the money Henry was spending on celebratory jousts, banquets and pageants, all on the promise of a marriage that would not take place in over a decade, if at all – Henry was still open to a friendship with the Holy Roman emperor.

Cardinal Wolsey had reunited the entire court in his palace, but also the all-time favourite dishes of both his king and his queen; baked lampreys and game pies stuffed with oranges for him, porpoise soup for her, and even a glorious roasted peacock. At some point during the meal, the bird pie turned out to be an actual pie of birds. The crust was cracked open, and instead of the usual smell of cooked meat and spices, ten very much alive birds were released from it and went flying around the great hall. The Queen laughed and the guests clapped, even Ella, who was trying to suppress the side of her that still cared about animal cruelty.

Ella was lying in her bed at the end of a long night of dancing when Henry discreetly joined her, getting naked under the covers and taking her in his arms.

'Did you enjoy tonight's festivities, my adored one?' he asked.

'Very much. The cardinal is a good host. I suppose anyone presenting you with quince marmalade is bound to be one,' she teased him and his unconditional love for this thick, sliceable jam.

Henry burst with laughter. 'You know me well! But that was an imprudent laugh. Do you think someone heard it?' he wondered.

'King Francis probably heard it.'

Henry laughed again. Wolsey had had built lodgings over no less than three floors to receive royal family and high-ranking guests, but Henry's laugh was loud and recognisable. Ella's instinct was to overthink and panic about the possibility of the Queen knowing from whose room her husband's laugh had come from, but the softness of Henry's lips on hers made her forget about it.

When Ella woke up the next morning, her body was aching from the dancing and the sex, but the corners of her mouth rose uncontrollably. If she needed tangible proof that the cardinal was aware of her relationship with Henry, the room she had been allocated for the night was it. The linenfold panelling of the walls had been hung with a deep red velvet embroidered with Henry's heraldry, from the lion and fleur-de-lys to the red dragon of Cadwallader and the greyhound of Richmond. In the corner of the room, a chair was covered with expensive Italian silk, matching the silken hangings of her heavy wooden framed bed. On the sideboard table by the door was a crystal clock. Henry's love for clocks, which were a luxury to own, was well-known.

He was still laying by her side, looking so peaceful that Ella could have stayed in this bed, watching him sleep, for the entire day. A noise in the room next door brought her back to reality. It was daylight already and she had to have someone come help her get dressed. She kissed him before sitting up and removing the covers, but was without warning, grabbed by the waist and pulled backwards. She was now lying on her back, feeling him hard against her thigh.

'They are all expecting you soon,' Ella managed to say under his pressing lips.

'Then they must all wait,' Henry retorted. She giggled as his hand caressed her belly, and opened her legs.

They did all wait. Even the Queen, who lingered with two of her maids at the end of the corridor to catch sight of the woman with whom her husband was now cheating on her. Under her silver damask gown, Ella's heart missed a beat. Maybe two. Her eyes filled with tears as she was faced with the magnitude of the pain, grief and betrayal she had just inflicted on a woman she respected and even loved.

The Queen walked towards Ella, her head held high but her chin trembling. Ella's body refused to move. She was still standing in front of the door when Henry exited the room. He bumped into her.

'Darling, why are you...' he started to say, but noticed his wife. 'Katherine, good morning,' he had the audacity to say.

'I had so very few friends,' the Queen declared, heartbreak in her voice.

Ella wondered what she meant. Maybe, she wanted to know why her husband had to pick one of her rare friends as a mistress when he had so many other options. Or, maybe, she was realising her mistake to ever consider Ella as a friend.

'Elizabeth, join the others,' the King told her.

'No. Please, stay,' the Queen disagreed.

Ella knew who to listen to. She barely even curtsied before escaping from the most awkward of situations, feeling like she could throw up any second but also somewhat amazed at the Queen's bravery for telling Henry no. Even in a world where he had been given everything he desired, even in a world where he had not picked up on the habit of beheading people every other day, it was never a good idea to tell Henry no.

Maud and Elsie were chatting with Blanche and Margery when Ella reached the great hall. For the first time in years, she thanked the heaviness of her gown. She would have barged in the room like an insane person if her outfit had been practical enough. Instead, she walked to her friends in the usual stiff way of high-ranked women sinking under the weight of luxury, but Maud saw right away that something was wrong and extended a hand.

'It is no secret anymore,' Ella quavered, briefly pressing Maud's for reassurance.

'Oh,' was all Maud could find to say. Elsie's teeth sank into her lower lip.

'My lady, if I may ask, what is no secret anymore?' Blanche asked.

'You may not,' Elsie immediately retorted.

Blanche's cheeks turned red and she looked down on the ground. Ella shook her head. 'It is but a matter of time before everyone knows,' she said.

'What is it?' Margery intervened.

'His Grace and I are in love. The Queen has just been told,' Ella declared, realising only now she had forgotten to put her friend in the confidence.

The light in Margery's almond eyes darkened. Ella felt guilty for keeping her out of the loop. The bigger the difference of rank between two people, the harder it was to maintain a healthy friendship. She was always spending more time with Maud and Elsie than with Margery. Ella was about to apologise when she read on her friend's face that she was not upset for having been lied to; Margery was looking at Ella as if she had stolen something that was not hers to take.

'You had the Queen's friendship and trust,' Margery stated, her voice cold as ice.

'Mistress Margery, remember your place,' Elsie snapped.

Ella wanted to assure she had taken no offence, but she knew that if she opened her mouth she would break down, sobbing at the truth of Margery's criticism. She watched the woman who was her friend a minute ago apologise and curtsey to her with an air of disgust on her face.

Word travelling faster at court than anywhere else, everyone knew everything before the Queen returned from her conversation with

Henry, her face pale and her eyes red. She disappeared in the chapel without a word.

Ella's throat filled with the bitter taste of vomit. She escaped with Maud and Elsie to the part of the gardens that was not undergoing works. It was cold and windy, but she needed to clear her head from the agony she had just read on the back-stabbed woman's face. After nine years of marriage and mistresses, the Queen had grown more or less accustomed to Henry's infidelity. Her misery was not caused by him. It was caused by her, Elizabeth White. Guilt overtook every vital organ in Ella's body and she bent forwards, her hands on her thighs. But her stomach, crushed by the fitted bodice, was empty.

The Queen did not deserve any of this. She had been sold in marriage to a foreign family, uprooted and married to some prince before she could master his language, widowed, then married to his brother whom she genuinely adored but had helplessly seen being unfaithful with several women as she grieved the loss of four of their six children.

And now, one of her friends is sleeping with him, the voice inside Ella's head reminded her.

But what about me? Ella thought. She did not deserve any of this either. She had travelled five hundred years into the past by mistake. Her entire life had been taken away from her. She had fought her way through it, but it had been taken away from her all over again when she had lost her job, been separated from the one she loved most and married off to a stranger. Again, she had fought her way through. She had learned to appreciate what she had rather than what she had not. Security over freedom. Wealth over love. And Nicholas had been taken away from her too.

For eight years, she had let other people decide what she was supposed to do with her life. Going to Henry's room that summer night, deciding to let herself feel something, had been a pure act of selfishness. But also of kindness to herself. She had made a choice, by herself and for herself. However sorry she was for hurting the Queen, she could not and would not regret it. She had put her own happiness first.

Henry did not bother with discretion when he joined her in her room that evening. Every single person under the roof of Hampton Court Palace was aware of their affair. He did not look ashamed of it at all. Ella took the deepest breath she had taken all day when he hugged her, his strong arms around her, enveloping her with the smell of orange water of his soap.

'It must have been a challenging day for you, my adored one.'

'I am fine. Please, do tell me what the Queen said. She has not spoken a word to me all day.'

'Katherine shall not bother you, I promise.'

'Henry, please, I shall not have any peace until I know what she said to you,' Ella begged, seeing on his face that he would have preferred to skip this part.

He sighed. 'She was not pleased. She wished to know if my love for you was true or carnal. She shed some tears when my answer was that it was the purest love I had ever borne anyone.' It was Ella's turn to sigh. She had no trouble imagining how destroying it must have been for a wife to hear those words from her husband. 'I am aware that it is sometimes preferable to keep some truths away from a distraught woman but I could not suffer for her to think I did not love you,' he explained himself, which was something he never did.

'I love you too. Please, tell me more.'

'I was not of even temper when she dared to ask me if you had consented to it,' he said, repulsed at the idea of raping a woman and even more that anyone could think him capable of doing so. Henry was many things, but not a rapist. He would have never forced himself on anyone, although it was more because of his deep need to be loved by all than because of his respect for a person's body and choice.

'Pain was asking, not her. Christendom knows how kind your soul is,' Ella reassured him.

'Indeed. I said something I did not mean then, but I have been thinking about it ever since, and I mean it now. I wish for you to be my sole mistress and for your position to be recognised.'

'What a French thing to say!' Ella joked.

But Henry was more serious than ever. He wanted her to become his mistress in an official manner, which was common for kings of France but had never been done by any English king before. Royal mistresses were like royal bastards, more or less hidden depending on the King's will. Not necessarily a secret, but never in the spotlight.

Ella sat down, processing the information. What Henry was offering her could possibly provide her with as much influence as Wolsey and the Queen together. If Henry's love for her was public, there was nothing courtiers would not do to please her and stay in *her* favour. What she would want would be what Henry would want. Ella chuckled, amazed. Henry was giving her every ounce of decency and respectability that he could afford to give her now that everyone knew she had had sex outside marriage with a man married to another woman.

The enthusiastic voice inside her head reminded her it had never been done before. Future records would mention her name as the first ever woman to be recognised as a king of England's mistress. Henry was giving her the world.

She looked up to him, only to find him waiting for her answer, a worried wrinkle between his eyebrows. Getting up on her feet, Ella caressed his cheek. He took her hand in his and kissed it with ardour.

'Are you certain this is what you desire?' she double-checked.

'There is so much love for you inside my heart it cannot contain it all. I am yours, you are mine, and my desire is that everyone should know,' he said.

'I can hardly think of anything that would make me happier,' Ella replied. She laughed as he pulled her up in his arms and made her twirl around the room.

'My love! My mistress! Elizabeth, my most adored one, you shall not be dowager duchess anymore. I shall make you Duchess of Exeter in your own right.'

'It is more honour than I deserve!'

'Nonsense. You deserve it all and more,' he retorted.

His happiness looked so genuine that, for the first time since they had begun their relationship two months earlier, Ella was the one to initiate sex. As a man living in the sixteenth century, Henry's view of sexual activities did not involve any acrobatic positions, oral sex, anal sex, or even women taking the lead, but as she started to take his clothes off, he kissed her passionately and ended up naked well before she did.

Queen Katherine revealed no emotion at the ceremony during which Ella was created Duchess *suo jure* of Exeter, in the presence chamber of Richmond Palace. Everyone that mattered was there to witness her accomplishment. All the nobility – with Norfolk and Buckingham in the front row. Ella had even asked that Maria, pregnant with her first child, and her husband travel back to court for the occasion. Every mouth that had once talked behind her back, spreading false rumours about who she was, was now open in bewilderment as she became her most influential self.

Ella had paired her green velvet gown with a kirtle of cloth of silver, as a nod to the royal colours of green and white. In its own way, it was sending the message that she was now Henry's most trusted, most faithful, most beloved subject – she was Henry's. And Henry was hers. His hose and shoes were of green velvet, his doublet of cloth of silver encrusted with diamonds and emeralds. They were a team.

Courtiers understood it. Overnight, they started to show her as much reverence as they showed their queen. They were hoping she would put in a good word for them during her private moments with Henry.

And Ella loved it.

She loved the power she held in her hands. It was indescribable. She could change the life of a man or a woman, for the better or worse, with only a few words. She was rewriting future Wikipedia pages with pillow-talk. She had never been so important. People could not disagree with her, ignore her, or leave her. All they could do was show their respect and admiration for her if they wanted their lives to improve. It was intoxicating.

There were times when Ella felt as if she were queen indeed. The actual one was spending so many hours praying in solitude that most courtiers no longer expected to see much of her. Once, Ella had made the incoherent dream of writing a letter to her father, with Pan on her lap and the blue sapphire ring on the hand that held the quill, informing him of the death of Queen Katherine and signing it *Elizabeth the Queen.*

She had never told Henry of it. The rule that viewed as treason the mention of his death applied to his wife too. Besides, like the vast majority of his subjects, Henry believed in ghosts and the devil, but also that a nightmare was the product of an evil spirit – the night mare – entering one's head and that the things seen or heard during one's nightmare were actually really there. If Ella had told him about her dream, he would have gone mental. Pretending to panic with him about a spirit messing with her head in her sleep was simply not something she was willing to put up with.

But this dream happened twice more before the New Year of 1519 and Ella came to wonder what would happen if the kingdom woke up one day to find its queen dead. Katherine was a popular consort, and although her love for Henry had become unrequited, she was still his first love and the mother of his children. That she would be deeply mourned was without question, but the voice at the back of Ella's head wanted to know only one thing: would she have a shot at queenship if it happened?

As Ella's destiny was to live and die five hundred years earlier than she thought, it would have been more interesting to do it with a crown of her head, but the obvious answer to her question was frustrating. Henry's grandfather, King Edward IV, had married for love an Englishwoman of genteel but unexceptional birth, Elizabeth Wydeville, and had created such hostility at his court that it had led him to be temporarily deposed and exiled. Kings of England were not supposed to marry one of their subjects. Kings of England were supposed to marry foreign princesses. They had to marry for wealth and diplomacy, not love.

A marriage with Henry was unlikely. 'Which might not be such a bad thing,' she reminded herself out loud one night.

Out of his six marriages, in that parallel reality that was somehow both in Ella's past and future, Henry had married for love a few times. He had also killed for it. Ella could never forget that queens Anne Boleyn and Katherine Howard had both lost their heads at his demand. It had to be better to live as Duchess of Exeter than die as queen of England.

21.

THE MOST HAPPY

1519

Almost like a renegade, Ella left the palace with Henry one cold morning of February, leaving queen and court behind to spend some quality time together as a couple. Nicholas Carew had surrendered his house of Beddington in Surrey to his royal friend for them to stay there for a week. Ella was to have Henry to herself. Better still, they were planning to share a room.

There was a lot of sex. But Ella also discovered what it meant to live with a Henry free from royal duties. Spending time in his company could never be without a certain amount of decorum, but the mood was so gentle that, as days passed, she noticed the servants grow more calm and relaxed even in his imposing presence.

They played and sang together every day after breakfast and she sketched a portrait of him while he was writing her a poem. As the snow was falling outside, covering the red brick house with a veil of sparkling white, they went to the kitchen and baked apple fritters together. He laughed loudly as the cook struggled to recover from the surprise, and even served him a pint of ale. The following morning, he let Ella replace his barber and shave him.

She could not remember a time when she had been so completely happy. The day before they were supposed to leave, a radiant sun was melting the snow and they went on a wild ride on their horses through the gardens to see which was faster. Despite Ella's best efforts, Henry's had a more confident rider on its back and was winning. Her grey horse reached the cavern first, though, and she looked back at Henry with consternation: 'you let us win!' she complained.

'Would you have rather lost?' he cackled.

'Yes! This is cheating!'

'I shall let you lose on the way back to the house, then, but let us see this from the inside first, as we have yet to discover it,' he decided, pointing his chin at the cavern.

He helped Ella down her horse and led the way inside. She had not visited many grottos in her life besides the underground one in twenty-first century Leeds Castle or the shell-made one in Margate. This one was radically different than anything she could have expected. A succession of four small rooms, one of them so low Henry had to bend forward, the grotto was patterned with uneven stones of different shades from brown to a light pink. Ella was holding Henry's hand, appreciating the intimate atmosphere and the rays of light that managed to peep through some of the rocks and turned the inside of the cave almost pink.

'It is beautiful', she whispered.

'Indeed. I believe it would look remarkable in my gardens of Richmond. Would that be to your taste?'

'You decided to build something similar for yourself the second you set foot in here.'

He laughed, his open mouth eating half of his face, and they both looked up and around as his laugh resonated inside the cavern. 'I love that you always speak the truth to me,' he said, turning to her.

'I love that you always let me,' she replied. 'I love you, Henry.' He bent forward and kissed her tenderly before they both realised their bodies wanted more than a brief kiss. Standing there, in a secret place, shrouded in a magical pink light, they wanted more.

'Here?' he asked between kisses.

'Why not?' she said, already catching her breath and placing his hand on her breasts.

The sex that followed may not have been the most comfortable Ella had ever had, but it was so passionate that neither of them minded. The sewing along the neckline of Ella's dress broke and, as a multitude of pearls were sprinkled everywhere at their feet, they chose to ignore what the servants who had followed them would hear.

Henry and Ella came back to the house giggling and Ella went to change her gown. Her pearls were still scattered around the pink grotto and, as two servants were helping her change into her gown of green satin, she considered asking one of them to get them back for her, wondering if it was worth the humiliation of explaining how she had lost them.

'My lady, where are all the pearls gone?' a little girl of about ten years old asked, holding in her arms the blue fabric that had been ripped of its jewels.

She was told off for impertinently addressing her without having been invited to but Ella silenced the complains. 'In the cavern, across the gardens,' she replied. 'What is your name?' she said.

'Mabel, my lady.'

'For how long have you worked here?'

'Four years, my lady.'

'And you are?'

'Eleven, my lady,' she stuttered, blushing under Ella's scrutiny.

There was little to no chance that Ella had ever met that child before, but something about her felt familiar – her impertinence, probably. The girl had tightened her grip on the gown and was looking apprehensively at the woman finishing to smooth the embroidered cuffs coming out of Ella's sleeves.

'Do you know where the cavern I mentioned is?' Ella asked the girl. She nodded.

'Answer, child!' the woman barked. Ella did not remember her name, but she irritated her.

'Quiet,' she snapped. 'Mabel, you are to go to the cavern. Take one of your choosing with you. Bring me my pearls. I shall give you and your friend some once you are back. Quick, now, it must be done before it is dark.'

The young girl's eyes did not even bother to check with the other woman this time. She put down the gown on the first piece of furniture she found, curtseyed and left the room in a silent hurry. An air of disapproval appeared on the woman's face and Ella demanded for her to go away.

One morning at the end of March, Ella was getting ready to celebrate with Henry and the court her first Annunciation as the royal mistress. She moaned in pain as her bodice was tightened. She sent everyone out of the room. It had been over two weeks. Two weeks without a number two! Ella refused to share her digestive troubles with Henry, or even with any physician, since not a single one of them knew about medical privacy, but her bowels were starting to hurt. There was to be a feast today, and although it was Friday and that one did not eat meat on Fridays, she was feeling sick at the thought of having to digest all the trout, sturgeon, eels and other fish that would be on the table.

She was so desperate that she sent for Maud. She would have sent for Elsie as well, but she was recovering from the birth of her baby boy and had not been churched yet. Ella was sitting by the window when Maud arrived. She curtseyed and Ella waved the formalities away with a grimace.

'I am in need of your help,' she announced.

'My dear, you do not look so well,' Maud exclaimed.

'Give me your word that you shall never speak of this to anyone,' Ella said.

'I give you my word.'

'I have not been able to relieve myself for a fortnight.'

'Jane Popincourt once shared that senna does wonders,' Maud told her as naturally as if they were chatting about soap scents. 'And, when I was expecting my William, I used to eat a handful of prunes every night. In fact, the same was done whilst I was expecting my daughters. I seem to always find myself with this problem when I am with child. Elizabeth, when were your last courses?'

'I am not with child.'

'When?'

'I expected it to happen ten days ago. Eleven, maybe. But it does often happen later than it is supposed to.'

'It is true. It is also difficult to know for sure if one is with child before it quickens inside the womb,' Maud admitted, looking like she was merely saying it to make her feel better.

Ella sighed. If only she could have popped to the supermarket and peed on a stick. Out of nowhere, she missed the twenty-first century with a violence she had not felt in years. Her mind started racing, panicking over a possible pregnancy. Henry had been her lover for seven months and his sexual appetite had been considerable compared to her late husband's. Or, maybe, it was her own. They could not take their hands off each other, and if she used to calculate her ovulation window during her marriage to Nicholas, she had let go of this habit in her current relationship. She and Henry had sex every single night they spent together. That was a lot of opportunity for her to conceive.

Inhale, exhale, Ella reminded herself. She took a deep breath, trying to chase the memory of Inez's cold corpse away.

'Do I still have your word that you are to never divulge our conversation?' she asked Maud.

'Of course.'

'What if I was with child but did not want to be?'

'My friend, I am aware of your fears of motherhood, but I beg you to not do this!' Maud cried, falling on her knees and grabbing Ella's hands.

'Inez lost three babies and her own life to motherhood,' Ella said and freed her hands more harshly than she intended to.

Maud got up and sat next to her. 'It was a tragedy. She died. My mother died, too. I shall always mourn them, but may I now remind you of the fate of Jane Appleton? How long her agony lasted after she had taken those devilish herbs?' she reminded her with terror in her eyes.

Ella closed hers as she remembered the awful screams of the maid of honour. A couple of years before, the unmarried fifteen-year-old had ingested a mixture of plants supposed to terminate the unwanted foetus inside of her. It had worked so well it had killed the mother too. Ella hopelessly looked around the room, as if the answer to her situation was hidden somewhere the scarce pieces of furniture and would come to her.

It was 1519. Abortion was both as reliable as contraception and as hazardous as childbirth. In desperation, Ella burst into tears. Maud took her hands back in hers and held on to them tightly.

'Elizabeth, please, do not weep. All will be well. Look at me, I am the mother of three children! And Elsie has just been safely delivered of a son. I cannot say that fearing childbirth is foolish, but I do believe you fear it more than you should,' Maud tried to reassure her.

'I might not even be with child,' Ella murmured, half-convinced.

'You might not. My advice would be to keep your suspicions to yourself at least until April. If your courses have not happened by then, you…' she paused. Her eyes widened brusquely. 'This unborn child is the King's!' she exclaimed, her hands abandoning Ella's to fly to her mouth, as if the identity of the father had only now come to her mind.

Ella would have laughed if her predicament had not been so delicate. She closed her eyes, wondering what Lolly would have said about her granddaughter having been knocked up by Henry VIII.

For some years now, when Ella had been reminded of the fact that she existed in a century that was not hers, she had not been able to help but wonder what her presence alone had destroyed. A person being the product of a conception that had happened at a precise moment, the list of names that her time travel had erased from history probably did not stop at Henry's illegitimate child.

But now she was carrying another one of them. A replacement to the never-born Henry Fitzroy. It was the fourth of April, and if a few prunes a day had helped Ella with her intestinal problems, it had not made her period reappear. Her breasts were so tender that she did not need a pregnancy test anymore. She was pregnant with a child that would have, if it was to live, two parents born five centuries apart. It was slightly insane.

Ella did not know how to tell Henry. She had no idea whether or not he would be happy at the idea of becoming the father to a child that could not ever be in the line of succession. Maud and Elsie, the latter being now churched and back in public life, were both pressing her to tell him. So was John Colet, whom Henry had recently appointed as Ella's chaplain as well as his own, on her request. He was standing silently by her side as she watched Henry fight with his five-year-old son with wooden practice swords. Pan was dozing in her arms, his body inflating and deflating at the slow but regular rhythm of his breathing.

'His Grace is a good father,' she told Colet to give herself some courage.

'Indeed. And my lord the Duke of York shall be an equally good brother,' he replied, watching Arthur's sword dance. His round cheeks were red with effort, his blue eyes radiating with happiness.

'Is it your belief that His Grace shall be pleased?' Ella asked.

'Elated, I am sure. My lady must not fear,' Colet affirmed.

At the end of his lesson, Arthur waved at Ella and left with his lady mistress. Colet surreptitiously disappeared when Henry came to give Ella a kiss on the lips. He always knew how to read a room.

'Arthur is doing well at sword-fighting. He shall be a fine soldier,' Henry told her.

'He will bring glory and pride to the kingdom of England, I am certain,' Ella replied in a way she knew Henry would like, although her mind was far from thinking about Arthur's possible future military career. 'My love, I am with child,' she blurted out.

'You are?' he asked, grinning. His laugh filled the space when she confirmed. His grip now as soft as if she were made of glass, he took her in his arms and kissed her on the forehead. 'My adored one, how wonderful! When shall we meet our child?'

'This winter, I believe. Before December. Are you happy?'

'The most happy. Are you well? You must rest as much as possible now,' he mansplained, his concern about her health and the health of their unborn child so genuine it surrounded Ella with a sensation of safety. For a second, she forgot why she was terrified.

'I am well. I am not experiencing any sickness yet.'

'Good, good. Darling of mine, a child! Are you as delighted as I am?'

'The thought of childbirth frightens me,' she admitted.

He kissed her again on the forehead. 'Only the best shall be appointed to attend you, do not fret.'

Ella had to fake a smile. Even the best of this era sometimes needed convincing when it came to wash their hands.

22.

TAINTING THE DIGNITY OF THE QUEEN

1519

Ella's pregnancy was still a secret when she attended the marriage of her namesake, Elizabeth Bryan, to Sir Nicholas Carew. Elizabeth was the sister of Sir Francis – who seemed to have abandoned the idea of marrying at all since she had rejected him – and the former mistress of Henry himself. He had deserted her bed before his affair with Bessie Blount and Ella did not think of her as much of a threat. Besides, worrying about the Queen's imminent reaction to her pregnancy did not leave any room for anything else. She had managed to convince Henry that he had to tell Katherine in private before they made her pregnancy known, and he had asked her to tell his sons.

At the end of the ceremony, Ella took the boys and their cousin Margaret to the garden. She was not sure how they would take the news. Hal, especially. The eight-year-old was very attached to what was right and what was wrong, and Ella was painfully aware that a man was not supposed to start a family whilst married to somebody else. Hal had reacted positively to the romantic relationship between Ella and his father, but a sibling was a different story.

'I have some news,' she said, making them all sit on a bench and standing in front of them.

She smiled through her fears. The Tudor gene was a strong one. The three of them were pale skinned with freckles on their noses and had big blue eyes framed with gorgeous ginger hair. Ella thought about the child-to-be in her womb and wondered if it would look like the three royal children facing her or more like herself, with green eyes and light brown hair. If it was to live, at least.

'Happy news or sad news?' four-year-old Margaret asked.

'You shall tell me what you think. I am to be a mother later this year,' Ella told them.

'Congratulations, dearest Bet!' Hal exclaimed and jumped on his feet to hug her. Arthur and Margaret imitated him. 'Have you told Father?' Hal wondered.

'I have. He is delighted. My dears, do you understand what this means?'

'A new sibling. I hope for a brother!' Arthur cried, holding his fists tight under his chin.

'I shall like a sister best,' Hal disagreed.

'Are you all pleased?' Ella asked, astounded than none of them had asked about Katherine.

'I am! I shall not be the youngest anymore!' Margaret smiled.

'You have always been like a mother to me. I am much pleased with this new sibling,' Hal said, looking at her in the eyes as if he could read all the extent of her anxiety. Ella hugged her beautiful boy close to her heart.

There was no word strong enough to describe her relief. She could live without becoming a birth mother but she could not live without the love of her miracle boy. She had not given birth to him but she had given him life. He had died once without her and had taken so many people down with him, but he was alive now, with this magnificent mind of his. As unmotherly as it sounded, he was more important to her that the foetus growing inside her.

And Ella could not forget that there was no prenatal care available. No vitamins. No water. No balanced diet. Vegetables were said to be the food of the poor, and although she had started to change the courtiers' minds about them, she still had to eat fish or meat about twice a day. And there was ale and wine. It was low in alcohol, but it was not water. She had very little hope the child would ever be born, never mind healthy.

Queen Katherine was pale as a ghost. She headed silently to the chapel. She had still not spoken a word to Ella since that morning in Hampton Court Palace, and this pregnancy was not to make things any easier. Ella wished she could have told her she did not particularly want this child either, but it would not have made her humiliation more bearable. Katherine had gone from first English queen to ever be divorced, put away and stripped of her title to first English queen to ever have to suffer the indignity of her husband parading his mistress in front of the court – and soon their child. Ella was not sure which was worse. In both versions of her life, Katherine had been betrayed by the people she loved and trusted, dishonoured for the world to see.

Ella walked back to the Queen's apartments. Her pregnancy had only been announced to a select few; Henry's younger sister and brother-in-law, Maud and Elsie, John Colet and Cardinal Wolsey. The other courtiers were far from guessing what was happening underneath her bejewelled gown and the women in the household did not even notice when she entered the room. They were too busy encircling a young and lively blond woman speaking with a French accent.

'Who is that?' Ella asked Elsie.

'The newest maid of honour to the Queen, my husband's niece,' she replied with disdain. 'Well, I do suppose Boleyn is my niece also,' she conceded.

Ella's heart dropped down to her feet like a free-falling lift. Ella used to see Thomas Boleyn around court before he was appointed Henry's ambassador in France, but she had never really thought about the day she would come face-to-face with his daughter. For years now, she had been in the household of the queen of France. Far away, across the channel. Yet, there she was now, transferred to the queen of England's household.

Anne Boleyn.

Ella's teeth clenched. Considering Henry and Katherine were both almost completely different people from their portraits, it was not such a shock that the woman looked so little like any painting she had ever seen of her in her old life. But she was there. The woman for whom Henry had fallen head over heels. Whom he had chosen to be his queen instead of the Queen. With whom he had changed England forever, at least in Ella's birth world. Ella touched the skin of her neck, thinking of how the now happily chatting maid had once seen her life end. On a scaffold. In blood and violence.

'Elizabeth, do you need to sit?' Maud asked, alarmed.

Of course I need to sit! That girl is going to take Henry away from me! Ella would have loved to scream to her face. 'I am fine,' she said.

'We all now have to suffer Mistress Mary's presence, I am afraid,' Elsie complained.

'I thought her name was Anne?' Ella grabbed her by the arm.

'Anne is the younger sister. I do believe she is still in France. That one is Mary. Every man at the French court is said to have ridden her,' she explained.

Mary Boleyn, of course! The other Boleyn. Her blond hair should have made Ella realise that the newcomer was not the famous dark-haired queen of her memories. She felt a certain shame in having forgotten Mary Boleyn's existence, but blamed it on what people from the twenty-first century called pregnancy brain.

The king of France once called her the great and infamous whore, Lolly's words came back to her granddaughter's mind. Ella chuckled, amazed and relieved. It was Mary Boleyn!

'I heard King Francis himself had her in his bed,' she said to regain some self-composure.

'Such a loose woman!' Maud despaired.

'A strumpet,' Elsie agreed. 'I suppose I should be pleased for my husband, as he loves them all,' she added.

Ella was about to remind her that Mary was her husband's niece when she remembered something else Lolly had said: *when she left the French court for the English one, she became a mistress of Henry VIII.'* She frowned.

'I shall talk to the King and have her removed,' she declared, and left the room.

She would not let Mary Boleyn become Henry's mistress, especially not now that she herself was pregnant and thus forbidden to sleep with him. People strongly believed a man's penis was mighty enough to hurt a foetus inside a womb. Henry had always had a mistress to get through his wife's pregnancies, and if he had promised her he would only sleep with Katherine until their child was born, Ella was not convinced she believed him. Mary Boleyn had to go.

On her way to Henry, Ella stumbled upon Cardinal Wolsey and realised it would be easier to let him find a way to get rid of Mary without creating any tensions between Henry and his friend Thomas Boleyn.

'My Lady Exeter. Are you well?' he enquired, his hands joined in front of him.

'Very well, I thank Your Eminence. May I have a word?'

'Of course. First, allow me to congratulate you on the delightful news I received from the King regarding your situation', he said, smiling.

Ella knew that he was one the rare men at court who would never, even for a second, think ill of her. With two children of his own from a woman he had recently married off to someone in the country because she had become an embarrassment to his social status, he could only sympathise. Ella remembered what Hal had told her one day during one of their clandestine conversations about religion: 'it seems to me that the Church turns a blind eye when suitable.'

They started walking together and Ella thanked him for his well wishes.

'Your Eminence sees me rather dismayed. I have just met the young daughter of Sir Thomas Boleyn,' she told him, and read in his brown hooded eyes that he knew perfectly well what the problem was.

'She is notorious. I do not believe His Grace has been made aware of her history at the French court,' he said, as he could not be heard criticising Henry's decision to bring Mary home.

'It is very dear to my heart that she should not taint the dignity of the Queen.'

'Your devotion to Her Grace is unparalleled. I shall do what is necessary.'

'May I remind Your Eminence of the King's affection for the girl's father…' Ella started to say, trying to tell him he could not send Mary back to the queen of France like a plagued dog.

'My lady can be assured that I shall find a suitable match for the young Boleyn,' the cardinal replied, and then chatted inconsequentially about the weather until he had walked her back to the Queen's apartments.

Ella ignored Mary Boleyn for the rest of the day, too worried she might come to like her, which would double the guilt she already felt for playing with her life. If there was one person in the room who was tainting the dignity of the Queen, it was not Mary. And yet, it was Mary who was about to be sent away. The poor girl had not done anything wrong, but she was soon to be married to a man she had likely never met.

She will never get to sleep with Henry, Ella said to herself. She smiled.

Less than a week later, Mary Boleyn was married to William Carey, a wealthy courtier and a distant cousin to Henry. On Ella's advice, they were given a large house in Lancashire as a wedding present. It was far enough from court to dissuade them from coming too often, and as soon as Mary found herself pregnant, she would be stranded there.

She would be too busy running her household and raising her children to even think about coming to court anymore.

Ella celebrated her success with the order of a carcanet made of gold and emeralds, with H and E letters intertwined. After Bessie Blount, she had sent yet another one of Henry's known mistresses away from him, their life and their relationship. She might not be a queen, but Henry would not be anyone else's but hers.

It was the end of June before Ella found any happiness in her pregnancy. The past weeks had been a succession of disagreeable symptoms. It had started with the realisation that her two favourite things were making her nauseous, to the point where she had to vomit right away: marzipan and the scent of orange water used to perfume Henry's clothes.

As soon as Henry had banned both from the court for the duration of her pregnancy and had supplied the palace with ginger to help with her symptoms, she had developed an obsession with bananas, which were simply not known to the England of 1519.

And, as if her nausea and frustration were not burdensome enough, her body had decided to reduce her bladder to the size of a lentil and bring back her dear friend constipation into her life.

For a man born in 1491, Henry was of surprisingly great emotional support. Not a single day went by without him telling her how beautiful she was, asking her what he could do to please her and reminding her how much he loved her. They had not had sex ever since he had found out about his unborn child, but she often caught him staring appreciatively at her breasts. They seemed to be carrying foetuses of their own as they had accompanied her belly in its growth spurt – Ella had even caught Elsie staring at them.

Ella was torn between her hurry for this pregnancy to be over and her terror of the actual day she would have to give birth, but something changed at the end of June. It was one of the first warm and sunny days of the year. Ella and Henry were sitting together in the gardens of Greenwich Palace, on a bench underneath the arbor, enjoying the privacy that the leafy arch was providing them. Henry was humming the latest song he intended to write, accompanied by the buzzing of the bees busying themselves in the vine overhead, and Ella was reading. As she turned the delicate page of her book, she felt a little twitch in her stomach.

Did he hear anything? she thought, her cheeks flushed, convinced she had just had a wind in his presence. The flutter happened again, only a few seconds later. Ella closed her book and waited for the next one. It was as if popcorn was gently popping inside her.

'Henry!' she exclaimed when it happened a third time.

'What is it? Are you unwell? Is it the child? Tell me!' he started to panic.

'I think our baby likes when you sing!'

'Oh, has it quickened?'

'Yes. I wish you could feel what I am feeling!'

'What is it like? I have often wondered.'

'It is almost as p… butterflies,' Ella said, remembering at the last second that Henry had no idea what popcorn was. 'Or bubbles. It fades almost as soon as it appears. It is odd, yet very pleasant.'

Henry took her hand and kissed it lovingly but Ella was too shaken up to notice. She was about four months pregnant and, for the first time, the part of her that hoped for a miscarriage had disappeared. She was not scared of anything happening to her anymore. Only the baby mattered. There would be pain, there would be blood. There might be even death. But it would all be worth it if the tiny little being she was growing inside her was to live.

Ella smiled as one more popcorn popped and did not even bother to open her book again. Her hands on her belly, she understood that she was so in love with the sensation that she had already become addicted to it. It was her baby. Her sixteenth-century baby, born five hundred years before her. And she would do anything to keep it safe.

23.

THE ANGRY BEAST
1519

Ella was heavily pregnant when she spotted young Mabel in the palace. Elizabeth Carew had grown so attached to the little servant in her husband's service that she brought her anywhere she went. Ella put down her quill and looked at her without really seeing her, thinking about how she had nothing in the world but a kind mistress.

According to Elizabeth, the girl had been taken in her husband's service when she had become an orphan. He suspected her to be his illegitimate half-sister, but his father refused to admit to anything. The poor girl was nothing, and ever since Ella had felt her child's first kick, her heart was in her mouth every time she laid her eyes on her. She picked up her quill and added an extra line to her will, bequeathing a more than generous sum of money to the Carews to be spent on the girl's dowry if she herself came to die prematurely. Money could not be taken to the grave anyway.

Feeling lighter than when she had started to draw up her will, Ella put her hands on her large belly and silently promised her child that, even if she died, she would not do so before delivering him or her safely into the world.

Henry's appeasing words came back to her mind: 'our child shall be acknowledged and raised alongside Arthur and Margaret, whether you live through the birth or not.'

Ella took a deep breath. Her baby was all that mattered.

'My Lady Exeter, Her Grace wishes to talk to you,' she heard a voice behind her but barely had the time to understand what it meant before the Queen entered the room, followed by the Countess of Salisbury. Ella curtseyed as low as she could before Queen Katherine showed her to a chair.

'I have something to give you, my lady,' the Queen said as the countess reverently gave her what turned out to be the supposed girdle of the Virgin Mary.

Ella's eyes widened. She did not believe there were any genuine holy relics. As far as she was concerned, the mother of Jesus had not dropped her belt as she ascended to Heaven and what was now in her hands was not holy. But the Queen believed it. And she was giving it to her.

'Thank you,' Ella murmured.

'The girdle of Our Lady was given to me for the birthing of my children and eased my sufferings, as it did for His Grace's most gracious mother Queen Elizabeth and His Grace's sister the queen dowager of Scotland. It is my hope it shall ease your sufferings too.'

'Your Grace is very kind,' was all that Ella managed to say. She cleared her throat. 'May I speak privately with Your Grace?' she asked.

The Countess of Salisbury left the room. Before Ella opened her mouth, the Queen raised her palm towards her.

'I have come to the realisation that the King's love for you is a blessing as it brings him joy. You have my gratitude and my best wishes for the health of your child.'

'Your Grace must know that it was never my intent to cause harm. I am deeply sorry.'

'Do not be. My husband now looks at you in the way he used to look at me. I am content to see such love in his life. It is my hope for us to be friends again.'

Ella was still staring at the tapestry on the wall long after the door had closed behind the Queen. She had always known her to be of remarkable kindness but would have never guessed she would one day come to her with a friendship offering. Somehow, she would have liked it better if Katherine had kept on despising her until the day she died.

'Her husband is the father of my child,' Ella murmured, taken aback.

It is not kindness if she has no choice but to make peace with what Henry wants, the cynical voice inside her head insisted. Ella sniffed inelegantly. Henry wanted to be seen with his mistress in public without having to deal with his wife's feelings, so the Queen had suppressed them. After almost a year, she had come to terms with it. She had been taught all her life that pleasing her husband in all things was her duty; that was exactly what she was doing. She was putting his happiness before hers.

Ella could have seen sense in the situation had the Queen done it for her sons' sake, in order for the six of them to become some sort of reconstituted family. But the truth was a lot sadder: the Queen was only sacrificing herself for the sake of her cheating husband.

2017. It was mid-morning, mid-week, mid-Winter. Westminster Abbey was desert, allowing Emily and Ella to wander around in a peaceful silence. In the Lady Chapel, where all Tudor reigning monarchs but one were buried, Emily stopped. She grievously stared at the effigy of Elizabeth I, with her golden crown and her convex nose. It was the first time she visited someone's resting place since her husband's death.

'Do you know that her half-sister, Queen Mary I, is buried under there too?'

'Bloody Mary?'

'Do not call her that. Her contemporaries didn't. Look over there. There is something in Latin, I am sure you can translate it for me.'

Ella went as close as she dared. The monument was protected with a black and gold gate but reading the plaque was still possible.

'Partners… in throne and grave… here rest we… two sisters, Elizabeth and Mary, in the… hope of resurrection,' she attempted to translate. Her grandparents had always insisted on her learning Latin and it was finally proving useful. 'I thought they did not get along well?'

'Mary's mother, Katherine of Aragon, lost everything when Henry VIII chose Elizabeth's mother, Anne Boleyn. Mary was willing to love her half-sister, at first. Rivalry and religion took them apart. Mary's rule was neither as long nor successful as Elizabeth's but she suffered so much throughout her life. They broke her spirit for her to recognise the validity of the annulment of her parents' marriage. Poor health, both physical and mental. The unhappiest of the Tudors.'

'I feel bad for her. And for her mother.'

'They loved each other so much. Queen Katherine had lost all her babies, so when Mary was born healthy, it felt like a miracle. She loved her more than life itself. As much as I love you.'

Katherine of Aragon was now so obsessed with her prayers that she had never tried to connect with her sons. Hal and Arthur loved her as part of their filial duty. When they had questions to ask, though, or achievements to boast about, Hal went to his tutor and Arthur to his lady mistress – or they went to Ella.

She had lost all her four babies, so when Mary was born healthy, it felt like a miracle. The Queen had become the mother of a healthy child a lot sooner this time. Ella did not think she viewed either of her sons as miracles at all. She had to feel for her. The boys had someone to love them as a mother, but Katherine did not have anyone to love her as a child was supposed to love its mother.

She had missed out on so much over the years, and she had not conceived since her last miscarriage, four years before. Half the court thought she was already barren.

Henry visited Ella one last time before her confinement. They spent the evening sitting by the fire and Ella wished he would never have to go. It was as if there was not enough air in the room every time she thought about spending an entire month away from him. It was not a battle she could win. Henry's paternal grandmother, Lady Margaret Beaufort, had written ordinances to follow at the birth of a royal child. Although this particular baby would have no royal title, Henry was determined to follow each and every step.

He looked at her lovingly. 'You are the most beautiful,' he said.

I feel like a whale, she thought. 'Thank you,' she replied.

'Are you comfortable?'

Ella nodded whereas she could have given him at least ten reasons why she was not: her swollen ankles, the pressure on her bladder, the ache in her back, the hurt in her pelvis when she walked, the stretch marks on her belly despite moisturising, the eternal constipation, the regular sleepless nights worrying about the health of her unborn child, the lack of convenience in gowns for pregnant women no matter the extra panels added to them, her exhaustion, her fear of death. Surely those were ten reasons already!

'I know about your worries, my adored one, but all will be well,' he comforted her. As usual, he was reading her mind.

Easy to say when you do not have to push a watermelon out of your vagina without peridural, decent medical equipment or trained doctors, she was close to retort, but her baby chose this moment to send a kick. Ella extended a hand towards Henry.

'Put your hand here,' she told him.

He stood up and ran to her chair. His face lit up when he felt the next kick and he laughed. It was the one thing in her pregnancy that was not getting old. The kicks were often uncomfortable, but on the days her baby barely moved, Ella could not resist the temptation to press her bump on strategic points until it made her child kick. She could not go to sleep without it.

Henry kissed her and went back to his seat. He was still struggling to accept that Charles, the king of Spain, his wife's nephew, had beaten him in the election to become the new Holy Roman emperor. There had to be a part of him that had always known his own elevation would have been a long shot, but Ella knew he would never admit it. The late emperor had now been succeeded by his own grandson, who was also the son of the Queen's sister.

Henry's only consolation was that the king of France had also been beaten. Ella was silently thanking whoever had made the decision to not elect Henry's rival, who had been a serious candidate. She would have never heard the end of it.

He sighed, as he always did when his mind was racing about something. 'Are you thinking about the Empire?' Ella asked.

'Yes. Wolsey's advice is now to strengthen further the alliance with France, as to support each other against the emperor,' he replied.

'I agree with him.'

'You often do. You are both my most trusted counsellors. He wishes for a state visit, for I to meet Francis and my son to meet his bride.'

And for I to meet Anne Boleyn, Ella said to herself.

'It is a good idea. You should invite Francis here, to show him the greatness of your court,' she told him.

Henry would never resist the possibility of blowing his frenemy's mind. Besides, since a meeting with Anne Boleyn must inevitably happen at some point, it was a lot preferable to arrange it in England, where Ella was the second highest-ranked woman, rather than in France, where she would merely be a guest in a stranger's home.

If she made it through childbirth, of course.

Henry had decided that Ella should give birth in Eltham Palace, in order to honour the place where they had first met. Exactly as his grandmother had demanded, Ella spent a month there, secluded from the world and from men. Her attendants were exclusively female, and her rooms were darkened by tapestries hanging over the walls and all windows but one. She was growing mad, waiting for her child to be born in the dark, surrounded by crucifix and tapestries that were supposed to depict calming romantic scenes. According to Henry's late grandmother, violent scenes were to upset both mother and child, but the only thing Ella was upset about was how they prevented the daylight from coming in.

When the day came, Ella was more than ready. Until she realised how painful contractions really were, at least. The resounding pain diffused through her stomach to her back. It was like being stabbed a thousand times over with a sharp knife, suffering from the worst period cramps of her life and fighting against the urge to relieve herself in front of everybody. All at the same time.

The moments of relief in between contractions were never long enough for her to properly rest and shortened more and more each time. Breathing heavily whilst staring anxiously at the baptismal font in the corner of the room, in case her baby was not deemed strong enough to survive and needed to be baptised immediately, Ella could see the full picture of labour: a long, exhausting marathon, for which she had not trained nor had been told where the finish line was.

As her latest contractions had unquestionably been the most painful thing she had ever felt, Ella both laughed and cried when, the baby's head pressuring all the way down, ready to come out, she understood that she was entirely at the mercy of whatever was pulling the strings of her life. The worst pain was yet to come and there was nothing she could do to avoid it. She had lost all control over the situation, and even over her own body.

'I cannot do it!' she howled.

Someone grabbed her hand. 'You can and you shall,' Elsie said.

Ella brusquely felt the need to push. She did not think about it twice and pushed as strongly as she could.

'It is time,' Maud calmly told the midwife, who rushed to her bed.

'Wash your hands!' Ella screamed.

'The child is coming, my lady!' she retorted.

'I am aware! You are not touching me or my baby with unclean hands! It is the King's baby! Wash your hands, now! Or lose your head!' Ella shouted like a madwoman.

She meant to apologise to the midwife for threatening her with execution, but her body decided to push once more and she stopped thinking about it. Her body had taken over. Hand in hand with her brain, it was taking care of everything for her, leaving her free to endure pain without actually having to decide when to push and when to rest.

It was an endless suffering. The angry beast was twisting, pushing and pulling all at once, trying to free itself from her body and ripping it apart from inside in the process.

It was loud and bloody. She cried, she screamed, she begged for it to be over. Tortured by this burning ring of fire between her legs, she pushed it out, feeling the head of her baby ultimately manage to get through. Followed by a singular, slimy sensation. And a cry.

It was over. Ella burst into tears, overwhelmed by an emotional liberation so intense she could barely think about anything else than the fact that her body had done what she had thought to be impossible. And that all that was left to do now was rest.

But then she saw Maud cleaning up the baby. Her baby. And she stopped being just Ella. She became a mother. She became so obsessed with this tiny little human being, who had felt so gigantic inside of her, that she did not hear Elsie send a young maid out to tell Henry's messenger about the birth of the child, nor did she even feel the next contractions that pushed her placenta out of her body. It was her baby.

Her daughter.

24.

DIVINE GRACE
1519-1520

When Henry entered the room, Ella was in bed, holding their baby in her arms. She struggled to take her eyes off her, but when she did, seeing the happiness on his face made her own complete. He sat on the side of the bed as delicately as he could and waved the ladies out, then kissed her hair and used his index finger to caress the cheek of his daughter.

'She is as beautiful as her mother,' he commented.

Ella smiled. 'I feel so grateful. She is healthy.'

'She is a gift from God, sending us His blessing.'

'The grace of God,' she murmured.

If there was a god, their affair should have been punished, not rewarded. If there was a god, this was divine grace. Time stopped for a moment, as it became clear in Ella's mind that the part of her name she had rejected for most of her life and the baby she had considered getting rid of were a perfect fit.

No one would ever forget that her daughter was Henry's. His Grace's daughter. Grace.

'Henry, I have a request,' she said, aware that the Queen had never had a choice in the names of her children.

'Anything for the mother of my daughter.'

'I would like her to be named Grace.'

'Grace… I thought of Elizabeth, as her mother and mine. Grace. Grace Fitzroy. *Fille du Roi.* The King's daughter.'

'Are you happy with it?'

'There is no better name for her,' he said. 'The cardinal and the Duke of Suffolk shall be her godfathers. The Duchess of Norfolk, her godmother,' Henry declared.

Although arrangements had to be made for the christening, he decided to stay a little longer. He took the baby girl in his arms so carefully that the concentration made his mouth open. He was pride and thankfulness personified. Ella rested her head on his shoulder.

The room where her daughter had been born was like an armour protecting their family. A newborn's life was the most feeble thing in the world, but Ella refused to think about it. With Henry by her side and Grace in their arms, she had never felt so safe. It was the three of them against the rest of the world.

Grace was christened in the palace chapel. Congratulations rained upon the parents, and when Elsie brought her goddaughter back to her mother after the ceremony, Ella was prouder than she had ever been in her life. She had made this perfect baby from scratch. It was the strangest thing to remember that, in the history that Ella had known, Grace had simply never existed. Her life, her future, was only a consequence of her mother's own journey across time nine years before. No ring, no daughter.

The corner of Ella's mouth lifted up. She had not spared a thought for her grandmother's ring for a while, now.

'I cannot imagine a world without my daughter in it,' Ella told Maud when she brought her supper in bed.

'Children are the most wonderful blessing of all,' her friend replied.

'It was difficult for me to understand, in the past, as you spoke of the joy of being a mother. I understand now,' Ella admitted. 'You do recall my feelings were… conflicted,' she mentioned her considerations on abortion.

'And today you would gladly choose death to protect your child from harm,' Maud finished her sentence for her.

Ella nodded. Grace was swaddled in her blue-painted wooden cradle, sleeping, oblivious to the world around her. Her mother let go a loud breath. Protecting her baby girl was now her job.

Ella had thought the first months of motherhood would be the most challengingly beautiful of her life but they turned out to be the most frustrating. Although she would have loved to breastfeed her daughter, Henry was adamant it was not the work of a noblewoman. She had not insisted, knowing disagreeing with him never led to anything, but cried herself to sleep every night for the entire month of her lying-in before her churching, which would mark her return to public life.

There was a woman out there, that Joan Browne person, bonding with her baby in her place, feeding her whilst she had to dry her own breast milk. Ella had seen the Queen do it and it was now her turn to wrap her breasts tightly, binding them as to make the milk dry.

Less than three weeks after Grace's birth, as Elsie was bringing her a bowl of some vegetable broth, Ella smelled the sage in the mixture and grimaced.

'Sage is not required anymore, my milk has dried,' she said in a robotic voice. 'Everybody but the Duchess of Norfolk, leave,' she demanded.

The room emptied. 'I am a bad mother,' Ella moaned.

'Your daughter is well taken care of. You have appointed Lady Carew as her lady mistress and said yourself you had complete trust in her abilities. Do remind me how many rules you have made her promise to apply?' Elsie asked, stroking her thumb on her friend's hand as she held it.

Ella chuckled. 'A hundred and three. Even the King thought it was a bit much.'

'A hundred and three rules! On what the wet nurse may or may not eat, on what must be done when the baby cries, on how she must be held, on hygiene, on clothing, on time managing, on record keeping…'

'I am afraid of what might happen to her in my absence,' Ella tried to explain herself.

'I know. It does not sound like being a bad mother.'

'Thank you, but I wish I could have fed her myself. Elsie, I have never even bathed my own child or changed her soiled clothing.'

'Neither have I, and I am an excellent mother,' Elsie retorted with her usual assurance. 'You are a duchess and the mother of the King's daughter. A duchess is not to dirty her hands. There are women of low birth for that. Do not worry yourself.'

Ella faked a smile and changed the subject. The truth was that she used to nanny someone else's child, and now other women were paid to take care of her own. She could have felt better if she had been in need of childcare because of a demanding job, or health worries, but it was as far from reality as possible.

A duchess is not to dirty her hands. But a duchess is now full of guilt, Ella thought.

A part of her was aware that she had little to complain about. In the twenty-first century, most mothers of newborns – and hopefully fathers too – were sleep deprived. In the sixteenth century, if one was from the lower classes of society, it was the same. In both, some women were battling postpartum depression, never diagnosed in the sixteenth century and still often overlooked in the twenty-first. The face of Nicholas sharing his late mother's story overlapped with the memory of Ella's own mother's face. She covered her eyes to make them disappear. She did not want to think about Nora's deadly experience of motherhood. Nor did she want to think about Nicholas and what he would have to say about his widow starting a family with his childhood friend.

The first thing Henry did after Ella's return to court life was to baptise his latest ship in their daughter's honour: "Lady Grace". Over the past month, Ella had come to resent him for taking Grace away from her so much when they should have been bonding, but seeing him publicly adoring their family mended things a little.

Living under a different roof to her daughter was not the motherhood Ella had ever imagined for herself, but it was her reality and she was making the most of it. She did not have a choice. Grace would never be in the line of succession as she had not been born inside the royal marriage, but she was the King's daughter, which meant that, in practice, she was given as much respect and attention as a royal princess.

Besides her set of rules that Elizabeth Carew was working hard to respect, Ella did not have a say in very much.

At least, Grace's birth had further extended her mother's influence. There was not the slightest doubt in every single courtier's mind that Ella was "the mother of the King's daughter". Grace looked so much like Henry that it was impossible to ignore she was a Tudor. Pale skin, blue eyes, red hair. Henry was delighted. Ella could not help but feel betrayed. She had carried her for nine months and suffered for hours to deliver her into this world, only for her to be the spitting image of her father.

Henry was so proud of Grace that, when she turned six months old at the end of May, he had her brought to court with her siblings for the king of France's state visit.

Ella wanted everyone's eyes to be on her, especially Anne Boleyn's. Her women helped her in her gown of gold and crimson brocade, with her silken cream kirtle underneath. The French hood was of the same fabric as the gown, with pearls sewn in a single row along the front edge and a double along the back. Her girdle was also made of pearls and ended its course with a large ruby pendant. She smiled as one of her ladies adjusted her bodice jewellery, a single row of pearls around her neck, gracefully connected at the front to a gold brooch with a bright white pearl in the middle. She looked like a queen.

The French had been delayed due to poor weather but arrived in Greenwich just in time for the magnificent banquet Henry had planned for their first evening. They were escorted by Henry's sister and Charles, who had picked them up in Dover. As soon as the king of France came into view, his laugh resonated all around. He and Henry hugged like old friends although they had never met before, tapping each other's backs over their thick and luxurious clothes. Ella silently cursed when she noticed King Francis was three or four inches taller than Henry, which was not to be received well by him. Henry was the tallest at court, but his rival had to be about six feet six.

As if they were one big functional family, both men presented their wives, children and mistresses to the other, in a mixture of French and English. English was not widely spoken at the French court, whereas every courtier in England had been taught at least rudiments of French. Ella had prepared herself to speak only French during the visit. King Francis was showing his friendship by speaking Henry's language.

'My dear Duchess of Exeter. A profound pleasure. If it pleases God that the Lady Grace inherit half of her mother's beauty, she shall one day be the most wonderful creature throughout Christendom,' he complimented her.

There was a mischievousness in his eyes behind his exquisite manners. His aura, oddly captivating, was both refined and chaotic and could explain why Mary Boleyn and many other women had fallen into his bed.

When he presented his own "sweetheart" to Henry, the queen of France forgot to hide her irritation. Ella pressed her lips against one another. Queen Katherine had built a tower around her heart to survive her renewed friendship with her husband's mistress, but Queen Claude was another story. Ella had only just met her, and she already felt sorry for her. The King's mistress was tall and graceful, but she herself was suffering from scoliosis and strabismus. One could only imagine the things people said about their queen in her own court.

Henry and King Francis decided to not say a word of politics until the morrow, so they could enjoy the evening. Henry had gone all in, with a glittering pageant and even a lion. Pop had always refused to take his granddaughter to the zoo, horrified for the animals to be in cages when they should have been running wild and free. Ella had to ignore the ache in her heart as she watched the king of the jungle walking around the great hall on a leash held by four men.

The following morning, nine-year-old Hal was formally introduced to his young future wife, Princess Charlotte, a dark-haired toddler of three-and-a-half. Ella had accustomed herself to a lot ever since she had travelled to this era, but the betrothing of children was still a difficult pill to swallow. She looked away from the awkward moment, and attempted to spot the infamous Anne Boleyn. The ladies in Queen Claude's household all looked so much alike that she gave up, but asked King Francis's mistress in French later on, during the archery contest.

The Countess of Châteaubriant squinted for a moment. 'Celle en noir, avec le menton pointu et les cheveux foncés,' she replied – *the one in black, with the pointy chin and the dark hair.*

'Difficile de croire qu'elle soit du même sang que sa soeur!' Ella exclaimed – *difficult to believe she is of the same blood as her sister!*

'Sa soeur est plus jolie, mais celle-ci est plus respectable,' the countess declared – *her sister is prettier, but this one is more respectable.*

'Je suppose que ce n'est pas un tel accomplissement,' Ella joked – *I suppose it is not such an achievement.*

Ella immediately felt ashamed of herself for slut-shaming Mary Boleyn, especially when she herself was someone's mistress, but the countess laughed.

Pretending to be entertained by the contest, Ella could not stop herself from glancing at Anne Boleyn. Although quite pretty, her hair was too dark and her skin not pale enough to be considered a beauty by sixteenth-century standards.

Henry must have fallen in love with her for so much more than her looks, the voice inside Ella's head concluded.

Ella was torn between a jealousy that made her want to strangle Anne Boleyn in front of everybody and a compassion that made her feel nauseous when remembering her historically violent fate.

Once the contest was over, Ella took her daughter in her arms for a walk in the gardens. The French countess, whose name was Françoise de Foix, decided to accompany her.

'Permettez-moi de vous féliciter pour la naissance de votre fille,' she said – *allow me to congratulate you for the birth of your daughter.*

'Je vous remercie,' Ella answered – *I thank you.*

The countess looked at Grace for a moment, pensive. 'Le Roi Henri doit vous aimer profondément,' she stated – *King Henry must love you deeply.*

'Vous devez certainement partager cette félicité avec le Roi François,' Ella replied – *you must certainly share this felicity with King Francis.*

'François m'aime tant qu'il ne m'a jamais laissé le choix,' Françoise retorted – *Francis loves me so much that he never left me with a choice.*

The blue-eyed woman did not give any detail regarding the start of her relationship with the French king but her nervous smile spoke for her. Ella's brain suddenly remembered that Lolly had told her twenty-first century historians were not sure Mary Boleyn had consented to being a mistress to King Francis. Ella held Grace tighter against her chest, frustrated at the powerlessness forced into what her contemporaries called the weaker sex.

'Il n'y avait pas de femmes à la cour avant la mort du Roi Louis, mais "une cour sans dames est une année sans printemps et un printemps sans roses" selon François,' Françoise quoted her lover – *there were no women at court before the death of King Louis, but a court with no ladies is a year without spring and a spring without roses, according to François.*

Ella found nothing to reply. There was nothing to reply.

But Françoise was one of these people who shared their entire life story to complete strangers, or she simply needed to talk to someone she would not bring back home with her. For twenty minutes, Ella did not open her mouth. She was not sure that Françoise noticed, too busy telling her all about how her forced relationship with the king of France had caused a feud with her cousin, Germaine de Foix.

Françoise and Germaine were the respective granddaughters of two brothers. Françoise had married the French Count of Châteaubriant, and Germaine had married King Ferdinand of Aragon, Queen Katherine's father, after the death of his first wife. Germaine had been very unimpressed when Françoise had become King Francis's chief mistress. Through her mother, Marie of Orléans, she was the niece of the late king Louis XII of France – Queen Claude's father.

Ella had to mentally draw a genealogy tree to understand who was who but, once she did, could understand why Germaine was upset that her paternal cousin was causing so much sorrow to her maternal cousin. A thought she did not share with Françoise.

'Parlons un peu de politique, comme les hommes. Donnons-nous l'illusion de contrôle sur nos vies,' she decided – *let us talk about politics, like men. Let us give ourselves the illusion of control over our lives.* 'Pensez-vous que cette visite se clôturera par un nouveau traité?' she asked – *do you believe this visit shall end with a new treaty?*

Ella was about to be the one confiding in a stranger. She meant to share that, the Holy Roman emperor being Katherine's nephew, an alliance with him might renew the influence she once had over Henry. She wanted to confess that she needed a stronger friendship with France in order to avoid it. But Françoise did not actually care about politics: before Ella had even opened her mouth, she changed her mind and asked if she was aware of the paternity of Germaine's two-year-old daughter.

'L'empereur du Saint-Empire est son père,' she replied when Ella made clear she did not have a clue – *the Holy Roman emperor is her father.*

'Mais… l'empereur n'est-il pas le petit-fils du Roi Ferdinand?' Ella asked rhetorically – *but is the emperor not King Ferdinand's grandson?*

Françoise confirmed and chuckled at Ella's disgusted face, but told her that the girl would of course never be acknowledged. She also admitted that Germaine was closer in age to the father of her child than to the man she used to be married to, but Ella only pretended to listen. She was still trying to digest the information that a man had had a child with his grandfather's widow. In comparison, her own family situation was very healthy.

Ella realised Françoise did care about politics after all when, as it was time to part, she looked at her in the eyes and promised that, for as long as King Francis would not tire of her, she would do her best for him to seek England's friendship over the Empire's. Ella promised to do the same.

She did not have to wait for long to fulfil that promise. Henry decided to spend the night with her but did not seem to find sleep after sex. Ella could not hear him snore.

'Henry?'

'I am awake.'

'Why?'

'The emperor wrote to me. He wishes for us to meet. An alliance would be advantageous, and he gave his word that he would support Wolsey's candidature for the papacy when Leo dies.'

'I must be naive, but I do not understand why he would do that. Surely, he has a candidate of his own already. Why is he helping you instead of himself?'

Henry turned around in the bed. Despite the darkness surrounding them, Ella could see that his eyes were wide open. 'You proved to me long ago you were as wise as a man. Tell me what you think,' he said.

'I do not trust the emperor, my love. Did you know he conceived a child with Ferdinand's widow?' she asked.

'I did. He is still in his youth, merely twenty years of age,' he reminded her, as if it was a sufficient explanation for sleeping with the widow of one's grandfather.

'I do not trust a man who imprisons his own mother and makes himself king in her place,' Ella counterattacked.

'Queen Joanna, Katherine's sister… yes. But a woman, especially one who has lost her sanity, is unfit to rule a kingdom,' he pointed out.

'It is a struggle for me to believe that Queen Joanna is mad. The intensity of her grief may have made her so,' Ella conceded, remembering the chilling news that the woman had had exhumed her dead husband's body to kiss his feet, only to then travel around with the coffin. 'But Henry, please, tell me. Would you have imprisoned your mother had she lost her sanity or would you have tried to help her?' Ella went on.

Almost twenty years after her death, Henry's mother, and the woman he had named her after, was still and would always be the woman he loved the most in the entire world. Ella knew she had won him over.

He sighed. 'Trusting a man who behaved so cruelly towards his mother…' he murmured, probably more for himself than for Ella. 'I shall not make a decision regarding an alliance with him before this state visit comes to an end,' he assured her.

Five minutes later, Henry was snoring. Ella smiled. The king of France could not pride himself with much more integrity than the Holy Roman emperor, but Henry did not need to know that. One invited women to his court to rape them, the other had his mother locked up so he could wear her crown, but only an alliance with the latter could weaken Ella's influence on Henry.

For days on end, life was but a succession of banquets, pageants, contests and jousts and, on the ninth day, Ella and Françoise exchanged a secret smile when their respective lovers signed a new treaty. Henry and Francis agreed to not make an alliance with the Holy Roman emperor for the next three years, vowed to support each other against their enemies and even set up a new lucrative trade between their two kingdoms.

The most thrilling for Henry was the promise of a marriage between any hypothetical daughter he might have with the Queen to Francis's heir and namesake, who was about Grace's age. Henry being Henry, he was confident that he would soon father the future queen of France. He even gifted Ella a gold brooch with an amethyst fleur-de-lys to thank her for the role she had played in the completion of the treaty. Of course, no one at court dared to remind him his wife had not conceived in over four years.

25.

TEN YEARS 1520

Henry was so determined that his descendants would rule the kingdom of France that, as they were riding together, he told Ella she was free to take Grace for a couple of weeks in the countryside. He did not explain the reason behind his offer and did not have to: he had to sleep with his wife as much as possible if he wanted their daughter to sit on the French throne, and it would be much easier if his mistress was out of the way. For a split second, Ella thought about pushing him off his horse. But jealousy was useless. Giving him an ultimatum, Katherine or her, would be counterproductive. It was 1520. She knew her place.

She took Grace, but also Maud, Elsie and their children to Godinton House, a grand red-bricked house near Ashford that she had purchased with Nicholas from the Toke family. Ella had always loved its large garden, especially the multicoloured wild flowers all around, and it soon appeared that the Parr children found it perfect for their play time.

'I am with child again,' Elsie broke the news about a week after their arrival.

'Congratulations, my dear,' Maud said. Ella smiled but did not say a thing, knowing what Elsie thought about creating a new life with her violent husband.

'I thank you. I hope for a girl, although my husband wishes for another boy,' she told them, looking down at her son in her arms. 'Elizabeth, my husband and myself agreed on enquiring about the betrothal of our children, if it was something the King and you were pleased to consider.'

'Your Henry is only one year of age, and Grace not even that,' Ella retorted. 'I have decided to keep her hand free until she reaches sixteen years of age and the King approved... after some convincing from me.'

Maud smiled, amused, but Elsie repressed a sigh. 'I will tell him.'

'No, do not worry yourself. I shall write to him. The Duke of Suffolk also shared his hope to betroth his son to my daughter, as they are cousins. He was met with the same answer.'

'Grace is the King's daughter, she was bound to have many suitors,' Maud commented.

'Yes. Ultimately, she will marry whom His Grace wishes for her to marry. In the meantime, it is my desire for her to be untroubled with betrothals and it will be thus until she is sixteen,' Ella repeated, determined to protect her red-headed treasure from the marriage game for as long as she could. Her daughter was not to meet the same fate as the late Viscountess Lisle.

Elsie was about to reply something but was interrupted by a letter and a parcel brought from a man wearing the royal livery of white and green. Ella put Grace in Maud's arms and opened the letter first, holding in her hand the mysterious velvety box.

The eleventh day of June, 1520.

Mine own darling, I send this letter to enquire of the good health of you and our daughter. The plague is into London. God be praised, there is no sick person at court. Do not frighten yourself, good sweetheart, but I beg you to remain in the country until all danger has gone and keep the duchess with you in remembrance of the promise which you made me.

By this bearer I send you this diamond, in the hope of you understanding how greatly your absence grieves me. My mistress whom I esteem more than all the world, I am yours, wherever I am, and I wish you in my arms always.

For lack of time, I make an end of my letter.

Written by the hand of him, who is, in heart, body and soul, and always will be, yours. H. Rex.

Ella smiled and folded the letter. He would never say so, but he did feel some remorse for sending her away. She only realised the extent of this guilt when she opened the box of black velvet. There it was, in all its splendour, the majestic diamond offered by the late king of France to his young new bride. The Mirror of Naples.

Elsie forgot all decency and screamed in the middle of the gardens, making her son cry. Ella ignored them, staring at the smooth and shiny black diamond, wider than any she had ever owned before, and its large yet delicate pearl, whiter than snow. She could not believe she owned it. A distant memory of the day she had come into the ownership of her grandmother's ring came back to her mind. Only briefly. She did not care anymore about finding the ring. It was, quite literally, from another life. This one mattered more.

'How fortunate to be loved as such!' Elsie moaned, openly sick at heart with the lack of love in her own marriage.

'Indeed,' Ella agreed, feeling somewhat guilty.

And keep the duchess with you in remembrance of the promise which you made me, Henry had written. Elsie's husband had first refused for his wife to leave court with their son but Henry had insisted on it. Not because he wanted Ella to spend some quality time with her friend, but because he had made her promise she would investigate some allegations against Elsie's father.

The Duke of Buckingham was rumoured to have made some very ill-advised boasts about his ancestry during the French state visit, and saying Henry was upset about it was an understatement. Buckingham's mother was sister to Henry's grandmother, Queen Elizabeth Wydeville, which made him the nephew by marriage of King Edward IV.

Most importantly, through his father, Buckingham was the descendant of the eighth son of King Edward III. Henry, of the fourth – John of Gaunt. But there was always a but. John of Gaunt's child whom Henry descended from had been born illegitimate. So had been his three younger siblings. Their mother, Katherine Swynford, had only become John's wife years after their births. King Richard II had legitimised them but had excluded them from the line of succession, and this, Ella believed, was the issue. It was not spoken of, but it was there, just beneath the surface.

In Ella's eyes, Buckingham had always been insufferable, but never that stupid. How easy it was now to suspect him of planning a rebellion against Henry, like his father before him had planned one against King Richard III! It was now down to her to find out what Elsie knew about his intentions, and she was not so thrilled about it. But Henry had not left her with a choice.

She decided to be blunt. Elsie complaining to Maud that her husband was never presenting her with any gift, and that the last time a man had offered her something was her father for her wedding, was the occasion she needed.

'May I ask you something about him? Your father?' she said.

Elsie nodded, uncomfortable. 'Is this regarding...' she started, then hesitated.

'His words during the visit of the king of France, yes,' Ella finished her sentence for her. 'It is. Dear friend, you must tell me if treacherous actions hide beneath incautious words,' she demanded, both as kindly and firmly as she could.

Elsie's face drained from its colours. She tightened her grip around her son, and Ella took her daughter back from Maud's arms. Silence was total for a moment, until baby Henry sneezed and that his nose had to be wiped. It seemed to release his mother's mind from wherever it had gone.

'My father is a loving cousin, subject and friend to His Grace. His words were indeed quite unwise, but I refuse to believe him guilty of treason,' she explained. Her voice was trembling, but her eyes seemed to be telling the truth.

'I believe you. Please do forgive me, I simply must protect my family,' Ella told her, realising as she spoke that Elsie might have been doing the exact same thing.

Elsie exhaled loudly. 'I understand. Elizabeth, I have never been in my father's affections nor in his ear. There is little of the way he conducts his daily activities that I am aware of. I can only say that I believe in my soul that his love for His Grace and for the princes is pure.'

'I believe you,' Ella repeated herself.

The voice inside her head was pointing out that a man plotting to overthrow his king would try not to draw attention to himself beforehand, as to keep the element of surprise.

But what if Henry is right to suspect him? What if nothing is done and he is overthrown, what would happen to you and your daughter then? Ella could not silence the other voice, more paranoid.

'What are His Grace's thoughts on the matter?' Elsie asked, alarmed.

'It has not been shared with me,' Ella lied.

To everyone's relief, the outbreak of the plague turned out to be a brief one. Grace and Ella were soon reunited with Henry. Because of his emetophobia, being around him often was the safest place to be, as he never let anyone with as little as a cold near him. In truth, since the sweating sickness, Ella was growing more and more like him. She could still picture herself collapsing to the floor. She could still feel the wetness of the sheets on her back, drenched in her sweat.

She would never forget Dr Alcaraz's words. "*The Duke has contracted the sweat and has departed to God, my lady, I am very sorry.*" She could hardly believe Nicholas had been dead for three years already. It was as if, the older she was, the quicker years passed. When September came,

Ella faked a headache and stayed in bed all day to process the tenth anniversary of her journey through time. It had been ten years.

Staring at the ceiling, her hands crossed over the soft covers, Ella tried to remember the person she used to be. The grieving millennial, with no clue of what her life was supposed to be like. A lost girl at war with her father over a ring, meeting a sixteenth-century king in a dirty dress and reminding him without an ounce of reverence that there was a moat around his palace. Ella chortled at the memory.

So much had changed, so much had happened. She had been married and widowed. She had had to pretend being in love with her husband and had fallen in love with someone else's. She had become a mother. She had stared at death in the face. She had climbed her way up the social ladder, and now most men had to bow to her and their wives and daughters had to curtsey for as long as she wanted them to.

The girl she used to be would not have recognised her. She was a different person, confident enough to involve herself in politics but also in other people's lives. She was shaping a different history than the one she had learned in her school books.

A different history for a different girl.

Ella Buckley and Elizabeth White were not the same person. One was free as a bird, the other had to ask for her lover's permission when she wanted to see their daughter. One was a nanny struggling to pay the rent of her studio, the other was moving from one royal palace to another. One bought her clothes in charity shops, the other was walking around wearing the most splendid fabrics and jewels, but was forbidden to uncover her hair.

Ella sat up. 'Your are Elizabeth White, Duchess of Exeter,' she said out loud.

Comparing her life as Ella to her life as Elizabeth was pointless. She was the mother of the King's daughter. Ella Buckley was dead. She had been dead for so long Ella was not even sure she could remember how to be her.

Henry celebrated Grace's first birthday with the commission of her mother's portrait. With the Mirror of Naples pinned on her gown of gold and crimson brocade, Ella posed for hours, still and quiet, feeling more like a queen than the Queen herself. She could not stop her mind from wandering off to the future, thinking about where her portrait would end up. How brilliant would it be to have her face hanging in a London museum, seen by thousands of tourists on a daily basis, admired and talked about for centuries to come!

The sexagenarian foreign painter was not quite done yet when Henry entered the room but packed up when asked to continue his work in the morning. Ella massaged her face to wake up her zygomatic muscles. Henry sat next to her.

'I have news, my adored one,' he said. 'Our beloved Pan is dead.'

'Oh, no! Such dreadful news. How?'

'Old age. I am sorry. I know you loved him.'

'I did. So did you.'

'We shall both grieve him. Darling Elizabeth, I wish to share some other news with you. Katherine is with child. It has quickened this morning and shall be born in the spring.'

Ella froze. She had prepared herself for the faint possibility of it happening, but was irritated that Henry had given her so little time to accept the news of Pan's death before slapping her in the face with his wife's pregnancy. There was a difference between knowing the father of her child was sleeping with another woman and seeing the proof with her own eyes: a baby bump walking around the palace. Henry's gaze was on Ella, scrutinizing, waiting. She had no other option but to tell him what he wanted to hear.

'Congratulations to you both,' she eventually spoke.

'It was my thinking that, if your heart was aching for Pan, you would not find my wife with child so distressing,' he admitted.

'How kind of you,' she replied, fighting the urge to punch him in the face.

'Are you unhappy?' he had the effrontery to ask.

'No. I am delighted for the Queen, whom I love, to be with child,' Ella replied with a sarcasm Henry did not detect.

'I hope for a girl, to have a grandson one day ruling the kingdom of France,' he exclaimed with such joy in his eyes it forced Ella to remind herself why she loved him so.

As Henry was lost in the vision of a perfect future, with his own flesh and blood on the throne of France, Ella listed what she loved the most about him. His passionate personality. His entertaining company. His curious, clever mind. It was impossible to stay mad at him, especially when she could see so much of Grace and Hal in him. Arthur was growing up to be more composed, distant and delicate like his mother.

In order to be loved by Henry and safe at his court, Ella had to pretend she agreed with his belief that men were superior to women. It was not even his fault. Everybody shared this conviction, even most of the women. It would take centuries to change people's minds – five centuries would not even be enough. But it was the price to pay to live here and Ella had accepted it. Somehow, and despite all his paternalism and his sexism, she genuinely loved him.

They were made for each other. But, as she watched him tell her all about his plans for the baby growing in his wife's womb, she still wanted to punch him.

26.

WHAT HIS HEART MOST DESIRED

1521

The larger the Queen's pregnancy belly, the more irritated Ella was. She could not help it. For the first time in his life, Henry was preparing this new birth as if the unborn child was female. He had already prepared the letter he would send to the king of France, announcing the birth of his future daughter-in-law. He was obsessed with this child and was showering its mother with presents and attentions.

Ella understood why the king of France did not want her daughter for his son. She might even have cried hysterically at the idea of marrying her precious girl to the son of a royal rapist, but part of her also loved to imagine Grace sitting on a throne, her bright red hair crowned with gold and diamonds.

When Ella entered the Queen's apartments one cold morning of January, shivering despite the many layers of her outfit, she faked a smile when she realised Henry was, of course, already there. Her dishonest smile froze when she saw the dried tears on his cheeks. He was sitting there, in the middle of the deserted room, his back rounded as if he was carrying the world on his shoulders. He looked so devastated that Ella took him in her arms without even asking what had happened.

'Katherine has been delivered of a girl, but it was too early,' he confirmed her fears in a murmur, his head resting against her chest.

'I am sorry, Henry,' she said.

She did feel quite guilty. She had spent so long wishing this pregnancy had never happened, angry at the sole sight of the pregnant queen, and now the innocent baby was dead. Henry's dream of a daughter on the throne of France had just been shattered in a million of pieces, but every single of Ella's thoughts was for Katherine. She had always felt sorry for each of her pregnancies that had ended in blood and tears, but this one hit different. Ella was a mother herself. She could not begin to imagine the pain Katherine was in. Losing one baby was surely traumatizing enough, but it had kept on happening. She had lost five babies.

Ella's eyes filled with tears that Henry interpreted as tears of sorrow for his broken dream. He thanked her for her compassion and kissed her before leaving the room, as the arrangements for the birth had to be cancelled and the king of France had to be made aware.

Without thinking, Ella walked to the Queen's bedchamber. The Countess of Salisbury tried to tell her that she did not want to see anyone, but they heard her weak voice behind the door and Ella came in. Katherine was sitting on her immense bed, her long hair lose, looking so petite and frail that only the greyish colour of her hair could tell she was not a sickly eight-year-old child.

'Lady Exeter…' she said, and took a deep breath to compose herself. 'Why are you here?' she asked.

'I beg Your Grace to forgive me for my intrusion. I was distraught to hear about the princess. I am sorry,' Ella replied, understanding too late that, despite their official friendship, she was the last person the Queen would have wanted to see.

'I am a forgiving soul,' she said, locking eyes with her. 'I have forgiven you for taking my husband away from me and betraying the trust I had placed in you. I have accepted the love my husband and my sons bear for you. I have welcomed every burden the Lord has sent me. I believe God shall never send me what I cannot bear,' she told her with a shake in her voice. She paused and looked away as a tear rolled down her cheek. 'God has blessed my marriage with two healthy sons and He has blessed you with a daughter, who shall forever be a reminder of my failure to give my husband what his heart most desired.'

'I am sorry…' Ella repeated, at a loss for words. Katherine stayed quiet and Ella curtseyed before retreating from the room.

Had the situation not been so excruciatingly sad, it would have been comical. Both at school and with her grandmother, Ella had learned about the fate of Katherine of Aragon, the abandoned queen, whose only crime had been to fail to give her husband a son. This time, she had given him not one, but two. It still was not enough, because what Henry needed now was the only thing his wife had given him in another version of their life: a daughter. A diplomatic pawn. A child-bride. A future queen. Tables had turned, but Katherine was once again the most miserable of all.

Henry cried in Ella's arms that night. She let him, choosing not to remind him that his wife was grieving too and that they should have been through this process together. Her hands running softly through his hair, she silently repeated to herself that for one to be happy, the other had to be lonely. She would not let it be her.

'I was confident I would conquer France,' Henry reminisced about his younger self, miles away from Ella's thoughts.

'I know. The kingdom's finances cannot afford a war with France, and I am sorry for that.'

'They shall recover. And then…'

'You are a magnificent king whether you hold France or not,' Ella did not let him finish.

Henry did not answer anything. It was so unlike him to not accept a compliment that she escaped from his embrace to look at him straight in the eyes. She took his face in her hands.

'You are a magnificent king,' she said once more. 'Maybe, God intended for you to find glory in England, not abroad. To be the caring father of all Englishpersons, protecting them from harm and need. To spend money on the prosperity of your people and your kingdom instead on the conquest of foreign lands. Henry, my love, you do not have to be a conqueror to be remembered as the greatest king England has ever known.'

Ella stopped talking, aware that Henry was unlikely to believe her. Conquest was power and kings sought it more than anything else. Especially Henry, whose hero was Henry V, the conqueror of France a century before. He had put his desperate need for conquest and glory on pause for the sake of the kingdom's finances and for the treaty, but it was clear he did not believe his wife would ever lead a successful pregnancy again.

'What are you thinking about?' she asked him after a moment.

'Without a daughter to marry Francis's heir, should I give up on the alliance with the French?' he replied with another question, his mind having already shifted from his subjects' happiness to political warfare.

'Surely, it would put Hal's betrothal to Charlotte in jeopardy.'

'Yes. She is not the only eligible princess in Europe. My grandchildren shall never rule over the kingdom of France if Katherine does not give me a daughter. The treaty is not as advantageous for England without it.'

'Yet, if you and King Francis both commit to it, at least until Charlotte becomes princess of Wales, it might just strengthen Hal's claim to the throne of France. Thanks to you, he could take back what is rightfully England's,' Ella told him, horrified to sound so convincing when, deep down, she did not believe for a second the kingdoms of France and England would ever be joined.

What she needed was a reason to stop Henry from reconsidering the alliance and falling into the arms of the Queen's nephew. It worked. He kissed her fervently on the lips.

'Do you believe it?' he asked.

'I do,' she lied.

Everyone at court was muttering that the way for Henry to have a third child in wedlock was to wait for the inevitable to happen and marry again. It was treason to mention the death of the Queen, but she looked so thin and fragile, so weak, that it seemed even a soft wind could have blown her away. Besides, most courtiers had lost their patience with her ability to produce a healthy girl. Henry VII had fathered two and had placed them on the thrones of Scotland and France, which was something Henry was unable to do.

Ella was powerless to stop the cruel gossip. All she could do was barking at them to be quiet, but she knew they always picked up where they had left things as soon as she was out of earshot. Katherine barely ever left her closet anymore, praying day and night that God would come to her rescue, as if it would make a baby girl appear in her empty womb.

When Elsie went into labour, Ella loathed herself thinking that it would be best if the child was to not survive. It was just for a minute, and it was in the hope of alleviating some of the guilt on Katherine's shoulders, but she had thought it and knew she would never forgive herself if the child was indeed to die. But Elsie gave birth to a healthy baby girl, christened two days later in the Queen's honour. Ella and Cardinal Wolsey became godparents of the little Katherine Howard, the namesake of Henry's fifth wife in the history that would never be, and Ella caught him looking at the newborn girl with envy and frustration.

Nostalgia came like a crashing wave at the beginning of May as Ella watched a bonfire from the palace window. Every year, on the fifth of November, Lolly and Pop would take her out in the evening to drink a hot chocolate and watch bonfire and fireworks celebrating Guy Fawkes's failed attempt on the life of King James I. Ella gasped when she realised that James I was once Henry's great-great-nephew. She was not sure neither he nor Guy Fawkes would be born this time.

The Cardinal and the bishop of Rochester, at Henry's urging, were overseeing the burning of all Martin Luther's works found in England. Henry had gradually become more and more upset about

Martin Luther over the past year as the priest had published three books following his theses, all attacking the abuses and excesses within the Church. Unsurprisingly, he had been excommunicated, but he had publicly incinerated the very papal bull that had excommunicated him, making it quite the social event.

Ella heard the disapproving snap of someone's tongue and did not have to turn around to know it was John Colet. Henry was unaware that his chaplain and the mother of his daughter were the ones responsible for the wide circulation of Martin Luther's books around court, capital and country. Ella never asked Colet any questions. She simply provided the money for the works to be printed and for the people involved, from printing to distribution, to be paid. Who these people were, and how they did it, was none of her concern. Witnessing the spreading of Luther's words around her was enough to know that her money was being put to good use.

'Had he been an Englishman, Luther would have already met a similar fate,' Ella commented in a murmur.

'We must then thank the Elector of Saxony for his protection,' Colet replied on the same tone. Luther owed his life only to Frederick III, of whom he was a subject.

'Indeed.'

'My lady, first reports mention that the King's search has been thorough. I am led to believe very few copies remain.'

'More shall be made in due course. His Grace's anger is strong,' Ella told him, recalling Henry screaming all over the palace after each publication. 'It is best to bide our time.'

Colet agreed. Neither of them had a death wish. They watched in silence as the hungry flames devoured the so-called heretic pages.

Reading outside without shivering for the first time that year, a large old tree shielding her from both the sun and the wind, Ella did not see Hal come and jumped when the ten-year-old sat next to her.

'Forgive me for frightening you,' he apologised. She smiled and closed her book, then noticed the deep wrinkle between his eyebrows.

'You seem troubled.'

'I had an uncomfortable conversation with Father about Martin Luther. He has been summoned by the emperor to formally renounce his,' Hal paused as if in pain, 'unsuitable', he continued, 'views on the Pope and the Church, but boldly refused. My poor father is distressed. I have decided to keep silencing my opinions.'

'That is wise.'

'Father said that by one man's disobedience, many are made sinners. He believes Martin Luther to be encouraging heresy and thus to be a threat to God's order. He wishes to see him burned at the stake.'

'Your father's sentiments cannot surprise you, Hal.'

'They do not but they sadden me. He said he would write a book to defend the Church against the attacks from Luther. Bet, do you believe I should have debated with him?'

'Ten-year-old boys do not debate with kings. You did well not to.'

'I do not think it is fair for him to write a book defending his faith when other people who defend theirs can be burned at the stake for it,' he said, making Ella more proud than she had ever been. 'As long as one lives virtuously,' Hal went on, 'what one believes should not be a cause for execution. You have my word, Bet, that once I am king, I shan't ever burn one at the stake because of faith alone.'

'With your compassion, kindness, and intelligence, you are to become the most glorious, awe-inspiring king England has ever known. I agree with your words and am very proud of you,' she told him.

The smile that appeared on his face was an invaluable treasure. Ella took his hand in hers and, as if they were alone on a deserted island, he put his head on her shoulder. They stayed quiet for a moment until they spotted Maud's son, eight-year-old William, playing with two other boys that Ella failed to recognise. Hal kissed her on the cheek and ran to his friends.

He had not even reached them that Ella felt a presence behind her. Getting up on her feet, she almost fainted when her eyes met Buckingham's.

'My lady, what a pleasure to find you here today,' he said with a terrifying smirk.

'Your sentiment is much reciprocated, my lord,' Ella replied, fighting the urge to vomit at the thought of what he might have heard.

'It warms my heart to be the witness of such a close bond between my lord the prince and you,' he told her, then bowed and started to walk away. About fifteen feet away from her, as Ella was starting to believe they may not have been overheard after all, he turned around. 'I trust you are aware that endangering the prince's eternal life shall be considered and punished as high treason, you heretic bawd,' he insulted her with evident delight.

And he left her there.

Ella found herself incapable of suppressing the urge anymore and vomited behind the nearest bush. Her hands on her stomach, she then tried to slow her breathing down, but it was easier said than done. Heretics were burned at the stake. Traitors of noble rank were usually beheaded. Ella was not sure what was supposed to happen to people guilty of both. She vomited some more when she pictured herself kneeling on the scaffold, waiting for the axe to cut off her head and end her life in a puddle of blood. Imagining a death by fire was worse. Ella fell onto her knees.

'What is to happen to Grace?' she murmured.

She thought she knew Henry so well, yet she could not tell if he would decide to forgive their child for having a treacherous heretic as a mother or if he would repudiate her and watch as she led an impoverished life, ending in complete misery.

'Calm down, think rationally,' she said to herself, loud and clear.

Henry loved Grace. And Henry loved her. She was the true love of his life, or so he liked to say. Buckingham was not. Henry did not like him. He was annoyed that his skills did not match his rank, he shared very little interests with him, and he feared how close to the throne he was. Henry had never trusted him.

But he trusts you, Ella reminded herself.

Buckingham had no proof. Hal would never do or say anything to harm her in any way. It was his word against hers. She may only be a woman, but she was not any woman. One could not accuse the mother of the King's daughter without strong evidence.

You cannot let him plant the seed of doubt in Henry's mind, the voice inside her head warned her.

Ella had to agree with it. She loved Henry with all her heart, but anyone finding the right words at the right time could easily persuade him of pretty much anything. Henry could be convinced of something one minute and guarantee the contrary the next. The painful truth was that he was so certain that the people around him lived only to serve and please him that it made him an easy target for manipulation.

You have to find a way to silence Buckingham if you want Grace to have a future, she decided before walking back to the palace with a dark light in her eyes.

27.

LITTLE WHITE LIE 1521

Options. Ella needed options.

She could not buy Buckingham's silence. She would find herself at his mercy. Besides, he was wealthier than most and had hated her from the beginning. He had no reason to keep quiet.

She could not blackmail him either. She did not have any information about him that she could use to ensure his silence. Elsie had been of no help in figuring out if her father had been planning a coup. She was either a fantastic liar or did not know anything.

This is not what matters, Ella understood as she walked past a couple of maids of honour, who curtseyed low before her.

What mattered was that Henry distrusted Buckingham so much that he had made her investigate him. After all, Buckingham had waited for the visit of Henry's royal rival to remind the entire court of his ancestry, and thus that his claim to the throne was serious enough to be considered.

Ella walked to Henry's privy chamber with both relief and resignation. She knew what she had to do. She walked through ten of the twelve rooms of his royal apartments, only to find him working on his anti-Luther book in his study with Sir Thomas More, who was one of his friends and personal advisers. Also a lawyer, author and philosopher, he was a brilliant mind and someone Henry admired very much, but also a ferocious opponent to Martin Luther.

She sat down on a chair in the corner of the room and put her best distraught look on her face, but did not bother to listen to what More, in his usual black cloak, was saying. Henry was doing it enough for the both of them. He was writing frantically, drinking his friend's every word just like the Queen used to drink Fray Diego's. Ella frowned as she realised Henry's book would actually be partially written by Thomas More, but quickly made the line between her eyebrows disappear when Henry stopped writing to look at her.

Seeing the pretend distress on her face, he asked his adviser to leave them alone.

'My adored one, what is the matter?' he asked, concerned.

'I beg you to forgive me for interrupting you in your important work.'

'Nonsense. You are upset. Tell me how to fix it.'

Ella sighed. 'I am afflicted by the conduct of the Duke of Buckingham…'

'Buckingham!' Henry growled.

'He talks and walks around your court as if it were his own. Henry, my love, I do believe that inside his heart, he thinks himself to be the rightful king and it is frightening to me,' she explained, looking as fragile as she could.

'I do not want your mind to be troubled by him. He shall never harm me, you, or our daughter.'

'How can you be so certain? The man has always loathed me, ever since I was but a maid of honour. I am so very scared of him.'

Henry's eyes shut and his nose crunched as his eyebrows sunk in a frown. He hated the frustration of not being able to protect the mother of his child – the weaker sex – from a threat as much as treason itself. Except that there was something he could do to protect her, and they both knew it.

'I have thought for some time of having him arrested and questioned. Now, seeing you so distraught because of his behaviour, my mind is set. Head to your chambers, sweet darling of mine. You need rest. Do not fear, tonight Buckingham will sleep in the Tower,' he promised.

Once back in her apartments, Ella sat on her bed and stared at the miniature painting of Henry that he had previously given her. She had manipulated him to cause the downfall of the father of one of her best friends. Buckingham should have been innocent until proven guilty, but whether or not he was indeed planning a rebellion against Henry was irrelevant. The only way for Ella to save her head was to make sure he lost his first, and quickly.

Henry was a man of his word. Buckingham was arrested on the grounds of 'imagining and compassing the death of the King,' taking everyone by surprise. Even Norfolk looked like he had had no idea of what was going on with his father-in-law.

Colet approached Ella in the great hall and stood by her side in silence for a moment as they watched courtiers exchanging their stupor with one another.

'His Grace shared with me my lady's fear regarding the latest occupant of the Tower,' he eventually said in a low voice.

He had put two and two together, Ella realised. They both knew her to be so powerful that very few things could make her fear for her life. With what he knew of her heretic views and activities, it was not such a wild guess to link everything together.

'It is of the utmost importance that the duke be silenced,' Ella whispered.

Colet did not reply. He bowed. Ella's forced exhale turned into a sigh of relief. If Henry came to hesitate about executing his cousin, his chaplain would bring him back to the right path.

The man of God had not yet disappeared from Ella's view when she spotted Maud and Elsie. The latter, as could be expected, looked dreadful. Buckingham may not have been the best father to her, but he was still her father.

'My friend, do not look so concerned. I am certain your father shall be well served by the court,' Ella heard Maud's attempt at reassuring words once the two women were close enough.

'I am not. His Grace seems much, oh so much displeased. I wish I could go see my dear mother!' Elsie cried.

'You must ask the Queen to go to her.'

'My husband has forbidden me to leave his side for as long as my father's fate has not been determined.'

'And he is right,' Ella intervened. She had planned to stay as quiet as possible, too worried to let anything slip, but she could not let Elsie beg to go back to her mother. 'Because of your marriage, you are no longer a Stafford. You should praise the Lord for it. If your father is found guilty of high treason, he will bring dishonour on his family. You must stay here if you wish for your reputation to remain what it is.'

Ella disgusted herself as she advised her friend to choose a husband who abused her over her own mother at such a bleak time, but it was the only way that Elsie could avoid Henry's wrath. Buckingham's fall would probably take his family down with him. Only her marriage to Norfolk would prevent Elsie from losing favour.

Still in the middle of the great hall, Elsie fell onto her knees and grabbed Ella's hands: 'I am begging you to come to my father's help! There must have been a mistake. My father loves His Grace and the princes. Please, I am begging you to help! You have His Grace's ear, love and trust. Please, beg him to be merciful towards my father!' she implored, tears jumping out of her eyes.

Ella could feel everyone's eyes on them. She had not yet managed to formulate a reply when an irritated Norfolk swung by them and forcibly put Elsie back on her feet. 'My lady, please do forgive my wife for this display of emotion,' he apologised between his teeth, still firmly holding a distraught Elsie by the arm.

'My lord, forgiveness is not required. Lady Norfolk may rest assured that I shall do my best to help in this matter,' she lied to Elsie's face before escaping, so her friends would not see the self-disgust on her face.

There was no question whether Buckingham would be found guilty of high treason. He had to be, because she needed him to be. And she had just promised his daughter she would try to save him.

Ella pushed away the guilt to the back of her mind when she saw Cardinal Wolsey walking briskly towards her. He looked concerned, but there were no yeomen of the guard with him, which meant Buckingham had not said anything yet to his gaolers regarding what he knew about her heretic influence on Hal.

'Lady Exeter, I trust you are aware of the Duke of Buckingham's arrest,' the cardinal said without introduction. She nodded. 'I find myself in a complex situation and in need of your aid,' he told her.

'I shall do my best to help Your Eminence,' Ella said.

'The duke is, to my humble view, an innocent man. Imprudent and foolhardy, yet innocent. The King's displeasure is such that my fear is the duke shall soon lose his head. This would cause an uproar in the capital, as he is rather well-liked by the common people.'

'Your Eminence is requiring of me to soothe the King's displeasure,' Ella guessed.

'Indeed. My lady, there is nothing my influence on the King can do to save the duke from the scaffold, but your influence has yet to find its limits,' he admitted.

'His Grace has very much a mind of his own,' Ella retorted, but both of them knew it was a little white lie. 'It is unlikely I shall succeed in this task you are putting upon me, but I shall do what I can,' she lied once more.

The cardinal expressed his gratitude, blind to the fact that nothing in the world would ever make her beg Henry to be merciful towards a man who could destroy her and her daughter. The years-long feud between Buckingham and herself could only end in blood. His or hers. Ella would not rest until the axe fixed her problem.

The very evening, Cardinal Wolsey received an anonymous letter accusing Buckingham of having listened to prophecies compassing the King's death. It was high treason. The timing was too great to be a coincidence, but Henry did not care and the cardinal chose to ignore it.

John Colet refused to confirm what Ella guessed about the identity of the letter's author.

As a member of the nobility, Buckingham could not be tortured. For days that felt like months, he refused to talk. Henry was growing so frustrated with the lack of tangible proof that he ordered that Buckingham's officers should be tortured instead of their master. Ella knew that Buckingham's fate was sealed. The pain of the rack was so excruciating that at least one of these men would say anything to make it stop. Ella wanted to tell Henry they did not deserve to be tortured for something their master may or may not have done, but she could not face what her future could turn out to be if her enemy was not executed.

Ella could not eat, nor could she sleep. Haunted at night with the unknown faces of men being tortured because of her, spending the day terrified of Henry asking her why his prisoner was accusing her of corrupting his son. But he did not, and the men's torture was soon to stop as two of them broke down and reported how their master had repeatedly said that, if something was to happen to the King and his sons, it was surely God's will that he ascend the throne. Whether or not it was true and whether or not he had plotted to make it happen, it was enough to have his head cut off.

Buckingham was tried by his peers and condemned to death. Standing in the Tower by a window overlooking the scaffold, waiting for him to be taken to his execution, Ella was joined by Elizabeth Carew, her daughter's lady mistress.

'Where is my daughter?' she asked her.

'The King does not wish to watch the execution and has requested some time with Lady Grace. I was given permission to come here, which gives me much satisfaction,' she told her.

Ella looked at her for a moment, unsure of what made any execution so joyful, until Elizabeth Carew explained Buckingham had once insulted her mother. Ella nodded. She could not judge. She could barely understand what she herself was doing there. She felt this sick need to see the man who threatened her entire life die. She had to witness his last breath so she could start breathing again. She knew it would devastate her. She knew she would never forget what she was about to see. Yet, she had to see it.

She grabbed Elizabeth's hand when Buckingham appeared to be taken to the scaffold. The woman's rings were hurting her palm but she could not stop squeezing. Buckingham calmly addressed the people who had come to see him die. Ella tried to read his lips and failed. He took off his gown and said a few words to the executioner before going on his knees. A servant came to blindfold him. Ella held her breath as he willingly laid his neck on the bare wooden block.

It took three blows to sever his head from his body. Ella refused to blink. Not until she saw the head roll down in the straw. The blood was flowing from the headless body, dripping to the ground from the edge of the scaffold. Ella started to weep.

The executioner picked up the head by the hair and showed it to the people before gathering his belongings, which now included the dead man's gown. And, abandoning both the head and the headless corpse behind, he left.

Ella slowly loosened her grip on Elizabeth's hand. Both women grimaced when blood started to reach their fingers again. Elizabeth saw her tears and asked if there was anything she could do to help. Ella could not find anything to reply.

She had just killed a man. Her mind was blank. All she could do was stare at one of the rings on the hand of her daughter's lady mistress. A locket ring. With an engraved gold hoop. And a hexagonal sapphire. Ella meant to ask where she had found it but her legs refused to carry her any longer and she fainted.

28.

A WORLD OF ILLUSIONS 1521

The next couple of days were hazy. Ella witnessed what unfolded from the execution as if her soul had detached from her body. If he were watching from Purgatory, as a convicted traitor, the dead man saw his children disinherited, his widow impoverished and all his titles and lands forfeited to the crown. Henry kept Stafford Castle for himself because he looked forward to hunting in its deer parks, but gifted Thornbury Castle, another of Buckingham's grand residences, to Ella, although she knew she would never go there. She saw his severed head every time she closed her eyes.

You would not hesitate if you had to do it again, the voice inside her head reminded her.

It was right. Ella wanted to feel guilty, but she did not. Not really. Not fully. Besides, there was no room for it; all she could think about was the ring.

Elizabeth Carew had told Henry that Ella had fainted because the brutality of the execution had been too much for her, and she had gone with that. There might even have been some truth in it. Ella had never witnessed an execution before and would never forget those few seconds between the first and the final blow, Buckingham's head hanging by a thread from his body. It was too horrifying a sight to ever forget about it.

But the true shock had come from Elizabeth's hand. Ella had not seen Lolly's ring physically for over a decade but she had also never seen this design on anyone else. Elizabeth's was not a mere lookalike. It was the same ring. She had shared having inherited it at the death of her mother-in-law, the same way Ella had inherited it at the death of her grandmother. It was Lolly's ring, Ella was sure of it.

It had to be why she had not been able to find it. She had travelled back to a time when it already belonged to someone else. The ring could simply not duplicate itself.

Ella sneered inwardly. *Simply.* There was nothing simple about her situation, and she was restless. Lolly had always been so confident that the ring had not left their family since it had been made, but Ella knew very little about her family tree. For two days, she had tried her hardest to remember what her grandmother could have said about Nicholas and Elizabeth Carew, whom she believed now to be her relatives, if not her ancestors. It had been as useful as talking to a wall.

Henry's snoring covered Ella's loud sigh. She smiled. It was too dark to see anything, but she knew his face so well that she did not need to look at him with her eyes. Her smile vanished when she reminded herself what the reappearance of the ring could mean. She still did not know how it had made her travel back in time or how it had gained its powers. She used to want to know. She used to care. The answer had lost its appeal as years had gone by.

Years ago, she would have given anything to return to the twenty-first century. Part of her would always want to. Ella moved closer to Henry, hoping for his beloved smell to calm her mind. Her life was here. Now. Whether she had wanted it or not, she was a sixteenth-century peeress of England, and she had got used to that life. She had created a life, too. She could not willingly remove herself from Grace's upbringing. She could not give up on being part of it. She was not her mother. She would not leave her daughter alone.

Henry snored louder. She would not leave him either. Or Hal, or Arthur. And it was impossible to bring them with her. Even in the unlikeliness of the ring being able to make several people travel at the same time, England needed them right here, right now, and Grace deserved to grow up with her father and her siblings as well as with her mother.

'I am staying,' Ella murmured.

She closed her eyes, at peace with her decision, and even chuckled in the dark at the thought of Henry having to adapt to a more modern life: earning his living, going to the supermarket, hiding his true identity. That last requirement would be especially painful, if not impossible.

'Fuck,' Ella swore as dozens of images she would have preferred to never have seen came to attack her brain.

She sat up on the bed. Buckingham's head rolling away from his body. Inez hallucinating on her death bed. Herself, agonizing from a disease that had no cure nor explanation. Nicholas's tombstone. Katherine and her dead babies.

Ella was in her early thirties. If she lived in the twenty-first century, she would still have her whole life ahead of her. But it was the sixteenth, and she was already middle-aged. Ella wanted to wake Henry up and ask for his opinion, but she could not. She lived in a world of illusions, where people curtseyed and bowed to her without knowing her real name, where she had to lie every day, about everything, even to the father of her child. It was lie or die. And yet, even with her lies, death was still everywhere.

Buckingham's head was still displayed on a spike when his daughter came back to court after burying the rest of his body. Ella's heart sunk at the sight of her friend's mourning clothes. She faked a smile and took her friend's hands in hers.

'Dear Elsie, it brings me much joy to see you again,' she said, fighting the shake in her voice.

'And I. Your friendship eases my pain in this time of sorrow.'

'Time heals everything, you will see.'

'Please, allow me to thank you for your help. It did not have the result for which I hoped but I know that you held only kindness in your heart for me.'

'You do not need to thank me,' Ella retorted, uneasy. Chances are Henry would have listened if I had actually asked him to reconsider, the voice inside her head threatened to say out loud. 'I am sorry.'

'You have always been such a dear friend to me,' she said. 'More than a friend,' she corrected herself, blushing. 'The love I have for you surpasses all other things.'

Ella's eyes widened. 'Elsie…'

'It was my intention to never speak of it as it brings me shame, but my father's passing replaced it by the fear of departing to God before telling you.'

'Do recall your own words on the day I shared being the King's mistress with you. One cannot choose where one's heart goes to is what you told me,' Ella replied softly, understanding only now what she had meant to say that day.

Elsie's face illuminated. Her hands, still in Ella's, were sweating because of the emotion. Or maybe Ella's were, because of the guilt. 'Am I to understand that your heart sings the same song?' she asked, hope incarnated.

Ella freed her hands – too brusquely, perhaps. A grimace invited itself on her face until she pushed it away. Elsie took a step back and looked down. Ella did not know how to apologise for her reaction. Or to apologise for not seeing who her friend was before being told. Elsie's sexual orientation was not illegal. There were homosexual people at court. Sixteenth-century people were gay, too. But they had to be so privately. Gossip was common and accepted, if only it stayed exactly this: gossip.

'My love goes exclusively to the King. Even before, it never went to the members of our sex,' Ella explained, sticking to the facts. As the mother of the King's daughter, she could not allow rumours to circulate.

Elsie attempted to look at her in the eyes but failed. Her mouth opened but no word came out. In Ella's mind, the axe fell down on Buckingham's neck, again and again, endlessly, relentlessly. She escaped to her apartments, leaving Elsie and her complicated, unrequited feelings behind to fend for themselves. She was incapable of dealing with the guilt Elsie's very existence brought to her life. She could not imagine their friendship moving forward. Elsie was the constant reminder of what she had done. And now, Ella would be nothing more to her friend than the one who had rejected her love with so little care.

When Henry joined her that evening, Ella was staring at the ceiling, trying to prevent herself from blinking to burn the image of Buckingham's headless corpse from her mind. He laid down next to her, holding his head with his hand, his elbow sunk in the feather mattress.

'My adored one, what is it?' he whispered.

'Nothing. I am sorry for having stayed in my apartments today.'

'You are allowed to do all that you want. Darling, you are upset. I desire nothing more than seeing you happy once more. Tell me what has happened.'

Ella turned her head towards him. His eyes were staring at her, penetrating her soul, determined to have an answer. She hesitated. She would have given up so much to tell him the truth and unburden herself. However, the love they shared would not prevent her from getting arrested, tried and executed for heresy, treason, or both.

But she could not bring herself to lie to his worried face. She burst into tears.

Henry took her in his arms and waited for her to let it all out. There was no other option, as it seemed there were too many tears in her body for it to function properly. Ella was sniffing disgracefully and soaking his clothes with her tears. He did not mind.

'Tell me,' he repeated with a kind voice when her body stopped shaking against his.

'Edward Stafford…' she said, remembering at the last second not to call Buckingham by a title of which he had been posthumously stripped. 'I do think about him more than I should,' she confessed.

'You have the kindest of all hearts, but he was a traitor and deserved to die.'

'I do not wish to make you unhappy…'

'I am not.'

'Every time I close my eyes, I see the axe… and his head… and so much blood…' she finally opened up, her body starting to shake again.

Henry tightened his grip around her. 'You should have not seen his execution. I myself do not enjoy witnessing a man lose his head,' he admitted.

'You do not?'

'This beheading was but the fourth of the past twelve years. I neither relish men being executed for treason, nor that they committed it in the first place,' he pointed out.

Ella did not answer. Lolly had told her Henry had most likely known Anne Boleyn to be innocent of the crimes she was accused of and had sent her, his own wife, to the scaffold anyway. The Henry who was now holding her in his arms was different. He had not been tortured by the lack of sons, he had not obsessed over finding the perfect wife who would give him his male heir, he had not been hurt in his manhood when the woman he had broken with the Pope for had not given birth to the promised prince. In this version of history, he was just Henry, a man with the peace of mind of believing Buckingham to be guilty of compassing his death. Ella could not say the same.

Karma was real and had the face of Anne Boleyn. Before the end of the year, Henry's wife from another lifetime was transferred from the household of the queen of France to the one of the queen of England and made Ella question herself about whether or not something or someone was punishing her for orchestrating the death of a man. Dark hair, dark eyes, dark dress, twenty-year-old Anne Boleyn was going to destroy her life like she herself had destroyed Buckingham's.

Ella faked a smile as the envoys from Rome arrived to court one day to present Henry with the papal bull giving him the title of Defender of the Faith, but all she wanted to do was defend her own territory and jump down Anne Boleyn's throat. The Pope had been so pleased with Henry's book against Martin Luther he had made one of his dreams come true: to have his very own title, given by the Holy Father himself. Henry was over the moon, like a child having been given a gold star by the headmaster. Ella was still struggling to accept that this pious man, willing to do anything to stay in the good graces of the Pope, had in some lost version of himself broken with him, declared himself Head of the Church of England and been excommunicated in the process.

All in order to have the opportunity to father sons from Anne Boleyn. Everything was about Anne Boleyn.

That oblivious young woman, always laughing, with not a clue of what she was remembered for in the twenty-first century – being the first queen of England to ever be beheaded.

That kind, devout maid. That elegant, charismatic, sharp-witted rival. As irritating as it was, Ella had soon realised Anne Boleyn had such a set of qualities it was impossible to dislike her. She may not have been the most discreet woman in the Queen's household and seemed to love a good gossip more than anything else, but her company was always enjoyable. Somehow, she was both opinionated and naive, adamant she would stay a virgin until the day she married the true love of her life.

'How lucky she would be if the love of her life came to also be her father's choice,' Maud said one day, summing up everyone's thoughts.

Every time Ella's eyes laid on Anne was a reminder that she had to get Lolly's ring back, although she did not want to use it. She only needed to have an escape route should things go wrong because of Anne. She wanted to control whether or not she would one day have to witness Henry's burning love for Anne.

Unlike her sister Mary, Anne's reputation was so spotless that Ella could not find an excuse to have Cardinal Wolsey send her away from court. She would have preferred her to be the manipulative woman she was supposed to have been, the one who had stopped at nothing to become queen of England, with her sixth finger and her aggressive determination, but what Anne was actually trying to hide under her large bell sleeves was nothing more than an odd little wart on her thumb and had clearly never been thinking about replacing Katherine.

2018. Emily had taken her granddaughter to an open-air play at the Tower of London, recounting the last days of Henry VIII's second wife. With the Shard pointing to the sky behind the wooden stage, the actors in their period costumes seemed to be coming straight from 1536, when Anne Boleyn had lost her head. As they bowed to the audience, Ella noticed the emotion in her grandmother's eyes.

'Are you okay?' she asked her when they started to walk away.

'Yes. It is difficult to think about her fate as she was innocent.'

'She was the reason Katherine of Aragon was put aside, though. I mean, she knew what Henry VIII wanted to do and she stayed anyway.'

'She was not the reason why the Queen was put aside. Henry VIII was. Tell me, darling, what other options do you think she had but to stay?' Emily asked. Ella shrugged, knowing a history lesson was coming. 'If a woman was known to have lost her virginity before her marriage, she could give up on making a good one. This was the only reason why Anne Boleyn refused herself to Henry VIII. She could not have predicted that he would get rid of his wife. It had never been done before. By the time she understood what was going on, everyone believed she was his mistress.

Her reputation was gone. Besides, the King would have had to give his blessing for her to marry anyone else. Do you really think he would have given it?'

'Maybe not. She was too far down the road,' Ella admitted.

'She was so far that turning back was impossible! She was no homewrecker. The only thing she had any control over was her virginity. It is the King who decided he needed to remarry.'

'But she wanted to become queen, didn't she?'

'Well, first: who wouldn't want to?' Emily joked. 'Ella, she had no alternative. Her only chance to have a decent future was with the King.'

'It is sad to love someone so much and then… this,' Ella waved at the Tower.

'He never loved her. From the moment he decided he wanted her, he pursued her, even though she refused him. No means no, but he could not accept it. He was obsessed. Obsession is not love. It is why it ended up in so much violence,' Emily told her.

Ella looked painfully at Henry, laughing with his namesake and friend, Henry Norris. Anne Boleyn had been treated appallingly, both historically and by history, and it was on him. Ella had to decide between trying to do right by Anne and risking the collapse of her entire world, or protect it in doing everything she could to get rid of her. Anne deserved happiness, but the longer she stayed at court, the more chances Henry had to notice her romantically. Ella was not prepared to live her life in fear of it happening one day.

A fleeting thought came to remind her that slipping something deadly in Anne's cup of ale could not be that difficult, especially if she managed to get the ring back. Lolly's poison locket ring had turned out to be a hair locket ring, according to the current owner. Not purchased to murder people, then, but it did not mean it could not be used as such. Ella shook her head, horrified. She had killed one person too many already. She would have to find a way for Anne to live away from court and from Henry, with her head on her shoulders.

29.

HEARTLESS DEED 1522

Grace, Arthur and Margaret were playing outside under Ella and Elizabeth Carew's close supervision when a letter was brought. Ella smiled. Soon after his eleventh birthday, Hal had been sent to Ludlow Castle, where every prince of Wales was meant to learn how to govern. The boy had since been sending many letters to Ella, so many in fact it was not rare for her to receive two or three at the same time, but there was only a brief one that day.

The fourteenth day of April, 1522.

Most noble and dearest Elizabeth. This letter shall be short, as I must hurry myself to archery practice. In much secrecy, I have attempted to cut the length of my hair. I pray God it shall grow long again hastily. I am certain my lord father the King would not approve of my foolishness. I must beg of you to withhold this information from his gracious self.

Your absence is for me a great burden. I miss your presence but find comfort in reading your

cherished letters and respecting your kind recommendations about my cleanliness and diet.
Your most devoted son,
Henry P.

Ella burst out laughing, picturing her eleven-year-old-boy clandestinely cutting his own hair and finding out with horror he was no barber. Saying Henry would not approve was some understatement.

'Are you amused by us, mama?' Grace asked, twirling with her cousin and her brother to see who could spin the longest without feeling dizzy.

'I am, sweetheart, but also by your brother's letter,' she replied.

'I would like to see Hal again,' the girl said.

Grace was two and a half years old and her speech was more advanced than any other toddler Ella had ever met, even Hal, at this age. Ella was boasting with pride every time her brilliant daughter opened her mouth. She meant to reassure the girl that she would see her eldest brother soon but noticed Henry approaching, not looking so pleased.

'Children, put an end at what you are up to and go back inside with Lady Elizabeth,' she demanded.

Elizabeth Carew grabbed the girls by the hand and Arthur trotted behind her back to the palace. Henry did not seem to notice his children or his niece and sat down next to Ella with an irritated sigh, taking his head in his hands. She waited, wondering how upset he was. The angrier he was, the more advised it was to keep quiet.

'I wrestled with Bryan,' he declared.

'The man must be much bruised,' Ella attempted a joke.

It worked. Henry laughed. Whatever had caused this temper, most of it had gone in his wrestling match with Sir Francis Bryan.

'Jacques Lefèvre, some rogue from Etaples. A protégé of Princess Margaret, the sister of King Francis. The scoundrel translated the Bible into the French language and had it printed. The devil's puppet!' Henry barely contained another outburst of anger.

It was not difficult for Ella to appear as shocked as Henry expected her to be. She was jubilant, of course. But still alarmed. That the French king's sister herself had something to do with the translation was unexpected. As far as Ella was concerned, France was as Catholic as England, and although fearful Henry might come to reconsider the alliance because of it, she was grateful that this princess had made history despite being of the so-called weaker sex.

'Do you believe Francis agrees with that nonsense?' Henry wondered.

'That Frenchman is a protégé of his sister, not his own,' Ella reminded him.

'Perhaps,' he conceded.

Ella stared at him for a second, gauging the peril she could find herself in if she tried to convince him to follow Margaret's example. He could accuse her of being a heretic.

If Henry decides to authorise the translation into English, it will prepare the kingdom for the religious reforms Hal is to bring one day and make things easier for him, the voice inside her head persuaded her. Ella took a deep breath.

'My love, may I speak freely?' she asked.

'Always.'

'Please do forgive me if it displeases you, as it is but a naive thought.'

'Do not fret. I am always eager to listen to you.'

'Would it be so wrong to publish a translation into the English language?' she asked, mentally crossing her fingers that Henry would not repudiate her for her heretic boldness.

There was a pause. 'Religious doctrine is not a matter to be interpreted by the ordinary person, Elizabeth,' he eventually retorted.

'Yet, Francis is the first king of France during whose reign a translation of the Holy Bible is published. It shall be his legacy,' she said, hoping the rivalry he shared with King Francis would push him to the right direction.

Henry took the time to look at her. 'Is it your wish that I do the same? That I let laymen preach wrongly translated Scriptures to unknowing souls?' he asked.

It was rhetorical. He was incredulous. Ella had failed.

She grabbed his hand. 'I beg you to forgive me. I overheard a servant say the powerlessness against death brought by the sweating sickness and the plague had weakened the faith of many. It was very ignorant of me to think that reading by themselves a translation of the Bible in English could strengthen it,' she apologised.

Henry relaxed – only slightly. 'You have a kind and charitable heart. Darling, persons who have benefited from a proper education do not need a vernacular translation,' he said.

And those who have not? Ella thought.

He read her mind. 'The persons who have not been taught Latin, even in the possession of a vernacular translation, would still be in need of a man of God to explain to them the appropriate doctrine, or they would understand it incorrectly and would be endangering their immortal souls.'

Ella apologised once more and thanked him for his clarification. Telling him anything different to what he wanted to hear, especially on a religious level, was too risky. Henry smiled, satisfied, and declared that his love for her made it easier to forgive her.

The translation of the Bible was not a cause Ella could fight for today. For a brief moment, she had thought she would succeed, but it was not possible. Henry went back to the palace, but she decided to stay behind. In silence, she observed a little sparrow flying from one tree to another, making her both hungry and sickened to have ever eaten such an adorable thing.

'My lady?' the voice of John Colet brought her back to the present moment. Ella was not sure how long she had stayed outside by herself. There were now more clouds in the sky than when Henry had come to her.

'Master Colet. Sit with me,' she said.

His black robes did very little to conceal his weight loss. Ella had been so focused on herself that she could not remember the first time she had noticed it, but it was now so obvious that she had to enquire about his health. He smiled, enigmatic and quiet.

Maybe the regrets of his secret role in Buckingham's execution are eating him alive, Ella's inner critic told her.

Or it was something else. As if it had only happened in a dream, a blurry memory came back to Ella's mind as she remembered how Pop had similarly lost a dramatic amount of weight in a matter of weeks. She looked at Colet's emaciated face. As her chaplain, he knew so much about Elizabeth White, but she did not know a thing about him. Maybe, he did not regret anything. Maybe, it was cancer that was eating him alive, like it had with Pop.

After a moment of silence, Ella told Colet about her conversation with Henry. He listened without interrupting her.

'The King rightly fears that a vernacular translation would involve a corruption of the Scriptures,' he stated.

'I understand this. But why not appoint a trusted scholar, like yourself, to begin a faithful, respectful and authentic translation, that His Grace would oversee himself?' Ella asked.

'One day,' he said.

But not today, she translated him silently.

As a strict follower of the rules, Elizabeth Carew cleaned her hands several times a day, always taking the ring off when doing so. Ella, convincing herself she was only taking back what was hers, jumped on the first opportunity that presented itself and snatched the coveted jewel as she walked past. Elizabeth forgot all about its existence when Grace started crying over a stain on her dress. Ella escaped the room, her heart beating so loudly in her chest she could have sworn anyone in the entire palace could hear it.

Rushing to her apartments to hide the inestimable ring, she bumped into Cardinal Wolsey. The man in red had spent the entire day giving her dirty looks from afar. Henry hid no secrets from his trusted friend and had told him how she had, the day before, attempted to lure him to the side of a vernacular translation of the Bible.

Ella had decided to ignore him. The cardinal had been in a foul mood anyway ever since the death of the late pope and the election of Adrian VI as his successor. The emperor had promised to put Wolsey's name forward, but – as predicted by Ella herself some time before – had ended up recommending one of his own men instead. If there was one thing the cardinal did not like, it was being made the butt of a joke. He had been lied to, publicly deceived, and he was still reeling.

'Lady Exeter, always a pleasure,' he said.

'The pleasure is mine, Your Eminence.'

'I have, only ten minutes past, been informed of the passing of the dean of St Paul's.'

Ella digested the information, resembling a fish outside of its tank for a second. John Colet was dead. She had spoken to him only yesterday. They had never been close, but they had been partners in illegality. And, although he had never confirmed it, he had helped save her life by anonymously informing on Buckingham to the cardinal. Ella clutched ever more tightly on the ring, now feeling utterly alone.

'I am very saddened and shall pray for Master Colet's soul,' she managed to let out.

'It is also my knowledge,' he ignored her response, 'that a forbidden copy of *De Libertate Christiana* has been found in his apartment.'

Ella fought hard to stay in control of her facial expression. *On the Freedom of a Christian* was the third of Martin Luther's works. It had been released in 1520, two years before. Henry had thought a good old bonfire had rid England of every copy. Colet and Ella, who had been working to circulate them widely beforehand, had agreed to stop for a while to avoid the wrath of both king and cardinal. Colet had never told her he owned one himself.

Careless man, Ella thought, but immediately regretted badmouthing the dead.

'Was my lady aware of it being in the late dean's possessions?' Wolsey asked.

'I had no reason to be.'

'Master Colet was your chaplain.'

'As he was His Grace's,' Ella reminded him. She would not let Colet's mistake become her problem.

The cardinal observed her for a moment. Ella did not look away. As much as she needed him to be, the man was impossible to read.

Is he suspicious? She wondered. But of what could he be? She had not been privately with Henry since the day before, but he had said he had forgiven her.

He could have changed his mind, the voice inside her head counterattacked.

'His Grace was disquieted yesterday, shortly after meeting with you,' the cardinal declared. He did not have to explain why. They both knew that they both knew.

'I was being naive, as is common among my sex. The King graciously forgave me,' Ella replied.

'Oh, but my lady is not naive,' the cardinal said with an obnoxious smile. What could have been a compliment sounded threatening. 'It is a source of embarrassment for me to have been unsuccessful at uncovering the identity of the persons responsible for the circulation of Martin Luther's heresy, here in England. I was of course unaware of the late dean's sympathies for it… as I was with my lady's.'

'Your Eminence be assured that I do not share Martin Luther's beliefs,' Ella retorted firmly. It was the truth. She did not believe in God, after all.

'You share his preposterous wish for the translation of the Scriptures,' he hit back.

There was no more smile. The ring was burning against Ella's palm. What exactly did he know?

'Your Eminence, am I under some sort of accusation? If it is so, I trust you have been wise enough to inform His Grace?' sudden fear made her snap.

'Of course not, my lady,' he replied, but Ella was unsure of which question had been answered.

Once back in her apartments, Ella threw the ring in Nicholas's old pair of gloves trimmed with fox fur. Lolly had always taught her that stealing was a heartless deed, but her hands were tied. Especially now that Wolsey suspected her of heresy. She went on to open a window, hoping to bring her breathing back to a more normal rhythm.

Ella did not waste her time wondering how and why her grandmother's ring had sent her to 1510, but she did torture herself about how to make sure it would send her back to the twenty-first century if she came to use it again. Picturing her life there after twelve years as a sixteenth-century-woman was obscure enough to think about travelling by mistake to 1210, 1810, or even 2110.

The wind was too strong to keep the window open. Ella closed it and rested her forehead on the cold glass. From her window, she could see Anne Boleyn and Henry Percy holding hands in what they surely thought was a discreet place.

Cardinal Wolsey distrusted her, Colet was dead and her questions were still left unanswered; but at least Anne Boleyn was in love, and Henry had not romantically noticed her yet.

Ella purposefully intruded on a secret rendezvous between Anne Boleyn and her special friend. The past night had been the third in a row that Henry had spent away from her. Ella was growing increasingly worried that the cardinal was poisoning his mind with his suspicions of heresy. Henry was always busy, or so she was told, every time she wanted to talk to him.

It only meant one thing: Anne Boleyn had to go. As a precautionary measure.

Anne's father, Sir Thomas Boleyn, was known to be concocting a marriage between Anne and her cousin, James Butler, in order to settle a family dispute over the Irish earldom of Ormond. One side of Ella's brain rooted for this plan. If Anne was to leave for Ireland, there was little chance she would ever come back to court. The other side was less enthusiastic. Any person living in the south of England in 1522 would view a life in Ireland as a miserable exile. Ella was not sure she was comfortable with the thought of Anne's second chance at life being spent this way.

Henry Percy, the twenty-year-old heir to the Earl of Northumberland, could solve this problem. It had been murmured for years that his father was planning to betroth him to the daughter of the Earl of Shrewsbury, but nothing had yet been made official.

The two lovebirds were awkwardly looking at Ella, unable to begin the conversation because she outranked them and unable to leave her sight without being labelled as rude by the mother of the King's daughter.

Ella smiled, doing her best to appear approachable. 'Do not look so frightened, there has been no offence committed,' she said, her shoulders shrugging under the red velvet of her gown.

Percy did not reply but Anne's eyes filled with relief. 'May I beg my lady to be so kind as to not tell a soul about this?' she asked.

'I give you my word that this shall remain a secret between us,' Ella promised. 'It is my recommendation that you should behave with the utmost discretion,' she added after a pause. 'To this day, I remember the King's terrible anger when the Duke of Suffolk married the French Queen without permission.'

'I was in the household of the French Queen then. The duke was much afeared for his neck,' Anne recalled, putting her hand on her thin neck.

'The King was merciful. It is a source of joy for I to know them so happy now, surrounded by their children in the country,' Ella said innocently before putting an end to the conversation.

It would have been quicker to remind Anne and Percy that they could marry behind Henry's back and beg for his forgiveness afterwards, but Ella would end up in trouble if it became known that it had been her idea in the first place.

The seed had been planted. They were young and in love. They would think so much about Charles and Mary living peacefully as a family that they would want to have this kind of life too. They would be fined by Henry, but forgiven, and Ella would insist on them being sent away from court for a few years as part of their punishment. And *au revoir* Anne Boleyn.

Only days later, the scandal of the unauthorised marriage of Anne and Percy exploded like a bomb, turning their immediate futures into ashes.

The Earl of Northumberland, who was the former Duchess of Buckingham's brother and already sick of the disgrace poured down on his family, was beside himself that his son had dared to tie himself to the daughter of a diplomat.

For Sir Thomas Boleyn, his last unmarried daughter choosing to marry for love over duty was a disappointment he did nothing to hide. He refused to provide her with a dowry.

A big knot formed in Ella's stomach as soon as she heard an outraged Cardinal Wolsey shout words about the newlyweds that should never come out of anyone's mouth, especially not from a man of God's. Percy was thrown out of Wolsey's household; Anne of the Queen's.

Ella had once again played with other people's lives. She wished she could have said it had been done so in order to give Anne the life she had always deserved, but if the then maid had not shown any sign of going further with Percy, Ella would have married Anne to her Irish cousin against her will and she knew it.

Anne and Percy had lost so much. Their positions, their parents' emotional and financial support, their reputations. The cardinal had publicly vowed to barre Percy from any route of preferment for as long as he would breathe. Virtually, Percy was left with nothing until becoming earl himself at the death of his father.

Ella was feeling so responsible for their situation that she did not even look up when Henry was announced to her apartments for the first evening in almost a week. He took off his hat and his doublet before coming to kiss her on the top of her head, so naturally Ella doubted for half a second that he had ever been upset at her. But his week of silence was the proof that Wolsey had shared his suspicions towards her with him. His decision to come back was the proof that Wolsey had nothing tangible against her.

'My adored one, why do you look so tormented?' he asked.

'I should have prevented this marriage, I should have told them these feelings were foolish,' she heard herself answer.

Realising what she had just said, Ella cursed silently and looked up. Henry was staring back at her, his gaze cutting through her skin and her bones like a well sharpened sword.

His cheeks turned red, the vein on his forehead popped, his eyebrows sunk in a frown, his mouth opened. Ella threw herself on the ground, her hands joint in front of her, bracing herself for the loud and indignant reprimand that was indubitably to follow.

Nothing came.

Henry's eyes were still on her. He was breathing heavily. His hands were in fists, resting on his hips. Ella knew he was trying to calm himself down before doing or saying something he would come to regret, which was a challenge for such a quick-tempered person.

For a minute that seemed to last forever, none of them moved. Ella's knees were hurting on the floor and her loose hair was in her face, but she was too frightened to move a finger.

'I have always been of even temper in your company and it is not my desire for it to change tonight,' Henry said between his teeth.

'I deserve your wrath,' Ella bowed her head down. She was shaking uncontrollably.

'You do. Your duty was to tell me, Elizabeth. This marriage cannot be annulled as it has been consummated, but it should have never taken place,' his voice trembled as he tried to keep it even.

'I failed you. I beg you to forgive me. I did not think they would be so senseless as to act on their feelings,' she had to lie. Henry could never know it had been her goal all along.

Henry closed his eyes and massaged his temples with an irritated moan. 'Thomas Boleyn's youngest daughter, Countess of Northumberland?' he then scoffed with a disdain that equalled a punch.

As wealthy and important as the earldom of Northumberland was for the kingdom, Henry had just sounded like Buckingham on the day she herself had become Countess of Nottingham.

In another life, you made her queen of England, Ella wanted to retort. 'What shall happen to her? To them both?' she asked instead.

'They are to be banished from my sight for as long as it pleases the Lord,' Henry replied, adamant.

'Henry, they will not be able to provide for themselves!' she cried, but he left the room without a word, slamming the door behind him.

She understood her mistake: he did not care. Charles and Mary had been forgiven because he loved them. They had married behind his back, but they were his best friend and his favourite sister. Anne and Percy were not. It should have cheered Ella up to realise Henry did not care for Anne at all, but it did not. He would never pardon them. He might not even pardon her.

On the bright side, as the newlyweds had not married into the royal family without his permission, they would not lose their heads. Which would have been a relief for Anne, if only she had known.

30.

THE EQUATION 1522

Anne had already left court with her husband when August drew to a close, but Henry was as upset as ever and courtiers were whispering behind Ella's back. She requested to spend a couple of weeks with her daughter in the country, away from the toxicity. His permission came too quickly for her to consider it good news, but as soon as she sat down next to Grace in the litter, she knew she had made the right call.

A few days were needed to reach Colwick Hall, the house in Nottinghamshire that Nicholas had bought to celebrate his elevation to the earldom of Nottingham. Alterations had been planned out straight away for the house to be considered grand enough for an earl, and then a duke. It was Ella's first visit since her husband's death, and she was not even sure she remembered what the house was like.

She looked at her sleeping daughter. Grace's sweet head was resting on her lap. 'What do you think my life would be like if Nicholas had survived the sweat, darling?' she wondered in a whisper.

'My lady?' Elizabeth Carew replied.

Ella resisted the will to roll her eyes. It had become so easy to ignore the immediate presence of people who were only there to serve her that her brain was sometimes shutting them out completely. Elizabeth had been sitting there, in her litter, for hours already.

'Do you believe His Grace would have professed his love for me had I not been a widow?' Ella could not help but ask her.

'It is not possible to know, my lady.'

'Have a guess.'

'His Grace's love for my lady is strong, pure and honest,' the woman only gave half an answer.

Ella sighed and opened the dark curtains of the litter. Outside, the sky was dull and grey, exactly like her prospects if Henry's strong, pure and honest love had been annihilated by her two consecutive mistakes – and the cardinal whispering in his ear that she may be a heretic.

Her near-death experience had shaken Henry up enough for him to come clean about his feelings, but she did not know if he would have done so had his childhood friend been alive. Both Henry and Ella would have had to make a choice.

You betrayed the Queen for Henry, you would have betrayed Nicholas too, the judgemental voice inside her head said.

'What would have been my late husband's reaction to my love for His Grace?' Ella asked Elizabeth, pretending to not see that her questions were making her daughter's lady mistress quite uncomfortable.

'My lady knew the late Duke of Exeter much better than I could ever pretend to,' she said.

Ella admitted that the woman was right. Legally, Nicholas could have beaten her out of indignation, sent her to a convent, or even pleaded to Henry that she should be burned at the stake. She refused to believe that he would have ever hurt her, but he would have been allowed to make such a request.

Grace snored, just like her lookalike father. She was oblivious to the bumps on the road. Ella smiled. The terrible truth was that her life was only better for the loss of her husband. As displeased as Henry was with her at this moment, he was the father of her child. She would never regret the choices that had led her to becoming a mother. Grace was Ella's greatest pride. As a child born in 1519 of a king and a noblewoman, she was bound to spend more time with her lady mistress than with her parents, but Ella knew she could feel that her parents' love for her had no limit.

Once settled in Colwick Hall, and for the first time in a while, Ella felt safe. The portrait of Nicholas, hung in her bedroom, was watching over her. She had taken with her just enough people to be properly attended without feeling overwhelmed or overheard. Elizabeth was officially there to help with Grace, but really because Ella wanted to get to know the woman who may be her ancestor. The woman had brought a few of her own servants too, including the fourteen-year-old Mabel. Despite their difference of age and rank, Grace had developed a close bond with her.

Ella was watching her daughter play with the girl's hair with a certain tenderness when she received a letter.

The first day of September, 1522.

My lady, I return you my most hearty thanks for the gold and the diamonds sent unto me and my husband by the goodness of your heart. I understand how great the trouble you have taken for me and I pray to ever be able to return this kindness, although the lack of certainty brings me sorrow. I shall always love you above all other persons, next to His Grace's illustrious self and my lord husband.

It grieved me to read the atonement in your letter, and in my boldness I must beg of you to cease all self-reproach and condemnation, as there is not a thing worthy of blame in your pure heart. My beloved husband found me deserving of the honour of becoming his wife and I shall carry the joy of this blessedness with me always. The great happiness that I feel in being loved truly by a husband whom

I adore is more fortune than my heart has ever deserved, and all that it has ever desired.

I pray God send you as good health and prosperity as I would.

Your most obliged and loving servant,
Anne, Lady Percy

Ella folded the letter with relief and satisfaction. Queen Anne Boleyn, the first queen of England tried and condemned to death, who had lost her head and her life for allegedly cheating on her royal husband with several men, including her own brother, would never be. She was now Lady Percy, banished from court but enjoying marital bliss. She had married for love. She was luckier than most women of the time.

On the day of Anne and Percy's departure for Lancashire, where the married and mother-of-two Mary Boleyn was waiting for them, Ella had discreetly put a purse of gold coins in Anne's hands. Shortly afterwards, she had sent another one, with some jewels and a few words of apology. Knowing Anne had received them and had some money to get through this chapter of her life was all that Ella needed to know.

Anne Boleyn's name was unlikely to be remembered, but Ella was not sure it mattered. Anne would keep her head, Henry would keep his wife, and England would have to work from there.

As days passed, a quiet, soothing routine came into place. It was Ella's first proper break in a while from the glittering chaos that was Henry's court. It was true that she had always rather enjoyed it; the people, the music, the entertainments, the luxury. But, with it gone, so were pride, greed, superficiality and rivalry. Ella was learning to appreciate this simpler life, aware of how precious those moments were. Any day now, she would receive a letter from Henry, allowing her to return.

It would all come back then. Elsie as a walking reminder of the heaviest secret that weighed on her heart. The cardinal and his mission to dispose of her by whatever means necessary. The constant threat of the end of Henry's love. The courtiers gossiping about her but begging her to promise her daughter's hand to their sons.

Ella would have given up all the jewels in the world if only it meant staying in Colwick Hall with her daughter for ever.

'Mabel, you must be more careful with your belongings!' the irritated voice of Elizabeth pulled Ella out of her thoughts.

The two women were enjoying the shadow of an old tree as the teenager and the toddler were making wreaths with flowers, leaves and small branches. At least, Grace still was. Mabel was now spinning around, trying to spot the large crack in the back of her dress like a cat trying to bite its own tail, and Elizabeth was about to give her a proper scowl.

'Elizabeth, please go inside and fetch a new dress for the girl. I shall pay for it myself,' Ella said, getting on her feet. She would not let anything disturb her peaceful retreat.

'Yes, my lady,' Elizabeth disappeared inside.

'I thank my lady for her bounty,' Mabel curtseyed low.

'Come near, let me see if it may be fixed. Turn around,' Ella demanded.

'I am quite certain it may be. I will do it myself right this evening. There is no need to trouble yourself for it,' Mabel stuttered, red-faced.

'Turn around, I said,' Ella repeated.

'I would rather not, my lady,' Mabel retorted.

Ella frowned. It was not so much about the fact that she had lost the habit of anyone telling her no, but more about the look of complete horror in the girl's eyes. Ella gently but firmly grabbed her arm and turned her around, now very curious.

She froze. 'What…' she started to say, but her mind refused to form any sentence.

'Please, have mercy!' Mabel sunk on her knees and cried when Ella, who had been holding her hair up to see what she was hiding in her back, pulled her back up.

Mabel was not hiding anything in her back. It was on it. On her left shoulder blade. A large, dark pink, skin pigmentation. A birthmark, shaped somewhat like Spain. Mabel was sobbing, probably terrified she would be accused of bearing the mark of witchcraft, but Ella could not have cared less about witchcraft. She cared about the birthmark she had seen too many times to even count. She made the girl face her once more, this time forgetting to be gentle.

'My lady, please...' Mabel begged.

'Shush. Look at me!' Ella took her face in her hands and raised her dimpled chin up.

Then she made the sobbing girl twirl again, holding her by the shoulders, staring at the mark like she had seen a ghost. The eyes were green, the mark was pink, and Lolly had come back from the dead.

2005. Emily took her granddaughter to the National Portrait Gallery one summer afternoon to hide from the heatwave. Ella loved to go to art museums to sit down in front of the prettiest painting in the room and copy it on her notebook. As she followed her grandmother into the Tudor room, Ella's eyes travelled from the Spain-shaped birthmark on her back to the coronation portrait of Queen Elizabeth I, sat down, and started to draw the crown.

'Her reign is one of the longest in history, but her birth was a disappointment. They had it all prepared for a prince and had to add "s" on the official letters because the baby was a girl,' Emily told her with an amused grin.

'There is nothing bad with girls,' Ella frowned.

'You are right but, back then, they thought boys were more important and that girls were not capable of anything great.'

'They were stupid.'

'Oh, no. They just did not know any better. She proved them wrong!' Emily pointed at the portrait. 'Her childhood was difficult, but she did become queen.'

'Why was her childhood difficult?' Ella asked as she kept drawing.

'Her mother died when she was little and her father remarried. People stopped treating her as a princess overnight.'

'But she became queen anyway.'

'She did. When her big sister Mary was queen, they disagreed on how to love God, and because of that, she was not safe. When Mary died without a child, making her queen, it was the chance for a new life. She had grown up bullied, with a dead mother and a father who did not love her as he should have, not knowing what tomorrow would bring,' Emily told her, caressing her sapphire ring with an air of melancholy on her face. 'Her life changed unexpectedly. She became what she was always meant to be.'

Ella and Emily observed the portrait in silence, the four-year-old thinking about how great it would be to wear a similar dress on her very first day of school in September whilst her grandmother was reminiscing about the moment her own life had changed so unexpectedly.

Ella let go of the girl and sat back down on the bench. She felt like vomiting, screaming, crying, fainting, all at the same time. She could not do anything but stare at her knees hidden under the luxury fabric of her gown.

Mabel was believed by Nicholas and Elizabeth Carew to be the illegitimate daughter of Nicholas's father, but Sir Richard Carew refused to recognise the paternity. She was a girl *with a dead mother and a father who did not love her as he should have.*

Lolly's maiden name came back to Ella, slapping her in the face as she realised her stupidity. Emily Richards. Her own made-up name, like Elizabeth White was Ella's.

She sniffed and stared at Mabel for a minute. She was a servant. She was poor. She was living her life *not knowing what tomorrow would bring*. Ella took a deep breath, unsuccessfully trying to clear her head.

'My lady looks pale,' Mabel said hesitantly.

'Emily Buckley… Richards… she never existed. She tried to tell me then. But I was only four!' Ella cried.

'I do not understand.'

'Of course not. You are not her yet.'

'My lady?'

'You must have stolen the ring…'

'I would have never done such a heartless deed!' Mabel panicked. Ella closed her eyes, hearing her adult grandmother echo those words in her head.

'You do not look like a thief… maybe you simply tried it on, like I did,' she murmured. The girl did not reply. She was looking at her like she had gone insane. 'Lolly was not wearing the ring around her neck because it was ancient and fragile, she was scared that it would force her back in time and become a servant all over again,' she realised.

'Mama?' Grace broke her trance.

Ella alternatively looked at her daughter and the teenaged version of her grandmother as if she were watching a tennis game. Grace was Mabel's great-granddaughter. It had to explain why they got along so well.

It also explained why Ella had felt like she had known Mabel already on the day she had met her. The green eyes and the dimpled chin should have been enough for her to figure it out. She had lived under the same roof as her dead grandmother's past self without knowing.

Mabel was Lolly. Lolly was Mabel.

Ella wanted to bury herself underground. The shame of not recognising the woman who had raised her was overwhelming. She could have taken her in. Supported her financially. Raised her from her condition. Given her a better life. But no. She had watched her miserable life from afar, from her silks and diamonds, with the solution to the girl's problems hidden in her late husband's gloves.

'I feel fine, sweetheart. I see Lady Carew coming back. I must ask you to stay with her,' Ella said, but took the time to hug her daughter tight and kiss her on the forehead before going back inside.

She had a plan.

Ella lied when one of the men escorting her back to court asked if she had received a letter from Henry requesting her return. The absence of that hypothetical letter was leading her to think he still was upset at her. He would not like to see her barge in without permission.

If you meet him without the cardinal strutting around, it should be easy to convince him that your undying love for him made your separation too difficult to bear, she thought.

She sighed. She did miss him and she did love him, but he was not the reason why she was on her way back to court. The ring was there, so well hidden that she had forgotten to take it with her to Colwick Hall. She needed it back. For the first time, she knew exactly what to do with it.

Her life changed unexpectedly. She became what she was always meant to be. It was what Lolly had told her all those years ago about Queen Elizabeth I – and about herself.

Somehow, Mabel had once before stumbled upon her mistress's ring and, accidentally, had travelled in time. Ella had once thought Lolly may have herself travelled to the past, but she had only travelled to the future. Ella could only guess what had followed. Mabel had discovered a completely different world. Where she did not have to serve anyone. Where she was free. Where she could choose. Ella loved her life in the sixteenth century but knew that her reality was millions of miles away from Mabel's. It was no surprise that the girl had decided to stay in the future.

The ring was the last gift Ella had received from her grandmother. She was now determined to give it back. Without it, Mabel could not become what she had always been meant to be: a woman in charge of her own life.

Ella smiled when Eltham Palace appeared after a long and boring ride. It was where the most important events of her life had happened, from her travel to Grace's birth. It was only fitting for it to be the place where the jewel that would change her grandmother's life for ever was kept.

As she entered the great hall, she silently begged for it to be empty, although she knew it to be close to impossible. Elsie proved her right: 'Elizabeth?' she heard her voice.

'Elsie. It is a pleasure to see you, and with child,' Ella said, noticing her slightly round belly.

'I thank you. May I ask for a few words in a more private environment?' Elsie asked and headed out of the great hall without waiting for an answer. The former friends walked in silence to an empty room. The wooden door shut with a loud thud behind them. 'It was my desire to meet with you first, as a token of our friendship, before talking to my lord husband as my duty commands me. Elizabeth, I found a note in my late father's belongings.'

'You see me confused,' Ella replied, already feeling sick to her stomach.

'My uncle Wiltshire was given the task of putting his affairs in order after his departure to God, but a particular piece of paper was overlooked until I myself discovered it. In it, my father accuses you of supporting Martin Luther's heretic views and of endangering the soul of the prince of Wales by requiring that he never burns a heretic at the stake,' Elsie told her, refusing to look at her in the eyes.

'This is scandalous,' Ella retorted with the conviction of a well-trained liar. Even beyond the grave, Buckingham was doing his best to ruin her.

'He acknowledges that he is incapable of accusing you of heresy, as the most influential person at court,' Elsie ignored her. 'He says this is the reason why he wrote down what he had overheard, so as not to forget any word of it until sufficient proof could be found. It is my understanding that his arrest prevented such findings.'

'Elsie, do not tell me you believe any of this!'

'I do not know!' she yelled. 'My father was never your ally, nor your friend. Quite the contrary! He may have been lying to bring trouble into your life. But the cardinal shared with my lord husband that some of Luther's works were found in your late chaplain's possessions... and that you attempted to convince the King to have the Scriptures translated!' she screamed, like these were the most atrocious words that she ever had had to pronounce.

'Your father's words are lies,' Ella defended herself.

'Swear it on Grace's life,' Elsie demanded.

'I swear on my daughter's life and immortal soul that none of this is true,' Ella replied, praying that Elsie did not see the disgust on her face from bringing her own flesh and blood into her dangerous lie.

'I must believe you, then. Please do forgive me. This was a convincing read,' Elsie admitted, taking her father's note out of her sleeve with a sorry smile.

Ella acted without thinking. She grabbed the paper and threw it in the fireplace, immediately regretting it.

'Elizabeth! No! What have you done?' Elsie shouted, reaching out for the note and burning herself in the process.

Wailing of pain and frustration, she watched as the note burned in the hearth. Ella pictured herself at the stake meeting the same fate. Two maids entered the room, coming to the rescue after hearing the screams. They curtseyed low when they saw Ella and left the room when she barked at them to go away.

'Tell me why you destroyed it,' Elsie said with a shake of anger in her voice. 'Was my father right?' she asked. Ella did not have time to answer before Elsie's eyes widened with pure horror. 'You never begged the King for mercy. My father had discovered your vile secret and you had him executed!' she accused her.

'This is outrageous! Your father was a traitor and I refuse to see my name tarnished because of his lies!' Ella hit back.

'Lady Willoughby was in the right… she tried to warn Her Grace but could not fight the evil inside your heart!' Elsie understood with obvious repulsion.

'The only reason Maria had for disliking me was the love Her Grace bore for me. I must insist that you cease this slander, otherwise I will see that you face the King's intense displeasure,' Ella threatened before storming out of the room.

Before the door closed after her, she heard Elsie saying to herself that her father had died an honourable man after all. She pretended that she had not heard anything.

Oblivious to anyone and anything around her, Ella rushed to her apartments and barricaded the door with a chair. Elsie knew. She knew everything. The proof was gone and her father was dead, his head and body rotting underground, but she would stop at nothing for the truth to be revealed. She would talk to her husband, who would share what he knew with Wolsey, who would in turn happily tell Henry. And *adieu* Elizabeth White.

'Why did you burn that letter?' Ella cried out loud.

Destroying it had said more about her guilt than the letter itself. She was done. It was the end. Like a hunting dog with a deer, Elsie would refuse to let it go. She would avenge her father and the indelible stain on the Stafford family name. She would never give up on what he had died for.

Ella's breathing became more erratic as she pictured Henry and Wolsey sitting down with Elsie and her husband, connecting the dots. How both Elsie and Wolsey had begged her to do whatever she could to save Buckingham from the axe, and how she had instead validated Henry's feelings and pushed him as far away from mercy as possible. Ella broke down in tears. Her guilt was too obvious, especially now that she had been seen destroying the words written by the man she had had killed.

And it was only a matter of time before the cardinal found the proof he needed about her involvement with Colet in the circulation of Luther's views around the kingdom.

'Hal…' she whispered between two sobs, taking her head in her hands.

Grace's future would be jeopardised for being the daughter of a convicted traitor, but Hal risked everything. Henry would never trust him to succeed him on the throne knowing that he had been manipulated by a heretic into rejecting some of the Church's teachings. Henry was to only get firmer in his religious views, but what if Hal refused to pretend a devout Catholicism? What if father and son, king and heir, openly opposed each other over it?

What if the only thing Ella had been creating for the past twelve years was the perfect recipe for civil war?

'Calm down,' Ella talked to herself. 'Elsie is the one threatening everything. She is the problem. She just has to be removed from the equation.'

Ella jumped on her feet and rushed to Nicholas's old gloves. Without Elsie, her children could still have the future they deserved. Ella took her grandmother's ring out and opened the lid. But then she retched. She could not do it. She could not poison a pregnant woman and the mother of two young children.

Who have you become for even considering it? the loathing voice inside her head wondered.

The next tear that rolled down her cheek ended its course on the ring. Ella wiped its surface. She stared at it for a while, until, out of the blue, everything became clear.

'Elsie is not the problem,' she murmured.

Ella Buckley had never belonged to this century. Elizabeth White was entirely fictional. Over a decade ago, believing herself to be stuck in the past, Ella had taken it upon herself to change history by saving Hal's life. Thanks to her, no one would ever have to die for King Henry VIII to have a son. But, knowing that Henry would now die without having brought religious reforms to England, Ella had decided that it was also her responsibility that his son would do it.

The eleven-year-old had seen the abuses within the Church. He was clever, well-informed and ready to tackle them. Ella smiled through her tears. She had dared to show him the beginning of the path. He did not need her by his side to follow it to adulthood and kingship. She had changed the course of history, for better or for worse. Now she had to go.

What about Grace? the voice inside Ella's head reminded her of her daughter.

Her resolution faltered. Her fingers came to pinch her nose in an attempt to prevent more tears to flood her cheeks. It was useless. She howled, sounding like an injured dog. She knew in her bones that her decision had already been made. And her heart ached for it.

She was the sword of Damocles over her daughter's safety. She had to leave her behind.

She had to abandon everyone. The man who had loved her more than any other and had made her feel safe and wanted; the miracle boy that was the pride of her life. She had to give up on being a part of their lives. She had to remove herself from their world without saying goodbye, and without ever returning.

The apple never fell far from the tree.

Ella exhaled sharply. She had to do it now, or she would never find the courage.

Without anyone to attend her, Ella struggled for a while to change into the costliest gown she owned, then went to open her jewellery box; she would need the finances to begin again whenever the ring was about to send her. She pinned the Mirror of Naples on her chest and picked out as many necklaces, bracelets and rings that she could wear. She switched her hood for the one encrusted with the most jewels. She folded the portrait she had sketched of her daughter on her previous birthday and slid it up her left sleeve. The drawing she had made of Henry at the beginning of their relationship found its place up her right sleeve. She put the ring on her finger.

Anxiety threatened to get the better of her when she remembered the extent of what she did not know about the ring: if it would work, how it had worked before, why the sixteenth century, and what if it sent her five hundred more years in the past? She would not survive the eleventh century!

'Maybe you will not survive at all. Maybe you will cease to exist, because Mabel never left,' Ella said out loud.

For a moment, the thought of closing her eyes and never waking up again felt incredibly sweet. So she did exactly that. She laid down on the bed and closed her eyes. She did not beg for the ring to send her to the twenty-first century. She stopped thinking. There was no more to fear, because there was no more to hope. Ella played with her grandmother's ring, turning it around her finger, tapping on the stone, opening and closing the lid, still feeling the tears flowing on her face, still hearing the fire cracking in the hearth, still smelling the pooch of lavender under her pillow.

Until the distant yet familiar sensation of falling off a cliff overwhelmed her.

EPILOGUE

THE ONE WHO FAILED

The lavender was gone.

Ella opened her eyes. The dark wood of the tester bed did not seem to have changed at first, until she noticed the carving. The geometrical shapes had been swapped for Tudor roses.

There was a certain heaviness on her finger. The ring had not disappeared. It had to be a good sign, or so she tried to convince herself. She took it off, but kept it in her palm. Ella slid her other hand on the soft fabric of the sheets, only to find out they were not so soft anymore. She turned her head on to one side. They were white. Minutes earlier, they had been red. Centuries earlier, in fact. Or centuries in the future? Her eyes set on the lamp on the bedside table. It was not lit, but she could spot a lightbulb. She had travelled again, and to the future this time.

'Well, I am still alive,' she said out loud.

As her voice echoed in the room, Ella noticed a hint of resignation in it – disappointment, even. She chose to ignore it and sat up on the bed.

During her time in the twenty-first century, she had visited so many beautiful houses, castles and palaces, once the homes of actual people, later opened as public attractions, monuments to a common national heritage. The red cord separating her side of the room, carpeted, to the other side, entirely bare, was an indicator that she was now in such an environment.

Besides the carpet, which had never adorned the floor of any of her rooms in the sixteenth century, some furniture had been added. A couple of chairs, a coffee table, even some shelves. On the other hand, the wooden chest by the door had vanished, as had the Italian silk that had previously been hanging on her walls – unveiling a simple, dark, linenfold panelling.

'Oh,' Ella could not help but let out when she recognised the sitter of the gold-framed portrait near the stone fireplace.

She got up on her feet. Her legs were still weak but walked her nonetheless towards what she had once only dared to imagine: her portrait, surviving to be seen and admired throughout decades and centuries.

There she was, as regal as she had ever looked, sitting still to commemorate her daughter's birthday. Ella's heart ached at the memory of Grace. She forced herself to focus on something else, anything else. Her hand went up to the Mirror of Naples pinned on her chest, mirroring the one painted on the portrait. She smiled, wondering what had been told for hundreds of years about this French crown jewel disappearing at the same time as her.

Faces appeared in her mind, one after the other. Hal. Grace. Henry. Arthur. Maud. Elsie. Margaret. Mabel.

Mabel. Ella had stolen her chance at a future, and now she was dead. Again.

The Mirror of Naples was not the only story Ella was dying – and terrified – to uncover. She had somehow survived travelling to a world where her father had never existed. Time had come to find out what had happened to her loved ones left behind.

The stairs were creaking underneath Ella's feet as she walked down, resonating loudly in the seemingly deserted place. Her hands were joined, fingers intertwined, resting on her lower belly, as an old habit.

She was trying to find the perfect adjective to describe the smell surrounding her, or lack thereof, when she saw a small, white sign at the bottom of the staircase.

'Shop,' she read aloud. 'With books to sell. That is what I need.'

The floor of the chapel was cold. Ella had collapsed there some time earlier, after her visit of the palace shop. She had since been staring at the magnificent, imposing black marble tomb standing on the left side of the room. It had her name on it. It was empty, but a part of herself was trapped inside.

The books she had stolen from the palace shop were laid in front of her. The traumatizing informations she had read from their back covers were like monsters under her bed; she was trying to forget about them, she was forbidding her eyes to look down. She could not think about anything but them.

Ella's body went into an uncontrollable spasm of agony and horror.

The life and death of Grace Fitzroy
by Vivienne Scott
Grace Fitzroy was the daughter Henry VIII never had with his queen. The "King's daughter" would have been a princess had she been born in wedlock, but her mother was the royal mistress Elizabeth White. The only bastard child of Henry VIII ever acknowledged, she was promised a comfortable life at her father's court. She was found guilty of poisoning Charlotte, Princess of Wales, wife of the future Henry IX, and beheaded. She was fifteen years old. From her birth in a royal palace to her death on a scaffold, this is the captivating and tragic portrait of a girl whose confessed murderous act was left forever unexplained.

Elizabeth White, Duchess of Mysteries
by Rosalie Berry

Centuries after her presumed death, Elizabeth White remains an enigma. Discovered in 1510 in the gardens of Eltham without any memories, she rose to the highest rank of nobility and became the first public mistress to an English king, but her sudden disappearance on 18 September 1522 plunged the kingdom into shock and confusion. What happened has been the subject of speculation for centuries. Did the mysterious duchess leave on her own account, taking the Mirror of Naples with her? Was she the victim of the all-powerful Cardinal Thomas Wolsey, as claimed then by the Duchess of Norfolk? And where are her remains buried?

From one Henry to another
by Louis Sylvester

The lifeless body of Henry VIII was found in his bed on the early hours of 19 May 1536, only a year after the king signed the order for the execution of his own daughter. He would have to wait nearly three hundred years for the truth about his death to be uncovered: he was asphyxiated. Fingers have since been pointed at his eldest son, Henry IX, but was the monarch really a murderer? In this book, we take a look at the upbringing of this phenomenal personality, well ahead of his time, and recreate the chain of events that ultimately fractured his relationship with his redoubtable father. From theological quarrels to notorious hostility, the key to Henry VIII's murder may be found in the implosion of his royal family.

Reformed minds
by Juliet Rose

The Reformation is a myth. There was not one, but a multitude of reformations: religious, political, societal, moral. When Henry IX, on 18 September 1536, pledged his Oath to nevermore burn an individual at the stake for heresy, England could have found itself in the epicentre of a seism, if not for its king's diplomatic skills. However, after a relatively peaceful reign, Henry IX's death is to reveal just how fractured the kingdom – and the world – really is. Doctrinal and theological debates under the reign of the father become violence and martyrdom under the reign of his son, Edward VI, who proclaimed himself Head of the Church of England two decades after "the King's Oath."

The consequences of the Reformation can still be seen today. Let us now determine the causes.

Ella looked to the other side of the room in a deafening silence. The tomb mirroring hers had her daughter's name on it.

And her daughter's skeleton in it.

And her daughter's skull, unattached.

The images of the Duke of Buckingham's head rolling down in the straw, then rotting on a spike, came shoving the taste of vomit at the back of Ella's throat. She took a deep, shaky breath, and exhaled loudly. There was no more strength in her to search for a definite answer, so she could only guess that Grace's body had been buried somewhere else first, and only later moved to the place of her birth. By someone who cared. Someone who was not Henry.

There were so many thoughts inside Ella's brain that a telepath would have struggled to hear anything that even remotely made sense.

She wanted to scream, she wanted to punch. She wanted to find Henry's remains, and desecrate them like he had desecrated the product of their love.

She was nauseous. She could not focus.

Anyone Ella had ever loved had either never been born or been dead for centuries.

There was so much silence. The palace was lonelier and emptier than she had ever known it. So was her heart.

Her partner and her daughter were both murderers.

'So are you,' she heard herself whisper.

Like magnets, her eyes were drawn back to the books in front of her. Grace was looking back at her mother from the portrait that had been chosen to illustrate the front cover of the book written about her. Ella's vision blurred. Grace's red hair, tucked underneath a blue French hood, disappeared behind the wetness of her pain.

How could a father do that to his child?

You are the one who failed her first, the ruthless voice in her head reminded her.

'Excuse-me, the palace is closed on Mondays,' an unknown voice behind her made itself heard.

Ella wiped her tears, then forced a chuckle. 'And who would you be?' she croaked, slowly getting back on her feet.

'Arthur Batley, site manager,' he replied. His eyes went from the books on the floor to the diamond on her chest, from the gold enamelled book at the bottom of her girdle to the precious stones on her hood. 'We manage historical costumed events centrally. You need to make an appointment at the Tower first,' he told her.

Ella smiled. She too had thought Henry to be a re-enactor, on the day she had travelled. 'Arthur. I have not enquired about him, but he is dead, too,' she said.

'Who is dead?' a soft-spoken voice intervened.

'Everyone,' Ella answered to the visibly pregnant woman standing next to the director. She had not noticed her, at first. Nor had she noticed the thirty-something-year-old man with them, a hand resting on some weapon hanging on his belt – or a walkie talkie, perhaps. A security guard was Ella's best, obvious guess.

'Were you hired by someone?' Batley asked.

'What year is it?' she ignored him, looking at the woman instead.

'It… is 1961,' she said hesitantly, but with a sympathetic, if cautious, smile. 'My name is Mary Batley. I am sorry, but as my husband said, the palace is closed today,' she added kindly.

A sign of the hand from her husband, similar to what Henry used to do, sent Mary Batley back to mutism. Ella looked down on the sapphire. It had sent her to the twentieth century. It would not be 2020 again for another sixty years.

'I will have to ask you to come to my office. What is your name?' Batley wanted to know.

Ella did not reply. Did she have to be Ella again? Or was she still Elizabeth?

Her silence lasted long enough for the security guard to decide to grab her by the arm and drag her out of the chapel. She stared at the tomb of her daughter until the last second.

*

ACKNOWLEDGEMENTS

I have heard that it takes a village to raise a child. The reality is similar when it comes to writing a book. To my village, thank you.

Maman, papa, thank you for the unconditional love. And for allowing my endless monologues about Henry VIII. I love you.

Pauline, Gaëtan thank you for your interest and your support, and for believing in me. Siblings love is one of a kind.

Luther, thank you for being my perfect little elf.

To my very dear friends, Ophélie, Anaïs, Luana and Ronja, thank you for being – sometimes against your will, I am afraid – involved from the very start. You heard all about the story in my head before it was even written. You read and replied to the thousands of messages every time I had a new idea, a concern, a doubt. You were my first readers, my first critics. Thank you.

Thank you, also:

To Matthew Kilburn, for his stellar – and very patient! – editing and proofreading of this book.

To Danna Mathias Steele, for creating the gorgeously perfect cover for Ella's journey.

I hope this novel is as entertaining to read as it was for me to write (and that some of you will reread it as many times as I had to rewrite it.)

ABOUT THE AUTHOR

Clemmie Bennett was born and raised in France, then moved to London to begin a career in childcare. She used her time of unemployment in 2020, brought by the Covid-19 pandemic, to fully focus on her writing before resuming her career – but hopes to be able to write full time one day.

Printed in Great Britain
by Amazon

38703260R00189